PRAISE FOR THE QUAKER BRIDES SERIES

Blessing

"Can love grow between a Quakeress widow, whose passion is nurturing the abused, and a man of means, who's striving for independence from his father? A relationship separated by the culture and values of 1848 explodes on the page in a story only Lyn Cote could pen."

DIANN MILLS, BESTSELLING AUTHOR OF THE FBI: HOUSTON SERIES

"Rich and rewarding! Blessing will captivate you from beginning to end. A unique and compelling plot and well-drawn characters will bring you back in history to Cincinnati, Ohio, where women's rights were nonexistent and racial tension permeated the city. I couldn't put this book down until I learned their fate. A must read!"

JUDITH MILLER, AUTHOR OF THE REFINED BY LOVE SERIES

Honor

"Strong in faith and determined to do what is right no matter the law, [Honor] is a spirited testament to the strength a wife can offer her husband. The unfolding of their sweet romance is a joy to read. . . ."

ROMANTIC TIMES

"With strong characters and compelling action . . . this story was highly engaging, and is one I would gladly recommend to my family and friends."

THE CHRISTIAN MANIFESTO

"Author Lyn Cote has carefully presented the situation of a period when women had little freedom and the Underground Railroad operated in secrecy. . . . I'm glad I met her heroine Honor, and I'll be watching out for more [of her] historical romances."

FRESH FICTION

"A wonderful story of a brave and strong woman, Honor is both a sweet romance and a lesson on the importance of doing what is right. The historical detail is fascinating, and the characters are rich and real. Highly recommended!"

GAYLE ROPER, AUTHOR OF AN UNEXPECTED MATCH

"Cote skillfully and deftly combines period details with a touching, heart-warming love story in a thought-provoking tale that will have readers eager for the next book in the Quaker Brides series."

MARTA PERRY, AUTHOR OF THE LOST SISTERS OF PLEASANT VALLEY SERIES

"In *Honor*, Lyn Cote has given her many faithful readers another story of suspense, surprise, and love that will hold their attention from beginning to end."

IRENE BRAND, BESTSELLING AUTHOR OF *LOVE FINDS YOU UNDER THE MISTLETOE*

Blessing

QUAKER BRIDES

LYN COTE

Tyndale House Publishers, Inc., Carol Stream, Illinois

Visit Tyndale online at www.tyndale.com.

Visit Lyn Cote's website at www.lyncote.com.

TYNDALE and Tyndale's quill logo are registered trademarks of Tyndale House Publishers, Inc.

Blessing

Designed by Stephen Vosloo

Edited by Danika King

Published in association with the literary agency of Browne & Miller Literary Associates, LLC, 410 Michigan Avenue, Suite 460, Chicago, IL 60605.

Scripture quotations are taken from the *Holy Bible*, King James Version.

Blessing is a work of fiction. Where real people, events, establishments, organizations, or locales appear, they are used fictitiously. All other elements of the novel are drawn from the author's imagination.

Library of Congress Cataloging-in-Publication Data

Cote, Lyn.
    Blessing / Lyn Cote.
        pages ; cm. — (Quaker brides ; #2)
    ISBN 978-1-4143-7561-8 (sc)
    I. Title.
    PS3553.O76378B58 2015
    813'.54—dc23   2015003183

Printed in the United States of America

21   20   19   18   17   16   15
7   6   5   4   3   2   1

To my dear friend Christine: wish you lived closer.

And to our beloved friend Gwen, may she rest in peace.

Chapter 1

SENECA FALLS, NEW YORK
JULY 19, 1848

On the high bench of the farmer's open wagon, Gerard Ramsay tried to take a deep breath, but the heaviness of life, a constant pressure over his heart, made it difficult—not to mention the July heat. Under the cloudless royal-blue sky, the New York countryside blazed green with healthy crops and full-leafed trees.

From the corner of his eye, Gerard observed with increasing chagrin his lifelong friend Kennan Buckley, who was sitting next to him. The man's expression radiated a kind of unholy glee.

Kennan's devilish sense of humor had lightened their boarding school and university years, but now that they were nearing thirty . . . Gerard almost asked, *This isn't one of your foolhardy pranks, is it?"*

1

The rough wagon lurched over a deep rut, and Gerard had to hold on to both his seat and his silk top hat. "I can't believe you talked me into this," he growled into Kennan's ear. "I left Boston for Saratoga for some horse racing and light flirtation at the springs—" another deep rut jarred them—"not this."

"Do you want to let your own cousin down?" Kennan retorted. "And of course, I had nothing better to do than bump along a country road in this heat."

Gerard sucked in hot July air and felt the starch in his shirt wilting in the blazing sun. "All right," he said under his breath. "The whole idea seems inconceivable."

"Well, conceive it. Stoddard Henry is in danger of becoming ensnared by a female—and a female who would lure him to a women's rights meeting. Have you ever?"

"I—"

"Whoa!" the driver announced. "Here we are, gents. The Wesleyan Chapel." The wagon rolled to a halt. The two horses flicked their tails high, swishing away irritating flies.

After Kennan, Gerard scrambled down from the bench, resisting the urge to rub his bruised posterior. He glanced around at the small town of Seneca Falls. He immediately recognized the chapel, a large brick building on the corner surrounded by tall leafy oaks and maples, with a few hundred people gathered around the door. So many standing outside in this heat and in this out-of-the-way village—the sight was startling. How had they heard about the meeting? "Look. Would you believe it—a crowd?"

"What did I tell you?" Kennan said, striding toward the building.

Gerard turned to pay the farmer. Kennan hadn't bothered.

But they'd been lucky to find this man and his wagon. When they'd arrived this morning on the early train from Saratoga, all the carriages at the station had already been taken. They'd persuaded this farmer, who'd been picking up a package, to bring them the few miles here.

"Gent, I'll be coming back this way in a few days." The farmer mopped his face with a large, frayed kerchief. "Should I stop and pick you up?"

Gerard hesitated. "Is there an inn here?"

"A few. The best is the Seneca Farmers' Inn—best food, clean sheets."

"When you come through, check for me—Gerard Ramsay—there, then. I'll leave word whether to find me or forget me." Gerard added an extra two bits.

The farmer beamed at him. "You can count on me, gent. I'm Jim Patterson. Everybody around here knows me." The man tugged the brim of his straw hat, pocketed the money, and slapped the reins.

Gerard hurried into the shade of the tall trees near the Wesleyan Chapel. He too took out his handkerchief and wiped the grime and perspiration from his face and hands. This crisis would have to land right at the very height and heat of summer.

The large crowd of women and, unbelievably, some men still waited outside the double doors of the chapel. Something odd was going on there. Two men were lifting a boy up to a window near the door. The lad opened the latch and slipped inside. Soon, to everyone's loud approval, he opened the chapel doors from within. No one had a key to open the chapel? What kind of ill-prepared meeting was this?

Gerard already knew the answer to that. A bunch of lunatics and radicals. He hurried forward, craning to see above the crowd, looking for his tall cousin.

"There!" Kennan shouted across the people now surging inside and gestured toward the door.

Gerard glimpsed his cousin—who, at the sound of Kennan's voice, turned just as the building swallowed him from sight.

Kennan jogged back to Gerard. "So did you see her?"

"No." Gerard felt irritation, hot and unpleasant like the summer air, roll through him.

"She's a very pretty blonde and she was right beside him."

Gerard chewed on this information. "I can't believe this is happening."

"Believe it."

Gerard started forward.

Kennan grabbed his arm. "Where are you going?"

"I'm going after Stoddard."

"Into that *women's* meeting?" Kennan's voice rose. "Are you out of your senses too?"

"Maybe he'll come to his senses when he sees me." Gerard pulled away.

"Suit yourself. And I'll do the same. I'm going to find a tavern and some cool, wet ale. Isn't that better than charging into bedlam? Stoddard will come out at luncheon."

Gerard shook his head as he hurried to the chapel door. At seven years of age, all three of them—Kennan, Stoddard, and Gerard—had been sent away to boarding school. Stoddard and Kennan had been unwanted stepsons and Gerard had felt like one. The three had learned to count only on each other, and the bond still held. He must find his cousin and stop him from making a fool of himself.

Inside the chapel, Gerard tried to glimpse Stoddard, but it was so crowded that he couldn't. And since the seats were all taken, he found himself obliged to stand in the back. When a woman stepped to the pulpit to address the congregation, Gerard felt his jaw drop. A woman speaking to a group of females and males—in public?

Astounded, Gerard stumbled back outside toward a bench in the shade under an old oak. What had Stoddard gotten himself into?

"Hey! Ramsay!"

The vaguely familiar Boston-accented voice stopped Gerard in his tracks. He turned to see who had called.

"It's been a long time," a stranger said, holding out his hand.

Suddenly recognizing him, Gerard felt a wave of disgust. Ambushed. Conklin had been a scholarship student at Harvard—the same university Gerard, Stoddard, and Kennan had attended. He forced himself to shake the man's hand. "Conklin, what brings you here?"

"Working." Conklin waved a notebook. "I'm covering this women's rights convention. Have you ever heard of anything so outlandish?" The man chuckled, mocking. "What is the scion of one of Boston's most swank—uh, I mean, most prestigious families doing here?"

Gerard stared at him, trying to hide his discomfort at being recognized by a journalist. This meant Stoddard's folly might be written up in the Boston papers. Worse and worse. "Just happened to stop here," Gerard said, attempting to smooth matters over. "I'm trying to find someplace cooler. Thought of the Finger Lakes."

"Really?" Conklin rocked on his heels, his expression amused.

"Really. Now if it's not against the law, I'm going to sit in the shade and relax."

Conklin studied Gerard for a moment. "Wish I could. But I have work to do."

Fuming, Gerard watched the journalist hurry into the chapel. He could only hope that Conklin wouldn't see Stoddard and would find more to write about than the fact that a Boston Ramsay had come to Seneca Falls on the same day that fanatics and lunatics had gathered for a big meeting, promoting the rights of women. *Unbelievable.*

Within him bloomed the urge to strangle Kennan for leaving him to deal with Stoddard alone. And a second urge: to throw a bucket of ice-cold water into Stoddard's face, shock him back to his good judgment. Gerard would have been happier staying in Boston, and he hated Boston.

❖

In a few hours, after Gerard had walked around the small town and settled back on the bench outside, people began to exit the chapel at the time for luncheon, and he rose to watch for his cousin. Finally he saw Stoddard's head above all the others. Gerard rushed forward. "Stoddard!"

Stoddard turned with a startled look, then pushed his way from the throng and hurried toward Gerard.

"Cousin, what are you doing here?" Stoddard gripped his shoulder, grinning but appearing puzzled.

"I met Kennan in Saratoga, expecting to see you, too, but he said you were here, so we came to find you."

Stoddard's grin tightened. "Came to save me from my own folly?"

What could he say here in this crowd? "Yes," Gerard admitted, leaning close. "How could you ever think coming to a meeting like this was a good idea?"

Stoddard chuckled in reply.

Gerard glimpsed Conklin, the reporter, dodging in and out of the crowd, heading straight for them. "Cousin, there's a Boston reporter here. Remember Conklin—?"

"Stoddard," a soft, feminine voice from behind his cousin interrupted Gerard.

A truly lovely blonde, dressed in the height of fashion and almost as tall as Stoddard, claimed his cousin's arm.

Beside her walked a petite Quakeress dressed in simple gray and white, her prettier-than-average face framed by a plain white bonnet. The ladies were arm in arm, but in total contrast. They looked to be from two different worlds.

Gerard snapped his mouth shut so he wouldn't blurt out any ill-considered words. Over the heads of the crowd, he noted that Conklin had been snagged and buttonholed by another attendee. Saved.

Stoddard chuckled, shaking his head at Gerard. "Ladies, may I introduce you to my cousin? This is Gerard Ramsay of Boston. Gerard, this is Miss Xantippe Foster—known as Tippy—and her friend, Mrs. Blessing Brightman, both of Cincinnati."

Blessing—an unusual name even for a Quakeress. And since Stoddard presented her by her given name and not her husband's, she must be a widow. Gerard commanded himself enough to accept the blonde's curtsy and both women's gloved hands in turn. "Ladies, a pleasure I'm sure," he recited the social lie.

"A pleasure? Truly?" Miss Foster laughed merrily as if he'd made a jest.

Gerard stiffened.

"Gerard Ramsay, won't thee join us for luncheon?" the Quakeress invited, speaking in the Quaker way and dispensing with any title, even *mister*. "Expecting that we might meet a friend, we reserved a table for four at our inn." Without waiting for his answer, the woman started walking briskly toward the main street, lined with shops and inns.

Stoddard offered his arm to Miss Foster and nodded Gerard toward Mrs. Brightman.

Gerard could not disobey years of training in proper manners. He edged forward as efficiently as he could through the crush of the surrounding crowd.

The Quaker lady paused, letting Stoddard and the blonde precede her. Then she gazed up at Gerard with a look that he might have used when trying to decide without tasting whether a glass of milk had soured. It unnerved him. He tried to step back but bumped against a stranger. He swallowed an unkind word.

She cocked her head, still studying him.

He'd had enough. He offered her his arm. "May I escort you, ma'am?" he said as if issuing a challenge.

She touched his arm and then began to walk on. "Yes, but I do not need to cling to thy arm. I am quite capable of walking unaided."

More startled than insulted, Gerard held back a sharp reply. As audacious as she might be, a gentleman did not contradict a lady. Peering ahead, he observed the possessive way the tall blonde clung to Stoddard's arm. He wanted to snatch up his cousin and run.

"I did not mean to be rude or uncivil," the Quakeress continued, walking beside him. "I'm sure thee offered thy arm simply from courtesy. But after this morning's meeting, I am afraid I see more clearly the prescribed manners between gentlemen and ladies as a form of bondage."

The equation of courtesy with bondage sent prickly disbelief rippling through him. "I beg your pardon." And with the press of the crowd threatening to bowl him over, he was forced to walk faster. What would this woman say next?

She looked up at him. A mischievous smile lightened her face, and he saw now that it was not just pretty but beautiful—big blue eyes, a pert nose, generous pink lips, and thick chestnut hair peeping out around her close bonnet.

Her smile did something to him, something unexpected yet welcome. The heaviness he always carried relented and he could draw breath freely. What was going on here?

"What is thy stand on abolition?" she asked, completely ignoring what should be the standard polite conversation between a man and a woman upon first meeting. They should discuss the weather and then move on to discreetly find out about each other's family connections.

He stared at her. Ahead, Stoddard was chuckling at something his lady had said. The sound wrapped Gerard's nerves tighter.

The Quakeress shook her head at him, still grinning.

"Very well. I don't mean to be impolite. I will follow propriety." She cleared her throat. "Gerard Ramsay, what brings thee to Seneca Falls this July day?"

He swallowed and tried to come up with a palatable conventional reply. He failed. "I'm against slavery," he said instead.

"I am happy to hear that, but I asked what thy stand on abolition is."

He was not accustomed to women who put forth opinions, and her tone, though cheerful, was almost cavalier, as if she was making fun of him. Usually, with him, people did that to their own peril. But this Quakeress had pushed him off balance. "You are in favor of abolition?" he ventured, trying to find his feet in this discussion.

She laughed softly, the sound reminding him of children playing. "Yes, I am in favor of abolition. Has thee ever heard Frederick Douglass speak?"

"No," he said, trying to keep up with her unexpected questions and her brisk pace without bumping into anyone.

"Would thee like to hear Frederick Douglass?"

"Who is that?" He looked down at her again, her face attracting him in spite of himself.

"Thee hasn't read his autobiography, *Narrative of the Life of Frederick Douglass, an American Slave*? It was published three years ago and has sold over five thousand copies."

Distracted, he wished he could overhear what the other lady was saying to his cousin. "I've not had the pleasure."

"Indeed thee hasn't read it, then. It is not a pleasure to read. It is as harsh as the slavery that bound him."

Gerard felt as if he were back on the wagon, only riding

over an even bumpier road. Though primarily concerned with Stoddard's flirtation, he scrambled to keep up with the Quakeress's odd conversation. "He's a fugitive slave, you say?"

"He is a free man of color who left the state and master that enslaved him."

Gerard gaped at her. Ladies didn't discuss slavery. No woman had ever spoken so frankly to him in his life. All his usual sangfroid evaporated.

"I see my direct manner has disconcerted thee. I apologize." She smiled and said in a sweetly conversational tone, "When does thee think this hot weather will ebb?"

His mind whirled, but he wouldn't bow in defeat. "Is this Frederick Douglass attending your . . . convention?"

"Gerard Ramsay, thee must make up thy mind whether thee wishes me to be conventional or not. I own fault. I started by speaking frankly as I do among people with whom I'm acquainted, not strangers like thee. But this morning's discussion of the Declaration of Sentiments has made me overbold with thee—one who is not at all acquainted with me."

She tilted her head like an inquisitive robin. "I apologize. Should we try to follow convention or proceed with frankness?" She looked at him expectantly as she continued walking. "Please choose. I do not wish to be rude."

He inhaled the hot, humid air. Her candor irritated him, and he would be cursed if he let this woman best him. He girded his defenses. "Mrs. Brightman," he drawled, "I must confess your conversational style is completely unparalleled in my experience."

She laughed once more, sounding almost musical.

Was this woman being artless or artful? He glanced at

Stoddard's companion again. The two women differed in costume, but did they both share this originality?

The foursome arrived at the besieged Seneca Farmers' Inn. Telling them to wait, Stoddard threaded his way through the crowd to the harassed-looking, aproned proprietress and then turned at the door to the rear arbor. "They saved us our table outside!" He waved them forward. "Come."

They followed a flustered-looking hostess to a table at the rear of the inn, just outside under a shade tree. She pointed out the bill of fare posted on the outside wall near the door, then left them, promising to bring glasses of cold springwater.

"Oh, this is so much cooler," Miss Foster commented as Stoddard helped seat her.

Gerard was at a loss. He was a gentleman and had duties as such. He never broke any of society's rules around ladies, no matter what he thought of them. Should he offer to help the unpredictable Mrs. Brightman sit or not?

The Quakeress peered up at him. "Which does thee choose?"

"What?"

"Should I sit with or without thy assistance?"

Her perspicacity nicked him. He swallowed his discomfort, his tight collar constricting his throat. He could not let her get the better of him. "I would feel unmannerly if I didn't assist you."

"Then please help me." She beamed at him as if this were all a game. Maybe to her it was, but Stoddard's being here with the blonde was serious to him.

He seated the Quakeress, then took his place and sent a tart, questioning look at Stoddard.

The waitress delivered the sweating glasses of springwater

and took their orders. They all chose cold sandwiches of ham and cheese. Then the four of them were left alone.

Gerard could not think of a word to say, an unusual occurrence. And each moment he watched Stoddard and Miss Foster interact with little glances and intimate smiles upset him more and more. This did not appear to be a mere holiday flirtation with which Stoddard was diverting himself. It was different because the woman was too. Had her sense of novelty ensnared his cousin?

❖

Blessing took her time sizing up Gerard Ramsay as he turned his attention to his cousin. Ramsay was of medium height, a good build, very expensively dressed yet without any dandyism. His dark-brown hair curled slightly, which gave him a boyish appeal, but his guarded brown eyes and cynical mouth warned her that he was not merely the proper Boston gentleman he seemed.

She tried to detect a family resemblance between the cousins but saw none. Fairer and taller, Stoddard Henry had red hair and striking green eyes. He was well dressed, but not as expensively as his cousin.

She'd ruffled Gerard Ramsay with her frankness. She hadn't meant to be rude, but the stirring phrases discussed this morning, regarding man's treatment of woman over the years, had tilted something inside her. *"He has endeavored, in every way that he could, to destroy her confidence in her own powers, to lessen her self-respect, and to make her willing to lead a dependent and abject life."*

That's what Richard had done to her. The old hurt twisted inside her, a physical pain. She drew in air and then sipped her cold springwater, quieting herself. The past had been buried with Richard. She was free now, forgiven. But the deep scars remained and could never be sponged away by anyone.

"So, Cousin, what did you think of this morning's meeting?" Stoddard asked.

"Sitting outside, I heard only snatches," Ramsay replied with a sour twist.

Both men spoke with Boston accents. She noted that, just like Stoddard, Gerard dropped *r*'s in most words and the *g* in words ending with *-ing*. She had heard this accent in other Eastern abolitionists and wondered why they didn't like *r*'s or *-ing*'s. Those living west of the Alleghenies certainly enjoyed the sounds.

"No doubt Mr. Ramsay questions your sanity, Stoddard," Tippy said lightly. "'Whatever are you thinking, man,'" she asked, mimicking a deep voice, "'going to a women's rights convention?'"

Blessing hid her smile behind her glass. "Tippy, don't tease Gerard Ramsay. It's not fair. As a gentleman, he can't contradict thee."

Ramsay glanced at her but revealed nothing of what he was thinking.

But Blessing could guess. Did he suspect that she, too, had reservations about this new romance between his cousin and her friend?

Tippy inhaled deeply and sat back in her chair. "I can't tell you how invigorating this morning has been. I have never felt so liberated before, so free."

Ramsay frowned.

"We are not being polite, Tippy," Blessing said, not un-sympathetic to the man from Boston who obviously dis-approved of today's convention. "Gerard Ramsay, please tell us about thyself. I confess I am curious."

The man shrugged. "A mutual friend saw Stoddard near Saratoga Springs and asked me to come and enjoy the Finger Lakes region. Said it would be cooler."

"It should be cooler here," Stoddard replied, touching his upper lip with his folded handkerchief. "After this conven-tion, I want to spend a few days relaxing by Cayuga Lake, near here. Mother has been taking the waters at Saratoga. That is how I met Miss Foster."

Blessing was becoming familiar with the accent. It was different but held a certain appeal.

"Yes, my mother was there also, drinking the waters," Tippy said, lifting her glass in a mock salute and taking a sip.

"When Tippy read about this meeting in the newspaper, she sent me a telegram," Blessing spoke up. "I set off immedi-ately from Cincinnati and arrived yesterday. I wish there had been more advance notice. I barely made it in time."

"You're both from Cincinnati?" Ramsay asked.

"Yes, we're longtime friends," Tippy replied, reaching for the Quakeress's hand. "Blessing is a very exceptional and interesting woman. I know my life would be very flat with-out her."

Blessing shook her head but accepted Tippy's hand. "Tippy, my life would be flat without thee." *And very lonely.* Tippy had been one of the few who'd persisted in being her friend during the dark years of her marriage. And there were not many others Blessing could trust with her secret missions.

Their food was served, and luncheon ended up being brief. Soon the four of them rose to cede their table to other hungry convention attendees.

"Well, Gerard," Stoddard said, looking mischievous, "I take it you won't be joining us this afternoon?" Before Gerard could reply, Stoddard went on. "I have a room here at the inn, and you can bunk with me tonight if you wish. Kennan, too, if he doesn't mind some crowding a bit."

"Thanks. I will stay with you and tell Kennan." Gerard turned to Blessing and Tippy. "It has been a pleasure to meet you, ladies."

"Don't you mean a surprise?" Tippy teased again.

"Mind thy manners, Tippy," Blessing scolded gently. She offered her hand to Ramsay. "I enjoyed our conversation, Gerard Ramsay. I hope thee finds something interesting and cool to occupy thyself with today."

Ramsay merely bowed over her hand.

The four walked through the noisy inn together and out the door, the women preceding the men. Blessing resisted the urge to turn around and glance once more at Ramsay. He had gained her attention, something few men did. Maybe it was the accent, maybe something more. But he had the same air of wealth and security that Richard had possessed. That alone was a warning to her.

She drew in the thick air and pushed him from her mind. Thinking of the afternoon of spirited discussion ahead, she took a quick step onto the dusty street and walked arm in arm with Tippy, who laughed out loud unexpectedly. Blessing suspected she knew the reason why.

"Stoddard, may I have a private word with you?" Gerard asked, realizing he sounded a bit desperate.

"Ladies, I'll just be a moment," Stoddard called after them. "I'll catch up with you." He drew Gerard into the greenery around the inn. "I'm going to the meeting. It's the most interesting, most revolutionary event I've ever attended. And you don't have to stay and chaperone me. I know what I'm doing."

Gerard steamed. "Do you? That reporter is here. He might include our names as attending this farce."

"You're not concerned about his mentioning your name. Just think how you'd enjoy the unpleasant jolt that would give your father. A Ramsay at a radical meeting." Stoddard paused. "And I don't care one whit if all Boston—indeed, all Massachusetts—knows I've attended a women's rights convention."

Gerard nearly swallowed his tongue.

Stoddard laughed and shoved Gerard's shoulder. "Go find Kennan. He's probably somewhere getting drunk. Then stay here or go back to Saratoga Springs or Boston, whichever you choose. But be happy for me, Gerard. I've found a woman who defies our dismal concept of womanhood and the bondage we considered marriage."

Gerard tried to interrupt, but Stoddard pressed on.

"And I'm not going to let Tippy or her exciting ideas slip from my grasp. I'm tired of my lonely bachelorhood and stifling Beacon Hill society. I'm moving to Cincinnati, Cousin. I'm going west!"

❧

Following the afternoon meeting and supper at the packed inn, Blessing mounted the narrow stairs toward the room she shared with Tippy. As Tippy's chaperone, Blessing did not think she needed to stand over the two while the younger woman said good night to Stoddard. They both were sensible. What did it matter if Stoddard stole a kiss in the gloaming?

A bittersweet memory of the first time Richard had kissed her spiked like a stitch in her side. He'd been so handsome, so charming, and she'd allowed that to sway her from all she believed. Trying to ignore the ache of guilt, she let herself into their room and immediately slipped off her shoes and stockings. Oh, to be free to run barefoot as a child again.

She shed her bonnet and gloves, moving to the open window and letting the soft evening breeze cool her. Fine linen tacked to the window kept out the mosquitoes and provided privacy.

Tippy came in and bolted the door behind her. "Oh, Blessing, isn't this wonderful?" Tippy danced in the middle of the room as if waltzing.

Blessing turned to enjoy her friend's happiness. "Is thee referring to the decision to include seeking the franchise for women in the declaration, or to a certain young gentleman of Boston?"

Tippy sank onto the bed with a gurgle of laughter. "Both!"

A crosscurrent of emotions kept Blessing by the window. She was happy for Tippy. She was frightened for her. Loving posed such a risk. Was Stoddard all that he appeared to be?

Or did his handsome face and quick smile conceal unforeseen heartache for Tippy?

"What did you think of Stoddard's cousin?"

Gerard Ramsay's handsome but world-weary face flashed in Blessing's mind. "He is interesting."

Tippy grinned. "How interesting?"

"Not as interesting as the day's events. I can't believe we got to hear Frederick Douglass speak."

"Not to mention hearing Elizabeth Cady Stanton and Lucretia Mott addressing a *promiscuous* gathering—men and women in the same audience! A shock the walls did not fall in." Tippy gave a small laugh. "My mind is bursting with all manner of ideas," she admitted. "I wish all men respected women as much as the men who attended the meeting today."

The sound of Stoddard's and Ramsay's voices, as they no doubt walked the hall to their nearby room, came through the door. Blessing thought again of Gerard Ramsay. He clearly didn't approve of the convention or of Tippy and Stoddard's friendship or of Tippy's radical ideas. Was it merely because Tippy was from Cincinnati, not from snobbish Boston?

"Blessing?" Tippy prompted.

She turned and smiled. "I'm sorry. I was remembering so many things from this day." *And wondering if thee will love more wisely than I.*

❧

BOSTON
JULY 24, 1848

"I cannot understand what you were thinking." Gerard's father, Saul Ramsay, slapped the folded and somewhat-mangled newspaper from a few days ago in front of Gerard at the breakfast table in their pale-blue-and-white morning room. The open floor-to-ceiling windows allowed a scant breeze inside, barely stirring the white sheers.

"What possessed you to go to Seneca Falls and on those particular two days? You were seen outside that ridiculous women's rights meeting. And I had to read about it in the newspaper and then field impertinent inquiries." His father's voice dripped with haughty censure.

Gerard stared at his father, his heavy-lidded, walnut-shaped eyes. Except for those, the two men looked so similar, but they had never liked each other. The heaviness over Gerard's heart plagued him most here. He'd only returned home to see his mother before—

"Well?" His father filled his cup from the sterling-silver coffee urn and then opened the matching chafing dishes on the sideboard, releasing the fragrance of bacon.

"I went to see Stoddard. He was in the district and it was convenient to pay a visit." In Seneca Falls, Gerard had stayed with Stoddard at the inn while Kennan had left the next day, going off with some friends to gamble at a horse race. Betting on horses was nothing a man given to drink should attempt. Kennan didn't appear to realize this. Typical. Troubling.

"I knew, of course, that Stoddard had gone to Saratoga Springs with my sister," his father replied.

Gerard nodded and tried to begin eating again. He had little appetite in this place, a house that had never felt like home.

"So what drew your cousin from Saratoga Springs to the Finger Lakes?"

A pretty blonde with advanced ideas. Gerard shrugged.

Long ago he had stopped trying to explain anything his father wouldn't like. It was easier on both of them.

His father began working his way through breakfast while Gerard nibbled his toast and sipped the good coffee.

"I'm glad you've come home, Son." The gravity of his voice did not bode well.

Gerard silently waited for him to continue. What was Father going to demand from him this time? Did he want another promise that Gerard would reform his way of life?

"I have been talking to the banker Briggs Mason. His daughter Cordelia has just come out this year. She is charming, sweet—the perfect candidate for your wife. Well connected, and she'll come with a generous portion. You've been the young bachelor around town long enough. It's time you settled down and came into the family shipping business."

Gerard hadn't expected this . . . yet his father had been making noises about Gerard's settling down over the last year or so. Did Father really think that he would go along with this plan, give up his independence and go into the bondage of a society marriage? "I see."

"The Masons have invited us to dine this Saturday evening. Your mother has agreed to make the effort to leave her chaise longue to go with us."

Gerard enjoyed saying his next sentence. "I'm very sorry, but I won't be in town this Saturday."

The vein in his father's right temple began to bulge, a sure sign of his irritation. "This is important. You can change your plans."

Gerard drained the rest of his coffee. Perhaps it was his

age, but he was tired of this fencing with his father over duties he never intended to assume. He decided not to use evasion again. He would tell his father the plain truth, go upstairs to spend an hour with his mother, and then leave Boston.

"Father, I'm leaving today for Ohio. I won't be going to meet Miss Mason or courting her. I am not settling down— not here. I might settle in Cincinnati." *Or not.*

"Cincinnati?" His father sounded more bewildered than angry. "It's a provincial backwater. Why would you even think of leaving Boston?" He made Boston sound synonymous with heaven.

"I have been living my own life for many years now. I expect to continue to do so. I will, of course, let you know when I arrive safely and where I can be reached." Gerard wiped his mouth with his impeccably white napkin and rose.

"I don't understand you, Gerard. Why must you be so . . . independent?" The way his father said the final word made it a slur. "We are a family."

Gerard gazed at his father. A family? When had they ever felt like a family? There were so many words he wanted to say, but he had no hope of their ever being heard. "I am the way I am, Father." *And you are the way you are.* He turned away.

"You will change your plans," his father snapped.

Gerard kept walking.

"If you leave Boston now, I will cut off your allowance." His father paused, obviously to let this sink in. "I said it's time you settle down and become active in the family business. If you don't, you can't expect to benefit from it."

Gerard slowly turned back to his father. "I have never had

any intention of going into the family business. And I plan to never marry."

His father gawked at him. Gerard bowed and left the morning room.

"You better reconsider this," his father bellowed. "I'll cut off your allowance. I will!"

The threat was serious, but Gerard would wait and see if it was legitimate or not. Upstairs, he knocked on his mother's door and was admitted.

His mother, Regina, reclined on her chaise longue as his father had predicted. Blonde with silver threads in her lush hair, the fragile-looking woman wore an elegant blue lawn dressing gown and matching silk slippers. "Gerard," she said in her breathy voice.

Gerard leaned over and kissed her soft cheek. His mother had been a beauty in her youth and still retained most of it even though she had been frail and ill since his birth. Affection for her stirred in him.

"You're leaving again, aren't you?" she said.

"You know me too well." He sat on the upholstered hassock near her.

"Where?"

"Stoddard is in Cincinnati pursuing a very pretty young lady, and I think I need to see what's going on."

She nodded, glancing away momentarily. Then she dismissed her maid.

This was unusual. He waited for the reason.

When they were alone, she took his hands in hers. "Dear, I am aware your father is planning a society match for you."

"I'm not going to marry to suit Father."

"I know that," she said, sounding amused. "But I do wish you could find a young woman whom you could love and respect. That's all I wanted to say. Sometimes I feel there is a hardness inside you." She pressed her hand to his shirt-front, over his heart. "I simply want you to find someone who pleases you, loves you."

Just under her touch, pain like a lancet cut deep into his chest. He drew her hand to his lips. "I hope the same thing," he said falsely, knowing those were the words she wanted to hear.

"Gerard, I need a favor. I want to go to my family's place in Connecticut for the remainder of the summer. Your father will not take me this year. And I . . . . I need to go."

Gerard wanted to say no, but something about the way his mother said the words caught his attention. Mother never asked him to wait on her. He paused, considering. Now he looked more closely. She appeared elegant as always but more feeble than the last time he saw her. And thinner. And her hair lacked its usual shine. "Of course, Mother." He didn't ask more. He didn't want to know more.

After informing her of what he'd heard and seen at Saratoga Springs, Gerard kissed her good-bye, and soon he was in a carriage on his way to the train station to make arrangements for a private car to Connecticut for himself and his mother on the following day.

His stomach twisted as he considered the delay in join-ing his cousin in Cincinnati. Unexpectedly at risk, Stoddard needed to be reminded that marriages were insoluble and unwise. The three of them—Gerard, Stoddard, and Kennan—had always vowed to shun society's prescribed bondage: wedlock. His father's choice for Gerard, the banker's young daughter, came to mind. The institution only brought misery. Let weaker, foolish men stumble into it.

Gerard would not allow his cousin to fall for a woman just because she had a pretty face and a clever mind.

Blessing Brightman's lively expression and pert questions flitted through his memory. He inhaled deeply and brushed her out of his thoughts. *Women.*

Chapter 2

Restless and aggravated, Gerard stepped off the riverboat in bustling Cincinnati weeks later than he'd originally intended. Both parents had disrupted his plan. His mother had delayed him and his father had retaliated, as promised, against his defiance.

After staying several weeks in Connecticut with his mother and conveying her back to Boston, Gerard had checked at the bank and found that his father had indeed cut off his allowance. His mother had discreetly given him a sum of money for his trip here, but now he would have to come up with a way to earn his own income. That was the price for refusing to consider the pretty Miss Mason as bride, for refusing a position in the family business.

And for going to help a friend.

Had he come too late? Had Stoddard already become publicly engaged to that suffragist? Or perhaps Stoddard had already come to his senses and would be more than ready to leave this dismal-looking river city that smelled like a packing plant.

Swallowing these questions, Gerard scanned the teeming, shabby wharf for his cousin. Had Stoddard received his letter?

Just then a familiar, tall, red-haired figure moved out of the crowd on the dock. "Gerard!" Stoddard waved as if they were still schoolboys, meeting at the train station after a summer apart.

His spirits lifted and Gerard couldn't suppress a smile. He strode along the gangplank and clapped Stoddard on the shoulder. "Cousin!" A sudden urge to tell Stoddard of how weak his mother had become bubbled up in his throat. He forced it down. No need to discuss that now. Or perhaps ever. Maybe he'd just imagined it.

"So you spent the rest of the summer at your mother's family's country place?"

"Yes. Too bad you didn't come. I was able to do some really good trout fishing." Gerard studied his cousin, looking for any sign that he regretted moving so far west and was ready to go home. "How did you stand the dog days of August here, so far from the coast?"

Stoddard shrugged. "I might as well get used to the summers here."

Gerard didn't like the sound of that.

Interrupting them, one of the porters set down Gerard's trunk and valises.

Stoddard's eyes widened. "You've come for more than a brief stay."

Gerard awaited his cousin's reaction.

"Excellent!"

Relief buzzed through Gerard. Even though it sounded like Stoddard still intended to settle here, he hadn't altered in any discernible way. This prompted Gerard to ask, "How's your friend, the pretty blonde suffragist?" He watched for evidence that Stoddard was still smitten.

Stoddard ignored his question and reached down to grip the handle of one of the valises. "Drayman!" He hailed one of the many small wagons along the pier. "Here!"

Stoddard's avoidance ratcheted up Gerard's tension. Then he glimpsed another figure he thought he recognized. In the distance he saw a woman dressed in gray Quaker garb.

For a moment the memory of the disturbing widow he'd met in Seneca Falls came to mind—once again. He took a step forward but then checked himself. Even if this person were the same woman, he had nothing to say to her. Whether or not she had been the most original, most outrageous woman he'd ever met.

Then another familiar figure slipped around the rear of the crowd and disappeared. "Kennan?" Gerard called out uncertainly.

Stoddard halted and glanced around to where Gerard was staring. "Kennan?"

Gerard blinked rapidly. "Thought I saw him but . . ." He regarded Stoddard, who sent him an odd look.

Gerard chuckled to cover his lapse. No doubt Kennan lingered in his mind, worrying him; that was all.

Soon the two sat beside the driver as he drove them to Stoddard's lodgings. "You're in luck," Stoddard said. "My landlady, Mrs. Mather, had a vacancy come up last week and I secured the room for you."

"I thought I'd stay in a hotel." Then the fact that his father had carried out his financial threat settled over Gerard again, souring his stomach. But before he'd blindly follow the steps his father laid out for him, he would go to hell and whatever might come after that. He swallowed the acid that came up his throat. Maybe a boardinghouse would conserve his dwindling funds.

Stoddard shook his head. "My landlady takes care of everything, and her cook is an artist. It's better than a hotel—not as many people coming and going. And she only rents to gentlemen." Stoddard paused to smirk. "Says spinsters are too particular and talk too much."

Gerard snickered at this yet was reassured by the sentiment. This sounded like the Stoddard he knew. "Appears like a good place for us." He wanted to ask about Tippy again, but Stoddard had let the first question go unanswered. He must be cautious or hazard pushing Stoddard even closer to the chit.

Before long the drayman was helping unload the baggage. Gerard paid the man, and soon he and Stoddard were in the boardinghouse's small foyer with the baggage around them.

A slim, middle-aged woman in a neat gray dress with white collar and cuffs bustled from the rear to meet them. "This is thy friend, Stoddard Henry?"

Gerard hadn't expected to meet another Quakeress here. Surely she'd have no connection to the first. A bit belatedly he managed a creditable bow. "Ma'am."

"Though I am Quaker and don't use titles, thee may call me that and 'Mrs. Mather.' This is business, after all." The woman eyed him up and down. "Stoddard has given thee a very good reference. The rules of the house are few but firm. I give every gentleman a key. Regardless of the hour, come in quietly and sober. No female guests are allowed over my threshold. Can thee abide by that?" She stared hard at him.

"Yes, ma'am." He grinned in spite of himself.

She sized him up another moment. "I'll show thee the room."

Gerard didn't know how, but he'd evidently passed inspection.

Stoddard carried the valises while Gerard dragged his trunk up the stairs.

"Here it is," the Quakeress announced.

Gerard peered over Stoddard's shoulder into a large, bright room in shades of gray and white with a bow window. It was simply furnished, evidently with a male tenant in mind: a fine shaving stand with a mirror rested near the window. "A good room."

"It is." The landlady turned to him, stated the rent, and informed him that he would have to pay the maid separately and that he could leave his laundry downstairs once a week for the laundress, also at extra cost. "I provide three meals a day—at eight in the morning, noon, and finally supper at seven each evening. If thee isn't coming for a meal, I expect to know as early as possible so I can tell the cook."

The lady definitely knew what she required, and he liked that. "I'll keep that in mind."

"See that thee does." Mrs. Mather bustled out.

"Glad you've come." Stoddard squeezed Gerard's shoulder.

Moved, Gerard couldn't find his voice, so he merely nodded.

"Even if it's just to rescue me from myself." Stoddard grinned.

His jaw clenched, Gerard didn't respond. He needed time and more information in order to figure out how to pry his cousin from this trap.

Stoddard's face suddenly lost its cheer. "Is Kennan coming?" All their combined worries about the direction their old school friend had taken came out in his low tone.

Gerard felt the same pall overcome him. "I haven't seen him since Seneca Falls." *Except for my lapse into imagination earlier.* "No word either." A moment of silence stretched between them. Gerard listened to the city sounds outside the window—peddlers calling out their wares, the creak of wagons and the hoofbeats of horses, the voices of children. Stoddard was as concerned about their old friend as he was. No wonder Gerard had imagined seeing him here. But what could they do to halt Kennan's descent? Nothing.

Gerard silently promised himself not to lose Stoddard, too. If he had to reside for months in this "provincial backwater" bringing Stoddard to his senses, it would be time well spent. But, he reminded himself, for all he knew, Stoddard's fascination with the pretty suffragist had already faded.

The thought of her Quakeress companion entered his mind till he booted it out.

◈

The next day, another that was sunny and warm, Stoddard suggested seeing some of the sights of Cincinnati. Gerard was pleasantly surprised when one of these sights proved to be an afternoon horse race just outside the city. His cousin had always loved horse racing. After all, Stoddard had met that pretty blonde in Saratoga Springs, which was noted for its races. As they stepped down from the borrowed gig, Gerard couldn't hold back a smile.

The open field carved out of the forest showed signs that this was not the first race held here. A track had been dragged and covered in sawdust. Jockeys walked their horses nearby. The familiar raucous excitement of men gathered around bookmakers livened the atmosphere. It was impossible not to feel it, catch it.

"Kentucky breeds really fine thoroughbred horses," Stoddard was saying. "The races can be exciting."

Gerard started toward the most reputable-looking book-maker, then paused. He needed to get his bearings. "Which bookmaker do you usually choose?"

Stoddard looked surprised. "I don't waste money on betting."

Since when? Gerard stifled his response. If he was right about who had caused this change, he needed to use subtlety. "Cousin," Gerard coaxed, "how much fun is a horse race if one hasn't placed a bet? Come on." He gestured for Stoddard to follow him and continued toward the bookmaker.

Stoddard came along but with such obvious reluctance

that Gerard silently cursed Miss Foster for her bluestocking influence. A gentleman was entitled to his entertainments. And leave it to a woman to take all the fun out of life.

"What's the favored horse?" Gerard called to the book-maker over the heads of other betting customers.

"Fate's Fancy in the third race," the man replied, handing out scribbled betting slips to the crowd. "Odds two to one."

"What's the long shot?"

"Kentucky Pride in the first race. Odds fourteen to one." The man turned to dicker with another customer.

Gerard pulled out his purse and shook out two gold dollars.

"Have you any idea what you're doing?" Stoddard murmured close to Gerard's ear.

Stoddard's words and concerned tone goaded Gerard. "Two dollars on Kentucky Pride!" he called out to the book-maker.

Stoddard's exclamation was loud and frustrated. "If you want to throw money away . . ."

A man's face at the edge of the milling bettors caught Gerard's attention. For a moment he felt the man's animosity like a punch in the gut. Holding up his two dollars to the bookmaker, he stared at the well-dressed stranger. Did he know him?

The crowd shifted, coming between them. Gerard accepted the betting slip without even looking at it, craning his neck. When the throng parted, the man had disappeared from sight. Who was he? Did they know each other from somewhere?

Gerard stepped back, still musing. Then he thought he

saw Kennan again, just a moving figure at the edge of the crowd near where the stranger had been standing. Unsettled, Gerard closed and then opened his eyes, blinking. "Did you see him?"

At his elbow Stoddard replied, "Who?"

"I thought I saw Kennan."

"Really? Where?" Stoddard was glancing around.

"Over there. I just glimpsed him. Or thought I did."

The two of them scanned the crowd.

"Must have been someone who looked like Kennan," Stoddard said at last with a shake of his head.

Gerard agreed with a curt nod, but his gut didn't believe it. And if Kennan was here, why would he avoid them? It didn't make sense.

Stoddard hailed a friend and hurried a bit forward. Gerard turned to follow him and found the man who'd stared at him with malice standing right in front of him. Blocking his way. "May I help you?"

"No." The man did not move.

"Have we met?" Gerard asked, nettled.

"Not formally. No." The man spoke with a familiar accent, but not the one Stoddard and Gerard shared. This voice held the flavors of both Boston and Ireland, Gerard thought. But he didn't recognize this man.

Not wanting to start a fight, Gerard could think of no reply except "If you'll excuse me, I must join my friend."

"Of course." The stranger grinned unpleasantly, turned, and walked away.

Gerard noticed that the crowd parted like the Red Sea, giving the stranger a wide berth, and then swallowed him up.

Stoddard touched Gerard's elbow. "Come, I want you to meet someone."

"Did you know who that man was?" Gerard motioned toward where the retreating figure had gone.

"I wasn't paying attention. Come on," Stoddard urged. "The first race is about to begin."

Gerard let himself be led away, but meeting this stranger left him feeling unsettled, vaguely troubled. He shook it off and shouldered his way to the front to watch the first race. A worry niggled at the back of his mind. Stoddard was right: When Gerard still had no concept of how to make a living here, why was he betting money he couldn't afford to lose? He could only hope Kentucky Pride would win.

❦

SEPTEMBER 2, 1848

In the autumn twilight a day later, Gerard walked sedately beside Stoddard. Miss Foster—Tippy—and her parents had invited them to dine. Apparently Stoddard was as firmly in her clutches as ever. Gerard wanted to grab his cousin and pull him away, head down the bluff to the wharf, where they could lift a glass and laugh and perhaps sing, forget the fact that neither of his horses had won their races the day before. Instead they were headed for a dinner party, a social obligation, a collar-tightening bore.

The girl's parents must be in transports over a catch like Stoddard Henry—a handsome, socially prominent, and well-educated man. Gerard sneered at the thought. But how could he counter their stratagems to gain such a son-in-law?

"I know you've come to save me from Tippy," Stoddard said baldly, blandly. "But I don't need saving."

Before Gerard could think of a reply to this sudden frankness, Stoddard called out, "This is the house." It was a three-story home on a corner lot with a large garden. And Gerard didn't like how his cousin's step quickened as if he couldn't wait to get inside. Gerard was depressed. Kennan in the bottle and Stoddard "in love." It was disgusting.

Stoddard all but ran up the steps, grinning like a fool.

A somber butler opened the door—a black man with a head of hair that resembled silver wool.

Gerard had rarely seen black servants. He studied the man.

"Mr. Stoddard, good to see you, sir," the butler said with a Southern accent.

Stoddard greeted the man and added, "George, this is my cousin Gerard Ramsay of Boston."

The butler bowed slightly. "Please step in, Mr. Ramsay. Welcome to Cincinnati, the Queen City of the West."

The grand greeting, spoken with evident pride, threw Gerard off stride. He nodded and gave the man his hat and gloves as he entered the home. Inside the house smelled of lemon oil and good food. Gerard's mouth watered at the fragrance of roasted fowl. Well, at least he might get a good meal here. If his stomach would let him enjoy it.

The butler showed them to the parlor, decorated in deep rose and white with heavy draperies at the windows and flocked wallpaper patterned with roses and vines. Clutter covered every exposed surface. On lacy crocheted table coverings sat porcelain figurines and daguerreotypes in intricate gilt frames, and oil family portraits hung on the walls. In the midst of all this feminine frippery, Gerard couldn't shake the feeling of being swallowed up by the sumptuous decor. On the other side of the parlor, three older couples and the daughter of the house waited for them.

Stoddard headed straight for a woman in lavender silk who sat on a chair by the cold hearth. "Mrs. Foster, I'd like to present my cousin."

The ritual of introductions proceeded according to form. Gerard sized up the Fosters, a middle-aged couple who appeared to be in comfortable circumstances. The husband was tall with side-whiskers, and his wife an older version of her daughter. The other two couples were of similar age and appearance.

"Mr. Ramsay," Tippy Foster, sitting near her mother, greeted him brightly. "I'm so happy you've ventured to the barbarous frontier."

"Xantippe," Mrs. Foster said reprovingly.

"Miss Foster, I see that you have not lost any of your sprightly charm," Gerard said, wishing he could say what he really meant.

As if she read his mind, the girl chuckled. "You are very adroit, sir."

An intimate glance passed between Stoddard and Tippy, and Gerard fought to hold his courteous smile in place.

"Miss Blessing," the butler intoned from the doorway.

Gerard turned and found the Quakeress standing there. The woman appeared to be ushering in daylight. The oil lamps seemed to dim and the overdecorated room to pale. He mentally stepped back.

The Quakeress moved purposefully into the parlor. She did not try to float across the room in that affected, aggravating way most young women did. Her measured, forthright gait irked him all the more.

And every head turned to watch her. Two of the ladies moved toward her with smiles and pleasant phrases on their lips, startling Gerard. A radical female would not have been welcome in any Beacon Hill drawing room.

Or was that true?

He had heard of people who had presence, but he had never known what that meant. Now he recognized it firsthand, though it still defied definition. He tried to analyze what about her seemed to reach out toward others. She was admittedly good-looking, and she dressed very simply but expensively in gray-and-white silk with a white widow's cap over her chestnut hair. Nothing outstanding that in itself should have called attention to her. If he could understand what her attraction was, perhaps he could counter it.

Because he would bet she was the one who'd lured Tippy Foster into radical ideas, and a beautiful girl with radical ideas was evidently the type that snared Stoddard. A bitter taste leaked over his tongue.

"Gerard Ramsay, we meet again." The widow offered him her hand like a man, behaving as if she were unaware that she was the center of attention in the room.

It irritated him, so he responded with an older and even more formal courtesy, taking her hand, bending over, and kissing it. "Madam Suffragist."

She chuckled.

The lilting sound grated on his nerves, and he tried to

come up with another way to catch her off guard. "How is the crusade for women's rights proceeding?"

"Slowly, much too slowly." Then she took back her hand and moved toward her hostess, effectively cutting him out.

He watched her, his annoyance deepening. Any other woman would have been chagrined at his provocative greeting and would have tried to downplay her radicalism. Why didn't she?

"I'm sorry not to arrive on time, but I was detained," the Quakeress said.

"Your work is very important," Mrs. Foster replied. "Don't apologize."

The other ladies murmured similar sentiments, sounding sanctimonious.

Her work? What else didn't he know about this woman? A particularly painful spot in his stomach began to flare, burn. He thought longingly of the small tavern he'd glimpsed near his lodging. He could be there now. Perhaps finding someone for a game of cards or chess.

Then he overheard Mrs. Brightman murmur to Tippy, "I received a letter today with important news from a woman we met in Seneca Falls. I'll call on you tomorrow to discuss it."

Gerard was intrigued. A letter from one of those radical suffragists? Perhaps Miss Foster would accomplish his mission for him. Certainly more outlandish behavior from this young lady could not fail to wipe the mist of blind love from Stoddard's eyes. As he thought this, he sent a particularly generous smile to Tippy.

The mystery was how this Quakeress and this young lady

of society became friends and why the Fosters hadn't protected their daughter from such a woman.

"Dinner is ready," the butler said from the doorway.

Soon, in a large dining room decorated with wallpaper
depicting the Parthenon in Greece and alight with a crystal
chandelier, they settled at the white-clothed dining table, lit
by candles and gleaming with polished silver. Miss Foster
and Stoddard sat across from him. Mrs. Brightman had been
seated to his right. The master of the house sat at the head
and the lady of the house at the foot, with the other guests
ranged along the sides. Just a happy family and their guests.

Gerard opened his crisp white napkin and placed it in
his lap, dreading the long, many-course dinner ahead. Social
chatter always needled him while at the same time boring
him. *But I must learn all I can about this family, all that is
useful to me.*

"I used to go to Saratoga," Mr. Foster said toward the
end of his wife's drawn-out story about how Tippy had met
Stoddard there. "Great horse races."

Gerard beamed at the man. "Nothing like a good horse
race. Stoddard took me to one yesterday. I take it Cincinnati
doesn't have a formal racetrack?"

"No, but those races are held in outlying towns from time
to time," one of the other men said. "If a Cincinnati man
wants a regular racetrack, he must go across the river."

"Really?" Gerard said.

"And that's close enough, if you ask me," Tippy snapped.
"Men betting on horses and losing money that should feed
their children."

Prudish busybody. Gerard held his tongue.

The other ladies busied themselves with their napkins, trying to ignore this lapse of good manners. Young debutantes were not supposed to censure gentlemen, and especially not at dinner.

Gerard regarded the girl, smiling with his teeth and hiding his animosity. "One can't outlaw every enjoyment just because some abuse it. I've always enjoyed horse racing."

"The lower classes lack self-control. That's all, and it's not going to change no matter what people say." Mr. Foster took another spoonful of the just-served beef consommé.

Gerard was aware that the woman beside him had gone very still. No doubt she agreed with the daughter, not the father. Blessing Brightman was a meddler if he ever saw one.

Tempted to say more, he decided to wait to pursue the topic till the gentlemen were left alone with the port after dinner. The idea of a permanent racetrack suddenly presented itself to him in another light. This might be an opportunity to address his most pressing need: a new source of income. And if he were forced to stay longer in Cincinnati than he'd anticipated, he might as well turn it to his monetary advantage. From what he'd seen yesterday, a new track would have no shortage of patrons. Here was a need he could meet.

Yes, a permanent racetrack just might prove to be an ideal investment. And it certainly would exasperate Miss Tippy Foster and perhaps Mrs. Blessing Brightman too.

Gerard smiled and, in spite of his touchy stomach, continued eating the excellent dinner, planning his course toward profit and vexation of the bluestockings. Abruptly, the memory of yesterday's horse race brought up recollections of the stranger who'd eyed him with such hostility. The unsettled feeling rose within, but he dismissed it.

❧

Later that evening Blessing climbed down from her town carriage. Night was one of her busiest times. Gerard Ramsay crossed her thoughts, engendering so many varied feelings. But she couldn't deal with them right now.

Judson, her driver, stood nearby. His dark, wrinkled face was barely visible in the night. "Miss Blessin', I gon' stay right here and wait for you. You call out if you need me." He said this every night at the docks, always wanting to protect her.

Her mind drifted back to the previous hours at the Fosters' and, before she could forestall herself, to Gerard Ramsay. A very handsome and disturbing man. *He doesn't like me, and I shouldn't care.*

A passerby jostled her, and she immediately checked her pocket for her small purse. *Nothing gone.* Pickpockets and purse cutters abounded on the wharf. She brushed Gerard Ramsay out of her mind and turned, only to nearly bump into Mr. Smith.

Her breath caught in her throat, and she hoped it didn't show. Mr. Smith liked to catch her by surprise, upset her if he could. She knew she stuck in his craw. "Good evening," she said, making her voice cool and unruffled in complete contrast to the latent anger he always managed to inflame within her.

"If it isn't the widow Brightman, out doing good among the poor sinners," he replied, his voice shaded with a sneer but so subtle that to rise to it would put her in the wrong.

She attempted to smile, but a scene from the past glimmered within—Richard, sobbing with regret the morning after a night's binge in this man's company. The pain of that memory clutched at her. "May I help thee?"

"Help me to where or what? Perdition?" he mocked her.

She gazed at him wordlessly. Smith regularly sought her out and taunted her. This man had done her great harm through her husband, and she still struggled to forgive him. It was hard to forgive a man who was always busy enticing others down the path to destruction.

"As much as I'd like to stay and chat, ma'am, this is my time to do business." He bowed his head and walked off, whistling. Smith's so-called bodyguard—the man who beat others at his orders—followed behind like a faithful dog.

In Smith's wake, Blessing tried to loosen her tension by drawing breaths of increasing depth.

Then one of the night watches who patrolled the wharf to keep order approached her. He'd been standing in the shadows, no doubt waiting for Smith to leave. No one wanted Smith's attention. Blessing and Richard had found that out the hard way.

"Mrs. Brightman," he greeted her respectfully.

In definite contrast to Smith. Irritated with herself for letting the man get under her skin yet again, she smiled at the tall young man in uniform. "Good evening."

"One of the *women* asked me about you and your work with orphans. She has a child that needs a home."

Another illegitimate child nobody wanted, another life she might save. As usual, Blessing simultaneously experienced a lift of thanks and a pang of regret. "Thank thee. Where is the child?"

"I'll take you there, ma'am."

She nodded her gratitude and walked beside him to one of the many brothels on the quay. A line of men waited at the door. At the sight of her, they melted into the darker shadows.

"I'll be near if you need me," the night watch said. "Her name's Ducky Hughes. You'll find her on the landing, third door."

Blessing touched his arm and then walked through the open door and scaled with caution the slanting staircase by the light of a few candles in glass wall sconces. At the stench of filth, she resisted the urge to cover her nose with her scented handkerchief. She tapped on the third door.

It opened with caution. "Yeah?"

"I'm looking for Ducky Hughes."

"Who's asking for . . . Ducky?"

"I'm Blessing Brightman."

The door opened, revealing a thin, worn woman in a scanty, soiled dress. "You the Quaker lady?"

"Yes, I am."

The woman waved her inside. "I hear you take in kids."

"I have a home for foundlings and orphans and others."

"I been taking care of a friend's newborn. She died a month ago. I can't do it anymore. But I want him safe and fed."

"I understand. Is there no other family for the child?"

The woman let out a sarcastic grunt. "None who wants him. Will you take him?"

Blessing drew in a breath. "Of course I will." Her mind went back to Seneca Falls. That meeting had not just been about winning the right to vote for women but also about securing women equal status. Society's double standard had forced many a young woman into a life of prostitution. Why could a man sow his wild oats and still be accepted in parlors and churches while a woman who made one mistake became condemned to a life like this? And if women could work at honest jobs and earn enough to support themselves, would any seek this life?

In short order the woman wrapped the baby in a ragged blanket and placed him in Blessing's arms. "I'm glad I heard of you. I was worried about what would happen to him."

"No need to worry. Thee may come and visit him if thee wishes."

"I can?" The woman sounded first startled, then suspicious. "Really?"

"Certainly. The house is on Seventh Street and Washington. The one with the fenced-in garden." Blessing sized up the woman. "Now, does thee need anything? There's room for women there too."

The woman shook her head. "I do all right."

Blessing wished she could counter this, but if the woman wanted to remain in "the life," she could do nothing to help her. "Thank thee. We'll take good care of him." Blessing turned and headed out.

A man leaned in the open doorway. "Glad to see you're doing something with that brat. But, Ducky, this Quaker scared away all your customers."

Every word from this excuse for a man ground like sandpaper inside Blessing, but she didn't let her disapproval show. *Brat* was a kinder term than *bastard*, which, unfortunately, this infant probably was.

The woman grunted again in disgust. "They'll be back."

The despair concealed within the woman's sarcastic tone touched a raw spot in Blessing's own wounded heart. Why wouldn't Ducky leave this man who rented her out at night? Was it just despair or fear that kept her here?

Passing by the man, who sneered at her, Blessing realized once again that while she moved among the people who inhabited the wharf, she did not understand what caused them to live as they did. This life was not simply the result of poverty. She knew poor men who loved their wives and cared for their children in spite of need—and poor women who did the same. Perhaps those who lived at the wharf were the "poor in spirit."

Blessing carried the infant down the stairs and out of the house. The child needed a bath, clean clothes, and food. She could provide all of those things, but what of the things she couldn't provide—a family, a sense of self-respect, a respect for God and man? Who could supply those? A thought she'd entertained for a while nudged her. Perhaps there was a way she could provide this child with some of those things. She glanced at him in the scant light. In spite of his thinness, he was a handsome child with blond down on his head like a duckling. He opened his eyes wide as if studying her also. She grinned at him and he gave a little kick, almost smiling back.

The night watch stepped out into the gaslight's illumination and pulled the brim of his cap in politeness.

"Thank thee! I have the child." At that moment, Blessing

caught sight of a familiar figure on the other side of the pool of light.

She gasped, flooded with dismay. So this man not only disliked independent females but also abused helpless women himself.

Gerard Ramsay was unable to hide his shock. "What are you doing in *this* part of town at this hour?"

Blessing stared at him. In her arms, the baby in the bundle whimpered as if also unhappy with Ramsay.

"Everybody knows," the night watch said in a stiff tone, "that this lady is a very respectable widow. She works among the poor on the docks. We look out for her. Now go about your business, sir."

"Thank thee," she said to the young man. "This *gentleman* is new to Cincinnati."

"I didn't realize that suffragists also worked for the poor," Gerard said in a disparaging tone.

His tone fired up her indignation. "My work includes helping those women who are most mistreated by the unjust laws and prejudice we women must endure. How else would I work for women's betterment here and now? Lobbying for new laws while ignoring present abuses would be negligence."

Gerard snorted in response.

Then Blessing recognized with distinct displeasure that Stoddard Henry stood behind Gerard.

"Mrs. Brightman," Stoddard stammered.

Unable to think of anything to say to him, she walked toward her carriage. She felt Gerard's gaze follow her till her driver helped her into the carriage and turned it to head back up the bluff overlooking the river.

Mr. Smith came to her mind. In spite of Gerard's apparent proclivity for the vices of the wharf, she hoped he wouldn't meet up with Smith. It occurred to her that both men spoke with similar accents, so Smith must have come from Boston too. She hoped that was all they had in common.

What did Gerard Ramsay think of her now? She certainly knew what she thought of him. Perhaps she should warn Tippy that Stoddard's cousin was luring him to the wharf with all its temptations and pitfalls. Or maybe he didn't need luring. It was possible she had misjudged Stoddard Henry. Was he just another privileged wastrel, wearing the mantle of respectability? Like Richard? Like Gerard Ramsay himself?

Chapter 3

THE UNWELCOME IMPACT of meeting a lady—and especially that lady—down here at the wharf worked its way through Gerard in cold waves. He watched her enter her glossy-black closed carriage and drive away. Only then did he exclaim, "Why in heaven's name is she down here?"

"I told you," the night watch said with impatience. "If you're so upset to see a lady here, what are *you* doin' here?" With a sound of derision, the officer stalked off.

"I said this was a bad idea," Stoddard said. "And nobody tells Blessing Brightman where she can go or what she can do."

Could nothing go right? Gerard shook off his exasperation. The idea of the racetrack had taken root, and he knew the wharf was the kind of place he must begin his research. He'd need two kinds of investors: the respectable and the disreputable. In the process of making it happen, he didn't want to brush up against some ugly customer who had already decided to do the same.

But the thought of meeting the Quakeress here had never crossed his mind. His thoughts still raced. What was the widow doing carrying a baby?

"I don't come down here," Stoddard said. "My days of venturing into places like this are long past. I thought the same was true for you. We were young and stupid when we frequented the Boston docks. It's a wonder both of us survived some of those dangerous nights. And came away without catching a disease."

In the dim moonlight Gerard stared at his cousin, realizing he half agreed with Stoddard, a startling thought. Nonetheless, the man's superior tone grated on him. Was Stoddard going to become one of those stuffy men like Gerard's father? Had his cousin forgotten how many of the socially prominent possessed feet of clay? "So you really are getting respectable."

"You are respectable and I am respectable. I just used to do things that I now see were foolish. And wrong. We're nearly thirty, man. Getting old enough to know better."

Gerard decided to adopt an honest approach. "Just a few drinks. I still want to broach the topic of a permanent race-track with this strata of society and see what the reaction is."

Stoddard grabbed him by the shoulder. "You don't mean that you are serious about that idea?"

"Yes, of course I'm serious."

"Why?"

Gerard did not want to reveal the truth to his cousin, but

he always had, so why stop now? "Where can we go and talk in private?"

"Home?"

Gerard shook his head. He couldn't go home yet. The restlessness that goaded him to seek bawdy humor and drink was roiling up inside. "How about that tavern a few blocks from our boardinghouse?"

Stoddard assented, and after a brisk walk, they entered the one-room tavern. The windows were open to let in the evening breeze, and a few lamps lit the interior. The clientele was mostly men—honest workmen, from all appearances—who stood at a short counter talking to a man in a white apron. The place hummed with quiet conversation. Gerard and his cousin sat at a small, round table and waved to the man.

Soon a woman who seemed to be the barkeep's wife, a white kerchief tied over her hair, delivered the ale they'd ordered.

"So what do we need to talk about that we couldn't talk about at our lodgings?" Stoddard asked after his first sip of ale.

Gerard hesitated. "That widow, how does she come to be in your friend Miss Foster's company? I would think they would move in different circles."

Stoddard stared at him. "They would have moved in different circles if Blessing hadn't married Richard Brightman. The marriage was quite the sensation, I'm told—a dashing society bachelor and a pious Quakeress. But why do you care?"

"It's just odd. How does she move in society? Where does her wealth come from?"

A group of men nearby laughed suddenly. Stoddard waited for quiet before replying, "Her husband left her his fortune: two breweries and much prime real estate."

"She was married to a brewer?" Gerard couldn't mask his amusement. "When he died, were there no male relatives to handle the estate? A woman left in control of a fortune—what was her husband thinking?"

Stoddard's expression closed. "You'll have to ask Mrs. Brightman. I'm not a gossip."

At Stoddard's reproving tone, Gerard decided to come to the point of why he wanted to pursue the racetrack without delay. Hang the troublesome widow. "When I visited my mother, my father said he'd all but chosen my future bride and told me it was time to come into the family business."

"Oh?" Stoddard raised an eyebrow.

"And if I didn't, he would cut off my allowance."

Stoddard considered him, smiling grimly. "So you need a new source of income."

Gerard was gratified that Stoddard was unsurprised that he hadn't fallen in with his pompous father's plans. "Now you see why a racetrack appeals to me?"

Stoddard took his time with another swallow. "I could get you many interviews for good positions here. My future— ah, Mr. Foster is well connected. You're educated, a gentleman. I don't see the need to set up a racetrack."

Gerard felt the old exasperation rise in him. "But none of those positions will spite my father like a racetrack will." He said the words with a twisted satisfaction. His father would pay for trying to force him to dance to his tune. He didn't want to dance to any man's tune—not his father's, not an employer's. He would make his way on his own terms or know the reason why.

Stoddard drained the last of his glass and rose, looking down almost sternly at Gerard. "I have already spoken to Tippy's father, and I have his permission to pay my addresses to her. I expect that we will be married before a year passes. Though I hope you will wish me happy, I doubt it. I'll see you in the morning. See that you don't turn up drunk at Mrs. Mather's. She'll put you out." Stoddard left with a wave to the proprietor.

Shaken by his friend's stern declaration and abrupt departure, Gerard sat alone, holding the thick glass of ale in both hands. So it had come to this. Gerard lifted his glass, rose, and moved to the counter. Well, here was as good a place as any to begin the spadework for his endeavor.

"Evening," he began after introducing himself to the barkeep. "I know it's near the end of the season, but are there any horse races coming up near here?"

❦

Blessing's orphanage sat on the far south edge of "respectable" Cincinnati, near Little Africa. Though she spent much time here, she'd decided to maintain residence in the house where she had lived with her husband, over a mile farther away from the river. Yet, once again, she didn't know when she'd be able to return home for the night.

In the washroom off the kitchen on the first floor, with her sleeves rolled up, Blessing finished bathing the baby boy. He lay in her arms, so very thin and so quiet with sunken eyes, but still he managed to keep his attention on her. Had she brought him here in time? Or would he expire as so many undernourished babies before him had?

She wondered if he'd ever had a bath. He was eaten up with diaper rash. But the woman had kept him alive. How easy it would have been to let the infant die. Blessing tried to shut out the memories of other children she hadn't reached in time. She said a prayer for this child to survive and for the woman who'd cared for him to find peace and safety. Blessing drew in a breath to hold back the tears that wanted to come. The infant tried to grip her finger as if clinging to life.

Would she ever become accustomed to the way the world treated unwanted children? No child should be unwanted. But how could she possibly prepare this child for a world that would always look at him with scorn? She finished bathing him and wrapped him in a towel. This little boy was affecting her more than usual, and she wondered why. Gerard Ramsay's face came to mind. That didn't make sense. He had nothing to do with this child or with her.

Her friend and coworker Joanna, slender and pretty with caramel skin, entered the room. Joanna was in charge of the children's care here, and she and Blessing had grown up together and been as close as sisters—until Blessing married Richard Brightman. That had separated them for a time.

"I got his clothing." Joanna laid out a worn but clean blue flannel blanket, gown, cap, and diaper on the dressing table.

Glad of her friend's company, Blessing carried the listless infant to Joanna, who deftly cradled the child. The boy still did not cry or make a sound, but merely stared up at them.

"Probably has never felt clean before," Joanna murmured.

She began to hum to the baby as she unwrapped him from the towel and started dressing him.

"I've sent my driver for the wet nurse." Blessing leaned her head against Joanna's shoulder, seeking comfort for her low spirits. Joanna's father and mother worked for Blessing's parents, Samuel and Honor Cathwell. Before that, Joanna's mother, Royale, had been Honor's slave. Together Royale and Honor had left Maryland to come to a free state. When Blessing had moved to the city, Joanna had come along as her day maid. Joanna had been engaged to Asher, a lifelong friend, for three years, but he didn't yet have the means to wed.

Blessing rolled down her sleeves. She and Joanna had been born only a year apart. Blessing was glad to have a friend who understood her work, her life. Still she wondered how long before Joanna married, began her own family, and left the work here, left her.

"How is that Miss Tippy doing?" Joanna asked, lifting and patting the child.

"I'm worried."

Joanna looked up. "Why? Is it about that man from Boston that's making up to her?"

"Yes." Blessing chewed on the worry again. "I just don't want her to make the mistake I did . . . with Richard."

Joanna gazed at her. "You were younger then."

Blessing half smiled sadly. "Tippy is younger now."

"Does this Boston man she interested in act like your late husband?"

Blessing considered this. She'd seen him at the docks tonight, but it was the first time. "Stoddard makes it plain that he wants to court her."

"If I remember rightly, Richard Brightman did more than that. He wouldn't leave you alone. Sending flowers every day. Little love notes. He didn't hardly give you a chance to think."

Scenes from her whirlwind courtship with Richard played in her mind. He had done whatever she wanted, whatever pleased her. Said he would die if she didn't agree to be his wife. She'd been so innocent then. "I should have known it was too good . . ."

"To be true," Joanna finished for her.

"I'm still assessing Stoddard Henry." Blessing sighed and switched her mind back to the present. "This baby doesn't have a name," she said, not putting her fear for the child into words. Would they choose a name only to etch it on a small tombstone?

"Well, we don't want to repeat a name." Joanna looked thoughtful and her humming lowered. "How about Luke?"

Blessing considered this, stroking the child's baby-soft skin. "It's a strong name and has a good feeling about it. What surname shall we give him?"

"How about Green? Simple. Easy to say and spell."

Blessing bent down and kissed the baby's forehead, wishing she could make up for the fact that he'd not been welcomed by proud and happy parents. Only one woman had cared about him or his mother enough to keep him alive. She blinked away tears again. "Welcome, Luke Green. May God bless thy life. May thee be a willing worker, honest and kind. May thee be strong enough to live and face this world."

"Amen," Joanna agreed.

Then the back door opened and their wet nurse, Theodosia, as dark-complected as Joanna was light, came in and shed her shawl. In short order she gathered the child from Joanna, sat down, and began to nurse him. "He's nearly starved. I can't stay long. I left my others sleeping. My aunt will look in on them."

A young widow with two little ones under four, Theodosia supported herself through her work for the orphanage.

"I think you should consider moving here," Blessing said once more. She still didn't like sending babies to Theodosia's neighborhood, even though it was close to her own. Little Africa was always a target for ruffians and violence.

Theodosia frowned. "I got a safe place and don't want to lose it."

Blessing didn't press her. Theodosia and her children spent their days here, and every evening she took the nurslings home with her. She liked to remain somewhat independent. And after all, Blessing couldn't blame her—she herself needed time away from the weight of this place.

After the child had eaten till he fell asleep, Joanna handed Theodosia a cloth bag holding clean clothing and diapers. The baby in her arms, Theodosia nodded and headed outside to the waiting carriage, bidding them good night.

Joanna sighed, bid Blessing the same, and left for her room upstairs. A nearby church bell tolled eleven times.

Wishing Joanna would have stayed up for a chat, Blessing sank down at the kitchen table, suddenly bone-weary. Joanna was in charge of the orphans' needs, but Blessing bore the ultimate responsibility not only for the orphans but also for most of the people who cared for them.

The orphanage had a staff of six. Four were former slaves or the children of former slaves: the cook, maid, laundress, and of course, Joanna. They were all at risk of kidnapping and violence, so she'd hired a white gardener/handyman and his wife, who had left North Carolina because of their anti-slavery sentiments and were needed here to protect the others when Blessing was absent. Even free people of color had no legal rights in Ohio.

She realized she was in an odd, reflective humor. Meeting the men from Boston at the wharf had stirred her up some-how, though how the two men passed their time was really none of her concern. But should she warn Tippy that the man she loved might be guilty of frequenting the dens by the river?

❦

Later, after returning to her own home, Blessing struck a match and lit a candle to guide her way to bed. Then she heard a quiet knock at her kitchen door. The very stealth of it galvanized Blessing. Candlestick in hand, she opened the door.

Two people slipped inside but remained in the shadows, away from any window. Blessing recognized one of her visitors, a young man from Joanna's church, and with him was a petite black woman. Blessing didn't need to ask why they'd come. Another runaway.

"All the other stations are being watched," the young man said. "Can she hide here till it's safe to move her?"

Blessing didn't waste words. "Follow me." She led the two swiftly up the stairs to the second story and into the attic. There she ran her hand across the wall until she found the catch that opened the secret door. She waved the woman inside. "I'll bring up food and water soon."

The runaway slave nodded. "Thank you, ma'am." She slumped, exhausted, onto the pallet along the wall, giving one last shudder of fear.

Blessing saw by candlelight the woman's face—it was lovely. And then she understood why the other houses were being watched. She rarely hid slaves; her home was reserved as a last resort, thus making it safe for the most-wanted runaways. This woman was no doubt some master's prized mistress, and he was willing to pay top dollar for her return— probably four to five times the usual bounty on an escaped slave.

"Thee'll be safe here," Blessing said, sickened by the woman's plight, and shut the panel.

The young man pattered down the steps behind her and, back in the kitchen, peered out the dark window.

"Perhaps thee should stay too," Blessing cautioned. "The watch might take thee up for being out at night." Or he might be set upon by ruffians.

"That might be best," he agreed.

She waved to the back door. "Thee can sleep with the driver over the carriage house. He has an extra bed."

He nodded his thanks and hurried outside. She closed the door and sank onto a chair at the kitchen table, wearier than ever. Head in her hands, she felt all the evils in this world piling up around her. The face of Gerard Ramsay came again to her mind, and she couldn't help the sudden indignation that welled up inside.

Did privileged Gerard Ramsay comprehend the realities of life? Babies were being born into poverty and worse. Women were living in bondage to procurers. Black men and women were fleeing soul- and body-destroying shackles. And all he could think of was having a good time. If he were here, she would shake him till his teeth rattled.

She *would* warn Tippy not only about Stoddard's appearance by the river, but that Ramsay was a bad influence on the man she wanted to marry. Resolved, she shoved away thoughts of Ramsay—a spoiled, probably dissolute gentleman—and prayed for the little baby with the whimsical expression who might not live through the night and the desperate runaway hiding in her attic. Spiriting her from the city unseen would be a challenge even for Blessing. The Lord would need to provide a way—Blessing couldn't think of one.

❖

SEPTEMBER 3, 1848

As church bells rang the next morning, Blessing walked toward the meetinghouse for First Day worship, troubled and feeling her lack of sleep. Did some slave catcher guess that a runaway might be hiding in her house? She had the sensation she was being watched, followed—an impression she had experienced often even as a child, since her parents' home had frequently harbored runaways.

With effort she concealed her unease, especially resisting the urge to glance over her shoulder. But whenever she heard a sound that would have naturally prompted her to turn around, she obeyed the urge. More than once she thought she glimpsed a man slipping out of sight. Hiding her anxiety, she met other Friends also on their way to meeting and exchanged quiet greetings. Still, uppermost in her mind was how to smuggle away the runaway in her attic.

Blessing caught sight of her father helping her mother down from their wagon, and she hurried forward, her spirits lifting. Her parents did not drive into town for meeting every First Day. Maybe they could take the runaway home with them. Better to get the woman away quickly while the catchers kept vigil in the city.

She waited till her mother was standing beside her father before she greeted them, using both her voice and her fingers in sign language since her father was deaf. Grateful for the subtlety of the signs, she explained her need without speaking.

Both parents kissed her cheek in greeting but responded that their hidden room was already occupied and that their house was being watched by two slave catchers at the moment. Joanna's parents, Judah and Royale, had stayed home on watch.

Mulling over this disappointing news, Blessing also greeted her younger sisters and brother, along with her honorary cousin, Caleb. They entered the meetinghouse as a family. When she looked around the quiet place, unadorned and plain, Blessing was comforted. All the long years of exile during her marriage—nearly six—she had missed this place of solace, missed being close to God and his people.

As Blessing followed her mother to the women's side, she prayed silently. Where to take the runaway and how to smuggle her out unseen wouldn't let go. She kept trying to give the problem to God—and then snatching it back.

❖

Gerard Ramsay woke to the pealing of the Sunday church bells. He groaned and rolled over, pulling his soft pillows over his ears. He'd been careful not to drink enough to slur his speech or cause him to sway as he walked, but he'd imbibed more than he'd intended.

Guilt niggled at him and he pushed it away. He was not going to sink into the bottle like Kennan. And his evening had been productive: he'd gleaned many facts about racing in the Cincinnati area and had gotten the names of a few local bookmakers, men who could give him even more information about racing and the players and powers around here.

The Quakeress came to mind again, uninvited. The way she'd examined him at the docks and the way she'd looked at Stoddard. Perhaps he'd accomplished his goal already. If Blessing Brightman informed Miss Tippy Foster that her true love frequented the riverfront at night, that might be enough to break their romance in two.

Gerard closed his dry, gritty eyes and tried to go back to sleep in spite of the infernal bells calling the hypocrites, dressed in their Sunday best, to sit in the pews and judge each other.

❖

Sitting on the same bench as her mother and her four sisters—Jamaica and Constance, both in their early twenties, and nine-year-old twins Patience and Faith—Blessing began centering herself, the traditional way Friends prepared themselves for worship.

Several years earlier, many Quakers had decided to adopt the ways of worship of other Christian churches, with a set program including music and a sermon. However, she and her parents were Hicksites and had kept to the old ways, still following the tradition of worship tuned to the Light of Christ.

She began to seek God's peace. One by one, worries rushed over her like waves—Gerard Ramsay, Stoddard Henry and Tippy Foster, the poor woman who'd given her Luke last night, the baby's thin body, and the frightened escaped slave hiding in her attic. She prayed over each one and tried to dismiss it from her mind, sending all of them to God. The tension she'd come in with began to ease.

All around her, the other Friends were doing the same. Or she supposed they were. What person could really know another's thoughts? But that deep quiet of meeting began to settle over the large room. Even the children rested against their mothers or fathers. Although a few babies whimpered or fussed, their noise didn't disturb the process of letting go of the world and entering God's peace. Her worries continued to bob up and she continued handing them to Christ.

Across the room on the men's side, her father, Samuel Cathwell, rose from his position beside her brother, John. This was a rare occurrence. Her father, who had been deaf since a childhood illness, did not speak often because his voice sounded odd and it embarrassed him. Blessing waited, filled with a special love for this quiet man.

Instead of speaking aloud, though, he began signing, and her mother interpreted the motions of his hands aloud for the congregation. "Sometimes I tremble for our nation," she said. "The scourge of slavery has cost many lives and will cost many more. A deep blindness, born of greed, has covered the Southern states. I long for God to find a way to end it without bloodshed. That is my prayer."

A murmur of agreement ran through the meeting. Even those who didn't approve of helping escaped slaves could agree, as no Friend wanted violence. Her father sat down. The stillness resumed except for the cries of one baby. His mother rose and left the meeting, murmuring to the child.

Blessing considered her father's words and prayed in agreement for slavery to end soon and without violence. But how that could be done only God knew.

As much as Blessing longed to be centered within God's peace, her mind began to disobey her again, bringing up scenes from the past months. Meeting Gerard Ramsay in Seneca Falls, dining with him at the Fosters', bumping into him at the riverfront. *Stop,* she ordered herself. Then a plan began to form in her mind of how she might help two birds at risk with one stone. A sweet, devious smile curved her lips.

❖

Gerard rose from bed long after breakfast had ended. Sitting on the side of his bed, he scrubbed his face with his hands, but that did nothing to alleviate the ache behind his eyes or the frustrations circling through his mind.

When Blessing Brightman had recognized him last night, the look she'd given him . . . Another meddling reformer who would tell him how to live his life and enumerate his sins. How could he disarm her? Spike her guns while he peeled Stoddard out of Miss Foster's gloved mitts—assuming Blessing's own words didn't do the job? A plan began to form in his mind. He chuckled. Military history class had taught him one thing, at least: always attack on the least-expected front.

❦

The next morning Gerard drove up to Blessing Brightman's impressive home and tied his rented horse and gig to the ornate iron hitching post shaped like a horse's head. Sure of success, he ran lightly up the steps and knocked. Women were so easy to manipulate.

Before long he was waiting in her parlor.

The widow entered, not making much effort to conceal her unease or lack of pleasure at seeing him there. "Gerard Ramsay, what may I do for thee?" she challenged him.

"I think we started off on the wrong foot, Mrs. Brightman." He crafted his most charming smile, the one he used on the wives of pompous men—wives he was trying to seduce. "I've hired a gig and would like you to show me Cincinnati and a little of the surrounding area. It will give us an opportunity to become better acquainted. Will you join me?" He said the last as a light dare. Would the woman come or demur?

She stared at him for a long moment and then did something he hadn't expected: she chuckled. "What a kind invitation. I have a friend visiting me whom I was going to carry to her next destination, about six miles from here. I dreaded driving back alone."

"A friend?" he stammered. He wanted to have Blessing to himself in order to ply her with flattery and pique her interest in him.

"So kind of you," the widow went on, ignoring his question, moving toward the door. "We'll be down in a trice. Thy gig is at the front?"

"Yes." He watched her leave and regretted coming.

Within minutes he was helping both ladies onto the seat of the one-horse gig. The other woman, her face concealed by a close-brimmed, veiled hat, crowded them a bit on the seat, but he didn't point this out. He'd offered and he was stuck.

Following the widow's directions, he drove out of town in silence.

When the silence became heavy, Blessing asked, "So Stoddard Henry is thy cousin?"

"Yes. He's the son of my father's sister. We were at boarding school together."

"How interesting. I received my education at home, and then, at fourteen, I was sent to a Friends' school for girls in Pennsylvania for a few years. After graduation I taught school in Cincinnati—before my marriage."

"Really?" He'd spoken to very few educated women—even fewer who had actually worked at a profession. Of course, teaching was one of only a handful of professions open to women, and typically to those who were unmarried and without funds. From her and from what Stoddard had told him, he extrapolated that the pretty teacher had charmed a wealthy man. "You married well, then?"

She laughed as if he'd told a joke. "Yes, I suppose thee would think so. Richard Brightman owned two breweries."

He hadn't expected her to admit this, so he stared momentarily. Again he wondered how a straitlaced Quakeress had agreed to marry to a brewer. "I see."

She laughed again. "I doubt it. I sold the breweries upon my husband's death and invested in other concerns."

"It was unusual for you to inherit, wasn't it?"

"Yes."

Steaming at her slightly mocking attitude toward him, Gerard drove on, trying to come up with a way to turn the conversation in the direction he'd planned for it to go. He'd come to charm the widow in order to bend her to his own purposes, and now a prim stranger—a silent chaperone—sat stiffly beside her, and Blessing was laughing at him in a way he didn't understand. And didn't like. How fast could he drive six miles?

But wait—surely he would have better odds with the woman once they were alone. And they would necessarily be alone on the way home. Perhaps he could delay their return so that she might be mildly compromised from being in his company alone after dark.

He brought up a fresh smile and began to quote poetry, a ploy he usually found successful in charming ladies.

❖

Later that afternoon, after they reentered Cincinnati, Blessing relaxed. Except for the presence of Gerard Ramsay, so unexpected but so providential, everything had gone exactly to her plan. And the effectiveness of the runaway's impromptu disguise: the veiled bonnet, along with a wig, gloves, and white rice face powder, was an extra precaution. His company had added zest to the whole experience. No one would suspect someone like Gerard Ramsay of helping a runaway. She suppressed glee at successfully using him as the means to her own end.

"You're in a lighthearted mood," Gerard said.

Since she was listening for it, she heard the tinge of irritation concealed in his words. "Yes, I am. It's been such a lovely ride, doesn't thee think? I'm so glad we had a nice breeze. I almost hate to return home."

"I'm glad you've enjoyed my company," the man had the nerve to say. "Perhaps we can take another ride soon. You still haven't shown me around the city."

Her house came into sight. "Thee strikes me as a man who can find his own way around, but I do thank thee for driving my friend to her next stopping point."

He didn't reply to this, merely pulled up the horse outside her home.

Before he could offer to help her down, Blessing slid off her seat and down the step. "Thank thee again." She waved and was up the steps without waiting. She turned back for one more look and saw Ramsay staring at her. She couldn't help herself—she grinned.

Letting herself in, she ran up the stairs to the attic. She caught Tippy sitting on a chair and reading a book by the small attic window. "Didn't I caution thee to listen for someone entering the house and to take cover?"

"I heard the gig stop outside, and I know your step," Tippy said, looking up from her book. "Did the disguise work? Did you get the runaway to the next station?"

"Yes."

Tippy leaped to her feet. "And Mr. Gerard Ramsay of Boston never guessed that he was aiding and abetting a fugitive slave?"

"Yes!" And that seemed to be the signal for both of them to dissolve into laughter, an outburst of relief and triumph.

The arrival of the runaway had tabled Blessing's plan to warn Tippy about Stoddard Henry—for now, at least. Instead, that morning she'd summoned Tippy with a note, asking her to come wearing a hat with a thick veil. After Tippy had arrived, Blessing had clothed the runaway in Tippy's dress, hat, and gloves and had been preparing to drive off to a nearby small town where she knew of another station on the Underground Railroad, used only for high-risk escapes. And later Tippy would slip away home, dressed inconspicuously. But there was still the worry of being stopped—and if they were, Blessing would be hard put to conceal her companion's identity, disguise or no.

Then Gerard Ramsay had arrived, and Blessing had sensed immediately that the man from Boston had come to charm her. She was a young, wealthy widow, and this had been tried before. In the moment, though, he met her needs exactly. What could be more natural than a couple and their friend driving along the road together? Even if they were stopped, Gerard would naturally be the one to answer any questions. She smiled to herself. Gerard was indeed a very handsome man of considerable means, and no doubt accustomed to easily ensnaring gullible women. *Well, Gerard Ramsay of Boston, I'm not gullible. In fact, I gulled thee today.*

Chapter 4

Soon Tippy, in disguise as Blessing, was headed for home in Blessing's carriage. Weary, Blessing had just sat down to tea in the back parlor when her housekeeper announced that Mr. Stoddard Henry was in the front hall asking to see her. The accepted hours for social calling had passed, and her housekeeper, Salina, looked peeved.

Salina handed her his card. "He been here twice already today," the woman said in her laconic way. Salina's father had been a runaway slave; he'd been taken in by the Wyandot, who had still roamed Ohio thirty years ago. He'd married into the tribe, and Salina's features showed the blending of the two races. In her early thirties, Salina was tall and trim with high cheekbones. Most of all, she was imposing and a good gatekeeper.

Blessing sighed with fatigue. Presumably Stoddard was

worried she would tell Tippy about seeing him the other night. She gazed at the calling card in her hand, remembering the unpleasant incident. She rubbed her tired eyes and blinked to bring up moisture. After the long ride and the all-day tension, Blessing was in no mind to admit him.

Then with a shrug she relented for her sake as much as his. She would have no peace till she heard him out and could assess the truth about him for herself. Would he make the mistake of trying to charm her like Ramsay? "Show him in. But tell him I am about to leave for the orphanage and cannot give him long."

At the back of her mind, little Luke Green hovered. Since the night she'd recovered him, she'd prayed for his health in between prayers for the runaway's safety. Was little Luke better today or still failing? The thought of losing another child hitched her breath.

Stoddard entered and bowed.

"Please be seated, Stoddard Henry," Blessing said but did not offer him tea. "What may I do for thee?"

Stoddard sat, then leaned forward. "I will not take up your time with idle chatter but will come directly to the point. Saturday night I went to the docks with my cousin, hoping to deter him and bring him away."

The audacity of Gerard Ramsay's demanding to know why she was at the riverfront still managed to rise up and aggravate her. She knew a handsome face could hide much—perhaps a wounded soul? Was that why he'd caught her attention? No, surely not.

Scrutinizing Stoddard, she sipped her tea. "Why does thee tell me this?"

Stoddard half smiled. "Because I know that my . . . that Miss Foster is very close to you. I don't want you to report me to her before I've had a chance to speak with her myself."

Blessing stiffened, though admittedly this had been her plan. "I am not usually a talebearer."

He held up a restraining hand. "Pardon; I'm not expressing myself very well. And in this case you need not be. I plan to confess it to her, as I said. I have already been frank with Miss Foster about my previously careless lifestyle."

Previously careless lifestyle? Blessing considered him. "When will thee tell her?"

"I've already tried. I was told she was here visiting you. That is one reason I came."

"She was helping me with my work," Blessing explained, letting him assume she meant the orphanage.

Now he pinned Blessing with an intense gaze. "I have been shown a different way of thinking, of living, and I am no longer the man I was a few months ago. In fact, I had become disenchanted with the society life before I met Tip . . . Miss Foster."

Blessing listened to this speech in silence. It could be true, but it could be a confession meant to disarm her. Dramatically admitting to faults was another ploy that had been used on her by her own husband. Only time would tell if his words were authentic. Richard's hadn't been.

She chose to reply obliquely. "Xantippe Foster is one of the most intelligent, refreshing, and honest young women I have ever met. Her friendship means a great deal to me."

"I know." He did not remove his gaze from her.

She couldn't let her friend be fooled by a handsome face

75

that might easily hide a dark heart. "I would do anything in my power to persuade her not to notice a man I thought was unworthy of her." After a day of dissembling, speaking the truth was liberating.

A pause ensued. Blessing nibbled a slice of fruited cake to gather strength. The tall clock in the hallway ticked loudly in the silence. A wagon rumbled by outside.

"I'm glad Miss Foster has a friend as true as you are," Stoddard replied. "I would ask you one question. Have you ever seen me at the wharf before Saturday night?"

Blessing set down her empty cup in its saucer. "No, I have not. But I did see thee then—"

"Not for long. And not again."

Blessing had no more time for this. Worry for Luke goaded her. She rose. "I will consider what thee has told me, Stoddard Henry. Now I must go to the orphanage and check on the infant rescued most recently."

He stood also. "I won't keep you, but please believe me. My intentions toward Miss Foster are honorable, and I would do only good by her."

Unconvinced, Blessing offered him her hand and then, with a bow, he left.

"So you believe what he say?" Salina had returned after showing him out.

"Thee was listening?" Blessing asked in gentle reproof.

"I like Miss Tippy. That man want to marry her. Anybody can see how he looks at her."

Blessing smiled. "Thee doesn't miss much." She walked toward the door. "I must go to the orphanage. If anyone else calls, I'm not at home till tomorrow."

"Even that slick customer who carried that poor woman away today?"

She couldn't help but smile at her housekeeper's assessment. "Especially that slick customer."

Soon, with her hot, dry eyes shut, she rested against the plush seat of her own carriage. Memories of Ramsay's attempts to beguile her today had told her more about him than he would have guessed. What bedeviled him?

She'd originally been happy that Tippy had found a young man who was not put off by her forward ideas. Now she was simply worried. She would write to some abolitionist acquaintances who lived in the Boston area to discover more about Stoddard Henry and his cousin. Forewarned was forearmed. Tippy deserved the truth, needed the truth.

❖

Entering the orphanage kitchen, Blessing found Theodosia at the table, munching a sandwich and drinking a tall glass of milk with Luke in one arm. "Hello, Theodosia." Her heart beat faster. What would the report be on the infant?

"Miss Blessing," Theodosia said, inclining her head toward Luke, "he's been nursing 'bout every hour." The woman nodded at her plate. "I'm having to eat and drink more just to keep up."

Lightened by relief, Blessing smiled and sat near them. "Did thee take a nap? I don't want thee to become overdone."

"I did. Joanna took over my two little'uns and watched them with the rest while I napped most of the afternoon. This one just sleeps and eats."

The cook at the stove turned and smiled at the baby. "He

is a good one. Before long he be as fat a baby as anybody could want."

Except nobody wants him. Despair suddenly knotted Blessing's throat. For a long time, she had thought she might adopt a child or two from the orphanage. Maybe Luke would be the first one. He drew her in a special way.

She stroked his fine golden hair. He spared her a brief glance before going back to the important task of nursing. He already looked like a different baby from the one she'd rescued. Food and care had awakened his will to live. Blessing rejoiced.

❖

After dinner and on his way to follow up a racetrack lead, Gerard could not shake the aftertaste from his troubling day spent in Blessing's audacious company. Somewhere on the drive home, he had come to the realization that she was a complex and resourceful woman. His usual tactics might not work on her, but he wouldn't give up. She believed she was the equal of a man. That alone needed to be addressed. He would find a way to humble her, teach her to take her womanly place in society.

However, furthering his racetrack came first. In the autumn twilight the wharf had barely begun to stir when Gerard entered one of the alehouses, looking for a prominent bookmaker named Clancy. Gerard walked directly to the barkeep and asked for the man.

"Who wants to know?"

Gerard had already planned what he'd say. "A man with means and connections who has a business proposition which will benefit both parties."

The barkeep, who appeared as though he'd once been a boxer, looked him up and down. And then glanced toward the darker back corner. At a nod from the man there, he motioned Gerard toward a table. "Clancy's over there."

Gerard thanked the barkeep and strolled over. He sized up the bookmaker quickly. Clancy appeared to be on the dark side of forty, with rumpled clothing but a clean face and hands, as well as a fine gentleman's hat hanging on the back of his chair. A ham-fisted man stood behind him.

Clancy had also been sizing up Gerard. "Who're you? And what da ya want?"

Gerard pulled out a chair, sat down across from him, and paused to flick a particle of dust from his pant leg. Then he looked up at Clancy. "I'm Gerard Ramsay of Boston," he said, in no hurry. "I'm new in town and looking for a profitable investment. I was thinking it's a shame—" he lowered his voice slightly—"that Cincinnati doesn't have a permanent racetrack. I heard that you're one of the main bookmakers in town—"

"He's the top bookmaker," the ham-fisted man spoke up, "and a lot more."

Clancy raised a hand. "Go on, Mr. Ramsay."

"I thought you might be able to tell me if anybody else is trying to bring this into being." He sent the man a knowing grin, like a slice of crescent moon. "Since I'm new in town, I don't know whose toes I might be stepping on as I proceed."

Clancy tilted his head as if trying to see another angle of Gerard's face. Then, visibly stalling, he took a swallow of his ale. "I'll be frank with you, Mr. Ramsay." He leaned forward on his elbows. "Not only me but other gents have tried to get one going, but the city bigwigs are pushed around in this town. They got a God-fearing seminary here, and the holy don't think a racetrack is good for the city."

Gerard nearly rubbed his hands together with joy. However, he let nothing of this show. "That's where I can help you. I can get to the people who can make or break this deal. I move in society and can come up with backing and capital from investors who would publicly countenance the plan." He sat back and grinned. "Always follow the money. Virtue bows before profit."

Clancy chuckled, then laughed outright. "That's a good one. I'll remember that."

"So? Should I draw up a plan? Or is there somebody I should meet first?"

The bookmaker didn't hesitate. "His name's Smith. Mr. Smith. He's got a finger in every ripe pie in the city."

"And where can I meet this gentleman?"

"Come back here tomorrow night about ten. I'll see if I can interest him in meeting with you."

Gerard rose and reset his hat with a jaunty tap. "I'll look forward to it."

Clancy laughed again, a dark, mocking sound.

The hair prickled on the back of Gerard's neck. He ignored the sensation and walked smartly out into the street. Once outside, he felt a mixture of elation and trepidation, both a lifting and a tightening.

When one stirred a muddy pond, one never knew what might float to the surface. A few hair-raising memories from his nights haunting Boston Harbor came back to him. He always had his cane at the ready and knew how to use it, but he would resume carrying his pistol tomorrow.

"Gerard Ramsay, I see thee is starting early this evening."

Not again. The tart tone behind him broadcast exactly what Blessing Brightman thought he was starting early this evening. He wanted to tell her to mind her own business, but that wouldn't serve his purpose. His goal was to best this woman, so he turned and arched his lips into a mock smile. "Ah, the widow Brightman, doing good among the poor." He tried to sound approving, not scathing.

She only lifted an eyebrow at him. And stared.

He flushed and prepared to speak, to try to do better this time. But a shrill outcry caught both their attentions.

Without hesitation, Blessing picked up her black skirts and ran in the direction of the cry, into a dark alley—an alley that no decent lady would or should enter. Gerard cursed under his breath and chased after her. "Hold up!"

On her heels, he arrived at the source of the disruption. The sound of a rod whistled through the dank air. A blow landed with a thump. Another pained shriek.

"Let her go," the Quakeress commanded the rod-wielding man, who was beating a young girl.

"Go about your business," the man growled, and he struck the girl again. She wailed, begging him to stop.

The sight sickened Gerard. He moved closer.

Blessing thrust herself into the man's face. "Let her go. Or I'll call the watch."

The man threw the girl backward with such force that she hit the wall behind, cried out, and fell hard to the ground, where she remained still.

But Gerard was more worried about Blessing. He hurried forward to protect her.

"Go ahead," the man taunted her. "Call the watch! They won't do anything. She belongs to me, she does—"

"She is white and not a slave," Blessing said, not giving ground—indeed, moving closer to the man. "Who is she?"

The man hesitated for a telling second and then muttered, "She's my daughter, yeah."

"Liar," Gerard said before he could stop the word.

Glad for a target, the man turned to him, face aflame and hands fisted. "Mind yer own business!"

Gerard swung up his cane, aiming the point at the man's throat. "Is this young woman truly your daughter?"

"No, she ain't, and you know what she is too," the man tossed back. "From firsthand experience, right?"

Gerard's spine tingled, his face flushing hotly.

Blessing took a deep breath and faced the man squarely. "Go away. I'm taking her home with me."

"She'll be back tomorra night," the man jeered. "Her type allus is." He curled his lip and stalked away. "She'll be back!" he taunted once more.

Without hesitation the widow bent over the girl. "Can thee stand?"

"Who are you?" the girl stammered, panting, sprawled against the wall like a limp rag doll.

"I'm Blessing Brightman."

"Oh, I heard of you. You help people." The girl moved to rise but then fell back, groaning with pain and holding her arm against herself.

Blessing turned to Gerard. "If thee will help her to her feet, I can get her to my carriage."

"Where are you taking me?" the girl whimpered.

"To a place where you can have a good meal, clean clothes, and a warm bed for the night. Would thee like that?"

The girl nodded, then moaned, still protecting her abdomen with her arm.

Gerard did not want to touch this girl. She gave filthy a bad name. But a lady had made a request within his power, and he must grant it. Gingerly and at arm's length, he slipped his hands under the girl's arms and lifted her, then propped her against the wall. With his every move, her moans tore at him in a way he hadn't expected.

Without any reluctance, Blessing slid an arm under the girl's arms and drew her close. "Can thee walk if I help thee?"

The girl grunted her assent. "Just go slow," she whispered, panting. "Please."

Blessing took a step forward and the girl stumbled with her, wavering precariously.

Gerard knew he should ask Blessing to take his cane and then lift the young girl himself and carry her. But he found he simply couldn't touch her again, till she staggered and fell, taking the Quakeress down with her onto the filthy alley pavers.

He growled with frustration and thrust his cane toward the widow. "Here. I'll carry her." He helped Blessing up, then stooped and lifted the girl into his arms. She weighed barely anything. "Where's your carriage?" he gasped at Blessing, breathing through his mouth at the stench.

She hurried forward. "Not far."

Within a block, the carriage came into sight. Gerard picked up his pace, wanting to get this over with. The old, black driver scrambled down and opened the carriage door.

Gerard climbed inside just long enough to deposit the girl on the seat, then backed out quickly.

The Quakeress gazed at him through the dusk. "Thee is a surprising man, Gerard Ramsay. Just when I think I have thee figured out, thee does something unexpected."

He didn't like this at all. He wanted to captivate Blessing and then bring her down a step or two, not actually help her. "You can take the girl and clean her up," he retorted, "but there are two kinds of women. And she's the kind who will end up back here in a week."

Blessing Brightman drew herself up and held out her hand to her driver, who helped her into the carriage. Then she turned regally to face Gerard. "Thee is wrong, Gerard Ramsay. In truth there is only one kind of woman, but there are two kinds of men—those who respect women and those who debase them. Which kind is thee?" She sat; her driver shut the door and drove off up the bluff.

Gerard stood there, feeling a mix of shame and anger drift through him. That woman. He would best her yet.

❖

Reaching the rear of the orphanage, Blessing asked Judson, her driver, to assist the girl out of the carriage. With her charge between them, they helped her into the house and directly into the washroom. Blessing heard Joanna speaking to the cook in the nearby kitchen. Judson left them and went to park the carriage.

"What are you going to do to me?" the girl whimpered.

"I'm offering to let thee take a warm bath, and when thee is clean, I will call a doctor if thee needs one."

The girl leaned against the wall and gazed as if fascinated by the large tin tub across the room. "A bath?"

"Yes, with lots of warm water like in the summer, and soap scented with lavender. When clean, thee will feel better, and we can see if thee needs medical attention. I'll have a hot, nourishing supper prepared for thee too."

"What's this gonna cost me?" The girl hung back.

"Nothing. God has provided for me, and I share what he's given."

Then the girl moaned long and loud, and blood pooled on the floor beneath her.

"Joanna!" Blessing called out. "Send for a doctor! Then come quick!"

Blessing helped her to a chair. The girl moaned and gasped. As Blessing realized what was happening, her heart sank. Was this child even fifteen?

"What's happening to me?" she panted.

"I think thee is suffering a miscarriage." A child should never have to endure this.

Gerard Ramsay encroached on her thoughts. She wished he could be here to see what was happening. *There are two kinds of women,* he'd said. If only she could ram that lie down his throat.

❖

After several long, harrowing hours, Blessing, slumped in a kitchen chair, woke to Joanna's tug on her shoulder and her plea. "Blessing, you need to go to bed. It's too late for you to travel home."

Blessing blinked her sleep-crusted eyes. "Bed?"

Joanna helped her up. "The bleeding hasn't started again. The doctor has gone home. The girl is sleeping."

Blessing stood still a moment, getting her balance, feeling about eighty years old. The girl she'd brought to the orphanage tonight lay on a cot nearby. "Someone should sit with her."

"I will," Joanna said as she led Blessing toward the door like a child. "I'm going to put you to bed in the attic room, and I'll come down and keep watch over her."

"Thee needs thy sleep too—"

"I have help coming tomorrow. But you must sleep. I'm worried, Blessing. You need to rest more. Or you're going to make yourself ill."

Joanna's concern was gratifying, but Blessing could only mumble her thanks and, without further protest, give herself up to Joanna's care.

❖

SEPTEMBER 5, 1848

Blessing walked down from the attic late the next morning and entered the orphanage kitchen. She found Joanna spooning porridge to their patient, who still lay on her cot.

"Morning, Blessing," Joanna greeted her without turning.

Blessing recalled Joanna's tender care last night. She was blessed to have a staunch ally like this friend.

"What's going to happen to me now?" the girl asked in a weak, trembling voice.

"Thee is going to eat, rest, and get well," Blessing said, coming near and placing a hand on the girl's forehead.

"Then what?"

"When thee is better, we will discuss that. Thee is safe here. Please believe that."

"I never met nobody like you before." The girl stared at her as if she were a giraffe or some other exotic animal.

Blessing smiled. "What is thy name? So we know what to call thee?"

"I don't like my name," the girl said and swallowed another spoonful of the cereal.

Joanna spoke up. "What name would you want to be called? A new name might do you good."

The girl considered them. "I've always liked Rebecca."

"Then good morning, Rebecca," Joanna said.

The cook laid out Blessing's breakfast on the table. Blessing's stomach gurgled and Joanna chuckled. Blessing joined in, feeling the mirth loosen her own worries. "I'd best sit down and eat now."

As she enjoyed the delicious breakfast, Blessing watched Joanna minister to Rebecca. One more life saved, but the girl's future remained uncertain. Blessing must find her a home. But who would take in a fifteen-year-old who'd just miscarried an illegitimate baby? That list would be a short one indeed.

❦

That afternoon, during the polite hours for social visiting, Blessing arrived at the Foster home to speak with Tippy. The events of the night before still hung lurid in her mind. Rebecca seemed to be doing well, but Blessing knew how quickly she could take a turn for the worse if infection set in.

At the door, the butler told Blessing that Mrs. Foster and her daughter had been called away to Louisville to visit an ailing relative there. Blessing turned away but, before returning home, headed toward the bank. She needed to see her banker and discuss an investment in a new steamboat venture.

As she walked off, the events of the day before unrolled through her mind as thread on a spindle. Some days it seemed as if the world washed its evil against her in waves—cold, disgusting waves. What kind of life must Rebecca have suffered to bring her to her present circumstances? Even if the girl lived, Blessing had no certainty that she'd be able to help her leave the degradation of the past behind. But their God was the God of second chances. He'd given her one.

At the bank, she was greeted courteously and shown to the door of an office. Just as she turned to thank the man, she glimpsed Gerard Ramsay sauntering through the doors. Anger from last night rushed up inside her like steam in a kettle. She mastered herself and then told her escort that she needed to greet someone.

Blessing swept over to him. "Gerard Ramsay, thee seems to turn up wherever I am." She pulled a sweet and false smile.

"Ma'am." He doffed his hat and bowed to her. "Business at the bank?"

"That is usually the reason one enters a bank," she replied, rendering his question ludicrous. "Does thee know another reason of which I, a weak woman, am unaware?"

"I was merely making social conversation," he said in a tight voice.

Blessing was glad she'd irked him. She wanted to drag him to the orphanage and force him to visit poor Rebecca and to look in the faces of all the unwanted children she'd brought home over the past years. Did this man have even a thought for what was really going on in this city? Or was life just a round of self-seeking pleasure to him?

"Mrs. Brightman," came the low voice of her banker from behind.

"Thee must excuse me," she said. "I must keep my appointment."

Gerard bowed again and let the animosity toward this woman flow unheeded through him. She was annoying as a too-tight collar. He couldn't get last night's scene from the alley out of his mind. And now he couldn't even go to the bank without running into the pious woman. Her parting words from the night before still stung. Gerard had never struck a woman in his life.

He addressed the young man who had escorted Mrs. Brightman through the bank, and soon he was standing in his own banker's office. He executed his most charming smile and bow. "Good afternoon, sir. An excellent day for business, I hope."

He had tonight's meeting with Mr. Smith to prepare for by lining up bank funding, and nothing, especially not a meddling reformer, would stop him. The main objective behind the racetrack was, obviously, supporting himself. Embarrassing his father was a significant collateral benefit. Saul Ramsay would pay for interfering in Gerard's life, for cutting off his allowance. And if this venture also provoked the good widow, all the better.

❖

Late that evening a cool wind from the west chilled the back of Gerard's neck. The wharf was busy with people doing a night's business: prostitutes, beggars, and—no doubt—thieves, all preying on travelers. As he headed toward the tavern to meet Clancy, who was to introduce him to this Mr. Smith, the feeling that he was being followed or watched heightened Gerard's tension. He gripped his cane more tightly, ready to strike back if necessary. The light from the windows of the tavern drew him. He quickened his steps and entered.

Inside the door he halted. The place should have been crowded; it was empty. Not even the barkeep was present. *Something's not right.* Gerard turned to leave.

"Don't be goin' yet, *Mister* Ramsay." The voice caught him midturn. It was a low voice, but with the familiar accent of a Boston Irishman.

Gerard pivoted toward it.

A man had entered from the rear and was waving for Gerard to join him at a table in the back. Gerard took stock of him before approaching. He was tall with a fair complexion and thick black hair—what they called Black Irish. Handsome, he was dressed well, even expensively, with a gold watch fob dangling from his vest pocket. If he hadn't spoken, the man could have passed for a gentleman. And Gerard had seen him before—this was the stranger who'd accosted him at the horse race he'd attended with Stoddard. "Mr. Smith, I presume."

"One and the same." He gestured again for Gerard to join him.

Gerard moved forward and took the seat facing Smith. He didn't like having his back to the door, but he wasn't going to let this man intimidate him. "This place isn't doing very good business tonight."

"I wanted to meet you without interruptions." Smith reclined carelessly, his tone genial but his expression cynical.

Neither of them spoke for a moment. Gerard wondered whether it was really necessary to close the tavern for this meeting. Odd.

"Are we going to have a staring contest?" Gerard finally asked with a wry twist of his mouth.

"No, I'm just wondering why Saul Ramsay's only son is here in Cincinnati. I didn't think Ramsays ever went farther west than Saratoga."

Jolted, Gerard listened in wary silence. How did this man know about his family? "Have we met before?"

"Ha!" Smith responded. "I hardly think we moved in the same Boston circles."

Gerard couldn't think of any polite reply, so he merely inclined his head and waited.

"Your family is prominent enough to be recognized." Smith's lip curled.

Gerard accepted this with a nod, not wanting to pursue the subject. "Now can we get down to business?"

"What is your business, Mr. Ramsay?" Smith made himself more comfortable in the chair.

"I told that bookmaker Clancy that I'm interested in setting up a permanent racetrack somewhere close to the city."

"Ah, you're a man who loves the horses, hmm?"

"I like horses fine, but I like money more. I'm planning on using my connections, my social connections, to find investors—"

"So you don't have the capital?"

This question gripped Gerard because it revealed his one

weakness. He had the social position of his family, which meant something even here, but negligible funds. "My father is not a man to invest in a racetrack."

"Ah. Did he cut you off, then?"

Gerard fumed in silence.

"These little family disputes crop up from time to time." Smith waved a hand airily. "So you need investors? Is that why you've come to me?"

"I've come to you so that I don't step on anyone's toes. Clancy seemed to think I should talk to you. Are you interested in my racetrack venture, or are you pursuing something similar of your own?"

"A prudent man always thoroughly researches each venture." Smith nodded with a show of mock approval.

The man's condescension galled Gerard. "Well?" he snapped.

"I have considered a permanent racetrack but have not pursued it. This city has a strong reformin' tendency. Gets in the way sometimes."

"Right." Gerard leaned forward. "That's something I think I can circumvent. Men who would never publicly countenance a racetrack might—in private, between gentlemen—be interested in a discreet moneymaking venture."

"In private, between gentlemen," Smith echoed. "Ah. Yes, gambling always makes a profit . . . for the house. Or the track."

"A truth that many miss, to their own regret," Gerard observed dryly.

Smith gazed at him.

Gerard sat still, waiting for Smith's reply.

"I think we might be able to do business—"

"I don't need any—"

"But you do need me," Smith interrupted. "This town belongs to me, at least this part of town. You try to find your investors, and I'll line up the bookmakers and others you'll need."

"This is my venture." Gerard wanted this perfectly understood.

"Of course, but it's always best to have local cooperation, as you yourself must believe if you wanted to meet with me. I have my own connections."

Smith's ability to clear out an entire bar for a meeting gave him a taste of the influence this man must wield among this strata of society. Gerard just might have to keep on his good side. *After all, I am a prudent man.*

Gerard rose. "Very well. We have an understanding."

Smith stood also. "Indeed we do."

Gerard turned to leave—without shaking hands. He didn't want to let Smith think he viewed him as an equal, as a partner.

"Good night, Mr. Ramsay," Smith called after him, and again, to Gerard it sounded as if the man were mocking him.

Gerard kept walking, merely lifting a hand in farewell. He did not like Smith's tone. He did not like the fact that Smith knew about his family. He did not like Smith. But that didn't mean Smith wasn't necessary for Gerard to accomplish his goals.

◆

SEPTEMBER 11, 1848

Almost a week since her last attempt to visit Tippy, Blessing stepped down from her carriage in front of the Foster home.

Tippy and her mother had only recently returned from Louisville, and Blessing had been so busy with her work that she had not been able to come by. And then, yesterday, she'd received an invitation to attend a dinner party here tonight.

The dreadful fear that this social event might have been planned to announce Tippy's engagement clutched Blessing's heart with cold fingers. The butler welcomed her warmly at the door, and she moved into the parlor, her gray silk skirt whispering around her. The door between the rear and front parlors had been slid open, and everyone gathered in this spacious area. As usual, the men congregated at one end of the room and the women at the other. She glimpsed Gerard Ramsay with the men and turned away. The women were also divided among themselves, the older women in the opposite corner from the younger.

As a widow, Blessing often moved to mingle with the older women, but tonight she needed some way to get Tippy alone. If Stoddard were indulging in morally questionable behavior and Tippy did not discover it until after announcing their engagement, she would have no choice but to make an unpleasant public stir when she ended the betrothal. Blessing wanted to save her friend from that fate.

Blessing greeted her hostess and then moved through the crush of women to Tippy's side. The ladies there all greeted her by name and praised her new dress. The compliments stung since they reminded her that she had yet to completely return to her plain Quaker garb. She dressed in subdued colors, but for social occasions she could not forgo the urge to be in fashion. She admitted her vanity but couldn't curb it.

"Blessing, how good to see you," Tippy exclaimed and

pressed a kiss on Blessing's cheek. Tippy glowed with happiness.

Hiding her apprehension over this, Blessing smiled at her friend. She tried to think of some way to lure Tippy away to a quiet corner. And failed.

"What do you think of the new bachelor from Boston?" one young lady asked Blessing. "He's so handsome, and I love that accent. It's so distinguished, don't you think?"

Blessing made a polite, noncommittal sound. She'd expected Ramsay's entrance into society to spark a wave—or waves—of gossip and speculation. But she would not participate in it.

"He's from a prominent family, I believe," another woman confided in a low voice. "Of course, Tippy claimed the good-looking redhead before the rest of us even saw him."

Tippy blushed. Blessing bridled inwardly over the tactless remark directed at her friend.

"Well, we should probably thank Tippy," a third young woman said, "for her handsome redheaded beau brought Mr. Ramsay here."

The young ladies all tittered at this.

Blessing again did not reply. Heaven help any young lady who set her cap for Ramsay. If nothing else, she sensed his disdain for Cincinnati society.

Several more minutes of engaging in meaningless social chatter—much of it continued speculation about the handsome Gerard Ramsay—heightened Blessing's agitation over what this evening was all about.

Then Tippy's father called for everyone's attention, just as if he were about to announce Tippy's engagement.

Blessing recalled her mother's playful advice: when in a difficult social situation with no way out, faint.

She didn't need to fake it. With her corset pinching off her breath and her heart beating so fast, she felt faint. She stopped fighting the sensations, let them build. Spots flickered before her eyes . . .

Chapter 5

BLINKING, BLESSING WOKE to Tippy chafing her wrists and Mrs. Foster waving a disagreeable-smelling vinaigrette under her nose. She realized that she'd been carried into the small dressing room off the lone first-floor bedroom. "What happened?" she murmured, still dazed.

"You fainted," Mrs. Foster replied, giving Blessing an odd look. "At a very critical moment."

Everything rushed back. She'd stopped Mr. Foster's announcement, but she still must find out Tippy's—and Stoddard's—intentions.

"Have you been working too many late hours?" Tippy asked with evident sympathy.

"I think I can leave you two alone now and return to my guests." Mrs. Foster rose from her chair. Before shutting the door behind her, she sent Blessing a second suspicious look.

"Tippy," Blessing said, knowing she didn't have time to tiptoe around this touchy subject, "is thee planning upon becoming engaged to Stoddard Henry?"

"Yes." Tippy gazed at her, obviously bemused.

"Is thy father announcing it tonight?"

"No."

"Oh." Relief enveloped Blessing. Her throat had thickened, so she cleared it. "Tippy, is thee sure thee knows Stoddard well enough to become engaged to him?"

Tippy bubbled with laughter. "I know about your meeting Stoddard and his cousin at the wharf. Stoddard has told me all about his past. But it's past, Blessing. Be happy for me. I have fallen in love with a very good man. But it is too soon for us to announce it to the world."

Blessing realized she could say no more. Of course Tippy believed Stoddard. She was in love with him. Just as Blessing had believed Richard. Love blinded a woman until finally, one day, she couldn't lie to herself any longer. Blessing could only hope that Stoddard Henry had spoken the truth about his history, untainted by convenient lies such as the ones Richard had told her.

"Your father isn't announcing your engagement tonight, then?" Blessing asked, just to be certain.

"No, and I won't give away his news, but it's something quite different."

❧

Standing beside his cousin, Gerard had watched the dramatic fainting spell and had not been fooled. Blessing Brightman was doing whatever she could to stop the engagement announcement—at least, he assumed that's what Tippy's father had been about to announce. And for once he was in perfect agreement with her. In recent days, he'd been so busy speaking about his racetrack to potential investors—so far unsuccessfully—that he hadn't spent the time he should with Stoddard. After all, one of Gerard's main reasons for moving here was to lure his cousin away from the shackles of a respectable wife.

"That was odd," Stoddard whispered to him.

Gerard lifted a hand slightly. Let his cousin figure it out for himself.

"What have you been busy with this week?" Stoddard asked. "Except at meals, I've barely seen you."

"You know what I've been doing," Gerard said. And once again, he mentally shrugged off the misgivings he'd had after his first meeting with Mr. Smith. The man had left a sour taste in his mouth that he was having trouble washing away. And so far the gentlemen Gerard had met in his own sphere weren't inclined to invest in his track, and the bank had turned him down for a loan too. Though he needed to continue widening his circle of acquaintances, Ramsay promised himself that he'd spend more time with his cousin as well. "You're right, Cousin. I've been neglecting you."

Stoddard merely shook his head, grinning.

Mrs. Foster briskly reentered the parlor. "Friends, Mrs. Brightman is recovering from her dizziness. She begs that we go on with the evening, and she will rejoin us when she can."

Then the lady of the house, on the arm of her husband, led them into the dining room. The table, decked with flickering, fragrant bayberry candles, crisp with white linen, and glimmering with sterling silver, had been extended to seat twenty people. The chair beside Gerard remained empty. He wondered whether they had seated Blessing beside him again, perhaps so he would have someone he knew nearby. Irritation sparked within. He didn't want the provoking woman next to him. Gerard glanced about, trying to recall the names of the men he'd already been introduced to. Each man here could prove to be an investor in his future racetrack. Or know someone who would be interested.

The butler and footman had served and removed the first course before the two absent ladies reappeared. The scent of wisteria enveloped the widow, something Gerard had never noticed before. But what did perfume matter? He rose to formally seat Blessing just as Stoddard did for Tippy.

As he seated her, the woman sent him a wry glance over her shoulder. He recalled the day they'd met—her outrageous conversation. With a start, Gerard realized she had secured his interest then, and that marked her as a dangerous woman, not one he could brush aside like most of the others. He would never be able to dismiss her as a mere society widow, boring and inconsequential.

At the head of the table, Mr. Foster smiled at his daughter, who was smiling into Stoddard's besotted face. Gerard cringed inwardly at this.

"Come now, Foster," a burly man seated near the host said. "You've piqued my curiosity. Now that the ladies have returned, what were you about to announce?"

Gerard gripped the stem of his wineglass hard enough to

turn his knuckles white. It was nearly impossible for a gentle-man to break an engagement once it was publicly declared. *Not yet!*

"Friends, here in your company and the company of my dear family—" Mr. Foster stood and raised his glass toward his wife and then his daughter—"I have decided to run for state legislature as a reform candidate this fall. I ask for your support."

A stunned moment, followed by applause and well-bred words of encouragement.

❖

Blessing raised her glass and glanced at Gerard Ramsay on her right.

The man looked grim.

She watched furtively as he gained control of his features and cast them into a bright, congratulatory expression. Why didn't he want Tippy's father to run for office?

Then she recalled seeing Gerard at the bank. Perhaps he was trying to move ahead with his ill-advised scheme to start a horse-racing track. If he'd hoped to gain support from Mr. Foster and any of his set, this announcement would impinge on his plans. A reform candidate would not want his name linked to a racetrack.

Where was the elation she would have thought she'd feel over this setback for Gerard? Since everyone was still talking and backslapping, out of the corner of her eye, she continued to study the man. Due to the general chaos, she could do this for a few moments without stirring up his notice.

One thing became clear to her. Ramsay was not happy.

He even looked a little sickly. Too many nights drinking and carousing could lead a man to ill health.

A tiny seed of concern for him germinated. *He's as lost as the men his racetrack might bring to ruin.* This knowledge stiffened around her heart, just a simple band of worry. Was it possible to save Gerard Ramsay from himself? And why did that matter to her?

❖

SEPTEMBER 15, 1848

A few days later, Gerard entered the same seedy tavern he'd visited twice before, having received a message that Smith wanted to see him tonight. Gerard resented the barely disguised order and the way these meetings with Mr. Smith made him feel. It was a cross between the apprehension of entering his father's presence as a child and the intimidation of older, bullying boys at school.

Gerard kept his smooth outward mask in place and forced himself to show no sign of nervousness as he sat down across from the man. He needed Smith to navigate the murky waters of the bookmakers, but after the racetrack was up and running, they would see each other only in passing. Tonight, in contrast to their last meeting, the tavern was full of people, both men and women, drinking and talking in small groups. Gerard drew some comfort from the presence of others.

"So Foster is going to run as a reform candidate for the state legislature?" Smith said, his accented voice low and mocking.

"Yes, that simply means I must cast my net further into

society," Gerard said with outward composure. "I've just begun—"

A man at the bar laughed explosively, drowning Gerard's words and setting his teeth on edge.

"I'll give you the names of some men who might be ripe for our enterprise," Smith cut in.

Gerard did not like the *our*. "Again, I must insist that this is *my* enterprise. I contacted you strictly for your knowledge of Cincinnati racing."

"Don't worry, *Mister* Ramsay. I know our parts in this." Smith eyed him, a wry grin creeping over his face.

Gerard sensed the man was trying to make him nervous, but he resisted giving in. Smith might be dangerous, but only if crossed, and Gerard didn't intend to cross him. Besides, he had the security of cold steel—the very newest Colt—tucked in a leather holster under his arm. He waited Smith out.

Finally, after a long silence, Smith said, "I hear you are getting friendly with the good widow Brightman."

Gerard didn't like hearing Blessing's name coming off Smith's curled lips. He went for his best nonchalant shrug. "She amuses me."

"And she's attractive and very wealthy," Smith continued smoothly. "I can see why you're tempted." He chuckled in a way that implied carnality.

Gerard fought to avoid rising to the taunt.

"She is a thorn in my garden," Smith pronounced. "She disrupts trade and goes where she doesn't belong. If you can interest her—give her something better to do with her time—that would be a welcome development to many at the docks. And could also, in the end, make life easier for her."

The subtle threat in these words caused a reaction more powerful than Gerard could have predicted. "Mrs. Brightman is an unusual woman."

Smith laughed out loud. "She is indeed, and perhaps you are the man who can return her to her proper place."

"And what's that?" Gerard drawled, though the question played into Smith's hand.

"Under a man's . . . thumb."

Repulsed by the bawdy insinuation, Gerard stared at the man and rose. "I'll continue with my own plans. Good evening."

Smith nodded, smirking.

As Gerard walked away, Smith called after him, "I'll bid you good luck with the widow, then!"

Gerard ignored it. He wanted to best Blessing, not ruin her. Originally, he had planned to do a little drinking and discussing the racetrack here on the wharf tonight. Now, as he walked the quay, he just wanted to get home to his room at Mrs. Mather's.

But perhaps he'd stop at that neighborhood tavern near the boardinghouse and have a quiet drink with the barkeep. He would be glad once his racetrack was up and running, and he'd never have to associate with Mr. Smith or his ilk again.

Then he recalled something his cousin had mentioned over breakfast this morning, and an idea for making mischief with the widow began forming in his mind. She'd refuse, of course, but it would be amusing to tempt her. Especially since the "temptation" he had in mind was a far cry from what Smith had suggested.

❖

SEPTEMBER 18, 1848

Blessing was sitting in the orphanage kitchen holding Luke when the cook answered a knock at the back door. As always, this infant called to Blessing in a way none other had. Something in the child had touched her heart in an unusual way. Just as she was kissing his downy head, she heard a vaguely familiar voice say, "The widow said I could come see my nephew."

"Come on in, then," the cook replied.

Blessing turned to see Ducky Hughes, neatly dressed, entering the room. "Ducky Hughes, thee came." She couldn't keep the pleased surprise from her voice. So few of the orphans had any visitors. And perhaps Blessing might yet find a way to help this woman.

Like a doe about to venture out of the forest, Ducky hesitated just inside the doorway. She very obviously scanned the room, taking in Rebecca still lying on her cot. Glances of recognition between the two connected and then slid apart. Yes, they had lived—and suffered—in the same world.

"Come in and see the child," Blessing encouraged, not forcing the two to greet each other.

Ducky took a few steps forward but still stood back from Blessing. "Oh, Danny looks good." Her words were packed with relief and gratitude. She reached out but then pulled her hand back.

Blessing glanced over Ducky's shoulder to the cook. "Please pour our guest a cup of tea." She rose and nearly pushed the other woman into the nearest chair. "Would thee like to hold him?"

Ducky looked painfully uncertain. "Can I?"

Blessing set Luke in her arms. "Did thee call him Danny?"

For a moment, the woman said nothing, just gazed at the child in her arms. With her head down, she replied, "Yes, I named him for his grandfather."

"He is your nephew?" Blessing probed gently, making sure she'd heard right.

Ducky nodded, still not looking up.

The cook set a cup of tea, the milk and sugar pots, and a plate of fragrant oatmeal-and-raisin cookies in front of the woman. "I baked yesterday. Your boy's a sweet baby."

Ducky looked up. "He is. Thanks for the tea and such. Can't remember the last time I had a cookie."

Blessing didn't ask any further questions. She had found that just sitting in comforting silence often opened mouths shut by suffering. Many prized a sympathetic ear above rubies.

The cook also delivered a cup of hot tea to Rebecca and set one in front of Blessing, who sipped quietly and waited, hoping for Ducky to tell her more about this child and how he came to be here.

"My sister and me," Ducky began haltingly, "lost our parents when we were still kids." She lifted her head as if to meet Blessing's gaze but lowered her chin again. "They were respectable people. Afterward we stayed with a friend of our mother's until she died. Cholera." Ducky stared down at the tea in her cup, lost in sorrow.

"So thee only had thy sister?" Blessing prompted gently.

Ducky nodded and at last sipped her tea. "I'm glad I heard of you. I want better for Danny."

"Of course. What is thy family history? When he's older, Danny will want to know and be proud of his grandfather."

At this encouragement Ducky raised her head with a trace of dignity. "My dad, Daniel Hughes, worked as a cobbler. My mother's maiden name was Cummings. They come here from Syracuse, New York."

Blessing stored away this information. She had found that sharing parts of her own story helped visitors like Ducky feel understood, so she said, "I am blessed with four sisters and a brother. But as children, we did lose another brother and sister to measles. That was hard."

Ducky looked into Blessing's eyes for the first time. "Death comes for everybody."

"Yes." And sometimes it brought blessed relief. She gripped her cup, thinking what her life would be like if Richard still lived. Guilt twisted her stomach for being glad of his early death. *There is a way which seemeth right unto a man, but the end thereof are the ways of death.*

Both of them remained silent for a moment, and Blessing sensed Rebecca's rapt attention on her dealings with Danny and his aunt. "Ducky, can I help thee?"

"No, I'm fine." The answer was quick. "I'm just grateful you took in Danny."

"I'm glad thee came to visit him. I hope thee will again."

"I will if I can."

Theodosia came down after leaving her children with the others. Baby Luke—*Daniel Lucas Hughes,* Blessing mentally adjusted his name—sent up a yelp when he saw her.

Ducky finished her tea and, with obvious satisfaction,

watched her nephew nurse in Theodosia's embrace. When Ducky rose to leave, she had noticeably relaxed and looked refreshed. She turned to Blessing. "Ma'am, walk me out, please?"

Blessing wondered at this request but rose obediently to accompany her. Halfway to the gate that led outside the large garden, Ducky halted. She leaned close and said just above a whisper, "As soon as that girl is well enough to travel, you need to get her out of the city. Her pimp is a mean one, and I think he's killed girls that don't obey him. And he never gives up a girl he wants to keep. Everybody knows about this place. He'll come after her."

The words, spoken urgently, chilled Blessing. "I will."

"Good." Ducky hurried toward the gate. She opened it and turned back. "But you didn't hear it from me, right?"

"Right," Blessing agreed, following her.

Ducky impulsively grabbed Blessing's hand and kissed it. "Thank you for taking in my Danny." As if embarrassed by her own action, the woman rushed away, the gate flapping shut behind her.

After latching the gate, Blessing stood still, her hands pressed against the wooden slats as she prayed for Ducky— not only about her life but her soul. Then the need to take action to protect Rebecca asserted itself.

Blessing had to come up with some plan of escape for the girl. For now, she might need to hire a strong young man from Joanna's church to sleep in the carriage house with the driver. No man would try to break into the orphanage in daylight, but nighttime was a different matter. Satan did not give up his prey easily.

SEPTEMBER 22, 1848

Blessing paused inside her front door, pulling on her gloves as she prepared to leave. She had come to a decision about Rebecca and was taking action. She only hoped her plan would succeed in protecting the girl and providing her with a chance to change her life.

She turned to her housekeeper, Salina. "I'll probably stay the night. Or even another day after that. So don't worry about me."

"I never do," Salina said. "If I did, I'd have to quit. You always goin' to the docks at all hours—"

"Salina," Blessing cautioned.

"Yes, ma'am," Salina said sharply, almost saluting.

"When thee accepted the position—"

Salina stopped her with laughter. "We are a pair for sure. Don't *you* worry—"

Both of them were interrupted by the tapping of the brass knocker.

Salina moved forward to answer the summons yet only opened the door halfway, shielding Blessing from view. "Mr. Ramsay, good morning, sir."

"I know it's early, but I heard Mrs. Brightman was leaving town this morning and I wanted to catch her before she left."

Salina looked to Blessing, who came forward.

"Is thee keeping track of my movements, Gerard Ramsay?" she asked in a withering tone.

"When I need to." The man smirked at her and held out an envelope. "I've come to invite you to join me and

Stoddard and your friend Miss Foster in attending a play at the seminary."

"A play? At the seminary?" He'd certainly broached the unexpected.

Ramsay chuckled. "A bit unusual for such an institution, I confess, but it isn't a professional production. No paid actors. Or actresses. The students themselves have decided to perform one of Shakespeare's plays—*Hamlet*, to be specific—and have persuaded the seminary faculty that it is a worthy project. There will be only one performance, and I've already obtained four tickets." He waved them at her again. "Will you accept the final one?"

Blessing stared at him and the ticket he offered. He must know that Quakers and a number of other Christians didn't attend the theater because of the vagabond and loose lifestyle of many actors and actresses. While married to Richard, Blessing had gone to a few plays performed by traveling troupes, and she had enjoyed them. But she had returned to the meeting now. "Thee knows I cannot."

He tilted his head. "A lady who goes to the wharf most every night can't attend a cultural event at a seminary?"

When he put it like that, her resolve was hard to defend. Yes, she did go places that most Christian women would never frequent. But it wasn't as if she ventured onto the wharf for her own entertainment. The elders at her meeting had approved her work, though they did not like it much.

"I will leave the ticket with you," he said, laying it on the foyer table and replacing his hat on his head. "And will visit you again after you have taken time to consider my invitation." Then he bowed and left, whistling.

Blessing and Salina exchanged glances.

"That man up to something," Salina muttered.

"Yes, he is—all the time." Blessing tied her bonnet ribbons and walked outside, where her gig awaited. She must be off while the sun was still ascending. Rebecca already sat in the vehicle, looking fearful. Blessing patted her hand and smiled reassuringly, praying that this carriage would take the girl to safety.

❖

Blessing and Rebecca sat side by side in the gig as they threaded through the outskirts of the city. The cooler autumn weather was pleasant, so Blessing had chosen this open vehicle for the trip. The highest leaves of a few maple boughs were tinged with scarlet. Once the women were outside the city, aptly nicknamed Porkopolis, Blessing breathed in the sweet fresh air.

The girl beside her was still painfully thin, but her color had returned and the bleeding had stopped. Today, with Rebecca dressed in new clothing and a wide-brimmed bonnet, Blessing doubted anyone would have recognized her. She had told Rebecca little about the reason for this trip, but the girl appeared to trust her—or perhaps she was simply desperate enough to follow her lead.

As they neared Sharpesburg, however, Blessing decided it was time to explain her plan. "Rebecca, I am taking thee to visit my family."

The girl looked sideways at her but said nothing.

Blessing read the uncertainty and the fear that always lurked in Rebecca's eyes. "I want to warn thee before we arrive that my family may appear a bit different from most. My father became deaf as a child, and my adopted cousin, Caleb, is also deaf. So my family members all speak with their hands in a sign language."

"None of them talk?" the girl blurted out.

"They speak in words and sign at the same time—" Blessing demonstrated by signing what she was saying—"so that my father and cousin can understand what is being said. It puts some people off, so I hope thee will be kind."

Rebecca looked concerned. "I never been around deaf people before."

"My parents are unusual in another way too. Most others judge people based on their pasts, but my parents don't judge. Thee will be welcomed by them as an honored guest." She waited, giving the girl time to absorb this.

"Will they know what I've been?" she asked in a little voice.

"They may guess, but they will not comment on it or make inquiries. Thee isn't the first girl I've brought to them."

"Why do I need to be brought to them?"

"I don't think thee wants to go back to the docks, and thee can't stay forever at the orphanage without being found out. We must begin the process of helping thee find a better, secure way of life far from there."

The girl laughed mirthlessly. "I'm a fallen woman. Nobody wants me but . . . customers."

"Rebecca, all have sinned. I know society says that girls who have been prostitutes can never be forgiven or reclaimed. But I reject that, and so do my parents. They have helped two other girls in thy situation find respectable husbands."

Blessing didn't mention that a third girl, given the same chance, had never made it to Sharpesburg. Addicted to alcohol and laudanum, she'd run away from the orphanage and back down the bluff to the quay. But Blessing was confident Rebecca would not follow that path—in any case, as confident as possible under the circumstances.

Rebecca said nothing but did not look convinced.

Two deer emerged from the woods and stared at the gig, negotiating the rough road.

Blessing patted her companion's hand. "We need not look too far ahead. For now, thee will take refuge with my family. Thee will be safe there."

Rebecca shivered. "I don't know why you're doin' all this for me. I'm nothing."

The desolate phrase pinched Blessing's heart. She squeezed Rebecca's hand. "Thee has never been nothing. God loves thee, and he gives us new beginnings by his grace. Thee didn't choose the life thee lived, did thee?"

Rebecca replied with a sound of derision.

Blessing decided enough had been said.

Before long they arrived at Cathwell's Glassworks. As she glimpsed home, Blessing's heart lifted. Over the years, her parents' two-room cabin had grown to four rooms. And the nearby cabin where Joanna's parents lived had also doubled in size since she was a child. Before the gig arrived at the door, her mother had already come out and was waving in welcome.

"Mother!" Blessing waved back. Soon she was surrounded by her younger sisters. Then her father, Samuel; her brother, John; and her cousin, Caleb, all streamed out from the large glass workshop.

As always, coming home felt bittersweet, reminding Blessing of her marriage and how it had separated her from these dear ones for nearly six years. Amid the hubbub of greetings, Rebecca hung back beside the gig.

"And who is this?" Honor, Blessing's mother, finally asked with a smile.

Blessing introduced Rebecca and let her mother take over the hospitality. A look passed between Blessing and her mother, and she knew that Rebecca would be invited to stay. She could always count on her mother.

After all, Honor had never given up on her when she'd chosen to marry Richard and forsaken the meeting. And when Blessing had returned as the prodigal daughter, she'd been welcomed not with recriminations but with grateful tears and the fatted calf too. Not for the first time, she silently thanked God for the family she had been born to.

❧

After dark, when everyone else had turned in for the night, Blessing and her mother sat beside the low fire. Blessing had trouble believing at times like this that she had ever been tempted to turn away from her family. She'd been barely eighteen when she married Richard, yet youth explained only part of her reason for rebelling.

She'd mistaken the plainness of being a Quaker for hypocrisy and lifelessness. And as Joanna had said, Richard had laid siege to her, and before she knew it, she'd stepped away from family and faith.

Reunification with her family had brought with it the gift of conversations with her mother, a gift she no longer took for granted. Now she longed to discuss several people with Honor. Rebecca, of course, who was sharing a room with Blessing's two younger sisters; as well as Tippy . . . and perhaps Gerard Ramsay.

"I take it Rebecca was engaged in prostitution," Honor began.

"Yes. She just miscarried her first child."

Honor let out a sigh of weariness. "The poor girl. We'll do what we can for her. But she's still so young. And I think that children who have been perverted have a harder time breaking free. Their scars run deeper."

Blessing let a glance reply for her and gazed into the scant flames, gathering her words. Ramsay pushed to the forefront of her concerns. "Mother, I need thy advice on something that has come up—or, I should say, on a man who has intruded into my life."

"A man? Intruded?"

"Yes. He's from Boston, a wastrel from all I've seen. I keep bumping into him at the docks. He's the cousin of the man who is courting Tippy Foster."

"Ah, I see. What's thy question?" Her mother's calm voice soothed her. Did anything ruffle her mother?

"He's invited me to a play, *Hamlet*, that's to be performed by students on the seminary grounds."

"And he knows quite well that Friends do not attend plays."

Her mother, kind as always, did not mention her marriage to Richard Brightman or the tenuous place Blessing still held within the meeting. But it wasn't necessary. Blessing's thoughts were already there.

After her husband's death, Blessing had confessed her sin of becoming unequally yoked and asked for the elders' forgiveness, and she had been reinstated into the fellowship. If she went to this play, the elders might discipline her again. The mere thought pressed on her like bookends coming together. "I think he's trying to tempt me, to ensnare me."

Her mother looked worried for a moment but drew herself up. "Then thee knows what thee must do."

Blessing nodded. More and more when she was with Ramsay, she sensed a deep, festering hurt in him. She wished she knew what drove him to push the limits, flirt with sin. Also, she admitted her desire to see a performance of *Hamlet*, which she'd read in school. But this inclination was not enough to pull her from the fellowship. A highly respected Quaker like her mother might be able to attend the play and receive only a minor reprimand from the elders. But not Blessing.

Then an outrageous thought occurred to her. She chuckled. If she correctly suspected that Gerard Ramsay was trying to ensnare her, this might teach him not to test her. Did she dare?

Chapter 6

The early evening play was nearing its climax. Since it was an outdoor performance, benches had been ranged around a makeshift stage. In spite of the felicitous setting, everything about the production grated on Gerard. He could barely discern Shakespeare's poetic phrases due to the amateur actors' mangled lines and poor performances. In addition, a few boys whose voices hadn't changed yet had been drafted to play the female roles. Though Gerard knew this practice was common in Shakespeare's time, these boys didn't look happy about their parts. To a man who'd enjoyed professional theater in Boston, performed by accomplished actors and actresses, this amateur production rankled—a travesty.

But all of that wasn't even the worst aspect of this evening. A few days ago, Blessing had accepted his invitation, but she had told him she would come in her own carriage. He'd thought it was her way of keeping gossip at bay.

At the last moment before the play began, however, a white-haired Quakeress leaning on a cane had arrived with the ticket he had given Blessing. She'd introduced herself as Deborah Coxswain and explained that the younger woman had been detained at the orphanage. Apparently Blessing had graciously offered Mrs. Coxswain her ticket.

Stoddard, who had been vexed with him for enticing the widow to attend the play in spite of her protestations, had smirked at Gerard as he'd been forced to welcome Mrs. Coxswain to his theater party. So tonight Blessing Brightman had bested him. He'd steamed in barely polite silence ever since.

Just as Gerard was sure he could abide no more of this theatrical posturing, fire bells rang out, breaking over the dialogue. A trumpet sounded. Police whistles shrilled with alarm. Many men in the audience leaped to their feet and started running in the direction of the noises. Gerard glanced around, unnerved.

"They must be volunteer firefighters," Tippy said, sounding troubled.

The actors on the stage tried to go on with the play, but the wind carried the sounds of danger over the crowd. Then gunfire split the gathering twilight. The audience rose almost as one. The actors fell silent, staring in the direction of the unexpected sound.

"Cousin, we had better get the ladies home safely," Stoddard said.

"What's happening?" Gerard asked. "Who's shooting?"

"The noises are coming from the direction of Little Africa," Mrs. Coxswain said. "Something like this has happened before. I have a bad feeling." She sighed. "Will thee take me to Blessing's orphanage? If what I fear is happening, she might be a target."

Gerard couldn't make sense of the woman's words, but he offered her his arm and started helping her toward the carriages. People rushed around them. Deborah Coxswain, with her halting gait, slowed their pace.

"What's going on?" Gerard demanded of Stoddard, speaking close to his ear.

"Haven't you been reading the newspaper articles alleging that the presence of free blacks in the city is hindering trade between Cincinnati and the South? Even the mayor has declared this to be true."

A burst of gunfire exploded to the west. Some women shrieked and lifted their skirts, dashing off. A few men swung their ladies up into their arms and ran.

"I have read the dreadful articles," Mrs. Coxswain declared. "We've been afraid that there might be an outbreak of violence intended to drive the free blacks out of the city."

Gerard's head spun. "The mayor wants mob violence?"

"Toward Little Africa. And he can count on prejudice to fuel it." The woman's expression became grim. "Greed and hatred blinds many to right and wrong."

When they reached the place where the Foster and Coxswain carriages should have been, they found the vehicles gone. The street had emptied of people, carriages, and horses.

"Our drivers must have been forced to go on home," Tippy said above the noise of chaos, which was nearer now.

"The horses might have been bolting and could have hurt themselves." She moved nearer to Stoddard. "The drivers knew we had male protectors."

Stoddard drew Tippy's arm through his. "Let's start for the orphanage. It's closer than home. Though also closer to Little Africa. But we have no choice."

Gerard stepped over to the older woman and pressed his hand over her arm in reassurance. "How far can you walk?"

"As far as necessary," Mrs. Coxswain said with iron in her tone.

As the sun set, the red glow shading the sky in the direction of their destination raised Gerard's tension. People seemed to be running helter-skelter through the streets. More gunfire rent the air. Gerard wanted to run ahead, to see for himself what was happening, but he had to think of the lady he was escorting, who was bravely moving as fast as her advanced age let her.

Finally, as night closed in, the orphanage came into sight. When the four of them opened the gate, a deep, gruff voice from the shadows challenged them. "Who goes there?"

"Hello, Brother Ezekiel. It is I, Deborah Coxswain."

"Hurry in! We're guarding the front door and back gates. You'll be safe here."

Heading toward a lantern light, Gerard and Stoddard bustled the ladies forward. From the title the Quakeress had used to address the man, Gerard surmised he must be a minister. "What's happening? Where's Mrs. Brightman?"

"We tried to stop her, but we got word that Theodosia's block had caught fire," Brother Ezekiel replied as Gerard and the others drew up beside him. "Mrs. Brightman took my grandson to find Theodosia and bring her family out safely. I'm worried. Many of our people have already lost their homes to the fires, and many were beaten as they fled. Now they're hiding here in the basement and carriage house."

Gerard noticed that a number of black men with clubs stood near the entrance. His head whirled. He'd never faced a mob before. One sentence found his mouth. "You let Mrs. Brightman go to the fire?"

"You try stopping that woman," the silver-haired minister said as he helped Mrs. Coxswain up the steps.

Stoddard nudged Tippy to follow her. "We'll go find Blessing and bring her back."

Tippy turned. "I can come—"

"No. If I know you are safe here, I can go help our friend. Otherwise all my efforts will be spent protecting you."

Impulsively Tippy rose on tiptoe and kissed him. "Go then! Quickly. Find her!"

Stoddard kissed her in return. For once Gerard was undisturbed by their open affection.

As soon as Tippy had disappeared into the orphanage, Stoddard addressed Brother Ezekiel. "Where is Theodosia's home?"

Gerard listened carefully as the minister directed them.

Stoddard swung away. "Coming, Cousin?"

Gerard followed him through the gate, then jogged beside him down the street. "Doesn't the mayor know that any fires could spread beyond Little Africa?" Gerard's pulse pounded in his ears.

"He's a fool. One can't control a mob. And the fire might already be out of hand."

Soon Gerard actually felt the heat from the blaze. Flames leaping above the rooftops lit the night, garish and frightening, as if a portal to hell had opened.

"This way!" Stoddard shouted above the noise of yelling and the roar of the fire.

Gerard hadn't prayed in a long time, but he found himself beseeching God that they'd find Blessing in one piece and get her home safely. What kind of woman ran straight into danger?

They turned a corner, and by the light of the fire, Gerard saw her. She was trying to force her way into a house already aflame. He sped up, racing to her, and grabbed her arm. "Are you mad?"

"My wet nurse is upstairs!" Blessing cried, shrill with panic. "With her two toddlers and my newest orphan. I must save them!"

Gerard wrenched her backward. "Stay here." He shouldered his way through the door. Inside, the acrid smoke nearly choked him. He bent low, feeling his way toward where he thought the stairs might be, and found them fully engulfed in flame—impossible to climb. He rushed outside. Bent over double, coughing.

Stoddard grabbed his arm and dragged him to the side of the building. "There!" He pointed to a small upper-story window.

A woman's scream split the air.

Through his watering eyes, Gerard saw a black woman peering over the windowsill, an infant in her arms. Two children, just tall enough to see out the window, were visible beside her.

"Catch them!" the woman cried.

Without stopping to think, both he and Stoddard dropped their canes, stepped under the window with their arms extended.

"One at a time!" Gerard shouted.

The woman screamed again as she dropped the swaddled infant from the window. Stoddard caught him and swayed.

"Again!" Gerard shouted, the pandemonium around him fading as he concentrated on the next falling child.

The little girl landed in his arms, jolting him.

Blessing snatched her from him.

Then the woman let go of the third child. Gerard caught him as well.

"Take off thy coats!" Blessing ordered, wresting the boy from him.

Stoddard quickly obeyed after passing the baby to her, and Gerard followed automatically.

"Put them one atop the other and hold the corners. Tight!" Blessing directed.

The woman above shrieked. "My hem is on fire!"

"Beat it out!" Blessing shouted. "Then jump! They'll break thy fall!"

Gerard panicked. Break her fall?

Before he could consider what he was supposed to do, the woman came straight at them.

"Hold!" Stoddard yelled as he tried to brace himself.

The woman hit their coats, and the weight drove both men to their knees on the brick street.

Gerard gasped for air. "Are you all right?"

The woman rolled onto her knees and tried to stand.

"Help her, Ramsay!" Blessing shouted. She carried the infant in one arm and shoved the other children toward Stoddard, who swept them both up.

The mob was nearing. Gerard could hear their yelling and jeers. He grabbed his cane and Stoddard's, tucking them under his arm. Then he helped the black woman to her feet. When she staggered, he slid his arm under hers. He turned to Blessing. "Widow! Run!"

She obeyed, racing away from the burning house. He and his cousin rushed alongside her. The mob nipped at their heels, pelting them with rocks and pummeling them with curses. In a burst, Gerard shoved the two canes into the widow's hands. He swung the wet nurse into his arms. "Faster!" he urged.

Finally the orphanage loomed ahead. The widow raced forward to the gate, unlocked it, and disappeared inside. Stoddard ran in behind her and Gerard pushed the black woman after him. He turned and drew his pistol, facing the men who had chased them.

His abrupt movement caught them up sharply. They halted, staring at him as if dumbfounded.

"Go about your business!" Gerard ordered.

"That widow's got blacks living in there!" one of them challenged.

"That is none of your concern."

The men moved forward. Gerard lifted the pistol and took aim. They froze.

"Go about your business," he said again, evenly.

The men eyed him. The moon had risen now, so he could see their twisted faces. They outnumbered him, but his gun trumped their clubs. If they attacked, one or more of them could die or be wounded.

"It's a repeater. A Colt," one man observed. He cursed Gerard and turned away.

The others followed suit, melting into the night.

Gerard stood there, trembling and gasping from exertion. Alone at last, he entered the gate, securing it behind him. He looked up, and Blessing stood on the steps with a lantern at her side. He'd never faced such naked evil in his life. As his heart still pounded with the aftermath of danger, his respect for Blessing Brightman rose. He couldn't believe he'd come through this alive. Thank God.

He shoved his pistol into the holster concealed beneath his arm, aware of the black men guarding the gates and the back door. It was just as well they had stayed in the background as reserve troops. The thugs would back down when faced by a white man, but not by a black man. They would have rushed him regardless of the pistol.

Before he knew it, Blessing had run forward. "Is thee all right?"

"I'm fine," he murmured.

"Thee is not completely unscathed. Come inside." She took his hand, leading him. He didn't pull away, all his senses dazed by the recent events. And suddenly he registered stinging in various parts of his body.

Inside the kitchen, the brighter lamplight made him blink as his eyes adjusted. Every window shade was drawn. Black men ringed the room, and a few women hovered near the table, including Deborah Coxswain, who sat with the infant who'd been rescued. Blessing nudged him into a chair. Tippy was bending over Stoddard's head, dabbing what smelled like alcohol onto his face.

The black woman he'd carried here sat slumped in her chair. Her two children huddled on her lap. Another woman was comforting her and trying to get her to rise.

Gerard stood. "She's in shock. Is there a bed for her? I'll carry her."

"I can do that." A young black man approached. He'd been watching around the edge of the window shade. He nudged the toddlers toward one of the young women and carried the wet nurse out of the kitchen.

"Joanna, I'll come up soon," Blessing called after the younger woman. "Get Theodosia out of that burned clothing and wrap her in blankets."

Gerard let the widow push him back into his chair.

"I am going to wash the soot from thy face and then anoint thy wounds."

"Wounds?"

"From burning debris in the air. Thee suffered small burns and cuts all over thy face, hands, and neck."

"So did you," he said, touching her face. Her bonnet had slipped down and her bun had lost pins and sagged over her left ear. Black soot smudged her complexion. He stroked her cheek without thinking of propriety, trying to reconcile its softness with her staunch bravery. He was still in disbelief that she'd tried to run into a burning building. She was mad; she was fearless.

"My bonnet protected me. But thee lost thy hat, and—" she felt the back of his head—"thee must have been hit with a sizable stone."

He winced at her touch. "How has this all happened? Out of nowhere."

"Not out of nowhere," Mrs. Coxswain said. She gently rocked the baby. "Cincinnati is a main conduit for the Underground Railroad, and that angers slaveholding Kentucky, right across the river. Businessmen here are concerned about their profits."

"And the prejudice against free blacks is always there, just under the surface," Tippy added. "Some whites resent that, in spite of all the prejudice against them, their industry and skill succeed. They don't keep to their *place*, you see."

Gerard tried to take it all in, but the gentle yet confident touch of Blessing's hand as she treated his cuts claimed all his attention. Finally he caught her wrist. The widow was caring for his hurts when she needed tending as well. "Miss Foster, Mrs. Brightman requires your attention."

"Oh!" Tippy turned away from Stoddard and their murmured conversation. The young socialite shoved Blessing into a chair and accepted a fresh basin of water.

A black woman he assumed was the cook set cups of coffee and plates of sliced bread with butter and honey in front of Gerard and Stoddard. "Eat," she ordered.

He didn't argue. The coffee was strong, and the bread and butter did much to restore his strength. While he ate, he watched Tippy tend the widow's cuts and small burns. Blessing had closed her eyes and tilted her face upward. Her expression spoke of weariness and distress. He'd never met anyone like her in his life. She needed someone to protect her from herself.

He thought of the play and his motive behind inviting this woman to it. His machinations all seemed so ludicrous in light of subsequent events. This night had shaken him. Its images and sounds still blazed in his mind.

❖

Gerard woke suddenly, a crick in his neck. He found himself lying on a sofa in a strange parlor, his head propped on the stiff arm. Gray dawn was lighting the windows and the house was silent. He tried to sit up but found a small child sprawled half on his chest. Like a cold rushing river, the events of last night washed over him.

Had he really run into a burning building? Caught a woman and children dropped from a window, lost his hat, and faced down a mob with his Colt? This couldn't be real.

"His name is Scotty," Blessing's voice murmured through the dimness. "He was frightened and discovered thee here."

His mind scrambled before he could ask, "He's one of your orphans?"

"Yes."

Gerard carefully lifted the child, who must have been younger than school age, and sat up, extending his legs the length of the sofa. That the sofa was not as long as he was tall accounted for the crick in his neck, and in his current position he had nowhere to lay the child. He settled the boy on his lap, wondering why the child still didn't stir.

Gerard could hear the soft sounds of others sleeping in the room, people whose presence he hadn't fully registered until now. The dawn grew gradually brighter. He glanced down to see, dimly, the shapes of his cousin and Tippy sleeping side by side on the parlor carpet. As their chaperone, Deborah Coxswain was snoozing in a rocker across the room, her white hair stark in the low light. Tippy and his cousin lying so close, so intimate, did not upset him as much as he would have expected under normal circumstances. They looked right together.

He noticed that the widow, seated in a nearby armchair, was gazing at him. "I've decided thy cousin will not be a dreadful husband for Tippy."

He was startled by her touching on the same topic he had been thinking of. He didn't know what to say.

Blessing's face was still hidden in the shadows. She also had a child resting on her lap. "Who's that?" he asked, switching subjects. He gestured toward her child.

"This is Daniel Lucas, the boy I rescued the first time I ran into thee at the wharf. I have decided to adopt him."

Gerard didn't know how to respond to this. The child in his arms let out something like a whimper, and Gerard pulled him closer, reassuring him.

"What kind of man is thee, Gerard Ramsay?"

Blessing's question startled him. He stared across at her but avoided answering. "You are in a strange mood, ma'am."

"What kind of man is thee, Gerard Ramsay?"

Her repetition of the question irritated him. "What do you mean by that?"

"We are here alone in the gray dawn. Be honest. Why did thee invite me to the play, knowing that I couldn't go?"

"Why couldn't you go?" he said, not liking his own feigned ignorance or the defensiveness in his tone.

"My late husband was not a Friend. I was put out of the meeting when I married him. I won't do anything that will cause me to risk shunning again."

"The Quaker elders didn't like you marrying a brewer?" he asked with a sneer in his tone.

"Thee will not evade me. What kind of man is thee? Why did thee come to my rescue last night? Why did thee face a mob bent on destroying this orphanage and driving out those who'd come here for refuge?"

"I'm not a saint," he snapped, "just because I will not allow a woman and her children to be burned alive or allow a mob to attack helpless orphans. It merely means I was raised to be a gentleman. That's all."

"I think thee could be much more—"

"Don't try to reform me, *Friend*. I've always found that the prim and proper have a dark sin they're trying to make up for. What's your sin, Blessing Brightman? What have you done that you have to hide?"

A ray of true dawn light flared in over the curtains, casting itself full onto Blessing's face. Her expression grabbed him. She looked as if he'd jabbed her with a sizzling, white-hot poker. Gerard inhaled sharply. He'd hit the mark, all right. And found himself as astonished as she. What was the widow's secret sin?

❧

OCTOBER 2–4, 1848

Two days later, with all honest citizens hunkered down in their homes or their closed businesses, in fear for their lives, the mayor finally seemed to realize that he'd lost control of the mobs and that a city in lawless chaos was far worse for business than the presence of free black people.

The police issued a call for volunteers to help them regain

order. Deputized citizens formed patrols and arrested any man who was causing trouble on the streets. The city jail and courts were jammed, but peace was eventually restored.

On the morning of the fourth day, Blessing stood on the orphanage's covered back porch and rested her forehead against a post. She felt as if she'd been through a war. Now she must face the aftermath and whatever changes it brought. She tried not to dwell on Ramsay's question about her secret sin—a sharp blade in her side.

Brother Ezekiel, his family, and some members of his flock who'd weathered the riots at the orphanage approached her. "We want to thank you again for sheltering us."

"I wish I could do more," she said simply. "If any of thee needs a roof, come back. If we run out of room in the orphanage, there is always the loft above the carriage house."

"We will keep that in mind."

"I'm takin' my family out of Cincinnati as soon as I can pack," one man said. "We're goin' to Canada. We're not safe here."

Blessing couldn't blame them—but how would the Underground Railroad function effectively without free blacks in the city to run the stations? She didn't voice this. It was unnecessary.

The group left, walking close together, the women and children in the middle. The men all carried clubs or sticks.

Blessing left her place against the railing and sat on the top step. She hoped she never had to face anything like this again. But only God knew what lay ahead.

In spite of her efforts, Ramsay's question continued to haunt her every waking thought. *"What's your sin, Blessing*

Brightman?" In her mind, Richard's face stretched in shock, and she heard her own scream. She shut her eyes, forcing away the memory. Blessing knew that God could forgive her, had forgiven her long ago. But forgiving herself loomed as an impossible task.

She blinked back tears. Life would continue to go on, often lonely and exhausting on some deep level. She couldn't deal with the past right now. She had children depending on her, and she must press on regardless of past mistakes, past sins.

❖

Gerard was loath to visit the docks tonight, but he'd received a summons from Mr. Smith and, though affronted, knew he must go.

As he opened Mrs. Mather's door, Stoddard hailed him from the parlor. "Where are you off to?"

"You don't want to know."

Stoddard approached and stared at him. "The papers say men should still travel in pairs. People died in the riots, Cousin."

"I have my Colt."

"Who has your back?"

Gerard merely waved and marched off. He tried to put away reflections on what had happened during the riots. Yet the past few days had cast his mind into a darkness that wouldn't lift. Tonight he found himself alert to danger on the one hand, yet most of his mind was occupied with remembrances—flames leaping against the night sky, people running through the streets, a mob threatening an orphanage.

However, two stark memories bedeviled him more than

the others: the look on the widow's face in the light of dawn and the feel of a little boy seeking his protection. Once more he tried to shake them off, unsuccessfully. *"What kind of man is thee, Gerard Ramsay?"*

The docks were littered with debris, and Gerard noticed a greater number of night watchmen than usual, along with deputized citizens. The ugliness of the riverfront glared at him. He entered the same tavern as before and found it crowded. Many of the patrons sported bruises, burns, and cuts, just as he did.

He went directly to Mr. Smith at his customary table.

"Mr. Ramsay." The man greeted him in his quiet yet sneering voice.

Gerard wondered whether Smith practiced sounding this way or whether it was natural. "Evening." He took a seat across from the man, who, as always, sat with his back to the wall.

"You look a bit worse for wear," Smith observed.

Gerard shrugged.

"I hear you protected the good widow from the rioters."

These words dismayed Gerard. How did Smith know? "Having me watched?"

Smith chuckled mirthlessly. "I told you once that Mrs. Brightman is a thorn in my garden."

Gerard stared at the man. Did this mean that Smith had something to do with the mob that had followed them to Blessing's door? "I am a gentleman. When a lady requires protection, it is my duty to provide it."

This time Smith laughed out loud. "And what does the widow provide for you?"

The thick innuendo in the man's tone drew Gerard to his feet, hands fisted. "I do not know what you mean." The stiff words felt like nails on his tongue. "I came to discuss business, not to bandy about a respectable woman's name."

"Sit down," Smith ordered. "I have a few names for you. Men I think might be eager for a racetrack and for a sure investment. They won't deal directly with me but will probably do business with you, a *gentleman*."

Remaining on his feet, Gerard ignored the man's tone, bristling at the order to sit. "Always remember, Smith, I am your business contact and *nothing more*."

Something flashed in the man's eyes. Anger? Or darker than that? Smith visibly commanded himself. "Of course. Understand—I don't want to be associated with a Boston prig any more than you want to be associated with me."

Gerard accepted the list of names Smith held out and vacated the tavern. Outside the door he again felt a surge of caution. Maybe he needed to drop this racetrack idea. Smith was not a man he desired to fraternize with in any way.

"Well, hello."

The familiar voice halted Gerard. It was Kennan, loitering outside the tavern.

"So how did you enjoy the riots?" Kennan went on. "I had a great time."

Gerard was caught between several reactions—surprise, relief to see Kennan here and alive, and a desire to cuff him on the side of his head. Riots, fun? He mastered himself. "I knew I'd seen you around the city. When did you come west? Why are you here?"

Kennan ignored the first question but answered the second. "I came to an agreement with my stepfather. He will continue my allowance, provided I move away from New England. I'm the black sheep—" Kennan grinned with satisfaction—"and they want me out of sight."

Gerard looked at Kennan, suddenly understanding why his friend was drinking and running away from family. He, Stoddard, and Kennan remained the unwanted sons they'd been at boarding school. But he chose not to broach the subject at present. "When did you get into town?" he repeated.

"A while back. Wanted to see what drew stuffy Stoddard to this place. Frankly I can't comprehend its allure except for that radical blonde female he's besotted with."

"Exactly how long is 'a while'?" Gerard pressed.

"Oh, I saw you arrive."

Gerard recalled that he thought he'd spied Kennan on the wharf that day. "Why didn't you let me know?"

"You're getting as uptight as Stoddard, or so I thought till I heard you were trying to get a racetrack started. That will embarrass your father, all right. Well done." Kennan beamed at him. "Let's go have a drink to that."

Gerard did not like hearing his motivation said aloud. He studied his old school friend's face and noted his bloodshot eyes and unshaven face. The last thing Kennan needed was another drink. But Gerard couldn't say that.

When Kennan tried to draw him back into the tavern he'd just exited, Gerard resisted. "Let's go elsewhere. I don't like the company in there."

"You mean Mr. Smith?" Kennan chuckled. "All right. Lead on. Just make sure it's a place where they don't water the gin."

Gerard claimed Kennan's elbow and led him toward the neighborhood tavern on the rise above the wharf. He hadn't realized that Kennan knew of Smith. What did that mean for Gerard, for Kennan?

Chapter 7

Gerard woke and wondered if he'd died during the night. His head felt as if it had been split in two. He could barely open his eyes, and hammers pounded behind them. He slowly sat up. A mistake. Dropping to his knees, he quickly snatched his chamber pot and retched. When the heaving finally ceased, he slid to the floor and lay on the carpet, gasping for breath.

He tried to focus and clear his mind, but clarity eluded him. Flashes from the night before—raucous laughter, standing at a bar with Kennan, scantily clad women . . .

He groaned and the sound hurt his ears. What happened last night? Where had he been? What had he done to feel this way?

Gerard lay still, gasping for air and forcing his mind to work. Eventually he recalled meeting Kennan after his interview with Smith. They'd gone to his neighborhood tavern . . .

But they hadn't stayed there. He'd intended to go home afterward. Why hadn't he?

He rubbed his face with both hands. In his youth he'd often suffered morning-after spells from overindulgence, but he'd never experienced one where he couldn't recall what he'd done the night before. *What could have caused me to go on a bender? I must remember.*

He rose tentatively to sit on the side of his bed. The sun shone bright at the window, so he averted his gaze to the patterned carpet. Sudden thirst prompted him to try to stand to go downstairs. But he realized he must become more presentable before he could enter the kitchen and beg some coffee. His stomach lurched at the thought, but he knew he must eat something, and coffee would help his headache.

Moving like an old man so he wouldn't disturb his hammering head, he went through his morning routine and managed to shave using cold water, with only a few nicks. After finishing, he walked carefully down the stairs and headed toward the kitchen.

Just before entering, a thought occurred to him. Had his Quaker landlady seen him intoxicated? He'd been warned about her standards. Maybe he'd been lucky and she hadn't witnessed his arrival. How had he gotten home, anyway? Why couldn't he remember the night more clearly?

Gerard entered the kitchen, relieved to find the big-boned, red-haired cook alone. He eased down at the table in the center of the room. "I overslept. Do you still have coffee and something for me to eat? Please."

She eyed him suspiciously. "I be thinking ye dipped too deep last night."

Gerard stared at her, begging with his eyes.

"All right. You look that sick. But don't ye be expecting this again."

"I am under the weather."

"Is that what you call it in Boston?" She raised her eyebrows in starched disapproval. When she set a mug of coffee in front of him, he cringed at the sound. She looked at him with pity and made him some dry toast. "Try to keep this down, child."

"Thank you," he muttered. He nibbled the bread and sipped the steaming coffee, praying he wouldn't be sick again.

A knock sounded at the back door.

He steeled himself for more noise, but he didn't leave, not wanting to move unless he had to.

The cook let someone into the room.

"Mr. Ramsay, sir? I'm Mrs. Theodosia March."

Gerard looked up to see the woman who'd jumped from the fire into his arms. He rose cautiously. "Yes?"

"I come to thank you for saving me and my kids."

He raised a hand. "No need to thank me. Glad you're safe."

A familiar-looking little boy clung to her hand. But he couldn't be her son; he was white. Gerard tried to place the child.

Then the boy charged Gerard, grabbing him around the knees. "You're Mr. Ramsay. You 'tected us from the bad men." The little boy stared up at him.

Gerard recalled waking with this child on his lap in the

orphanage parlor. "Scotty?" he said, trying to avoid thoughts of his conversation with Blessing that morning.

"Yeah, I'm Scotty." The child grinned at him.

"Mrs. Brightman thought I'd be safer bringing Scotty along with me," Theodosia said. "No one would dare accost a nursemaid with her charge."

"I see," he said, patting Scotty on the head. So Theodosia still felt unsafe. He didn't blame her.

"Mister, can you come to my house and play ball?" Scotty asked.

Gerard patted the boy's head once more, unable to come up with a response to this.

"Scotty, you come on now. We're goin' home. Mr. Ramsay's a busy man."

Scotty looked crestfallen, but he waved and hurried to take Theodosia's hand. The two left.

The cook gazed at him as if trying to understand why the woman had come.

He sank back into the chair and managed to consume the coffee and dry toast. Rising, he thanked the cook, who merely frowned at him and waved him out of her domain with a wooden spoon.

He was walking through the dining room when Mrs. Mather approached him.

"Gerard Ramsay, a word in the parlor." The silver-haired landlady crooked her finger at him as if he were a child and marched ahead, expecting him to follow.

He had no intention of going against her wishes. Shame at his condition warmed his face, and he could not think of an excuse. He was no longer a callow lad sowing his wild oats.

Mrs. Mather shut the parlor door with a snap that was painful to his head. "Gerard Ramsay, thee was warned about how I expect my gentlemen boarders to behave themselves. Give me one reason that I should not send thee packing today."

In that moment he realized the import of what he was facing. Not only did he not want to leave this comfortable home with its good food and friendly boarders, but also he didn't want to lose this lady's respect.

"Mrs. Mather, I met with an old friend and brought him to the local tavern. I don't know what happened after that. But I have not overindulged like this for a very long time. Please give me a second chance, and it won't happen again. In fact, if it does, you won't have to ask me to leave. I will just go."

With lips pressed together, she stared at him like a disapproving teacher. "Very well. We will leave it at that." She quit the room.

He moved to the stairs. Images of provocatively dressed women from the night before dogged his every step. Ever since the evening he'd helped Blessing save the girl Rebecca from a beating, he'd been unable to look at women of the night the way he always had, the way society viewed them. The question now was what he had done with these women during the time he couldn't remember.

As he mounted the third step, the front door opened.

Stoddard walked in and barked, "I see you finally got up. I'm home early for *luncheon*."

Gerard stared at him.

"I've never seen you in such bad shape. Let's go upstairs. I want an explanation." Stoddard gestured for him to continue up the stairs.

Gerard couldn't reply; he had just enough energy to make it to his room.

Stoddard followed him closely and shut the door behind them before starting his attack. "Last night I stumbled across you lying in the gutter outside this house. What possessed you to get stinking drunk?"

"I didn't plan on it," Gerard mumbled. "Kennan—"

"Kennan?" Stoddard's voice rose.

"I saw him." Gerard rubbed his throbbing forehead. "At the docks."

"Kennan?" Stoddard repeated, then sat on the bed beside Gerard. "Here?"

Gerard nodded and regretted it. "I don't know what happened," he muttered. "I saw him and brought him up to Jenkins's place for a drink. After that, everything is fuzzy." He could feel Stoddard staring at him.

"Do you think you got some rotgut in one of those seedy bars?"

"I'm not sure." Gerard longed to lie down. "I just know that I didn't intend to go back to the docks with Kennan." With a look, he implored his cousin to sympathize.

Stoddard gazed at him, his expression shifting from disapproving to concerned. "You don't think Kennan might have taken you somewhere and someone put something in your drink—say, opium?"

Or put it in himself? Gerard thought the question he sensed Stoddard was skirting. How far had Kennan fallen? Would he do something like that to a friend? Then Gerard recalled that Kennan had been in Cincinnati for weeks without informing either of them—and that he knew Mr. Smith. Could Kennan be tangled up with Smith?

How and why had Gerard been left lying in the gutter in front of his boardinghouse? Nothing made sense. *If I could only concentrate.*

His cousin's words repeated in his mind. Gerard gripped Stoddard's arm. "Thanks for bringing me in last night." *Mrs. Mather wouldn't have given me a second chance if I'd been found in the gutter.* "I won't let this happen again." *I won't be in Kennan's company again.*

"I think you had better lie down." Stoddard touched his shoulder. "You really look sick. Have you been able to eat anything?"

"Toast and coffee." Gerard reclined obediently, soothed by his cousin's concern. Soon he felt Stoddard rest a cold, damp cloth on his forehead.

"I'll check on you later."

"Thanks." Gerard tried to relax and fall asleep. Maybe he'd feel better later. But doubts over what he'd done last night wouldn't leave him. The sound of laughter and images of those women with rouged lips and cheeks and dresses of black lace flashed in his mind.

Blessing Brightman's words floated back to him. *"There are two kinds of men—those who respect women and those who debase them."* He recalled the poor, beaten girl he'd carried to the widow's carriage that night not so long ago, and his stomach lurched precariously. Until that evening, he'd always assumed easy girls had enjoyed being with him. But had they, or was it all an act bought and paid for?

❧

OCTOBER 7, 1848

Saturday evening, still balmy in spite of the shortening days, Blessing let her driver help her down from her carriage in front of the Foster home. In contrast to her somber mood, the house glowed with lamplight in the October dusk. Tonight the Fosters were giving a party to celebrate the announced engagement of their daughter.

Though Blessing never wore her corset cinched tightly, she was having trouble drawing a full breath. *Dear Lord, is this of thee? Will Tippy be glad she married Stoddard Henry?*

She had no way of knowing, but she needed to trust in the Father and support her friend. If Tippy was making a mistake, she would need encouragement in the coming years. Blessing had isolated herself from everyone out of shame over her disastrous marriage. She would watch and make certain Tippy didn't fall into that trap.

Inside the brightly lit home, the butler and footman relieved her of her light shawl, and she entered the parlor, already full of cheerful guests. Tippy, in a new rose-colored gown lavish with cream lace, stood in front of the cold marble hearth beside her beaming intended groom. Both of them radiated joy.

Blessing felt the sting of tears and looked away, only to lay eyes on Gerard Ramsay. Her response to him was instantaneous, and her skin tingled with awareness. The gentleman from Boston, in conversation with a local businessman, stood against the wall opposite the couple. He glanced at them occasionally with no sign of joy. As usual, she felt the pull toward Gerard as if some invisible bond linked them.

Two ladies approached Blessing and entered into polite social chatter. Was she wearing a new dress? Its amber hue looked lovely with her hair. Wasn't it exciting that Tippy was marrying a man from such a prominent Boston family? And so romantic that they'd met at Saratoga Springs.

Blessing replied pleasantly and did not miss the women's glances back and forth between her and Gerard Ramsay. Were people speculating about whether they were becoming a couple? She couldn't think why anyone would consider that a possibility. Perhaps it was merely because she and Tippy were friends and Gerard and Stoddard were cousins. Did society hope to enjoy the gossip about another deliciously unlikely match?

"We all wonder if Mr. Ramsay will be staying in Cincinnati or returning to Boston," the older of the two ladies ventured with a questioning glance to Blessing.

"I could not say. I am so busy I rarely have time even to see my friends, much less newcomers." She didn't appreciate finding herself under even more scrutiny than usual.

The ladies smiled knowingly but were called away by another group of women who waved to them.

Blessing remained where she was. Theodosia had informed her that she'd gone to Prudence Mather's house a couple of days ago and had thanked Ramsay for his heroic act. Her wet nurse had reported that the man had looked as if he'd spent the night before drinking blue ruin.

Blessing pondered the many names people assigned to adulterated gin, cheap liquor that could kill. She hadn't realized Gerard had sunk to that kind of gone-too-far-to-care drinking. This thought caused a pang of concern she didn't want to feel.

The businessman turned and walked away from Ramsay,

and she couldn't stop herself from moving toward him. If Theodosia was correct, he seemed bent on self-destruction just as Richard had been. What drove a man to dangerous choices? Her own hasty decision to marry Richard Brightman should have shed some light on this question. She had certainly lived the truth of "Marry in haste; repent at leisure." But she'd been so very young, and it had all been so exciting after living such a sheltered life, just as Tippy had.

She hadn't been able to stop Tippy from becoming engaged to Stoddard much too soon. She doubted she would have any better luck turning Gerard Ramsay from a dark path that would be hard to retrace. But she must try. Surely this desire explained why he drew her to him. And she had an idea of something that might influence him for the good. He would probably decline, but she would issue the invitation anyway. He just might rise to her challenge.

❧

Gerard watched Blessing Brightman walk toward him. Dressed in a high-necked amber silk gown this evening, in contrast to the other ladies' bare shoulders, she looked prim, proper, and utterly lovely. However, her manner was determined, like a ship gliding toward its destined port. He wanted to move away, not let her dock beside him.

Of all the people milling about the parlor, he inexplicably wanted to talk to her both least and most. It was confusing. Nobody else in the room interested him, but this woman could annoy him faster than anyone, aside from his father. He swirled the wine in his glass and averted his eyes from her.

When she reached him, he straightened his shoulders and

lifted his chin. "Well, they're engaged," he observed, trying to alleviate her effect on him.

"Yes, they are." She moved to stand at his side, the wisteria fragrance subtle and alluring. "Doesn't thee know better than to go on a spree at the docks?" She spoke the words as she smiled and nodded to another lady passing them. "Theodosia said you looked like death on a hard day."

Her quip forced a chuckle from his dry throat. "Worried about me?"

"Some of the gin served at the wharf can blind a man." She lifted her plain fan and used it against the stuffiness around them.

Gerard didn't answer. He knew what she said to be true. But he didn't have to account for his behavior to her. It was difficult enough accounting for it to himself. The most troubling aspects of the night were twofold: first, that he couldn't recall anything of substance; and second, that afterward Kennan had evidently disappeared or gone to ground. Gerard couldn't shake the feeling that Kennan had a part in what had happened to him. Or had Kennan succumbed to rotgut and fallen dead in some dank hole?

He shook off this idea and dealt with the woman's tart words. "Then, Widow Brightman, I advise you not to imbibe the gin at the docks."

She shook her head at him, not responding to the barb.

Another couple passed by, greeted Blessing, and moved on. The woman glanced over her shoulder at Blessing and Gerard once more, a knowing expression on her face. Evidently their "association" was a topic for public conjecture. He bristled. Gossips.

"So, Gerard Ramsay, is thy cousin good enough for my friend?"

"I've been wondering the reverse of that myself."

"Well, let us hope so. Neither of us could stop them from taking this life-altering step."

"I can agree with you there. How did you know I opposed the union?"

"On the last occasion we were here together, the relief on thy face just as I fainted told all."

Her brazenly honest answer jolted him. "No matter how often we meet, I cannot get over your frank conversation. Do you talk this way to everyone?"

"Thee is not everyone, Gerard Ramsay. I still cannot make thee out." A group near them broke into spirited conversation, and she stepped closer. "When faced with danger or crisis, thee rises to the occasion. But in everyday life thee follows a course that can only bring disaster. What drives thee?"

That her assessment was correct again infuriated him. He stiffened. "My character and my endeavors are none of your business."

She swung to face him. "I urge thee to stay away from that man Smith. He is dangerous, and his main business is to ruin people and enslave them. He holds me in bitter hatred because he has been unable to bring me under his control. I've learned to see through his schemes. And I am too respected, too prominent for him to touch. But *thee* is playing with a consuming fire. This is not Boston."

Her words resonated inside him. If he never saw Smith again, it would be too soon. He tried to come up with a response to put her in her place, but a hard knot in his heart made replying difficult. "How do you know so much about my association with Smith?"

"I have my sources." She did not meet his gaze.

He wouldn't tolerate her intrusion, even as he was dogged by the knowledge that she was right. "Don't meddle in affairs that don't concern you."

"If you knew what I . . ." She paused and then continued, "I am going to challenge thee again. Thee invited me to a play. I am inviting thee to an upcoming meeting to hear James Bradley, one of the Lane Rebels, on his life as a slave."

A former slave? Associated with the radical Lane Seminary? What would this woman come up with next? "Trying to draw me into the movement for abolition?" he said with scorn.

"Trying to give thee something worthy of thy intellectual capabilities." Blessing smirked as she walked away.

He fumed and sipped his very good wine, barely tasting it. There was nothing worse than this woman who could pierce his armor by telling the truth.

Gerard had heard much of the Lane Rebels, a group of seminary students who were rabid abolitionists. He couldn't imagine what their parents must think of their debates and activities. In fact, if Gerard could ensure that his father would hear of his own attendance at such a meeting, he might be tempted to go. But this was a matter for later contemplation. For now, Gerard selected another gentleman from the gathering and approached him, ready to discuss his racetrack plans. He might as well take advantage of this social gathering for his own ends.

❦

OCTOBER 16, 1848

It had been over a week since Stoddard's engagement party, and so far Gerard had failed to drum up any interest in his racetrack venture among the gentlemen he'd become acquainted with there—or, to be honest, among any of his contacts. He knew the Fosters moved in a segment of society that leaned toward social reform, but he'd held out hope that some of these men would support reform with one hand while engaging in beneficial investments with the other. This not being the case, Gerard had at last decided to use the list of investors Smith had provided him. But it would be the final time he would ever take anything from Smith. From now on, he would proceed on his own.

So he'd reserved a room at a prominent hotel, ordered engraved dinner invitations, and sent them to the prospective investors from the list.

Tonight, with the sound of rain on the windows, he welcomed his eight guests into the comfortable dining room, with its velvety flocked wallpaper, ornate fireplace, and thick, claret-colored carpet, for a delicious meal. After dinner, over a fine port and cigars, he would outline for them his plans for a racetrack, including the two promising tracts of land he'd found when he toured Cincinnati's outskirts.

Dinner went off without a hitch, and all of the men were more congenial than Gerard would have expected from Smith's acquaintances. He'd made brief allusion to the racetrack early on, and at least a few of his guests seemed amenable. As he started the bottle of port around the table,

Gerard knew the decisive moment was almost here. He looked for an opening in the conversation.

"We had a bad week for business at the end of September," said a man with a pronounced paunch straining against his embroidered vest.

Another with thinning hair and a sarcastic expression accepted the bottle and poured. "But it got rid of a lot of our *unwanted* population. I've noticed a black exodus, haven't you?"

The other men all nodded with approval.

They couldn't mean what Gerard thought they meant. "Are you talking about the riot?" he asked.

"Yes," the first man said. "The mayor could have handled it more efficiently, but he got the job done."

Gerard recalled Theodosia's terror and felt again the impact of each child landing in his arms. Would these men have let them be burned alive? He stared at the group, unexpectedly repulsed. And disgusted. No doubt they attended church each Sunday. Hypocrites. Blessing Brightman's fierce expression flickered in his mind. Well, he'd met one real Christian here in Cincinnati. And she bedeviled him at will.

"We hear you're interested in Brightman's widow," another suggested with a sly grin.

Gerard jerked inwardly. It was as if the man had read his mind.

"Hope you have better luck with her than her late husband did," the man with the paunch said and laughed, making his belly shake. "Poor Brightman came to a sudden end."

"There was gossip that she had something to do with that

untimely and abrupt end," the gent with the thinning hair added.

A few men nodded. "That's what comes of a man leaving his fortune to his young wife," one said.

Gerard could not believe what was being hinted about the Quakeress. These men thought her capable of her husband's demise? Again their conversation repelled him. But he'd wondered about one aspect of this situation before, and now he had someone to ask. "Why did he leave her his fortune? Was she aware of that before he died?"

The man with the paunch shrugged. "Don't know—"

The pocket door to the private dining room slid open. And Blessing Brightman herself stepped in, dressed in her most sober gray Quaker garb, as if on her way to the meeting-house.

The jovial men were struck dumb.

Gerard nearly choked on his port. He couldn't believe it himself. Blessing had pursued him once more. How did she know of this dinner party? And to come uninvited to an all-male gathering—did nothing intimidate her?

"Good evening, gentlemen. I heard Gerard Ramsay was holding a meeting of prospective investors for his future race-track."

The men had risen as one in the presence of a lady. Their expressions were ludicrous but told a clear tale. They, of course, all understood the potential social consequences if this lady let it be widely known that they were investing in a disreputable gambling venture. Even in circles not prone to reform, public proclamation of this fact would be viewed with disfavor as not "respectable." Universal dismay registered on each face.

"Racetrack?" the one who had approved of the black exodus blustered. "That wasn't mentioned to me." He moved away from the table, feigning outrage.

The others joined in with a spatter of disgruntled *Or me's*.

Within minutes the men had thanked him for their fine dinner, remembered other engagements, and left.

Gerard helplessly watched them go and then turned to the widow. Blessing gazed at him without any gloating in her expression. As usual, she was studying him. He should have been very angry with her.

But in truth, he was glad in some ways to see the men go. He had no plans to admit that, however. "Well, Widow Brightman, how did you find out about my business dinner?" Though unable to keep the resentment from his voice, breeding dictated that he politely motion for her to take a seat before he resumed his own.

Blessing settled across from him. "Stoddard told me. And I'm glad I came. Every man in this room is no doubt beholden to Smith. If thee obtained thy capital from them, he would in actuality hold the strings to thy scheme. He would own thy investors, own thy racetrack, own thee. Is that clear enough?"

Gerard refused to cede victory to her. "I can handle Smith."

"Is thee so certain of that?"

He changed directions. "I still do not understand how you know so much about Smith."

A veil dropped over her features. She looked away.

He waited to hear her explanation.

"Smith is my adversary and has been for many years." Her voice was low and hinted at some unreadable emotion.

153

She looked into his face. "Thee must have realized by now that if thee joins thyself to him, only he will profit from this venture. Hasn't thee?"

"I don't see that at all," he retorted, holding in his irritation at her interference. "You act as if Smith were in charge of Cincinnati. From what I've heard, he's merely the most successful bookmaker."

She let out a sound of dark mirth. "His influence runs wide throughout the criminal class, and he is universally feared. He is relentless and unscrupulous toward any target. The men here tonight could have told thee that. I'm quite sure that each was sent a message that he must accept thy invitation tonight. Each man here *owes* Smith. And fears him."

Gerard hated her way of speaking openly of matters no lady should ever even acknowledge. "Do you never stop meddling, ma'am?" he snapped.

"I don't meddle. I shine the light into the dark corners of this city. Does thee really want to belong to Smith?"

"No, I don't." For once he told her the absolute truth. *But I don't have to.* He'd step back and give this some thought. Certainly there were some men in Cincinnati who didn't belong to Smith, were sufficiently discreet, and could be interested in his racetrack.

"Then pay the bill and let us leave this place."

Again her audacity stymied him. What other woman would do what she'd done tonight? And then act as if she'd done nothing more than drop in for a visit?

Marveling, he rose and obeyed her. There really was nothing else for him to do—not now, at least. As he finished paying, he recalled that he had only enough money left to support himself for two more weeks. Then he'd be broke and forced to ask his mother for more than she could spare of her private funds. The realization ignited his stomach. He might have to follow an unexpected course of action. After escorting the widow out and handing her over to her driver, he stepped back under the overhang at the entrance, eyeing the unwelcoming rain.

From her carriage window, the widow waved at him. "Would thee like a ride home?"

"Why not? It's the least you can do for me." Ducking his head and running through the rain, Gerard climbed in beside her, and the driver started off. Gerard shook the rain from his hat and swiped at the raindrops on his shoulders. He wished he could shake off Smith as easily.

Then he recalled how Smith had revealed that he was keeping close watch on Gerard. And more unsettling somehow, the man's marked animus toward Blessing. Her words tonight had affirmed this hostility. What grudge lay between these two unlikely people?

Rain pattered on the carriage roof as if taunting him. He might have been playing the fool, and this irritating woman had intervened. But he was unsure whether she did it to settle a score with Smith or to save Gerard from his own folly.

Blessing, mostly shielded from his view by the darkness, spoke without preamble. "I asked Stoddard why thee was pursuing the racetrack. He wouldn't tell me, but I could see that he knew thy reasons. Will thee tell me? I want to understand."

"Why am I of interest to you?" he snapped, her disruptive forthrightness still jabbing him with each breath.

"Ah, I am delving too deeply," she observed in that calm and maddening way of hers.

The rain continued to fall in a constant tapping on the roof. Gerard brooded in silence. "Let me say again: my life is of no concern to you."

"On the contrary, the lives of others are my main concern. Thee seems to be at odds within thyself. Thee has every opportunity to make a good life here in this city, but instead thee takes delight in flouting society—"

"You're the one who flouts society," he interrupted hotly. "Going to the docks at night, associating with . . . harlots and their bastards. Why does society tolerate you?"

In spite of the murky shadows, he felt her intense gaze upon him. "I am deemed an Original," she said in a light tone with a self-mocking edge. "A Quakeress who married into high society. I'm also fair to look at and very, very wealthy. I give much to municipal projects, such as the free library being built. I support political candidates. And if I weren't there to enliven society, whom would the ladies whisper about behind their fans? I amuse them, intrigue them. That is why I continue to be received."

After viewing her movements in society, unfortunately he couldn't refute her logic. He never had—yet.

The rain suddenly intensified against the carriage roof.

"Again I will invite thee to attend James Bradley's lecture with me."

He batted the invitation away like a fly and raised his voice against the falling rain. "How will that help me establish myself here?"

"More important, how will it help thee establish who thee is—here or elsewhere?"

Many hot words bubbled up. Gerard swallowed them down. His plan for tonight had been thwarted. After taking the measure of the men Smith had suggested—men who, Gerard had to admit, might have been his last resort—he was coming to a sobering conclusion. He would have to find employment.

Perhaps pursuing a career here could broaden his pool of acquaintances. He didn't have to give up on the racetrack completely, just take his time and do it without Smith and his ilk.

Still, he didn't want to let go of the possibility of striking back at his father for his overbearing ways. The sound of the downpour mirrored the way his heart beat whenever he thought of letting his father go unscathed after cutting off his allowance, all with the goal of controlling him.

But the Quakeress was right. He could make a good life here for himself away from his father's influence. Still, he must make his father pay for all the hurt he'd inflicted, not only on Gerard but also on his mother and anybody he deemed inferior to himself. His father did not deserve to prosper. He deserved judgment, and who could shame him more than his only son? His father had quoted King Lear to him more than once:

How sharper than a serpent's tooth it is
To have a thankless child!

Then another quote came to mind:

Living well is the best revenge.

❧

OCTOBER 20, 1848

Several days later, Gerard, with the Quakeress at his side, entered the small auditorium at Lane Seminary. The days were becoming shorter and shorter, so candle sconces flickered on the walnut-wainscoted walls, and a large chandelier glimmered overhead. He felt as if he were outside himself, watching a stranger. *Am I really doing this?*

As if she heard his thoughts, Blessing glanced at him. "Thee can always back out now."

The veiled taunt in her voice grabbed him around the throat. He shook off the sensation. "I am unintimidated, madam."

She had the nerve to grin at him.

The last week had been eventful for Gerard. He'd telegraphed his mother, and she had arranged for the transfer of some money into his bank account here. But he knew it was wrong to depend on her, especially in light of the strict limits Father placed on her funds. So in spite of this infusion of cash and with the racetrack still in the back of his mind, he'd faced the facts and gone to one of the businessmen he'd met at Stoddard and Tippy's party. The man had offered to interview him for a job in his steamboat firm. The position hadn't been a good fit, but the man had said he was sure there was a position for a Ramsay in Cincinnati. He would let it be known that Gerard was looking for employment.

I am looking for a job. That was just as unbelievable as his walking into this promiscuous meeting where both men and women would listen to a speaker—and a speaker with dark skin, to boot. His own discomfort offered him some satisfaction. If he couldn't yet embarrass his father by owning a notorious racetrack, he might do even better by dabbling in abolitionism, a radical cause that, according to Father, no respectable person would support. But after his dinner with "respectable" gentlemen here, perhaps this evening would be enlightening.

He followed Blessing into a line of chairs. Not for the first time, he noted that among the women who supported abolition, Blessing stood out as the most imposing in manner and pleasing in looks. In fact, he felt an odd stirring of pride that she would ask him to be her escort. She was indeed an Original.

Gerard sat beside her and tried to look as though attending a radical meeting to listen to an African speaker were an everyday occurrence in his life. Remembering Conklin, the reporter who had pegged him attending the women's rights convention, he looked around for any newspaper reporters in attendance. If he found one, he'd love to be quoted. He had to make sure his father found out what he was doing now. If he knew his father, the man was receiving Cincinnati papers in an attempt to track Gerard's doings here.

Gerard glanced around and glimpsed a few reporters and, unexpectedly, some familiar faces, and he nodded in acknowledgement. Many gazed at him a bit longer than was polite. No doubt because he and the widow had come together. Another factor that would irk his father, who thought Quakers were outlandish and appalling. *Better and better.* Why hadn't he thought of this ploy before? And it wasn't as though he minded her company. Not at all.

The meeting began.

Gerard waited through the introductions and settled in, hoping he wouldn't be unbearably bored.

James Bradley, a tall man near middle age wearing a sober suit, moved to the podium on the low platform. The white of his shirt gleamed against his dark skin. "Good evening, ladies and gentlemen. Thank you for coming this evening. But before I begin my lecture, I would like to open myself to questions."

Gerard was already impressed by the man's presence and eloquence. What had he expected? Not a man who could speak in an educated way. Bradley had been introduced as a graduate of Ohio's Oberlin College, but Gerard had thought that was mere honorary pretense. Evidently not. How had a former slave had the chance to go to college?

After an initial hesitation, one man rose. "I am a member of the American Colonization Society. I hear that you oppose our efforts. Why?"

Bradley gazed down. "I'm glad you brought that up. I think the basis of colonization is the flawed theory that people of white skin and people of black skin cannot live together in a free society. That simply is not true."

"But slaves are different from whites," the men said.

"Yes. They are enslaved, and whites are not."

"That's not what I meant. They are not able to take care of themselves in our modern civilization—"

"Slaves not only take care of themselves; they also take care of their white owners. I did not run away from my master. I bought my freedom through hard labor. How many slaves have you ever spoken to?"

The man raised both his hands in defeat and sat down.

Another rose swiftly. "I don't want to witness the amalgamation of the races. If blacks are freed and sent back to Africa, this will be avoided."

"Sir, my father was white," Bradley replied. "The amalgamation of the races takes place daily on the plantations of the South."

The audience gasped.

The back of Gerard's neck prickled with shock. James Bradley was more audacious than the widow beside him.

"Bradley, there are ladies present," the man blustered.

"And they understand, perhaps better than you can, the heavy burden their black sisters suffer. I was separated from my mother after birth and, while I was still a very small child, only saw her a few times before her death. I can only imagine her suffering."

Silence ballooned through the hall. Gerard thought of his own mother and how he'd felt when his father had sent him away to school at only seven. He remembered his mother's tears. And that was all inconsequential compared to what Bradley and his mother must have experienced. The old hurt roiled inside him. Of all things tonight, Gerard had not expected this man's address to touch him personally.

Bradley glanced around as if seeking any more questions. But his responses had prepared his audience to listen. The man did not charm; he challenged.

Gerard grappled with Bradley's words. If he'd ever given the plight of slaves and former slaves more than a passing thought before now, he couldn't recall it.

"I will recount my life as a slave in hopes that it will

inspire you to do all you can to work toward abolition."
Bradley paused, gathering the attention of the crowd. Then
he began his story. "A slaveholder bought me when I was only
a child and took me up into Pendleton County, Kentucky. I
suppose I stayed with him about six months. He sold me to
a Mr. Bradley, by whose name I have ever since been called.

"This man was considered a wonderfully kind master,
and it is true I was treated better than most of the slaves I
knew. I never suffered for food and never was flogged with
the whip, but oh, my soul! I was tormented with kicks and
knocks more than I can tell."

Listening in rapt silence, Gerard wondered how he could
have worried this speaker would bore him.

❧

Gerard sat beside Blessing in her open gig on the way home.
His mind whirled with all he'd heard.

"Well, I hope the evening proved interesting for you,"
Blessing said in her driest tone as they neared Mrs. Mather's
boardinghouse.

By moonlight, he was caught by the clash of opposites she
presented. Though she wore a plain bonnet and a drab gray
dress with a white collar and cuffs, moonlight gleamed on her
pale complexion, glinted on the shine of her dark hair, and
reflected in her large eyes. She was like a pearl displayed on
common linsey-woolsey rather than on the dark velvet she
deserved. It physically goaded him. "Why do you so often
insist on wearing black or gray?"

"I'm a widow and a Quaker. Those are the colors we wear
most."

"If God created a rainbow, I don't think he dislikes color. And I have seen you wear colors at parties, and very stylish gowns. Why do you consistently try to hide the fact that you are a beautiful woman?"

"Ramsay, this is not a conversation we should be having. Yes, you are right. I do like to be fashionable on occasion. I cannot deny it. Yet I am truly little concerned with whether people see me as beautiful or not."

"Except when it suits your needs. You said that yourself. Smith leaves you alone because society delights in the wealthy and beautiful Quaker bluestocking."

She sighed but with evident humor. "I cannot argue with my own sentiments. I have already admitted that. Thee is in a strange mood. What did thee think of James Bradley?"

Gerard was still too stirred and confused to provide a meaningful answer. "He gave me much to consider."

"I'm glad."

He glanced at her again. "Why did you invite me tonight?"

"I thought thee already knew the answer to that. James Bradley overcame being a slave. What is it that thee is fighting to overcome? What drives thee, Gerard Ramsay?"

Her prescience provoked him, but this was becoming so typical that he hardly reacted to it. They had arrived at his boardinghouse. He climbed down to the street and turned. "When you reveal your secret sin, I'll reveal what drives me." He watched in the scant light for her reaction. But she didn't flinch. He hadn't caught her at a vulnerable moment this time.

She stared back into his eyes without giving ground. "I suppose, then, that we will remain mysteries to each other for the rest of our lives."

He bowed, thanked her for the interesting evening, and strolled toward the door. Guilt at needling her nudged him, but he ignored it. So what if his comment was uncalled for? She had no right to intrude without expecting the same in return.

Chapter 8

BLESSING'S CARRIAGE was turning a corner, halfway home from leaving Gerard. A shaft of moonlight glinted on something small and bright on the carriage floor. Blessing reached down and lifted it into the scant light. A gold fob from a man's watch chain. She recognized it immediately. Both Stoddard and Gerard wore these, bearing emblems from their university. Blessing tapped the roof. "Judson, we need to go back to Prudence Mather's. Ramsay dropped something."

Her driver assented and turned the carriage. In a few minutes, Blessing came within view of the boardinghouse's front door. And was startled by what she witnessed.

A woman dressed in vivid red was forcing her way into Prudence's front door. The lamp by the door lit the woman's face. Recognition jolted through Blessing. She gasped.

"Don't stop," she urged her driver. "Keep going."

Judson didn't pause to ask questions, just drove on.

Blessing's mind raced, running through all the possible reasons for that particular woman to show up here. Only one solution explained this, and it appalled her.

"Judson, drive me to the alleyway two streets behind Prudence Mather's."

As he drove, she folded in her white collar and cuffs, concealing them. When the carriage stopped, she stepped quietly out and murmured to Judson, "Wait here. Call no attention to thyself."

Then, with her shawl covering her head and face, she moved surreptitiously through several backyards. A couple of dogs whined and came to watch her, but her gentle murmurs calmed them. She arrived at Prudence's rear entrance. Since it was not yet locked for the night, she slipped inside. And instantly heard raised voices. She hurried toward them.

"I'm going to send for the watch," Prudence was declaring.

Letting her eyes adjust to the light, Blessing paused in the doorway to the dining room. Prudence Mather, Gerard Ramsay, and the woman she'd recognized stood in a loose circle. "Prudence," Blessing said, "I don't think that will be necessary."

All swung to face her, wide-eyed.

Blessing continued, unperturbed. "Jewel, I know why thee is here."

The woman's expression mixed scorn with confusion. "How do you know my name?"

Blessing had never seen her up close, but Jewel was truly beautiful with black hair, dark eyes, and lovely olive skin.

Adorned lavishly in lace and wearing gold earrings, she was dressed in crimson satin at the height of style but with a plunging neckline beyond what bespoke of good taste. Yet her condition was obvious. She was with child. Again.

Concern caught in Blessing's throat.

"Well?" Jewel stared at her, both daring and caution in her voice, her eyes.

Blessing didn't bother to answer. "I have often wanted to speak to thee, but he keeps thee close."

Prudence stood, openmouthed.

Ramsay stared at Blessing as if she were speaking Greek.

"You have?" Jewel challenged, propping a hand on her hip. "Why?" The word slashed.

"To find out—" Blessing swallowed, moistening her parched mouth—"if thee wanted to leave him."

Jewel let out a sarcastic travesty of a chuckle. "Quaker, you beat all. And I don't have any idea of who you're talking about. The only man I have something against is this one." She gestured toward Gerard. "He—"

Blessing gazed at the woman's waistline. "Is he planning on killing this child too?"

Jewel's face went sheet white, and she staggered back a step.

Gerard caught her arm instinctively.

"Prudence, please shut the curtains," Blessing directed. "In case someone is watching. I must not be seen here tonight."

The older Quakeress obeyed, still looking astounded. "What is this all about, Blessing?" she asked in a low, confused voice. "This . . . *woman* claims she is with child by Gerard Ramsay."

"Ramsay, pull out a chair for the lady," Blessing said, dealing with the pressing issue. "She is faint."

He obeyed her with the same bemused expression as Prudence.

Blessing couldn't waste time. "I warned thee, Ramsay, that Smith would try to trap, control thee. Thee believes thee has finished with him, but he is not done with thee. He wants thee thrown out of this house, thrown out of society, humiliated. He is now trying to use Jewel, his mistress, to accomplish this."

Prudence gasped and pulled back as if confronted with a leper.

"How do you know?" Jewel whispered, sounding fearful.

"I know Smith," Blessing said, feeling the pinch of old hurt, anger. "I'm familiar with his ways. Now we both know the child thee carries is not Ramsay's but Smith's. I've heard the rumors about the child four years ago—"

"Don't," Jewel begged, lifting a hand for mercy. "Please."

Blessing stared at the woman, pity coursing through her. "Does thee want to be free of him?"

"I'll never be free of him." Jewel's voice was laced with bitter defeat. "Never."

"I have thought of a way. In fact, I have it all planned. I hoped someday I'd be able to reach out to thee, help thee."

Jewel stared at her. "Why would you care about what happens to me?"

Prudence sank into a dining chair, pressing a hand to her forehead. "I don't understand what's happening."

Ramsay remained standing beside Jewel, studying Blessing.

"Why would you want to help me?" Jewel repeated, each word desperate to comprehend.

"Because no woman should be under his control." Blessing's voice shook with vehemence. "I know many poor women are, but thee is in the worst position of all. Does thee want to be free of him? I can make it happen. Tonight."

Jewel stared at her, consternation wrinkling her forehead. She chewed her lower lip. "You can't."

"Not alone, but I know a way." Her voice had found its steadiness again. "I can do it. Will thee take this opportunity? Does thee want thy freedom? To save thy child?"

"What do I have to do?" Jewel asked, still uncertain.

Blessing turned to Prudence. "Does thee have some old clothing that we can use for this woman?"

The landlady goggled at her.

"We must move quickly. Please, Prudence. This woman's soul and the life of her child are at stake."

Prudence leaped to her feet and hurried from the room.

"You still haven't told me what your plan is," Jewel objected, looking dazed but leery.

"I have a way to smuggle thee far away, and I have someone there who will take thee in."

"Why are you doing this?" the woman asked for a third time.

Ramsay echoed the words inwardly. He tried to sort through all the widow had revealed. Regret writhed inside him. Smith must have tried to use Kennan to get him thrown out of this house, and now he'd sent this woman with her false accusation against him, once more attempting to get him blacklisted from respectable society. In associating with Smith, he'd sown the wind and now the whirlwind had come to claim him. Except Blessing Brightman was interceding once again. And again he was struck by her clarity and fearlessness, this woman who did not dishonor the faith she claimed. An anomaly.

Prudence returned with Quaker garb over her arm. "It's a bit wrinkled but clean. I was going to send a box of clothing to our mission in the Indian Territory."

Blessing grasped Jewel's beringed hand. "This is thy chance. Thee may never get another. Will thee trust me?"

Jewel rose. "I've heard stories about you. If anybody can get me away from him, you can. I'll try." She pressed a hand over her rounded abdomen. "I can't bear it—" She choked on the rest of the sentence.

Blessing looked to Gerard. "Ramsay, please step into the hall. Prudence, help me get her into this outfit."

Within minutes, Ramsay reentered the room and found Jewel had been transformed from a lavishly dressed woman of the night to a prim and proper Quakeress, wrapped in a gray shawl.

"Prudence, burn these clothes immediately." As Blessing spoke, she tied all the jewelry Jewel had been wearing into a white handkerchief and tucked it into the woman's pocket. "We must leave no trace that Jewel has changed clothing here. I doubt anyone will come asking for her, but if they do, tell them thee threw the hussy out the back door."

Blessing took Jewel's hand and led her swiftly toward the kitchen.

Ramsay rushed after them. "I'm coming too."

"Thee will only be in the way," Blessing said over her shoulder.

"I'm coming with or without your approval." He kept pace with her.

At the back door, she turned, glaring at him. "My carriage is two blocks away from here, waiting for me. The minute we reach it, we will leave the city."

"I'm coming," he insisted grimly. He couldn't let her go with no protection.

"Very well. Pull thy coat together and turn up the collar so the white shirt doesn't catch the light. Thee must move like a shadow. Does thee understand? Both of thee? No one must notice us."

He nodded grudgingly, reached around her, and opened the door. "After you."

Blessing stepped out first and paused, glancing around, obviously listening. Then she waved for them to follow. The three moved in a line: the widow, the mistress, and Gerard bringing up the rear. He was grateful for the clouds passing over the moon. Soon he was helping the two women into the carriage.

Pausing on the step, Blessing spoke quietly to the driver. "Number three," she said. "Quickly but without seeming to hurry."

As soon as Gerard closed the door, the carriage took off at a sedate pace. The driver was evidently accustomed to clandestine activities.

"The veiled moonlight should be just enough to travel by yet not enough to make our movements easy to detect." Blessing sat back as if at ease.

The woman next to her wrung her hands, moaning occasionally and trying to blend into the shadows and the carriage upholstery.

Gerard sat across from them, his hands clasped in strain.

He had many questions, but he would save them till they were out of town. He presumed that's where "number three" was located . . . whatever that signified.

❖

Far into the night, the carriage—which, after leaving the city streets, had been moving at a snail's pace over the rough road—finally rolled to a halt. Gerard peered out into the darkness and by moon and faint starlight glimpsed a lone house and barn.

"Ma'am, we're here," the driver said in a low voice.

Blessing leaned forward to open the door.

Gerard moved in front of her, barring her way with his arm. "Where are we?"

"I want to know that too," Jewel said, her voice shaking and tear-filled.

"We are at a safe place, Jewel. Ramsay, thee must stay here."

"I'm not staying in the carriage."

"Thee is an outsider. Thee won't be allowed in without my say-so."

He stared at her in the low light. He wanted to argue, but Jewel looked ready to faint with anxiety. "Very well," he agreed grudgingly. "But I will expect an accounting."

"Thee may get one . . . in time."

The widow led the mistress, now dressed as just another Quaker, through the dark to rouse the sleeping house. He watched in amazement as the door opened well before he'd have predicted. The two vanished inside.

An explanation occurred to him and he wondered why he

hadn't thought of it before. He had heard of the Underground Railroad. Could the widow be involved in that illegal activity? But the Railroad helped runaway slaves, not white mistresses.

Only a few minutes passed before the widow reappeared. After murmuring something to the driver about waiting, she rejoined Gerard in the carriage.

Her calm manner irked him. "What has happened?"

"I have spirited away Smith's pregnant mistress and saved thee from the censure of society."

Gerard stared at her, trying to make out her expression in the dim light. "And Smith is just going to let you? You've put yourself in grave danger, made yourself his target."

She ignored his warning, glancing out the window of the still-motionless carriage as if expecting something or someone. "He already considers me a foe. But he will never know that I had a part in this. I wish thee hadn't insisted upon coming. Now we must get thee back to thy house unseen—"

He tried to interrupt, object.

But she continued without acknowledging him. "Smith will be looking for her, but if thee is at home in the morning and both thee and Prudence go about thy normal business, what can he do? And how would he connect me to Jewel's leaving? He's not aware that I know of her. That is why I already had a plan to put into action instantly. I am sure he will seek her, but he will not find her."

Gerard threw his hands up. "I don't understand any of this."

"Does thee understand that Mr. Smith would do anything to ruin thee?" She kept looking out the window.

He followed her gaze. What was she waiting for? And why weren't they moving? "Why? I didn't use any of the investors on his list, and I haven't seen him since."

"Yes, thee has succeeded in slipping through his fingers. And thee would have been a prize for him: a gentleman from Boston whom he could manipulate, demean, torment." She paused as if holding in some strong emotion. "I told thee Smith lives to possess people, control people—especially those who are respectable. He wanted to see thy distinguished face rubbed into the filth of the gutter. He will still make attempts. Be on thy guard."

Gerard recalled what the men at his dinner said about Blessing's husband and his abrupt end. They'd suspected Blessing herself of doing away with her husband, but he was beginning to wonder whether they should have accused Smith instead.

Before he could reflect further, a shadow of movement near the house caught Gerard's attention. From around the corner of the building, a man who'd evidently shoved his nightshirt into his pants sauntered toward the carriage. He was leading a saddled horse.

Blessing pushed open the door and waved for Gerard to exit. "Take this horse. When thee reaches the edge of town, watch for a livery named Woolsey's—"

"No livery will be open in the middle—"

She spoke over his objection. "Go to the back door and knock three times, hard. When the door opens, give my name. They will take the horse. Then thee must walk home without being seen."

He tried to interrupt. This couldn't be happening.

She expected him to sneak back into town and leave her undefended? He wasn't a coward. "I will not—"

"Thee must be at home before dawn and go innocently about thy business. I doubt Smith will come to thee, but he will certainly have many people on the watch, so thee must be clever."

"I'm not leaving you."

"Gerard," she said, gripping his hands, "trust me. I will explain all in time. Two lives are depending on us, on our discretion, our ability to carry out this ruse. Trust me. Go. I beg thee."

The pleading in her voice silenced him. He held on to her, trying to make sense of this. Giving in, he squeezed her small, gloved hands in agreement and stepped into the night, ready to ride. "Where are you staying the night?"

"I have family near here. I'll be safe. Don't go near my house or orphanage for a time, please. Smith must not have cause to connect me to this event. Or I will be in danger more than I already am."

Gerard still wanted to argue, but he realized the widow was not going to take no for an answer. He must trust her. As he spoke quietly to the owner of the horse, preparing to mount, the carriage headed away.

On the lonely, chilly ride home, he went over the events of this extraordinary evening. Something about the place where they had left Smith's mistress stirred his memory. He'd been there before—or thought he had. Was this the same house they'd come to that September day when he'd driven her and a friend out of the city? Could that "friend" have been more than she appeared? Another prostitute? An escaped slave? He looked back on that day and his motive for taking Blessing Brightman for a drive. It seemed to be from another life. Could it be merely weeks ago?

❖

The next night, Gerard woke in pitch blackness. He lay listening and tried to figure out what had wakened him. Some noise? He strained to hear, feeling fatigue from lack of sleep. After leaving the borrowed horse at the designated livery, he'd reached home on foot in yesterday's dark, early morning hours. Exhausted but keyed up, he hadn't bothered to try to nap.

Due to the recent strange events, Gerard had been watchful all day, expecting some backlash. He didn't think the widow had yet returned to the city. But he'd followed her advice and had gone about what he thought was his usual routine for the day—going to various businessmen and discussing employment—steering clear of any tie to the Quaker widow. His landlady had exchanged a few strained and questioning glances with him, but she also had attempted normalcy. Wary still and prepared for anything, he'd gone to bed in his shirt and pants when evening arrived at last.

A muffled thump came from below, jarring Gerard from his reflections. He heard more sounds from the main floor, stealthy ones. He rose in one motion, drawing his loaded Colt from under his pillow.

As quietly as possible, he crept out of his room and listened in the hallway. Faint footsteps and other whispers of cautious movement came from below. He edged to the top of the stairs, letting his eyes become accustomed to the near-total darkness. Awareness prickled through him. Then, footsteps right behind him.

He swung around, prepared for a fight, and found Stoddard in his robe.

"What?" his cousin whispered.

"Intruders," Gerard replied and began to ease himself down the steps. Stoddard followed him closely. At the bottom they turned toward the kitchen, whence the muffled sounds emanated.

Stoddard leaned close. "I'll slip outside and come around the back."

Gerard gestured him on, heart pounding in his ears. He set each foot down with care.

"She's nowhere on the first floor and not in the cellar," a voice in the semidarkness said. Gerard peered around the kitchen doorframe. A ship's lantern with only one side panel open sat on the floor of the room. Two men conferred in the corner. "We got to try the second floor and attic."

"How will we be doin' dat without wakin' t'gents?"

"You won't." Gerard stepped through the doorway, his Colt drawn and pointed toward the two housebreakers.

They both cursed and rushed to the back door.

Perfect. As they opened the door, Stoddard sprang up in front of them and swung his cane at their heads.

Gerard raced to his aid. "Stop! Thieves!" he shouted repeatedly.

The men knocked Stoddard backward and trampled over him. They headed straight for the gate. Gerard pelted after them, but they escaped down the dark street. He didn't follow. He couldn't shoot men in the back, not even burglars.

He returned to Stoddard, who had not risen. "Cousin." Gerard dropped to his knee. "Stoddard?"

Stoddard moaned. "My head."

Gerard slid his gun into his pocket and helped Stoddard stand and stagger into the house.

Mrs. Mather, in her plaid flannel wrapper, met them just inside. "What's happened?"

"Intruders," Gerard replied, Stoddard's arm slung over his shoulder. "Do you have any restorative? As they fled, they knocked down my cousin."

A loud rapping came from the room off the kitchen, the cook's quarters. Mrs. Mather followed the sound and exclaimed, "Help! They've tied her up."

Gerard left Stoddard sitting at the kitchen table, head in his hands, and hurried to his landlady. She was lighting a lamp by a narrow bed. The cook, tied to a chair and gagged, lay on her side on the floor.

He realized at once what had wakened him. The cook had managed to knock her chair over, and the thump must have echoed through the house. He quickly righted the chair and unbound the woman. She clung to him, gasping. "Burglars," she muttered. "Burglars."

"I chased them away." He supported her.

"Ramsay," Mrs. Mather instructed, "assist Mary into the kitchen. I will bring up one of the small bottles of sherry I keep for medicinal purposes."

He did as he was told.

Soon they were all gathered in the kitchen. Mrs. Mather lit a lamp on the table and poured amber sherry into tiny glasses, one for each of them. "What happened, Mary?" she asked, once the woman had taken a fortifying swallow.

"I woke up with a hand over me mouth and a man holdin' me that tight." The cook trembled as she sipped the sherry.

"I've never had anyone break in before," Mrs. Mather declared.

Gerard gazed at the faces around the table, illuminated within the pool of light. He knew exactly who had sent the burglars to break in and whom they were seeking. He sent Mrs. Mather a pointed look.

His glance arrested her attention. Finally she murmured, "I see." She rose, dampened a cloth, and pressed it on Stoddard's head, where a nasty lump was rising.

"I canna stay here tonight," Mary declared. "I might be killed in me bed."

"Mary, thee isn't going to be killed," Mrs. Mather said. "Those men will not come again."

"How do ye know that?" the cook demanded.

"Because Gerard Ramsay is going to see to it," she said in a steely tone with a stern look in his direction.

Gerard stared back at her and wondered how he could manage that. Then came a pounding at the back door.

He went to answer it, his hand on the pistol in his pocket. "Who's there?" he challenged.

"The night watch. I heard shouts, and your house is the only one with a light on. Is something amiss?"

Gerard opened the door to a man wearing the night watch badge and holding an intimidating club. "Come in.

My cousin and I chased away a pair of burglars." He waved the man forward.

The young officer joined them at the table and jotted down the information they provided in a small black notebook he'd retrieved from an inside pocket. "I don't have much to go on," he admitted when they had all run out of the few details they had. "But I will report this incident, and there will be extra patrols on your block for the next week or so."

The watchman turned to Mrs. Mather. "And you can't think of any reason these burglars would target your house?"

She sent Gerard another of her pointed looks. "I'm sorry, Officer, but *I've* done nothing to draw attention to myself or my boardinghouse."

The officer rose. "I'm very sorry that you and your cook had to suffer this, but I promise we'll do what we can to keep your establishment secure. We'll even walk around your house twice each night if you wish."

"I think that would be advisable." Gerard stood and extended his hand to the officer. "I appreciate your response tonight."

The young man colored. "Just doing my job."

"Well done," Stoddard murmured.

Gerard walked the watchman to the door and locked it behind him. Back at the table, he helped his cousin to his feet.

Mrs. Mather attended to the cook. "Mary, thee will come upstairs with me tonight. Thee can sleep on the daybed in my room."

"Take my arm, Mary," Gerard said. The four of them trooped upstairs, Stoddard leaning heavily on the handrail and Mrs. Mather lighting the way with the lantern the burglars had left. Gerard saw the women safely to Mrs. Mather's chamber, then followed Stoddard into his room.

Stoddard sat on the side of his bed. "What just happened?"

"Burglars broke into our house and knocked you down."

"I know that. But who is the 'she' they were looking for?"

"Some things it's better you not know, Cousin. Believe me." He got as far as the door before Stoddard's voice stopped him.

"This has something to do with that villain Smith, doesn't it?"

Gerard turned, wondering how Stoddard had come to that conclusion, but he was too tired to try to make sense of it. "Good night, Cousin."

Back in his room, Gerard tried to think of what he could do to keep Smith away. When would Blessing Brightman return to face the mess she'd created? His conscience stabbed him at the thought.

For he'd been the one who had brought this to his own door. One couldn't dance with the devil and not pay. *Regret* was too paltry a word to describe his feeling over becoming involved with a man like Smith. In trying to pursue his own desires and strike back at his father, he'd stumbled into a serpent's nest. What would Smith's next move be? Gerard lay down on his bed, wondering how many more sleepless nights he would have to endure.

He considered all the possible avenues he could pursue to bring this to an end and finally realized that not reacting was his best course. Smith's mistress had come, undoubtedly at

Smith's behest, and she had left by the back door—and that was all he'd confess to knowing about her.

Blessing knew more, but she had effectively concealed her role in the woman's disappearance. At all costs, Gerard must ensure that Smith would never learn of Blessing's part in this.

Smith could likely replace a mistress with ease, but he'd been crossed, bested. To a man like him, such a slight must be repaid—with interest. And Gerard would no doubt be his target.

❖

NOVEMBER 1, 1848

Over a week later on a sunny, unusually balmy day, Gerard could no longer stay away from Mrs. Brightman. Curiosity over where Jewel had gone was eating him alive, and surely the most dangerous window of time had passed. He'd heard through Stoddard that Blessing had returned from visiting her parents three days after the intruders had broken into Mrs. Mather's house. Gerard had expected her to make some overture to him, but she had not. More importantly, Smith and his cronies had also kept away.

Gerard stopped first at Blessing's private residence and was directed to the orphanage. He'd intended to knock on the front door but heard the sound of children playing in the back garden. Recalling Scotty's invitation to play, Gerard chuckled, suddenly coming up with a logical excuse for his call.

He entered by the same gate where he'd stared down a mob during the riots. But now, in contrast to that night, the garden was filled with about twelve children. The oldest ones looked to be playing a game of tag. Two young women of color were swinging the littler children in seats that hung from tree limbs.

One of them noticed Gerard's arrival, but before she could make her way over, Scotty recognized him. "Mister, mister, you came!" The boy ran to him and wrapped his arms around Gerard's knees as before.

Gerard patted his head again, unsure what else to do.

"Mr. Ramsay, sir." The young nursemaid approached, greeting him with restraint. "What can we do for you?"

"I came to visit this young lad. He invited me to play ball with him."

The woman very obviously sized him up and then nodded, as if savoring some private jest. "Why, how nice of you. You are Mr. Ramsay, and I am Joanna. Scotty, go get one of the balls."

The game of tag ceased and the children all stared at him, gawking as if they'd never seen a man before.

Scotty quickly obeyed. "Mister, you stand there and I'll stand here, and you throw me the ball, okay?"

Gerard shed his coat and hat, hanging them on the porch railing. He accepted the ball and went to stand where Scotty had indicated.

"Hey!" another boy yelled. "I want to play too."

Soon Joanna had the children lined up so they could take turns catching and throwing the ball with Gerard. For the next several minutes, he was kept busy trying to toss the ball low and slowly enough for the children to catch, then chasing after their wild returns.

A loud chuckle caused him to look up. There she was, standing on the back steps. *Blessing.*

She grinned at him openly. He had rarely seen her in daylight without her head covered. Now her thick chestnut hair, braided and coiled, reigned like a crown. Her large green eyes danced with amusement and her smile dimmed the sunshine. He'd started their flirtation to entrap her, and here he was the one in danger of being snared. He grasped for control, tried to moderate his reaction to her. But he wanted to rush up the steps and pull her close . . . His lips tingled with their imaginary kiss. *Stop. Now.*

"How good of thee to come and visit the children, Ramsay." She sauntered down the steps as if she fully realized her effect on him. And found it amusing.

"I needed some exercise today." He couldn't take his gaze from her. If only he weren't hip-deep in children.

"He came to visit me," Scotty declared with obvious pride. "But I'm sharing him, Miss Blessing."

"Sharing is always good," she agreed, trying to hide her amusement. "I'm going to sit here and watch and see how well everyone can catch and throw. Please don't let me interrupt."

Her insouciance gratified Gerard, and he chuckled as he signaled for the play to continue.

After another ten minutes, his reprieve came.

"I think it's time for everyone to get a drink of water!" Blessing called out. "Ramsay, come sit in the shade with me."

The children complained a little but obeyed Joanna and the other nurse, who lined them up at the pump.

Gerard joined Blessing, sinking into the wicker chair beside hers. The cook came out of the house with two glasses of lemonade.

"Thy reward." Blessing raised her glass and saluted him. Never the dull, serious widow.

He drew in a long swallow of the tart lemonade and exhaled. He patted the perspiration from his brow with his handkerchief and allowed his gaze to rove over her—covertly, of course. Somehow she appeared elegant even in a simple dress. "What have you been doing these days, Widow Brightman?"

"Oh, the usual," she answered evasively. "I hear thee has found employment."

He nodded with a smug smile. "Yes, I am now with Cincinnati Fidelity, selling fire and life insurance."

"Definitely needed."

"So," he said in an undertone, "are you ever going to let me know what really happened?"

She watched the children, who had begun their game of tag once more. "I'm sorry about the break-in. I read about it in the newspaper." She continued before he could comment. "I was wondering if thee would like to borrow my copy of Frederick Douglass's book."

Her refusal to quench his curiosity annoyed him—but he'd expected evasion. That this woman might be involved in the Underground Railroad again suggested itself to him. But Gerard didn't want to delve into her radical activities, especially if they broke federal law. Surely Blessing would not do that. Regardless, she owed him the truth of what had happened that strange night. "I will not stop asking you until you tell me."

She didn't reply immediately. "I think it's best thee not know the facts." She spoke so low, he had to focus intently on her voice, shutting all else out. "Then thee can maintain ignorance. Mr. Smith may suspect that I had something to do with his . . . loss, but I have provided him no evidence connecting me to it. Yet I remain on my guard, as thee should." In spite of her serious words, she waved to the children and called encouragement as they chased each other around the garden, giggling and shrieking.

He chewed on her words, disgruntled. "Very well, for now. But sometime in the future I will demand to know the truth."

"Agreed. Again, would thee like to borrow my copy of Frederick Douglass's book?"

Her insistence grated on his nerves. "Why would I want to borrow a book I have no interest in reading?"

She met his gaze. "I thought after hearing James Bradley speak, thee might want to know more of slavery."

"What does any of that have to do with me, with you?" Gerard asked, returning his gaze to the playing children. "Why do you care so much?"

"How can I not care when so many suffer?"

He didn't know how to answer her. Of course there was great suffering in this world, but that wasn't going to change. One person's effort to right wrongs amounted to spitting into the ocean. Some emotion he couldn't identify roiled up inside him. "Don't you ever think about having a life of your own?" he snapped.

"I have a life, a full one."

He knew that he was flirting dangerously with wanting more of this audacious woman in his life. The idea was out of the question. She was clearly not a candidate for a discreet affair, and he wanted no wife. So they could share nothing more than . . . friendship. That in itself was an astounding idea. Men and women didn't become friends. Or did they?

He glanced at her. "Are we friends?"

Blessing laughed. "What a scandalous idea," she teased. "What will people say?"

He shrugged. He'd tried to shore up his defenses, but this unique woman could not be dismissed. "I hear we will be attending a wedding soon."

"Yes," Blessing said, her voice suddenly subdued.

"I am best man." His tone matched hers.

"I am matron of honor."

Silence ensued until Blessing spoke again. "I would like to invite thee to listen to another unusual speaker who is presently traveling around Ohio. And is scheduled to give an address at Lane Seminary."

Gerard felt the corners of his mouth lifting of their own will. He tried to imagine a more provocative speaker than James Bradley. "Let me guess. A radical suffragist?"

"Yes."

He drew in air sharply and shook his head at her nerve. "Why not?"

Going to listen to another speaker like Bradley definitely wouldn't bore him, and it would give him a reason to spend an evening with Blessing. Still, even with these ulterior motives, he sensed a shifting inside him, a realignment. The feeling was alarming yet invigorating. He'd never experienced anything like it and was unsure whether he wanted to.

Chapter 9

BLESSING ESCORTED GERARD RAMSAY from the orphanage in time for his luncheon at Prudence Mather's and a few appointments with prospective clients in the afternoon. After some prodding, the children lined up to go in for their meal. Blessing rose to go inside too but found Joanna blocking her way. Instead of entering with the children, Joanna had let the other nursemaid direct their charges.

"What is it, Joanna?" Blessing asked.

Joanna bowed her head as if praying and then looked up. "I have something hard to say."

At her friend's unusual demeanor, Blessing stilled, apprehensive. Resuming her seat, she patted the now-empty wicker chair beside hers. "Sit and tell me." But she really didn't want any more sobering or distressing news.

Joanna accepted her invitation. By now, the garden was

quiet with just the two of them, the southbound Canada geese honking overhead, and the chickadees chittering in the trees. Fall had come, and the leaves were just starting to show red edges.

"I am getting married soon," Joanna said, not looking at her.

"Asher?" Blessing named the young man who'd been courting her friend. She kept her tone light, but her tension increased. What she'd dreaded was coming true.

"Yes. He can finally support a wife, and he wants me with him."

"I understand." Leaden sadness weighed down Blessing's heart. "I'll miss having thee here every day."

"That's not all."

Blessing waited, wondering, her heart skipping.

"We're moving to Canada."

The words struck Blessing, a heart blow. "Canada?" she murmured, thoughts racing.

"Yes. Asher wants our children safe from kidnappers and catchers, so they can grow up in a place where their freedom isn't always in question. He's saved enough to buy us land and already has his team and plow. He's decided we shouldn't wait. We plan to marry next week and then go to Canada before winter and get settled. After we arrive, we'll hire out and find land to buy before spring planting time."

"That is a good plan." This unwelcome change ruffled through Blessing like the wind through the pages of an open book. "It's just so sudden."

"I know. I thought we'd wait till next year, but the riot . . . Asher is ready to leave and I must follow."

Blessing couldn't argue with that. She didn't blame Asher for wanting to protect his future family. "I will miss thee."

"I know. I missed you when you married." The sadness in Joanna's tone distressed Blessing.

She rested a hand on Joanna's arm, sorting through what she should say, what words she wanted to speak. She should just be honest, she knew. Her mother always quoted Shakespeare at times like this: *"Truth will out."* She drew in a breath. "Joanna, I missed thee too."

"I wasn't much welcome in your house when your husband lived. I've always wondered why. Will you tell me now?" Joanna met her gaze.

Blessing closed her eyes against the past.

"I've carried a hurt over that ever since," Joanna continued. "I want to clear it up before we part, maybe for the rest of our lives. Will you tell me, please?"

Blessing quieted her nerves as much as she could. Just recalling one of the occasions Joanna had come to visit her and Richard was enough to shake her. The entire time, she'd been afraid Joanna might guess that Richard was upstairs sleeping off another drunken night.

"Joanna, there was a reason I kept my distance from thee and my family back then." She mustered her courage. "My marriage was not a happy one."

Sounds expanded around them: people walking past the garden fence, two squirrels chirruping in an argument over acorns, the clopping of horse hooves.

"You didn't act happy," Joanna agreed. "We all knew something was wrong. But you pushed us away."

The old hurt and suffering swirled inside Blessing, an ache

that could still rob her peace. "I'd wed him against the counsel of my parents and had gone against the elders, been put out of the meeting. Too soon I realized I'd made a disastrous choice, but I had already married. I couldn't change that. I had promised to stay for better or worse." That awful feeling of being trapped in a box with no exit washed over her.

"You could have come home," Joanna said.

"No, I couldn't. Richard was my husband. It was a complicated situation." She saw before her eyes Richard's recurring bouts of remorse and repentance. No doubt it was during one of these that out of guilt he'd willed his property to her and unwittingly given her the wherewithal to do God's will in helping others. The personal pain and self-recrimination still held, though. Why had she always believed he would change? "I loved him." At first. But then . . .

"I've wanted to talk to you about this many times, but you have ever held back about your marriage."

Blessing faced Joanna. She wanted to deny this but paused before speaking. "Hiding the truth about my marriage," she said slowly, "became a habit. But my affection for thee has never faltered, even when we were distant. We were raised together. Joanna, I understand thy desire to leave this place, where thy skin color always stands against thee—"

"Asher and I know we'll face prejudice in Canada too, but . . ."

Blessing nodded her sympathy. "But I have been so happy to have thee here at the orphanage with me." She took Joanna's hand. "Thank thee."

"I have loved working with the children and with you—being a part of this good place." Joanna gripped Blessing's hand in return. "But it's time for me to have my own children. Asher and I have waited long enough."

Blessing nodded, at first unable to speak. Joanna's words brought to mind the special bond she felt with her latest orphan. "I must tell thee before thee leaves—I am going to adopt Daniel Lucas."

"Why do you always talk like you won't ever marry again? You're still young."

Blessing shook her head. "I'll not marry a second time." Memories of her husband crowded around her, as menacing as the mob that had gathered at her gate. She stood. "Tell me about thy wedding plans." She led Joanna to the house, holding the past at bay.

❖

NOVEMBER 10, 1848

Gerard entered the familiar Lane Seminary auditorium, alight with lamps and candles against the early autumn darkness, and as before, he walked beside Blessing Brightman. Again, the audience, composed of both genders, caused him an odd feeling of displacement. But he'd come because Blessing had invited him and because his attendance at the James Bradley lecture had made the Cincinnati papers from which his father kept tabs on him. He recalled how incensed his father had been over Gerard's merely being seen in Seneca Falls last July and found himself suppressing a smile. However, at the back of his mind niggled the thought that such a motive smacked of immaturity. *I've also come tonight because I want to hear what's said.*

This evening even more people than before turned to

watch them enter. Gerard was struck by the startling realization that he almost wished the gossip about himself and Blessing were true.

Blessing halted and exchanged a few words with an older woman. As always, his lovely companion stood out as an oddity in the room. Dressed plainly but expensively, she was a dove among crows.

As the two women conversed, once more Gerard wondered about Smith's mistress—where she was now. He didn't believe for a moment that the woman was still at "number three." On a few occasions, he'd been tempted to visit that house and see what he could find out there. But caution held him back. He would do nothing to endanger that poor woman or Blessing.

The older woman embraced Blessing and went to sit farther ahead.

Blessing turned and dazzled Gerard with a genuine smile. "Ohio has been chosen to host the second women's rights convention in 1850. I will be working along with several of the women here to arrange everything."

Gerard tried not to react. Another women's rights convention? Wasn't one enough? "I see," he said.

His cautious tone set her chuckling. She swept into the next aisle and sat down.

He followed, shaking his head.

"Is that why thee comes with me?" she asked. "Because I am so different, so radical?"

Gerard drew in breath and again shook his head at her. Indeed that wasn't the reason. He accompanied her in spite of this. She was becoming sunlight to him. He craved her presence. She had made his stale life interesting. He couldn't countenance marriage for himself, but they had become . . . friends. Mentally he took a step back. This was still alien territory for him. A man and woman becoming friends—unheard of.

He was saved from replying more fully to her question by the introduction of the first speakers. Two men addressed the gathering briefly—neither of them as inflammatory as Gerard had expected. But when the main speaker walked out onto the platform, Gerard's mouth opened involuntarily.

"Our main speaker tonight is Sojourner Truth." The man introduced her with a gesture. "I hope you will give your attention to her."

He was about to be addressed by a female *Negro* suffragist. Dumbfounded, he sensed the chair beneath him dropping as if an earthquake had shaken the foundation.

Then he felt Blessing's gloved index finger gently lift his chin, closing his telltale open mouth.

He sent her a glance that asked why she hadn't warned him. Being addressed publicly by a female was radical, shocking enough, but by a black woman? Were there no boundaries of decorum at these meetings?

Blessing smiled teasingly and faced forward.

On the platform, the tall, older woman dressed simply in black began her address. "I am speaking to you tonight about the rights of women. Some people say women don't need rights; they just need good men to take care of them." She paused for a wry grin that deepened the wrinkles on her face.

Her saucy words brought Gerard back to earth, his chair on solid ground again. Yet something unlooked for had caught his attention. The woman's inflection was not the Southern accent he'd expected. Rather, she spoke in a sing-song pattern that he identified as New York Dutch. Some elderly New Yorkers who'd been born into Dutch families there still retained the distinctive speech pattern. Why would a black woman—no doubt a former slave—speak with a Dutch accent?

"Many of you are taken aback that I, a woman, a *Negro* woman, would speak in public. But I've been through many changes in my life and I have much to say. I was born a slave *in the state of New York*. That should prove to all how much our nation has changed within our lifetimes. So is a black woman speaking out about the rights of all women really so unusual?"

Gerard wanted to stand up and declare, *"Yes, it is unusual."*

But the woman continued. "I am always amazed how little men understand how the world looks to a woman or a slave or a slave who is a woman. Would any man wish to live completely under the will of another?"

For a moment Gerard considered his father with his will of iron and how he had tried to control Gerard with his purse strings. No, Gerard had refused to be controlled. *So why am I here? Under my own will I would never have come.* And something about this woman captured his attention. He tried to let go of his preconceptions and just listen to this bold woman.

Sojourner Truth continued, facing them with her arms outstretched. "I am standing here before you because of Jesus. But I knew little of Jesus when I was a slave. All I knew of God was the Lord's Prayer my mother taught me in Dutch as a small child before . . . before I was *taken* from her." The woman paused, letting the impact of that simple yet devastating sentence roll through him, through them all.

Another unwelcome memory returned: watching his mother weep as she was driven away from him to go to a spa for her health. He'd come home on summer holiday looking forward to spending it with her. There had been no reason for his father to choose that moment to send her away. She'd been in poor health for as long as Gerard could remember, but his father had insisted. And he and his mother had been powerless to change that. He'd hated his father from that day.

The speaker sighed loudly. "That prayer was all I knew of God as I grew up. Yet somehow all I longed for was to please God, be acceptable to him. I made up my mind every morning to obey him, but every day I failed." She stared at them and, it seemed, peered straight into Gerard's eyes. "I could not please God on my own."

Gerard had never thought of pleasing God. God didn't enter into his life.

Sojourner Truth continued, gripping the podium with one hand as if for support. "So I was in despair. One night I fled from my master's house into the woods and prayed to God. How could I reach him? He, high up and holy; me, sinful and lowly. Then a radiant figure appeared before my eyes. I did not know who he was, but he said, 'I am Jesus. I will be your go-between to God.' I had not even known the name Jesus!"

The stunned silence all around pressed in on Gerard, and he could barely draw breath. Nobody talked like this, did they?

"Soon I ran away and found a Quaker meeting in New York City. I began learning who Christ Jesus is and of his light. My life changed. That vision has given me power, Christ's power—" she raised her fist—"to proclaim freedom, pursue freedom. How many people live in darkness? In bondage? Jesus wants us to be free—white and black, slave and free, male and female. Why should that be so strange?"

Gerard felt electrified. Freedom. Wasn't that what he wanted? Didn't everyone seek it?

❧

On the way home, Gerard found himself unable to make small talk with Blessing. After Sojourner Truth's speech, others had risen to speak, but his gaze had been riveted on the dark, wrinkled face of the woman who claimed to have seen God. She'd stirred his mind, not just his heart. New thoughts sprang up, challenging him. What *must* it be like to be a slave, to be a woman?

The carriage slowed in front of his boardinghouse. He still could not speak. He opened the door, but before he stepped out, in the darkness he searched for and found Blessing's hand.

In that moment he fully recognized the power of this woman's influence. His resistance to the new world of radical ideas she was opening to him was waning. The freedom it proclaimed beckoned him. Moved, he lifted Blessing's hand to his lips, kissed the soft kid glove, and pressed it to his forehead. "Good night, Widow Brightman."

"Good night, Gerard Ramsay." Her voice sounded subdued, thick with emotion, as if she sensed his turmoil.

Gerard stepped down and shut the door, then watched the carriage roll away. He realized that though he'd attended church most of his life, he knew little of what Sojourner Truth had spoken of regarding her vision. Had God used a unique means of communication to speak to this unusual woman? However, he understood some of what she'd expressed. He'd met Blessing Brightman, and nothing would ever seem the same in his life either.

❖

DECEMBER 13, 1848

The day had come for Tippy's wedding. Dressed in her best blue-gray silk dress and holding a bouquet of pink-and-white hothouse roses, Blessing stood in front of the Fosters' parlor fireplace, a step behind the bride. Tippy glowed with joy, and Stoddard's expression was so revealing that Blessing felt as if she were intruding on the couple in a private moment.

Ramsay stood to her left, just behind his cousin. She forced herself to focus on the minister, who was leading Stoddard and Tippy through their vows—not letting her gaze roam to the gentleman from Boston.

In the weeks since she and Ramsay had attended Sojourner Truth's lecture, they had met only in passing or when involved in the planning of this wedding. And she'd been grateful. She still felt the kiss he'd pressed onto her hand at the end of that evening at Lane. How could such a slight touch cause such chaos? Again her wayward eyes sought him.

Intruding into Blessing's thoughts, Tippy's voice trembled as she said, "I, Xantippe Elaine, take thee, Stoddard Albert, to be my wedded husband, to have and to hold from this day forward; for better, for worse; for richer, for poorer; in sickness and in health; to love, cherish, and to obey, till death us do part, according to God's holy ordinance; and thereto I give thee my troth."

As Blessing listened, she recalled Joanna's recent wedding and heard Joanna's lower and richer voice overlaying Tippy's. Joanna's wedding had taken place in Bucktown, a free black settlement near their hometown of Sharpesburg. Afterward Blessing's parents had hosted the wedding dinner at their place. Their large barn, decorated for the occasion, had been filled with the wedding guests from Bucktown and Cincinnati. The next day Joanna and Asher had loaded their wagon and left for Canada. Remembering the last glimpse of her lifelong friend peeled back a layer of Blessing's composure. She felt defenseless here.

Now Stoddard received the ring from Ramsay and slipped the gold band onto Tippy's finger. "With this ring I thee wed, with my body I thee worship, and with all my worldly goods I thee endow: in the name of the Father, and of the Son, and of the Holy Ghost. Amen."

Blessing's unruly gaze wandered once more toward Ramsay, who stood very straight and stiff. Did he still think his cousin was making a mistake? Blessing had finally accepted that Stoddard was likely what he appeared: an honest man with a good heart. She hadn't found substantial reason to doubt it, in any case. This conclusion eased Blessing's concern in one way and caused her distress of another kind that she couldn't or wouldn't analyze.

The brief ceremony drew to a close, and the minister presented the new couple: "Mr. and Mrs. Stoddard Henry." The sound of the final words sent a pang through Blessing. When a woman married, she placed all her trust in her husband because she legally became invisible from that point onward. Even a good man was rarely worthy of such a sacrifice.

Blessing wondered if Stoddard realized the gift he'd just received and the responsibility he had assumed. Bitter memories of her own powerless state after she'd married Richard stirred, but she turned from them, scanning the small gathering.

Since Tippy had been unwilling to wait months for her wedding, the affair was a small one—just family and close friends. Blessing knew most everyone here at least by sight.

But two people were new to her. Stoddard's mother, Frances Henry, and his uncle Saul Ramsay—Gerard's father—had traveled from Boston for the occasion. As Blessing stood in the short receiving line with the bride and groom, greeting their guests and thanking them for their good wishes, she watched these two strangers, very aware of Ramsay at her side.

From all appearances, Stoddard's mother seemed happy about the match yet a bit uncertain of herself among the cluster of strangers. Saul Ramsay looked as if he had descended from Mount Olympus and didn't like rubbing shoulders with lowly humans. She listened curiously for what he would say to the happy couple.

"Congratulations, Stoddard," Saul Ramsay said formally, shaking the groom's hand. "Best wishes to your lady." That was all—the polite phrases and nothing more.

As he approached Blessing in the line, she gazed at him. Even while bowing over her hand, he looked right through her as if she weren't there. And she sensed that, in truth, she did not want his notice. He was a man of arrogance, grasping for control.

Saul Ramsay then offered a hand to his son but said absolutely nothing—not in words. Nonetheless, the friction between the two was palpable.

❧

As they shook hands, Gerard endured his father's silent displeasure. Father would never make a public scene, but Gerard knew that, later today, he would have to suffer his father's venting his spleen over his cousin's "disastrous" marriage. Then the man would blessedly return to Boston.

"Gerard," his aunt Frances said as he kissed her cheek, "I'm so glad you live here so that Stoddard will have family nearby. I plan on moving here too."

"Oh?" He hadn't known that. "I like Cincinnati, Aunt Fran. A very interesting city with great potential."

His father humphed, moving away as quickly as courtesy allowed, letting all know that his mere presence here today was noblesse oblige.

Aunt Fran leaned closer. "You know that this will probably be your mother's last Christmas?"

Gerard tingled from his head to the soles of his feet. He managed to nod. Impulsively he leaned down and embraced her. "I'm glad you're here, Aunt Fran."

She squeezed his hand and blinked away tears.

The wedding dinner passed without incident—many flowery toasts, clattering silverware, and cheerful chatter. Gerard had been seated across from Blessing this time. He tried to keep from looking at her too much, a struggle. She was always attractive, but in her best silk she was beautiful. Nonetheless, Gerard wanted to give no hint to his father that he viewed her as anything more than Tippy's friend and a shocking radical. He did not want his father to think that he might be interested in her romantically, because it might lead Saul Ramsay to be rude to her today. His feelings toward Blessing were in flux.

In the weeks since Sojourner Truth's lecture, he'd stayed away from her simply because he wanted so much to be in her company. Now he once again felt the pull she exerted over him. It was physical, as if they were linked by an invisible bond. He glanced at his aunt and was arrested by her look of sympathy. The sad news she'd brought from home about his mother caught afresh in his heart.

The dinner ended. The party began to break up, and Gerard found himself leaving at the same time as Blessing. They met at the front door and paused simultaneously.

"May I offer thee a ride home?" Blessing said, pulling her woolen shawl closer around her in anticipation of the stiff wind.

As Gerard prepared to accept, his father rounded the corner. "Gerard will be riding home in my carriage."

Gerard gritted his teeth at the man's high-handed behavior, then lifted Blessing's hand to his lips and clasped it within both of his hands. He'd wanted very much to touch her and would not let his father put him off. "You looked lovely today, Mrs. Brightman."

Blessing nodded, slipped her hand free, and walked down the steps to her waiting carriage. Her grace and composure made him proud.

Gerard decided to go along with his father and get the big scene over and done with. His father looked about ready to explode with venom.

As soon as Father's hired carriage pulled away from the curb, he launched his attack. "I can't believe your cousin has married a pretty little nobody, here of all places."

Already out of patience, Gerard looked directly at his father. "I am not returning to Boston. So save your breath."

"I cannot understand what has possessed you to come to this provincial town."

The fact that you don't live here, Gerard replied silently, then changed the topic. "Is Aunt Frances really moving here?"

"Yes." His father sounded dazed. "She wants to be near her only son. I suppose that makes sense. Though why Stoddard doesn't bring his bride to live at the estate near Boston that he inherited from his stepfather, I can't understand. And why is he working at a bank? There's no need for that."

"He likes his job."

"And you? Do you like your job?" his father jeered.

"As a matter of fact, I do."

"Selling insurance."

"Yes, I am rendering that service to companies and individuals." *And I am free of your interference.*

"Going to make your fortune?" Father taunted. "Or going to marry one? I've heard you're often in the company of that Quaker widow. A *Quaker*, of all things."

Gerard had expected no less than scorn from his father. Tempted to lose his composure, he kept himself in hand. "Do you have to be so predictable, so commonplace?"

His father glared at him.

"Mrs. Brightman is an intelligent and interesting woman. We sometimes attend antislavery meetings and other lectures together—"

"Together." Saul said the word as if tasting vinegar. "Going to promiscuous meetings on outlandish subjects. What possesses you to do this? Just to flout me? Come to your senses and return to Boston. Take up your rightful place in the family business. I'll reinstate your allowance, and I'll take your opinion into consideration before presenting another candidate for marriage."

Gerard sat back, letting himself feel the rhythm of the team as it drew nearer to the boardinghouse. Not long ago he'd have relished his father's unhappy capitulation. But now he felt removed from it. "Actually, I have come to my senses—I think for the first time in my life."

"What does that mean?" his father snapped.

"It means I am finally discovering who I am apart from you."

"You're my son, and you always will be."

"True. That's blood speaking, and blood can't be denied. But I want my own life." He glanced out the window and saw they were pulling up at Mrs. Mather's house. "When do you leave for Boston?"

"Tomorrow on the first riverboat."

The carriage halted and Gerard moved to exit.

His father's arm came up, barring the way. "You'll come home for Christmas?" This wasn't a command but a request—and it was different, at last personal. It wasn't about Saul Ramsay but must be an unusual plea for his wife's sake.

"Yes, I'll come home for Christmas," Gerard replied. "I

wish you good travel, Father." Then he was standing outside, watching the carriage drive away. He wanted to go to Boston for the holidays like he wanted to have all his teeth drawn. But he must return for one reason. Aunt Fran's words echoed in his heart, wrenched already with sorrow. *This will be your mother's last Christmas.*

❖

DECEMBER 18, 1848

In the days following the wedding, Gerard had fought going to visit Blessing. Now, the day before he was to leave for his parents' home, he finally gave in. He could no longer deny that he was unable to leave without seeing her. Golden lamplight shone in her windows, and a wreath with holly and berries hung on her door.

Accustomed to the harsher winters of the northeastern coast, he felt that the December evening was unusually balmy. Kentucky lay just across the river, and the warmer climate was welcome while it lasted.

The housekeeper opened the door and reprimanded him. "Mr. Ramsay, the hour for house calls is long past."

Her bold remark forced him to chuckle. "I realize that, but I worked late today and leave tomorrow. I'd like to see Mrs. Brightman before I—"

Then Blessing appeared in the hall. "Let him in, Salina."

A new realization came to him. This woman was at ease with everyone, no matter their color, gender, or status. Blessing turned back into the rear parlor, the one usually reserved for intimate friends.

He hesitated, but the housekeeper was shutting the door

behind him and he couldn't just stand on the rug. He let the housekeeper take his hat and cane before following Blessing toward the rear parlor. If she had been a never-married woman, he could not have called on her alone at this time of the evening. But society accorded widows more freedom. Especially Blessing Brightman.

On the other hand, his calling after dark would be viewed as significant, a sign of interest in her. While his mind reviewed this, his feet carried him straight to her. He paused at the threshold of the cozy room. Pine boughs adorned the mantel, cradling glowing pillar candles, their flames shielded within tall glass globes. A fire burned in the hearth, cheery and bright.

Clothed in one of her simple gray dresses, Blessing sat in a Windsor rocker. She had just picked up her knitting. The scene warmed him in a way he'd never experienced.

"Mrs. Brightman, I apologize for arriving here late."

"Please make thyself comfortable, Ramsay."

He chose the seat opposite her, unbuttoned his coat, and drew in a deep breath of the familiar fragrance of bayberry. He allowed the peace, elegance, and charm of the setting to soothe him.

"Thee leaves in the morning?" she said, the click of her wooden needles balm to him.

"Yes. I don't really want to go, but I need to visit my mother. And then I will escort my aunt Fran back here so she can take up residence."

The lady nodded. "I liked your aunt very much."

No comment about his father. That sparked a chuckle. "Yes, she is a good woman who has known much sadness."

Blessing counted her stitches. "I'm happy that she and Tippy seemed to take to each other."

"She was quite fond of Tippy, and I'm glad she purchased a cottage so near Stoddard's new home. Aunt Fran deserves to have some happiness."

Blessing met his eyes. "I take it she was unlucky in husbands?"

He inclined his head. "But fortunate in her son."

Blessing sent him one of her sweetest smiles. "I believe that."

He forced himself not to reach for her hand. *What am I doing here?* Then he knew exactly what he'd come to discuss. "Do you think what that woman said actually happened?"

Blessing paused and looked up. "Who?"

"That woman we heard speak. Sojourner Truth. What kind of name is that, anyway?"

"Her real name was Isabella. She gave herself the name she bears now."

"I see. Well?" he prompted.

"Thee must be more specific. She said much that I believe." Blessing gazed at him.

"Do you really think she saw a vision of Christ?"

Blessing bent over her knitting and pushed down her foot to make her chair rock. "I am a Friend. We believe that the Holy Spirit guides us if we let him."

"But it could simply have been her imagination."

Blessing kept the rocker creaking in a gentle rhythm. "We are told, 'Ask, and it shall be given you; seek, and ye shall find.' Sojourner Truth was asking with a broken and contrite heart—a heart God promises not to despise. She couldn't read and didn't have a Bible. How could she find God if no one bothered to teach her?"

He thought of all the Sundays he'd endured church services. He'd never felt the presence of anything divine there. "It just seems . . . unbelievable."

"Before we had the written Scripture, God used visions and prophets. Yet not all such experiences are true. Friends depend on the Inner Light, Christ's Light, yet we are always guided by Scripture."

"How does one do that?"

She frowned slightly at him. "Thee knows the Scriptures. Who is the only mediator between God and man?"

He hadn't thought of spiritual matters for a long time, but the answer was on his lips immediately. "Christ."

"And in her vision, whom did Sojourner Truth see as the intercessor between herself and God?"

He closed his eyes, not needing to speak the answer.

"We are also told to test the spirits," she continued, her gentle voice easing the kinks in his taut neck muscles.

He opened his eyes. "How?"

She shook her head at him. "Thee knows. Did Sojourner Truth have her vision and then go back and slaughter those who oppressed her? No. Her life is not a shame to Christ but a pleasant fragrance. And indeed I believe it took a powerful meeting with God to help this woman gain the courage to do what she does. God found a willing heart and claimed her for his work."

Gerard smiled, still sorting her words. "You have all the answers."

"No, I don't. That much I know." She put down her

knitting. "Tippy confided in me that thy mother is not in good health."

Gloom fell on him. He looked away. "I fear this may be her last Christmas, as my aunt believes."

"I am so sorry. Mothers are irreplaceable."

He could not think of a response, so he merely nodded.

Salina entered with a tray and offered him a cup of holiday punch. He accepted it and relaxed in their companionable silence, listening to Blessing's knitting needles and the comforting crackle of the fire.

Passing time with Blessing like this both stirred and calmed him, a confusing mix. He gazed at her as she bent over her knitting and felt he would be content never to leave. The thought of kissing her came to mind, making his lips tingle.

At this thought, he roused himself to bid his hostess good night. But, remembering, he reached into his pocket and brought out a slim, leather-bound volume. "I saw this in a shop and thought you might enjoy it." He handed her the gift.

"*A Christmas Carol* by Charles Dickens. I've heard of it but haven't read it. I do like Dickens. His fiction has substance." She smiled up at him. "Thank thee, Ramsay."

Longing shot through him, forceful and demanding. He pulled her up and stood within inches of her, staring into her green eyes. He desired to say something to her, something she would think of while he was gone. But all his words had fled. He stroked her soft cheek with the back of his hand, wanting to kiss her. Again he could almost feel their lips meeting. But he stopped himself short. "Merry Christmas, Blessing Brightman."

She glanced downward and stepped back. "Godspeed, Ramsay."

The urge to draw her deep into his arms crashed over him. So he, too, stepped back from temptation. "Good night."

He left the parlor swiftly, not waiting for anyone to see him out. By the door, he gathered his things and hurried outside. The widow was becoming more and more special to him—something he hadn't asked for, couldn't afford. He wasn't the man for such a free-thinking woman.

As he walked quickly down the street, Gerard gradually became aware of footsteps behind him. Strange—the streets were nearly empty at this hour. He rounded a corner, but the determined footsteps followed him. He checked for his pistol and gripped his cane more tightly, ready to stop and defend himself.

"Mr. Ramsay." A gruff voice spoke from behind.

He turned and by the moonlight glimpsed, of all people, Smith.

Chapter 10

GERARD'S ALERTNESS leaped high. He searched for a tactical advantage. Ahead at the next house someone had left a lantern burning on their gate—no doubt waiting for a family member coming home late. He walked briskly to the lamp and stood in its light so that, perhaps, the people at home nearby could observe whatever happened.

Smith chuckled unpleasantly. "Trying to protect yourself?"

Gerard stared at the shadowy figure, ignoring his question. "Why are you here? None of your investors signed on with me, and I've given up the idea of the racetrack. Our dealings are done."

Smith stayed in the shadows. "You know why I'm here."

"I really don't," Gerard lied. Not only his own safety but also Blessing Brightman's might depend on how he handled this interview. And he couldn't forget Jewel, the woman who'd been debased by and escaped this man.

"You don't? Really?" Smith sounded disbelieving, mocking.

"No. The good widow scared off all those investors, and I finally decided to just get employment." He kept his tone light as if all this were not significant to him. "I think I over-estimated my talent for entrepreneurship. We have nothing to discuss, and I'm heading home now."

"I see you're getting thick with Widow Brightman. That's unwise," Smith threatened.

"I'm unlikely to take any character recommendations from you."

"I knew her unfortunate husband. She made his life a living hell."

Gerard didn't dignify this slur with a reply. He moved as if to depart.

"Didn't a young woman visit you at your boardinghouse?" Smith pressed, drawing nearer though still avoiding the light.

Gerard stared into the night, barely able to make out Smith's face. "A young woman?" He acted as though he were thinking. "Ah, do you mean that unfortunate young woman who falsely told my landlady that I had gotten her with child?"

"Yes." The word sounded ripped from Smith's throat.

"So you sent her? I wondered if you might have been behind that. I couldn't think of anyone else I know in Cincinnati who would try to do me harm in such a scurrilous way." Gerard infused his tone with contempt and adjusted his arm so he could easily reach for his pistol if necessary.

No reply came from Smith.

But Gerard felt the waves of his animosity and continued. "It didn't work. Mrs. Mather refused to believe her and ordered her from the house. The young woman left by the back door."

"That's not true." Smith's every syllable was laden with pent-up anger.

"I was there. You were not. She left of her own accord, out the back door, and that was the first, last, and only time I've ever laid eyes on the woman. Now I'm heading home. And, Smith, our business—our association—is done." He started away from the lamplight.

Smith grabbed his arm. "I'm not done with you, Ramsay. After I left Boston, I never thought I'd see you again—" Smith broke off.

"See me again? When did we meet in Boston?"

Smith barked an imitation of a laugh. "We never met formally, but I saw you." The words seethed with repressed fury and resentment.

Baffled, Gerard stared at Smith. "Where did you see me?"

"In front of your house in Beacon Hill, I saw you. Many times I watched you." Again the simple words were laden with hostility, and Smith still grasped his arm.

Gerard wanted to break free but couldn't without resorting to violence. And the man sounded irrational, unpredictable. Warning quivered over Gerard's nerves. Was there something wrong with Smith's reason? Angling his free arm, he shifted his pistol from its holster, still concealing it under his coat.

Smith must have felt the movement, but he did not loosen his grip.

Gerard stared into Smith's eyes, moonlight reflecting off them. "Why are you so concerned about that young woman? Didn't you just pay her to try to embarrass me? I did her no harm except to object to her lie." He continued improvising. "Why do you care where she went? Did she owe you money or something?"

"Something," Smith replied in an even darker tone.

"Well, I can give you no more help. Now are we going to be reduced to a public brawl or will you release my arm?"

Smith let go suddenly as if trying to jar Gerard off his feet.

Ready for any move, Gerard straightened his coat and sauntered away as if unconcerned that Smith stayed behind.

Just as he turned the nearest corner, he heard Smith mutter, "We're not done. This isn't over till I say it is."

He didn't let on that he'd heard. Smith could threaten, but he had no proof. There was none to find. The man had fallen back on conjecture.

Gerard tried to dismiss the lingering impression of seething anger and spite Smith left in the air, but he could not. Then he surprised himself with a silent prayer. *God, keep Smith away from Blessing.*

❖

DECEMBER 24, 1848

On Christmas Eve after supper, Blessing sat at the table with her family and Rebecca, waiting for the evening's annual event to begin. She gazed around her parents' home. Though very simply decorated, the home displayed her mother's style, elegant and welcoming.

A bookcase filled with colorful leather-bound volumes

sat against the far wall, away from the hearth and windows. The fireplace was flanked by settles with quilted cushions. On a large oval hand-hooked rug, two Windsor rockers sat in front of the fire with her mother's sewing basket on the floor between them. A few framed samplers embroidered with Scripture hung on the walls.

Their old wooden toy box sat in the corner, waiting for grandchildren in the future. That she would never bring home a child to delve into the carved horses, wooden blocks, and leather balls caught Blessing around her lungs. Then she recalled little Daniel Lucas, back at the orphanage, and she could breathe again. She had no doubt he would be welcomed here.

Ramsay's arresting face drifted into her mind, almost painfully. She forced herself to block out his image and sipped the sweet mug of wassail beside her, inhaling the scent of the cider, mulled with cinnamon and nutmeg—her mother's own recipe.

Many Quakers didn't celebrate Christmas at all, and definitely not as other Christians did with feasting and gifts. Instead her parents had always set Christmas Eve apart. It had become a night of reflection on the birth of Christ and a time to honor those who'd already gone to be with him. Tomorrow, on Christmas Day, they would hold an afternoon open house where friends from miles around would visit.

Much as Blessing tried, Gerard Ramsay was ever at the edge of her thoughts. She recalled his last visit and how close he'd drawn to her, how she'd feared—almost hoped—he'd kiss her. Her body awoke at his imagined touch. She drew in breath and regained control. He'd bidden her farewell and headed home to Boston for the holidays. And when he returned, she must once again set him at arm's length. She must not continue flirting with disaster.

Her mind shifted to the night he'd helped her and Jewel. Had the mistress he'd helped free reached her Canadian destination safely? The mail between Canada and southern Ohio was slow and irregular. Blessing sent another prayer heavenward for Jewel and her unborn child. And that God would help Blessing keep her focus on him alone. Nothing must impede her work. Certainly not this man from Boston.

The expected knock at the door sounded. Her cousin Eli, home from his position as professor at Oberlin College, left his chair and opened the door. Dressed warmly, Aunt Royale and Uncle Judah—Joanna's parents—came in, followed by their youngest children, pretty girls nearing marriageable age. Aunt Royale was still beautiful with her caramel skin and green eyes. Her husband, who worked with Blessing's father in the glassworks, was tall and solid-looking.

Blessing's mother rose and embraced Royale. Blessing also stood, greeting both of them by name. In plantation society, the titles "uncle" and "aunt" were accorded to older slaves as a sign of respect for their age. But that wasn't why Blessing had been taught to use these titles for Royale and Judah. The connection between the two families was long and deep.

Tonight all Royale's family appeared subdued. And Blessing thought she knew why.

"I'm missing Joanna and Asher too," her mother said, voicing the cause.

Aunt Royale nodded. "It's hard, but all those years ago we left our home in Maryland. Now Joanna and Asher want to be in Canada. It's for their family's best." She wiped a tear from her cheek.

Uncle Judah held a lantern, as did Royale and their daughters. They remained near the door, waiting.

Everyone at the table rose and started to put on their own shawls or jackets.

"Where are we going?" Rebecca asked in word and sign, which she was learning quickly.

"On Christmas Eve, our two families always go by lantern light to our family plot," Blessing explained, thinking of the few graves with the unmarked crosses that lay within the plot—runaway slaves who'd died hiding here. "We decorate the graves with wild holly and pine boughs to remember them on this holy night."

Rebecca looked frightened. "The family plot? At night?"

Blessing understood the common hesitation about visiting a graveyard in the dark. "We'll all be together. It's a quiet time and peaceful."

Rebecca still hesitated.

Caleb signed, "I'll stay with her. You go on."

Blessing watched as her adopted cousin rested a comforting arm around the back of the girl's chair.

"That might be best," Honor agreed.

As they set off into the chill night under a crescent moon, Blessing hovered near her parents. She murmured for her mother only, "I see that Caleb and Rebecca are becoming close."

"Yes, I'm glad. It's long past time he should have taken a wife."

"Will it be a wise union?"

"Yes, I believe so. Caleb has very tender feelings toward her, and Rebecca, though still very subdued, is healing."

"There's such an age difference between them—nearly twenty years," Blessing objected. An owl swooped overhead with a rush of wings.

"Yes, there is, but does that matter to the heart?"

Blessing let it go at that. If the feelings between Caleb and Rebecca were mutual and honest, she had no right to object. But was Rebecca merely looking for a home and a man who could protect her?

Again memories of Ramsay intruded. *I must draw away from him. Neither of us could prevent Stoddard and Tippy from marrying, and he appears to have given up on the racetrack idea. At least he knows the truth about Smith. I can step back from him now.*

Blessing's thoughts rang hollow in her own ears. She didn't want to distance herself from Ramsay. She enjoyed, craved his company, and being with him meant much to her. Too much.

❖

DECEMBER 25, 1848

To avoid arguing with his father, Gerard was hiding out in his mother's suite of rooms. Father had been spectacularly unpleasant at dinner. Now Gerard sat in a chair near the fire while his mother lay upon her brocade chaise longue. She had lost weight since he'd last seen her, and her pale-blue dressing gown hung on her. Her breathing was shallow and at times labored.

Gerard wanted to ask her what the doctors had to say

about her decline but couldn't bring the words to his lips. He also had not commented on the fact that she could no longer walk unassisted.

"Gerard," she said weakly, "you are the only good thing I've done with my life, and your father has obstructed my efforts for you at every turn." The comment came after a long interval of both of them staring into the flames in the rose marble hearth.

He could think of no reply, so he merely gazed at his mother, questioning.

"When she returned from Stoddard's wedding, your aunt Frances visited me. She was so pleased with her son's bride. I hear that while she is a pretty girl, her personality is what is most notable about her."

"Tippy is a bright girl and very charming."

"It seems she believes that women deserve equal rights with men."

Gerard tried to gauge his mother's opinion from her tone and failed. "She does."

"And so does her best friend, a Quaker widow in whom you have shown interest."

Instantly Blessing's face sprang to mind. She was smiling at him, teasing him. He buried his eager response. "Aunt Fran shouldn't let her tongue run away with her," he observed dryly.

"Frances liked her very much. Said she was honest and good. I hear she operates an orphanage. That's a fine thing to do. Many times I've tried to visit an orphanage here to offer my assistance, but your father forbade me. He just sent them money. He said he didn't want me exposed to 'such people.'"

Gerard could hear his father saying those words and meaning them. "Father didn't care for Mrs. Brightman."

She sent him a wry grin that said she understood. "I should have been stronger, Son." She sighed. "When my parents decided that Saul Ramsay would be my husband, I should have resisted. But I've never been strong like your Quaker widow, who doesn't seem to care what others say about her work. I protested but in the end gave in. I'm sorry."

Gerard leaned forward and captured her hands. "You've been a good mother. I've never doubted your love for me."

"Thank you, Son. But I'm not happy with how I've wasted my life. Perhaps if this ailment hadn't come upon me when you were just a small child, our life might have been different. But it did come, and soon it will finally take me to the grave."

Her words touched a spark to his fear. "Mother, don't speak like that."

"It's the truth, and I'm glad to have this time with you while I am still somewhat myself."

"I don't have to go back—"

"Yes, you do. You've broken free from your father, and I won't let my failing health interfere with that. In fact, Gerard, I don't want you to witness my final days. Let's enjoy this last holiday with each other. Then you'll go back to your independent life in Cincinnati and not let your father hem you in."

Her expression lightened. "Now tell me about these free-thinking speakers you've listened to. Your father was livid when he saw your name in the newspaper as attending radical meetings."

Ramsay smiled back. "You sound as if you'd like to go."

"I would. Please tell me what these speakers said."

And so he did, telling her first about meeting Tippy and Blessing in Seneca Falls, then recounting James Bradley's lecture and Sojourner Truth's. Finally he could tell she was lagging, so he rose and called for her maid. He kissed his mother's forehead. "Sleep, Mother. I'll visit tomorrow."

She responded only with a frail grip that caused him more distress. He returned to his room and found a note by his bed. He opened it and could not believe who had sent it. He hurried downstairs and found the butler. "When did this note arrive?"

"After dinner, sir. You'd already gone up to your mother's suite and I didn't want to disturb you. The messenger boy said that I should just leave it in your room. I know it's not the usual way, but a note this late in the evening . . ." The man looked worried as if he feared Gerard might be displeased.

"That's fine. It is unusual." *But then Kennan is unusual.* And should he go to the meeting the note proposed? After his "lost" night in Cincinnati?

❖

DECEMBER 26, 1848

Fluffy snowflakes fell in a gentle shower as Gerard arrived at Ticknor, Reed & Fields, a publishing house across from the Park Street Church with its imposing white steeple, the church where Gerard's family had held membership for decades. The note that had prompted him to appear here lay in his pocket.

Kennan stepped out from the leafless elms near the side of the church. Gerard's onetime friend looked haggard, unshaven, and rumpled. "Gerard."

Remembering how awful he'd felt for two days after their last meeting, Gerard hesitated. "Kennan."

"I chose a church so we could speak privately and you wouldn't feel . . ."

Gerard let a carriage pass, then crossed to the entrance of the church as Kennan drew nearer.

"Feel as if you might slip something into my drink?" Gerard asked, pinning Kennan with his gaze.

"You figured that out?" Kennan almost smirked but without any humor.

Anger flamed within. Gerard glared at him. But instead of speaking, he waved his friend through the white doors, out of the chill. Winter sunshine lit the cavernous interior of the church. He sat on one of the straight-back chairs, and Kennan took the seat beside him. The walls and floor breathed deep cold around their ankles and up into their faces.

"I'm sorry," Kennan muttered. "I didn't want to do it, but Smith—"

"Smith," Gerard snapped in an undertone. Even though the church appeared empty, someone still might be inside.

"Gambling got me. I owed him way more than I could pay. He told me he'd cancel half my debt if I could get you out for the evening onto the docks at a certain . . . brothel."

Each word galled Gerard. "Why did he want me at a certain brothel?"

"I don't know. Halfway through the night, I think someone else drugged me too. I woke up in an alley at the wharf, sick with an aching head."

"Serves you right. That's how I woke up." *After being dumped in front of Mrs. Mather's boardinghouse.*

"As soon as I was able to, I got on the next steamboat east. I reached Pittsburgh and was able to borrow money there from another old schoolmate to get the rest of the way home."

Gerard fumed in silence. Kennan had betrayed him and run away. He'd known Kennan had betrayed him, but each blunt fact was more bitter than the one before.

"Frankly, I couldn't face you after what I'd done. I don't know why Smith wanted me to get you down to the docks. But it couldn't have been good."

Gerard knew why, but he had no intention of explaining the scheme to Kennan. Thanks to Stoddard, Gerard's reputation had been preserved and Smith's intended scandal had been avoided. No need to rehash it or to satisfy Kennan's morbid curiosity.

"Are you still trying to get your racetrack started?" Kennan shifted in his seat as if the surroundings made him uncomfortable.

"I've broken with Smith." Gerard shivered with the chill. The idea of the racetrack still resurfaced from time to time, but Gerard knew it was unlikely ever to materialize.

"That was wise. I'm not going back to Cincinnati. I still owe Smith money, and I'm not giving him another penny."

"Good."

"I'm really sorry, Gerard. The incident made me realize that I was going beyond the pale." Kennan sounded sincere.

"Good," Gerard repeated and moved to rise.

Kennan stopped him with a hand on his sleeve. "Gerard, I tried to think of a way to make it up to you," Kennan continued in a lower voice, sounding urgent. "So I started watching your father. I thought the man can't be the plaster saint he makes himself out to be."

Gerard noticed the sudden suppressed excitement creeping into Kennan's tone.

"And I was right." Kennan grinned, his eyes alight. "Here, take this."

Gerard glanced down at the folded paper. He accepted it but with a feeling of uncertainty. Was this another ploy to ruin him? Could he take a chance on trusting Kennan again?

"How's Stoddard?" Kennan asked as he stood nervously, obviously ready to escape the church.

"Married." Gerard looked again at the paper.

"Poor sap. Don't let that widow catch you," Kennan said with a nonchalance that poked Gerard hard.

Kennan took one step away, then paused. "I did this to make up for . . . that night. I felt bad, really bad, about wronging you. You and Stoddard have always been my friends. I'm sorry I broke trust with you." Kennan gazed at him. "Go to the address on that paper."

"Why?"

"Because I could hardly believe it myself. There you'll find your father's clay feet. Merry Christmas." With that darkly turned felicitation, Kennan left as if escaping an enemy.

Gerard didn't follow Kennan. He sat in the silent church, listening to the muted street noises outside. Finally he unfolded the note. In Kennan's scrawl was an address, an address in Manhattan. What was this about? Did it have anything to do with Smith? Did his reach extend all the way to the East Coast? But Smith was from Boston, not New York. And Kennan had sounded honest about his remorse. His father and clay feet? Gerard didn't know what to think.

❖

DECEMBER 27, 1848

Blessing sat quietly in her own kitchen, staring into space, shortly after returning from her parents' home.

Salina came in, glanced at her, and sat down with a grunt. "What's ailin' you?"

The question shook Blessing out of her listless gloom. She chuckled. "Nothing really." Nothing she would admit to.

"Hmm." Salina sounded unconvinced. "I know what's got you down."

Blessing knew too, but she didn't want to hear anything about Ramsay said out loud. "Just a bit of loneliness after visiting my family," she alibied. "We were all there."

"Except for Joanna."

"Yes, that too," Blessing said, grateful that Salina hadn't added, *"And except for Mr. Ramsay."* Blessing rose. "I need to get busy and do something constructive, not just sit here."

Salina worked her way back to her feet. "You found anybody to replace Joanna?"

"No, but that's a good idea. I need to start looking. Theodosia has been helping with the children, but we need more help, someone in charge." Blessing headed toward the front hall for her shawl, bonnet, and gloves.

Salina followed Blessing and opened the door for her. "When that Mr. Ramsay comin' back?"

"I don't know," Blessing replied as if she didn't care. But she hoped soon—and then scolded herself. She must not let him into her heart. One husband was enough to last her a lifetime, and she sincerely believed that Ramsay wouldn't ever desire marriage. And in light of the fact that she'd never be unequally yoked again, the idea of Gerard's joining the Quaker meeting was even less conceivable than the idea of his taking a wife—and that wife being her.

❖

Though he'd resisted the impulse, Gerard found himself in Manhattan two days after Christmas, riding in a covered, horse-drawn omnibus. He would need to return to Boston before dawn in order to depart on time with Stoddard's mother.

Now, nearing the address Kennan had given him, he tugged on the strap connected to the ankle of the omnibus driver, and the coach drew to a halt. Gerard stepped out near the address. And felt like a fool.

He gazed around at the neighborhood, neither rich nor poor. A coffeehouse sat on one corner and a grocer across from it. The chill wind started him walking. He tried to act purposeful, but since he was uncertain about the nature of his destination, that was difficult. Most of the houses on this street were modest, two-story affairs. Some no doubt housed two families.

He located the house in question and glimpsed a woman walk out into the back garden. She was in her middle years with silver in her dark hair, plump and unprepossessing. She stooped over what looked like a dormant vegetable garden and began to dig with a spade. The woman unearthed three white tuberous vegetables.

Parsnips? Gerard seemed to recall that they needed to be left in the cold ground and harvested over the winter, though he had no idea where he'd heard this. The woman rose, shook off the dirt, plunged the spade back into the ground, and hurried into the house as if chilled.

He realized that he'd stopped too long and started up the street. A ruse came to mind, so he took out a notebook and paused at several houses in turn, gazing at them and jotting down notes.

Finally one woman, clutching her shawl around herself, hurried out of her house and accosted him. "What're you doing staring at my house?"

He lifted his hat politely. "I was just wondering if any of the homes in this area are for sale?"

"If you want to know that, you should ask a land agent, not loiter in a respectable neighborhood," she snapped.

"True, but I've often found that some people might be interested in selling but haven't spoken to an agent yet. Do you know if any of your neighbors might be moving soon?"

"No, and I wouldn't gossip about my neighbors if I did. Now move along." The woman waved him away.

What was he doing here anyway? An omnibus heading back toward the heart of the city approached. Gerard bowed to the woman and hurried to lift a hand toward the omnibus. The driver stopped and Gerard boarded, paying the fare.

Just as he sat, he saw another omnibus enter the street from the other direction and stop right across from his.

Gerard's bus was driving away when he saw someone he thought he recognized exit the other omnibus. His father?

He craned his neck to see the man who dressed like his father, walked like his father. The man headed straight for the house Kennan had identified—the house with the woman and the parsnips.

Turn around. Look toward me.

But the man didn't obey Gerard's silent commands. He walked directly to the door and entered the house without knocking. What would his father be doing here? As the omnibus rumbled away over the cobbled street, Gerard sank into rank confusion.

Chapter 11

JANUARY 17, 1849

Expecting Tippy and her family any moment, Blessing once again toured the first floor of the comfortable cottage across the street from Stoddard and Tippy's home. Tippy had asked Blessing to help her prepare the cottage her mother-in-law, Fran, would live in. Blessing had relished the diversion of ordering custom curtains and slipcovers, coordinating colors and prints, and outfitting and stocking the kitchen. But nothing had distracted her from thinking of the man she wanted to forget.

She'd heard that Ramsay had returned from Boston, escorting Tippy's mother-in-law. And for two weeks, he hadn't so much as passed her on the street. Absently, her fingers stirred the potpourri in a dish on a maple side table, the scents of lavender and rose oil drifting upward.

Unfortunately, the less she saw Ramsay, the more she wanted to see him. Was he avoiding her—and if so, why? Perhaps visiting Boston had reminded him of who he was. But she had liked who he was becoming much better. Too much.

A quiet sound alerted her that Shiloh had come into the room.

"Mrs. Henry'll be coming over soon?" Shiloh interrupted, obviously nervous to meet her new mistress.

Blessing turned and smiled reassuringly at the girl, one of Joanna's younger sisters. Shiloh resembled her mother, Aunt Royale, with her golden-brown hair and green eyes, and she matched the woman in beauty. "Yes. Stoddard's mother has rested up from the trip here, and everything is ready for the move into her own cottage."

"I hope I like her and she likes me." The girl looked down. This was Shiloh's first job and first time living away from her home in Sharpesburg. Fran had left hiring her staff to Tippy, and Tippy had turned to Blessing.

"Thee will do fine. She's a sweet lady."

Shiloh smiled, her lower lip quivering.

"Here they come," Blessing said, looking over her shoulder as she heard the lady and her party approach. She went to open the door. "Come when I call thee, Shiloh."

The girl disappeared into the kitchen at the rear.

Up the flagstone walk, Tippy led the quartet: herself, Frances, Stoddard, and bringing up the rear, Gerard. Blessing hadn't expected him and quickly hid her sharp reaction to seeing him again—the man she couldn't get out of her mind. She greeted the group with as much composure as she could manage.

"Here's your new home, Mother Henry," Tippy said. "We tried to arrange it comfortably for you, but you're welcome to make changes."

Blessing attempted to study Gerard without appearing to do so. However, his face was shut tight like a boarded-up house. Perversely, this remoteness merely caused her to draw a step nearer.

She was close now, but his complete lack of acknowledgment shoved her backward.

Halting, she swallowed hard.

The others were still discussing the house, oblivious to Blessing's angst. "We could always buy or build you something bigger if necessary, Mother," Stoddard said.

"No, I'm older now," Fran replied, scanning the main floor. "I won't be entertaining much, and this is certainly enough room for me."

At Gerard's persistent disheartening silence, Blessing felt her own face freezing into place.

"And you'll be taking most of your meals with us," Tippy reminded the older woman.

"Shiloh," Blessing called, anxious to move this forward and escape to her own home.

The girl appeared, her face lowered. "Yes, Miss Blessing."

"Mother Henry," Tippy said, "you've met Honoree, my housemaid. This is her sister Shiloh, your housemaid."

Fran approached her. "Hello, Shiloh."

Shiloh dropped a curtsy. "Ma'am."

Unaccountably, at that moment Blessing's gaze met Ramsay's. Blessing found she couldn't move, couldn't smile, couldn't speak. She tried to break the connection, knowing that she must not just stand here staring at him. A panicky feeling shook her.

Gerard broke away first, striding toward the rear of the cottage and looking out the window. "The cottage has a nicely sized fenced-in garden."

Why could he break their connection and not she?

Most of the others moved outside to view the winter garden. Tippy hung back, letting Blessing come alongside. Blessing hated the look of sympathy on her friend's face. *I must not behave foolishly about this man. My path is set*—was *set long before he came to town. And he can have no part in it.*

She accepted Tippy's hand and the two of them followed the group. Tippy squeezed her hand as if in understanding, and Blessing vowed not to allow her emotions to affect her like this again. *I should know better.*

❖

Standing at the edge of the garden, Gerard chided himself for giving in to the temptation to come today. He could have begged off, but knowing that Blessing would be here, he found he couldn't stay away. Until today he'd managed to elude her disturbing presence, but not his memories of her.

Confusion weltered within him—over her, over Kennan, over the house in Manhattan. Yet he found he needed to at least see Blessing, a concerning admission. Her pale cheek beckoned his touch, and his gaze strayed to the elegant curve of her neck. He slipped his hand into his pocket to keep from drawing near and reaching for her.

Since Gerard's return, Stoddard had been very busy with his new bride, their new home, the demands of his job. Gerard hadn't wanted to bother him, but he'd finally decided that he would, after all, confide in Stoddard about the address in Manhattan. He needed another opinion. And he most trusted Stoddard to give insight.

As he and Stoddard hung back by the garden's edge, the women strolled the path and the young maid pointed out the remnants of different plants and herbs that would bloom again. Even as he strove to ignore Blessing, the woman's graceful carriage claimed his attention.

"I need to talk to you," Gerard whispered into his cousin's ear.

Stoddard glanced sideways at him. "Does it have something to do with Blessing?"

"No," he snapped in a low tone. "I saw Kennan in Boston."

Stoddard swung fully toward Gerard. "Kennan? When?"

"Keep your voice down," Gerard cautioned, raising a hand. "He left a note at my home, and then I met him at Park Street Church."

"Park Street Church?" Stoddard didn't try to conceal his puzzlement.

"I know—not where I'd ever expect to find Kennan. Anyway, he admitted he drugged me that night."

The women turned back toward the cottage. Blessing was looking down as if avoiding him.

Stoddard growled under his breath. "Let's table this till we can be alone."

He and Stoddard followed Fran, Tippy, Blessing, and Shiloh back inside. The women went on up the stairs to view the large bedroom for Stoddard's mother and the small dressing room that had been turned into Shiloh's quarters. Unable to look away, Gerard watched Blessing's slender, stockinged ankles ascend the steps.

Gerard and Stoddard remained downstairs, standing side by side. "Kennan admitted he drugged you?" his cousin asked in an undertone.

"Yes. He owed Smith gambling debts he couldn't pay. Smith wanted me drugged—to get me thrown out of our boardinghouse, as we suspected."

Stoddard let out a sound of disgust. "I'm done with Kennan."

"I am too, but before we parted, he said that he'd wanted to make it up to me. That he'd been watching my father—and then he gave me an address in Manhattan."

"What?" Stoddard's face twisted in consternation.

From above, Gerard heard the women's voices and footsteps. "I tried to resist, but I ended up going there."

"What did you find?" Stoddard's voice was a heated whisper.

"A modest house in a comfortable residential section. And . . . I think I saw my father walk into it as though he belonged there. I mean, he didn't knock, just walked inside."

"You think you saw your father there?" Stoddard repeated, disbelief in his tone.

"Yes. My omnibus was just pulling away when I saw him—or a man who looked very much like him. I didn't see his face directly, but he walked like my father," Gerard said, his mind still resisting what he'd witnessed.

"This is troubling," Stoddard muttered. "What could your father be doing at a home in Manhattan?"

The ladies were coming down the stairs now, Aunt Fran

inviting them all to tea. Blessing walked past Gerard without a glance, and the slight stabbed him to the bone. He shook it off.

The widow might intrigue him, tempt him, but his confusion over his father had reminded him why he should resist temptation. His parents' arranged marriage had been unhappy, and Blessing's own previous match didn't inspire confidence. Yet how flat life tasted now without the audacious widow enlivening it.

❖

JANUARY 19, 1849

Answering a quiet knock, Blessing opened the back door of the orphanage and found Ducky Hughes standing there. "Come in."

The subdued woman followed her into the kitchen, and with a nod to the cook, Blessing requested tea and cookies for their guest. Ducky sat down at the table, looking nervous, more nervous than before. What was the matter?

"I'll go get Danny," Blessing said, hoping this would calm the woman. She returned in a few moments with the baby in her arms. She sat adjacent to Ducky. The woman was sipping her tea and nibbling a cookie, obviously tense. But she smiled as soon as Blessing turned Danny toward her.

"Oh, he's getting chubby. And he looks good." Ducky drew in a deep breath of relief.

"He's growing fast," Blessing agreed, noting that Ducky still seemed restless. "I want thee to know that I've started the legal process to adopt Danny as my own."

Ducky looked stunned. "Why would you do that?"

Blessing tried to come up with an explanation. "I don't know. I've just felt drawn to him from the very first night. I had always planned on adopting a few of the children. Danny will be the first." She could look forward to having a family of her own, not living a completely solitary life.

Ducky blinked away sudden tears. "I don't know what I can say but thank you."

The cook excused herself and left with her shopping basket.

Ducky looked around furtively and lowered her voice. "Are we alone?"

So Ducky was indeed going to tell her what was wrong.

Blessing glanced behind her and nodded. "Since it's raining, the nurses and children are in the parlor, drawing pictures and playing jacks."

Ducky leaned forward and lowered her voice even more. "I came to see Danny, but I also wanted to warn you." The woman paused and looked around again as if fearing to be overheard. "Smith is becoming . . . I don't know how to put it. He's always been bad, but now he's worse somehow."

Blessing stiffened.

Ducky sipped her tea and set the cup down. "His mistress left him, poor girl. I don't know how she managed to get away, but ever since she left, he's been really . . . dangerous," Ducky said, shrugging.

Blessing had known there might be reprisals over what she'd done.

"He's been heard saying things about you. My man, the one who protects me—" she looked down as if in shame— "he heard Smith's got it in for you. He told me because he

knows you took in Danny and knows I wouldn't want anythin' to happen to you. My man says for you to watch out
comin' down to the docks. Smith might try something. He's
dangerous," Ducky repeated.

Dangerous. Yes, Smith could be dangerous.

"I don't know why he should think you had anything to
do with Jewel leavin' him, but . . ." Once more the woman
shrugged.

Blessing also could think of no verifiable link between
herself and Jewel's disappearance. She was sure she'd covered
her tracks, though Smith no doubt had his suspicions. She
was a person he had not been able to twist to his purposes, in
spite of his every effort. And she certainly stuck in his craw,
though he couldn't have been more successful in destroying
her husband. It was through Richard's periods of confession
and promises to change and not return to the docks for long
nights of drinking and worse that she'd first learned of Smith.
The man had actually had the effrontery to attend Richard's
funeral and speak to her in veiled and insulting terms.

But her husband wasn't the only young gentleman Smith
had ruined. He seemed to target them in particular. Over the
years his ability to profit and coerce had only grown—to the
downfall of many like Richard Brightman.

Now, however, she'd foiled Smith's attempt to ensnare
Ramsay. Perhaps she shouldn't be surprised that he believed
her capable of interfering in his other enterprises as well.

She came out of her thoughts. "Thank thee, Ducky. I'll be
cautious. I won't come down to the docks alone."

"You might just stay away. I noticed you ain't been down
for a while."

Blessing sighed and felt the pinch of guilt. "I've been busy with other matters. Tell thy protector that I will heed his advice. I thank him."

"Good. I don't want anythin' to happen to you."

Blessing smiled and began to distract them both by telling Ducky about her nephew's progress in rolling over and smiling. The woman stayed for about an hour before leaving. Holding Danny, Blessing remained on the back porch, praying for wisdom on how to proceed. Danny prattled, watching a bird on a nearby branch.

The only person she really wanted to accompany her to the docks was Gerard Ramsay. But should she ask? She knew she shouldn't, if only because she so wanted him with her in this, wanted him with her—period.

❖

FEBRUARY 14, 1849

Tippy and Stoddard were giving their first dinner party on Valentine's Day. Blessing had guessed that Ramsay would attend, and here he was, right beside her at their dining table. Yet he sat as removed from her as if she didn't exist. She tried not to show how awkward this felt, tried to relax and act as if nothing between them had altered.

If she didn't know Tippy better, she would have suspected her of matchmaking. Blessing sincerely regretted the events and decisions—hers and his—that had drawn Ramsay more deeply into her life, her work. And obviously he was regretting them too. But she couldn't have let him go to destruction and done nothing. That she didn't regret.

Across from her sat Stoddard's mother and Tippy's parents.

Her father had won the legislative seat and had been recently sworn in, and now he was back from his inaugural session.

"I'm so glad your father didn't have to miss your first dinner party," Mrs. Foster was saying.

Everyone made agreeable sounds at this. Gerard's voice, so low and near, caused the hair on Blessing's neck to prickle. She hoped this special awareness of him would fade. Unfortunately the attraction to him was so similar to what she'd felt for Richard before they married.

The pleasant, inconsequential social dinner conversation progressed, and Blessing made suitable innocuous comments as necessary while Gerard remained impervious beside her. Her hand underneath the tablecloth so wanted to reach for his.

"The treaty with Mexico ending this dreadful war has certainly altered matters in the upcoming presidential election," Stoddard observed to his father-in-law as the second course was served.

Blessing listened with only half her attention. Over the past several weeks, on a number of occasions, she'd started to go to Prudence Mather's in order to consult with Ramsay over Ducky's warning about Smith. But each time she'd turned around and gone home. Somehow she hadn't been able to ask him to go with her to the docks nor to resume her usual independent nightly rounds. Some invisible barrier was holding her back. However, she wondered if she should warn him in spite of her worries.

"What are we to do with the vast southwestern desert we've won?" Ramsay challenged. "Was it worth the fifteen million dollars we paid?"

Though acutely aware of the sharp edge to his voice, Blessing couldn't let this go undisputed. "California is not to be despised. We now have gained Pacific ports," she countered, barely glancing at Ramsay.

She forged on, his intense gaze making her more and more uncomfortable. "But I'm worried what the Democrats in Congress may do to extend slavery into new territories." Her last few words trembled and she hated letting her discomfort show.

Maybe her preoccupation with Ramsay was growing all out of proportion because of his visit to Boston and his subsequent avoidance of her. Perhaps if she simply had it out with Ramsay, she could go on with her work. She should ask Ramsay to go with her to the quay. He would tell her to stop going to the docks, to stop her ridiculous activities. They would argue, and then she could break free of him.

Smith's threat had made her cautious, even a bit fearful to proceed with her work. But what did that have to do with her fascination with Ramsay? She didn't need him to go with her to the docks. If necessary, she could hire a bodyguard. Her thoughts chased each other around in confusion. *Stop.*

At that moment, as she lifted her napkin, their hands brushed. Waves of awareness tested her composure. *I must break free of this foolish attraction.*

"Yes," Tippy said, taking them back to the vast new lands just acquired from Mexico. "And most important of all—will these territories enter the country as slave or free?"

❖

Gerard found himself falling silent. He knew it shouldn't bother him, especially considering the two women in question, but the participation of ladies in a political discussion still threw him off his stride. But more than that, the widow's presence right beside him was weakening his ability to concentrate. His hand still vibrated from their chance touch. Maybe if he just stopped avoiding her, faced her, he could get over this preoccupation with her and move on with his life.

At the end of the dinner, Stoddard unexpectedly stood and lifted his glass. "We are going to have a special toast tonight."

Tippy blushed a bright, rosy pink.

"This news is just for the family and our closest friend—" Stoddard nodded toward Blessing—"but Tippy and I are expecting a blessed event before the end of the year."

Gerard sat, stunned.

The ladies all hurried to hug and kiss Tippy.

Gerard shook himself free from his stupefaction and rose. He lifted his glass. "To the blessed event." Another unwelcome proof his friend was moving deeper into family life, leaving Gerard behind, solitary, alone.

❖

The end of the evening came soon. While Stoddard walked his mother to her cottage and Tippy's parents rode away in their carriage, Ramsay stepped out into the chill night.

Blessing was waiting by the front door for her carriage to arrive. "Ramsay, may I drop thee at home?"

He'd heard the invitation force itself through her lips—out of social obligation, no doubt—and he didn't want to accept.

His own words came before he could stop them. "Thank you." He walked right beside her, his rampant senses surging to life. He helped her into the carriage and followed her inside. At her command it rumbled away.

Concealing all he was feeling, Gerard sat like a statue. Blessing sat opposite him just as stiffly.

"We haven't spoken privately since thy return," she said finally.

"I've been busy with business." *And preoccupied with my father. And avoiding you.*

"I'm glad you accepted my offer of a ride. I've heard some disturbing news . . . about Smith."

He stirred at the mention of the man. "He accosted me outside your home that December night I bid you . . ." He couldn't bring himself to mention more about the evening he'd nearly kissed her. "He accused me of having something to do with his mistress disappearing."

"Thee knew that might come."

"Yes, and I stuck to the truth. His mistress came, left by the back door, and I don't know where she went."

"Good." She looked away.

"I take it you know where she went."

"I only know she is no longer in Ohio," Blessing said, obviously choosing her words with care.

Her fencing sparked his temper. "I'm not going to tell Mr. Smith—"

"I'm just accustomed to taking precautions. One never

knows who might be listening." She glanced out the window, watchful. "Recently I've been warned that Smith is growing more dangerous and for some reason holds me responsible for his losing his mistress."

Gerard hissed his dissatisfaction. "What do you think he'll do?"

"I don't know. I haven't gone to the docks since Christmas. I've been busy with other matters, and now . . ."

A chill went through him. "You're afraid." He never thought he'd say that about this fearless woman.

"I am cautious. After losing Jewel, Smith is like a wounded bear. Unpredictable. Vicious. I do want to go back to my work at the docks, but perhaps—"

"If you don't go, he'll see that as an admission of guilt." *I should have kept my mouth shut. Why am I getting involved in this?*

A shaft of lamplight glanced over her face. Her expression was intense, anxious. He gripped the leather strap by the window, holding back once more from reaching for her.

"I hadn't thought of that," she murmured, again in shadow.

"Let's go tonight. I'll be your protector." His rash promise was out before he could censor it.

"Yes, let's go—but for a short time." She moved forward on her seat, toward him, suddenly eager. "And certainly I cannot let evil stop me from my work. If I do, Smith wins."

Caution contended against a burst of energy within him. Blessing's characterization of Smith as a wounded bear had been apt. He tensed. This dauntless woman needed someone to protect her. And only he understood the circumstances.

Blessing spoke to her driver, and he turned them toward

the docks. When they arrived, she let Gerard help her out. "I usually dress more modestly than this so I'm approachable," she murmured. "But let us walk the quay and see if anyone needs help."

Beneath her mundane words he detected a current of wariness. Under the cover of darkness, he checked his pistol. Since Smith had confronted him, he carried it every day. And he had his cane in hand as well. His senses became alert.

A night watch patrolling nearby raised a hand in greeting. Blessing acknowledged him.

The night watch fell into step beside them. "Ma'am, I've heard threats against you. Be very careful. No going into dwellings alone or into the alleyways."

"I am aware of my danger, Officer."

"Glad you brought a gentleman with you." The watch dipped his head and moved away, taking a stand in the low lamplight near a tavern entrance.

Gerard's senses heightened. But all seemed to be a quiet night on the waterfront. He and Blessing barely passed any streetwalkers, and no one approached them.

And then the man they were both thinking of stepped from a doorway before them. "Well, the Quaker widow and the Boston gentleman have come to face me together."

Gerard stepped ahead of Blessing to be ready to defend her if necessary.

Blessing didn't flinch at Smith's bitter gibe. "I was wondering if thee would greet me this night."

Smith rattled something like a laugh, but he sobered immediately. "I'm going to make you pay for your interference, Quaker."

"I have been interfering for several years on these docks."

Gerard wished she wouldn't taunt Smith. There was something more lethal than usual about this man in his voice, his agitation.

"Did you think to pay me back for your husband?" Smith sneered at Blessing.

What did Smith have to do with Blessing's late husband?

"I do not seek revenge, Smith, though thee did wrong me and my husband, as well thee knows."

"But I do seek revenge, Quaker, and I know what your parents in Sharpesburg are about," Smith said, ignoring Gerard's presence. "I am going to make life interesting for them, too, from now on."

"Then thee knows my father runs his own glassworks and my mother writes antislavery poetry. I can't see what thee can do about their endeavors."

"We both know what I mean," Smith barked.

Gerard didn't.

Blessing shook her head. "Have a caution, Smith."

"Or what? What will you do to me, Quaker?"

"I don't need to do anything. There is a way that seems right to a man, but that way leads to death."

Smith growled with anger. "Don't preach to me. You're going to regret what you've done."

"I believe I can say the same for thee."

Fearing she had pushed too far, Gerard took another step forward, his weight on the balls of his feet, ready to spring if need be.

Smith trembled with some obscure emotion, then spun on his heel and disappeared into the shadows.

Blessing turned to Gerard. "I think we should finish walking the length of the quay," she said, her voice cool, "and go home."

He agreed with a nod and continued walking beside her, trying to figure out what Smith had meant about her husband, her parents. Did he dare ask her?

He recalled vividly that night at his boardinghouse when, with his collusion, Blessing had helped that man's mistress escape his grasp. All the conjecture that had perplexed him over the past months rushed back, flooding him. Blessing's faith appeared to bolster her courage, but he didn't have that reserve. He suddenly wished he did.

Maybe it was time that he found out more about Blessing Brightman's family and what exactly happened at "number three." Knowledge was power, and he needed all he could get in her defense. He couldn't let this woman face a man like Smith armed only with Bible verses.

Chapter 12

FEBRUARY 21, 1849

At the end of his workday, Gerard went directly to Stoddard's house. Memory of his encounter with Smith wouldn't let him rest. He wanted—needed—more information on Blessing's family. Smith's words kept repeating in his mind. What did Smith know? And why was that knowledge a chink in the Quakeress's armor?

In a flattering yet matronly and subdued lavender dress, Tippy welcomed him with a fondness he didn't feel he deserved. After all, he'd come to Cincinnati expressly to prevent her from marrying his cousin.

Within minutes she pressed a hot cup of tea into his hands. Uncomfortable, he sat with her by a warming fire in the rear parlor, done in shades of rose. Tippy was tatting lace and humming to herself, leaving him to his thoughts.

He let himself consider how much his life had changed in the past six months. That July meeting in Seneca Falls had set him on an unexpected course. This consideration brought Blessing back to mind, the reason he'd come to visit Stoddard today. For his part in Smith's renewed enmity toward this woman, he felt responsible. But he was unsure how to introduce the topic. And unsure what they could do once it was introduced.

"Sometimes Stoddard has meetings at the bank after hours—or if the books don't balance, no one leaves till the daily accounts are correct," Tippy said, breaking into his thoughts. "Stoddard might be tempted to steal a penny, you see." She grinned, her fingers still busy.

Words he hadn't and didn't want to voice spilled out. "I want to know more about Blessing, about her family."

Tippy sent him an arch look. "What do you want to know?"

He was disgusted with himself. He couldn't blurt out, *Are they part of the illegal Underground Railroad?* "I don't know. She never talks about them."

"Blessing is a very private person in many ways," Tippy said. Then, looking mischievous, "However, your interest in her is common knowledge."

He grimaced at this news, but again the need to talk about what had brought him here, even in an oblique way, overcame discretion. "I've never met anybody like her." He heard the front door open, saving him from revealing more.

"Tippy!" Stoddard called. "I'm home!"

"I'm here," Tippy responded.

Stoddard entered the room, paused when he noted Gerard,

but went forward to kiss his bride. Only then did he turn. "Cousin, what brings you here?"

This was a terrible idea. He wasn't going to get answers, he realized; he was simply going to provide Stoddard and Tippy with yet more reasons to pair him with Blessing. Gerard scrambled to come up with a different reason for his visit. A thought that had lingered in the back of his mind moved forward as an excuse. "I wanted you to know I'm going to look around for some land to invest in. I've been saving and may be able to invest in the future. The racetrack obviously hasn't come through, but I might decide to breed thoroughbreds."

"Really?" Stoddard looked at him as if he'd just sprouted vines from his forehead.

"Yes," Gerard replied, not really prevaricating since the idea did interest him, though it would be years before he could buy land. "So I'm going to hire a horse on Saturday and ride for a bit out of town, get the lay of the land."

"Really?" Stoddard repeated.

"Really," Gerard said, rising, with no idea if he actually planned to do it or not. "I've got to get going." He felt like a fool.

"Stay for supper," Tippy invited, clearly amused at his discomfort.

"No, Mrs. Mather is expecting me. Good evening." He escaped before any more ill-considered words slipped out.

Stoddard followed him to the door, also grinning. "Why don't you just go see her? Stop fighting it. I find that marriage is nothing at all like we feared."

Gerard glared at his cousin and stalked out.

As he shut the door, Stoddard had the nerve to chuckle.

Gerard kept walking. The idea that had coalesced moments before recommended itself to him, and he indeed began planning a Saturday ride . . . but not for the sake of finding land. Smith had said Blessing's family lived in Sharpesburg. He must find out what road would lead him there.

Tippy and Stoddard could never learn of this. Gerard's teeth clenched at the memory of his cousin's parting shot. Stoddard didn't know half of what the good widow was doing, so Gerard would have to find out the whole for himself. He shouldn't take Smith's threats against the widow or himself lightly.

He had to know what it meant, had to know the truth—to be ready for what, he didn't know. He still wondered why Smith had chosen him as a target. Smith spoke with the Irish Boston accent and said he'd seen Gerard often in Boston. Could Smith's family have been servants at a nearby home? All this was a puzzle.

❦

FEBRUARY 24, 1849

On Saturday Blessing sat at her kitchen table after breakfast, the air still redolent of bacon drippings. She tapped her lips with one finger, thinking. Smith's threat and her musings over Ramsay chased each other around in her mind. She finally decided what she needed to do. Her parents had years of wisdom, and they would advise her.

"I will be gone until tomorrow," she told Salina, who'd just entered. "I'll write a note of regret to a social invitation I received and leave it on the hall table to be delivered."

"You runnin' away from that Boston man?"

Blessing chose to ignore this impertinent question. "On my way out of town I'll stop at the orphanage to let them know I will be away." Then she rose and left the kitchen before Salina could question her further. Yes, she was running away from that Boston man—an unwelcome admission.

She packed her overnight bag with her maid's help, left the house, and stepped into her carriage to be on her way. Judson drove to the orphanage and stopped in the alley behind the building. He helped her down and she walked quickly to the back door, where she entered.

Adela, who'd taken Joanna's job at the orphanage, rushed to meet her just inside the kitchen. Adela was Joanna's cousin through her father's side of the family. So she favored Judah and was tall and darker complected with large brown eyes, her best feature. "I'm so glad you've come."

The woman's urgent tone arrested Blessing. "I'm on my way out of town. What is it?"

Adela drew in a deep breath and looked relieved. "Good. We got another escaped slave who needs to get out of the city. Now. Today."

Blessing asked for no more explanation. "My carriage is at the back gate. Will the person fit?"

"Yes, it's a young girl."

"Let's go now."

Within minutes a girl who looked only around thirteen marched through the walled garden and out the back gate, shielded between Adela and Blessing. Under the cover provided by the open carriage doors, the girl climbed inside. Blessing let down the concealed door—a flap, really—in the front of her seat, exposing a small, padded berth. "It will be uncomfortable."

"Don't matter to me," the runaway muttered. "Just get me out of the city as fast as you can. Please." She slipped under the seat, curling up her legs to fit.

Blessing fastened the trapdoor, climbed in, and tapped the ceiling. The carriage rolled away instantly. Blessing had no trouble figuring out this young slave's dilemma. Beautiful and expensively dressed, she was appallingly some master's mistress.

The heavy responsibility for this young woman's safety settled over Blessing. As she rode through the city streets, she secretly longed to be free of the burdens she carried—orphans, runaways . . . the past.

❧

Gerard slowed his mount as he rode into Sharpesburg. He'd been intrigued by how few people lived in the miles just beyond Cincinnati. Along the way, one obviously lonely woman had come out to speak to him and had assured him that the population was growing all the time.

Sharpesburg appeared to be a small town with a few farmers and a blacksmith. Ahead he saw a sign that read *Cathwell Glassworks*. When he'd told Mrs. Mather he was going to ride around outside the city, she'd smiled and brought up Blessing's family without his saying a word. He hadn't appreciated her knowing look.

He must be more careful in the future. Previously he'd been relatively unconcerned whether people knew of his interest in the widow or not. She was an engaging woman, but being linked with a woman who might do any unconventional thing at any moment didn't recommend itself to him. He reminded himself that had a job now and was building his reputation in Cincinnati.

Yet he'd found himself drawn here to the glassworks. Only to gain insight on how best to protect her from Smith, of course. . . . He paused in the open yard. Small purple flowers bloomed all around in the wild grass. He dismounted and secured his horse to the hitching rail. What could be more natural than to stop and ask for a glass of water?

Gerard knocked on the door, and it opened before he could reconsider.

He suffered a shock. Gaping, he recognized the young woman who peered around the doorframe. Though she'd changed for the better, this was the poor beaten girl he'd carried to Blessing's carriage that night late last year.

The girl exclaimed wordlessly and shut the door in his face.

He stood there, vibrating with astonishment and still absorbing the fact that she was here.

The door opened again. This time a tall, very striking woman gazed at him. "I'm sorry. Rebecca tells me that thee knows my daughter Blessing."

So much for his ruse. "Yes. I'm Gerard Ramsay."

"Ah. Welcome, Gerard Ramsay." She said his name as if she already knew who he was. "I am Blessing's mother, Honor Cathwell. Won't thee come in?"

What else could he do? He stepped inside.

"Please warm thyself," the lady invited, gesturing toward the cozy fireplace. "Spring is coming, but the ride from Cincinnati is still chilling."

Gerard obeyed her suggestion, warming his hands and face. He sat in what appeared to be the cabin's largest space, a combined sitting room and dining room with a vaulted ceiling. Two doors at the far end no doubt led to bedrooms, and there was a loft over those chambers. He looked around, but Rebecca was nowhere in sight. "I hope I didn't upset the girl."

"Rebecca is shy with everyone. She said both thee and Blessing helped her the night she left her former life."

Such honesty, and spoken as if taking in a prostitute were commonplace for the Cathwells. "Yes, I happened to be . . . there." Now he'd admitted to being on the waterfront. Not a very respectable place.

"What brings thee to Sharpesburg?" she asked, sitting down and picking up a man's large plaid flannel shirt for mending.

"Curiosity." Why try to dissemble? This woman's sharp gaze was astute and penetrating.

She smiled. "Blessing has never mentioned thee. But Joanna told me about thee and how thee has helped my daughter. Thee protected the orphanage during the riot. I am grateful."

"Anyone would have done the same."

She knotted a thread and snipped it with small, silver-plated scissors. "We both know that isn't true. Otherwise the riots wouldn't have continued for three days unabated."

He was left with nothing to say. Or nothing he could bring himself to say.

Honor Cathwell threaded her needle again and bowed her head over her work. "Please take a seat."

Once more he obeyed, then stared into the flickering fire, unsure how to begin, regretting that he'd come. Thoughts, memories of Blessing, played through his mind. Here was where he could discover what Smith knew, but he couldn't bring that up out of the blue.

Finally Honor finished stitching the shirt and looked up. "My daughter is a singular woman, so I understand thy being inquisitive about her family. But thee would do better merely to ask her the questions thee might have."

Her insight silenced him completely.

The door opened. A woman of color entered without knocking, carrying a tray laden with food. Behind her came two white men, one who looked to be in his midthirties and one in his fifties. The latter was clearly Blessing's father—the resemblance was plain. Both men also carried bowls of food covered with crisp white dishcloths.

Honor rose. "I don't know if my daughter mentioned it, but her father and her adopted cousin are both deaf. They can speak but can't hear. We communicate with sign language."

Gerard tried to process this as he watched her agile fingers move quickly, greeting the men. She helped the woman set down her tray and distribute the bowls and platters across a large round table. Others, appearing to be more Cathwells, entered the room as well. Blessing's brother and sisters?

Honor introduced Gerard to the group in word and sign, then turned to him. "Thee will of course join us for our noon meal." It wasn't a request, merely a generous statement of fact.

He nodded, unable to take his gaze from her fingers.

The older man kissed Honor's forehead and approached Gerard with an outstretched hand. "Welcome," the man said in an odd voice. "I'm Samuel Cathwell, Blessing's father."

Gerard pulled himself together and accepted the man's hand. "Good day," he said, raising his voice as if to be heard. In the same second he realized how ridiculous that was. Embarrassment scalded his face.

The younger man also welcomed him in a similar voice. "I'm Caleb, Blessing's adopted cousin."

Honor summoned Gerard to sit in the chair beside her. Blessing's family and shy Rebecca gathered around the table. Samuel bowed his head and began to thank God in his unusual voice. In such a curious household, Gerard had half expected the woman of color to sit down with them, but she'd gone out with a cheery wave.

When the prayer ended, Gerard contrasted his own family to Blessing's unaffected and lively one. The two couldn't have been more different. As the younger members of the family began questioning him about his life in Boston and Cincinnati, something inside him softened.

Yet it was like being plunged into an interrogation, though not an unpleasant one because he understood its source. The younger Cathwells had a thirst for information about the world beyond this little bump in the road. And Blessing's sisters asked questions as intelligent as their older brother's. The food—sausages, corn bread, and a chunky sweet cabbage relish—was simple but excellent. He began to relax.

❖

Blessing looked out the carriage window and made a face. A strange horse was hitched in front of her parents' home. "Friend," she addressed the young woman hiding under her seat, "I'm afraid my parents have a visitor, so thee must stay hidden until I see who it is. In broad daylight I don't dare move thee into the secret room in the glassworks."

"I'm fine," the girl said in a tremulous voice, not sounding fine at all.

The driver halted the carriage and opened the door to help Blessing out.

"Just keep silent no matter what," Blessing cautioned the girl as she stepped down. "Judson, please stay here. I'll see if thee can drive the carriage into the barn so we can move her unseen. And I don't know how long it will be." Then she went to the door and entered the house.

She stopped just inside, petrified. Gerard Ramsay was eating cherry pie with her family. Her mind whirled.

"Blessing, what a sweet surprise," her mother said. "My second today." She smiled meaningfully. "Come in and shut the door, dear. Thee came just in time for dessert."

Just in time for disaster. Blessing's thoughts went immediately to the runaway concealed in her carriage. She couldn't move her till Ramsay had left or was distracted. The poor girl must be in pain curled up for so long. "Could Judson move my carriage into the barn?"

"I'm sorry, dear," Honor said. "Thy father has a large order he's been stacking there."

Blessing sent her mother a pleading look.

Honor caught it. "But perhaps thy driver could park the carriage near the back barn door and unhitch the team there and let them graze."

"Miss Blessing!" Judson's voice called out. The panic at its edge turned everyone's heads. Blessing hurried to the door. She opened it and her stomach dropped.

Slave catchers had arrived.

She moved quickly to confront them as they climbed out of their wagon. "There's no need to get down. Thee isn't welcome here."

Her family, including Rebecca, filed out behind her. Yet she was most aware of the two hard-looking men in front of her and of Ramsay so nearby.

One hitched up his belt, heading toward her carriage. "We're chasing a gal that run away from her master last night."

"I hope thee is unsuccessful," Blessing said, her parents and Ramsay drawing nearer to her.

"We know you folk help runaways," one catcher said.

"How is that?" Honor asked. "None has ever been found here."

"We been paid—" one began.

"Hush up," the other interrupted. "We think you got a runaway in your carriage."

"In my carriage?" Blessing repeated. Her family and Ramsay formed a half circle around the carriage door.

The second catcher pushed through. "Yeah, and we're going to look—"

"Does thee have a search warrant?" Blessing challenged, moving between them and her carriage.

"Don't need one to search a carriage," the other one asserted, shoving his way through.

"Thee is in error," Honor said, taking a step forward.

"That's too bad," one said. "We're looking. The reward should be a hefty one for this girl. She's supposed to be quite a looker. And you Quakers won't do nothing to stop us."

Blessing's mind raced. There must be nonviolent means by which she could drive these men away.

❖

Gerard watched this drama wordlessly, trying to figure out what was happening. But he didn't have time for analysis. Blessing's expression shouted, *Help!* He moved forward, placing himself directly between the two strangers and Blessing. Raising his fists, he said in a commanding voice, "I'm not a Quaker. Step away from the carriage."

One stranger chuckled in a nasty way; the other sidestepped him, pushed through the Cathwells, and opened the carriage door.

Gerard yanked the man back and slammed a fist into his face. The man dropped like a weight. The other landed a glancing blow on Gerard's ear.

Gerard grabbed him around the waist, knocking him down. The man reared up. His fists pummeled Gerard, who answered blow with blow. Gerard had boxed at university, but this slave catcher appeared to have years of experience in street fighting and was practically on top of Gerard now. Gerard began to give ground, protect his head, hoping to land a blow that would—

Then the man gasped and dropped to the grass.

Gerard glanced up in confusion and saw the girl Rebecca standing behind the man with a long-handled wooden paddle in hand. She'd struck his head from behind. "I'm not a Quaker either," she said.

Her imposition galled him. But, too winded to speak, he stood and stared down at the two men.

"Get the girl they want out of the carriage," Honor ordered. "We must hide her safely before they regain consciousness."

Blessing surged forward and climbed over the two catchers and into the carriage. Before Gerard's eyes, she let a girl out of a hidden compartment. Astonishment went through him in icy waves. Just as he'd feared, Blessing Brightman was involved with the Underground Railroad and evidently all of her family was too.

The runaway cringed, whimpering and trembling. She was finely dressed, a very beautiful mulatta and so very young that he was horrified any man would make her his mistress, if indeed that's what she was. It was indecent.

The girl bolted, obviously terrified. She disappeared behind one of the cabins.

Gerard bent over, gasping from exertion, trying to think what to do.

"We need to get her away from here," Blessing said. "These men will not listen to our objections. And someone else might come prepared with a search warrant." She paused.

"Thee's right," Honor agreed. "I should have thought of that." She turned and rapidly signed to her husband, who nodded and started running toward the barn. Honor rested a hand on Gerard's back. "Gerard Ramsay, what will we do with these slave catchers?"

"What will we do?" he asked, still trying to regain his normal breath.

"Yes, that's what she asked," Blessing snapped at his repetition.

Their gazes connected, and he could see she was thinking

the same thing he was—Smith. The men's mention of being paid had been the clue, but perhaps a misleading one. The slave catchers might have been paid by the girl's master, after all.

"Gerard Ramsay, can thee handle these slave catchers?" Honor repeated.

"I need rope. Quick." He straightened. "I'll tie them up. Drive them back to town in their own wagon."

Honor signed quick instructions to Caleb, who hurried off.

"And what then?" Blessing demanded.

"Turn them in to the sheriff for trying to search without a warrant and for attacking me when I tried to stop them. They've broken the law." *Just like you have, Blessing Brightman.*

"I'll come with thee," Blessing said.

"No, you'll stay here with your family," Gerard ordered. "Who knows what . . ." He didn't finish what he was thinking—*what Smith might try next, especially if these are his men.*

Blessing didn't argue but bit her lower lip, looking worried.

Caleb appeared with a length of rope, and soon the two limp men were trussed up and lying in the bed of their own wagon. Gerard turned to say good-bye but halted. He'd never seen Blessing wring her hands. He stopped and claimed them. "Stay here."

"The orphanage," she murmured, searching his eyes. "After thee has finished with these two, please visit and see that all is well. While I'm away, he might . . ."

Gerard understood her. He squeezed her gloved hands, wanting to pull her close and reassure her within his embrace. "I will make sure everyone is safe."

Then he became aware that his hold on her hands was

being noticed, so he dropped them and stepped backward. His bloodied knuckles stung from fighting, and a headache was beginning. But Gerard was momentarily unable to move, captured by the distress in Blessing's expression.

After securing Gerard's hired horse to the rear of the wagon, Caleb called out, "Ready!"

Gerard composed himself, thanked the Cathwells for their hospitality, and turned away from Blessing.

"Thanks for helping," Caleb said in that strange-sounding voice. Gerard shook his extended hand.

Gerard climbed onto the wagon, turned it, and drove back toward the city. He was aware that a Cathwell Glassworks wagon had also left the property and was headed in the opposite direction, but he dismissed it from his mind. The less he knew, the better. By law he should have apprehended the runaway and compelled her to come with him to the nearest magistrate. But he would not, could not have done that, even if a magistrate had been standing in front of him. The girl's youth and her obvious situation repulsed him.

Within a mile, the men behind him began to wake, moaning. Caleb had gagged them, a touch Gerard appreciated. He wouldn't have wanted to listen to them threatening and arguing all the way to Cincinnati. His mind stuttered over all that had happened, all that had been revealed within a few minutes' time.

Now he knew how Blessing had been able to spirit Smith's mistress away; he knew why she had connections at a place like "number three." No doubt Jewel had long since arrived somewhere in Canada. And maybe, in vengeance, Smith had hired those slave catchers to watch Blessing and follow her.

Again he saw the terror-stricken face of the young run-away, imagined the helplessness of her position. Ire forced its way up his throat. His knuckles, cut and bruised, tingled. He only wished he could have dealt out more punishment to the two slave catchers. Blessing might have broken federal statute, but now so had he. And he didn't regret it. God as his witness, he didn't.

❖

Late that Saturday night, Gerard finally was able to leave the Cincinnati jail. Leading away the horse he'd hired for the day, he walked beside Alan Lewis, the lawyer Honor Cathwell had told him to consult if needed.

The sheriff had been extremely reluctant to arrest the two slave catchers, who had been vociferous in their own defense. So Gerard had paid a boy on the street to take a message to Lewis. The lawyer had come right away and had insisted on the two catchers' being charged with unlawful search and assault. Though muttering darkly, the sheriff had given way to the lawyer and jailed the catchers.

"I'm sorry to say that those two catchers will probably go free," Lewis said now, finally penetrating Gerard's mind.

"But I can bring witnesses."

"And the jury will likely ignore their testimony. Have you forgotten the recent riots? The majority of people here don't like slave catchers, but they really just want the runaway problem to disappear."

This view chafed Gerard, but he couldn't fault this man for telling the truth. They shook hands and parted.

Gerard stood a moment on the cool, dark street. Blessing

had asked him to stop at the orphanage, but now he intended upon sleeping there. Anything could happen if it were left unguarded. First he'd stop at his rooming house to let Mrs. Mather know he'd be out for the night. He mounted the horse and started off.

Mrs. Mather met him at the front door, her face creased in concern. "I'm glad thee is home. Stoddard sent a boy to fetch thee hours ago."

"What is it?"

"His wife. They've called a doctor."

Gerard turned and hurried down the steps to his horse, heart racing.

Chapter 13

FEBRUARY 25, 1849

Still unsettled by Saturday's violent confrontation, Blessing returned to the city with her family to attend First Day meeting—nothing out of the ordinary that might even hint at wrongdoing. Obeying God instead of her own desires often frustrated her.

After meeting, her family climbed into their wagon and followed her carriage to her own home in the city for the midday meal. Staring out the window at the familiar streets, she watched families dressed in their Sunday best walking home from church on this sunny, mild day, unaware of and unconcerned for the desperate lives passing through their city.

And in another layer of unseen concern, she struggled over Gerard's involvement in her illegal activities. As soon as they'd eaten dinner, she planned to send a message to Ramsay and find out what had happened to the slave catchers. To him.

What would she say to him? Most people viewed the Underground Railroad with shock and disapproval. But he'd defended the runaway. However, had that just been the passion of the moment? He'd helped Rebecca too, though— much against his wont.

As she led her family up her front steps, she chided herself. *Just as well if he's disapproving. This should erect a higher, firmer wall between us.* Though that might be the sensible view, she found it hard to face.

Salina opened the front door to them, her expression somber.

Blessing inhaled sharply. "What is it?" Had Ramsay been hurt?

"Your friend is bad."

"Gerard?"

Salina shook her head. "No, Miss Tippy."

Blessing paused, her thoughts reeling. "What's wrong?"

"Shiloh sent word that sweet young gal lost her baby last night."

Blessing staggered. From behind, her father braced her. For a moment she couldn't think, her heart lurching. "Tippy," she whispered.

"Salina," Honor said, "I think a strong cup of coffee is needed."

Waving for them to follow her, Salina led Blessing and her family straight into the dining room; then she went on into the kitchen. Within minutes she returned, balancing a coffeepot, cups, sugar, and creamer on a tray. Blessing's sister Jamaica hopped up and helped Salina set her burdens down and serve the coffee.

"The cook got plenty of fixin's and a couple of chickens roasting," Salina said. "We thought you might bring your family here for Sunday dinner."

Blessing's head began throbbing. She rubbed and stretched the muscles at the back of her neck to loosen them. "Mother, Father," she said and signed, "I must go and see if there is anything I can do."

"Go on, dear." Her mother patted her arm gently. "We'll stay here, eat whatever thy cook has prepared for us, and then go on home. Don't give us another thought. We'll be praying for Tippy."

Blessing rose and hugged her parents in turn. She bid the rest of her family farewell and headed out the door. Salina had evidently assumed that Blessing would go to the Henrys' once she heard the news. Judson was still out front, waiting for her.

When she arrived at the Henry home, her courage nearly failed her. But she walked resolutely up to the door and was met by Honoree, Tippy's housemaid and Shiloh's sister. "How is she?" Blessing asked, shedding her bonnet and gloves in the foyer.

"Bad. It's not just that she miscarried," Honoree replied in a low voice. "She was terrible sick before, and that's what caused her to miscarry. The doctor thinks it might be cholera."

Cholera. The floor dropped out from beneath Blessing. She clutched the arm of the hall tree. Death usually claimed cholera's victims.

"The doctor isn't letting just anybody in to see her, and no one is supposed to touch her. Her mother and father are away." Honoree was wringing her hands in distress.

Blessing rallied. "Has anyone sent for them?"

Honoree nodded. "A messenger has been sent. But it'll be days before they return from Kentucky."

"I want to see her."

"Come." Honoree led her up the stairs to the second-floor landing. The door to a spare room stood open, and as she passed, Blessing glimpsed Stoddard sitting in a chair and holding his head in his hands in evident despair. Gerard sat on the seat adjacent to him, speaking in a low voice, his hand on Stoddard's back.

Blessing was grateful Gerard was present and comforting his cousin. But her whole concentration turned to Tippy. Honoree opened the master bedroom door and Blessing entered.

On the canopied bed Tippy lay, pale and shrunken. Her mother-in-law, Fran, sat in a chair by the fireplace, her head bowed in obvious prayer. A familiar black-frocked doctor, one Blessing respected, stood at the end of the bed. They exchanged nods.

"Don't touch her," he cautioned in a low voice.

"How bad is the cholera?"

"It's a light case, I think. And Mr. Henry called me immediately, so I was able to start treatment of saline injections right away. But it's a violent disease and has taken its toll. She lost the child about eight hours into it. She's also lost a lot of blood."

Each sentence pounded Blessing's already-throbbing

head. Resisting the urge to take Tippy's hand, she dropped to her knees by the bed and began praying for her friend to be spared. *Father, Tippy's found a good husband who respects her. Please let her live. Let them have many good years together.* Then her mind drifted back to Gerard and Stoddard sitting together. *Help Ramsay comfort his cousin.*

❧

FEBRUARY 26, 1849

About to leave his room for work on Monday morning, Gerard received a note from the lawyer Alan Lewis that the two slave catchers he'd brought in Saturday night were already scheduled to appear before a judge and Gerard must come to testify. A change of plans on top of everything else.

He rubbed his gritty eyes. After staying very late at his cousin's house, he'd barely slept. Tippy was still fighting for her life, and Gerard feared his cousin might lose her. He hadn't realized how much he himself cared for Tippy, so endearing and pert, until now, when she might be wrenched from them.

Sick in spirit, Gerard hurried to the courthouse downtown to do his part against the unscrupulous slave catchers. Never before in his life had he ever given any thought to such men. Now he was involved with two. He entered the walnut-paneled courtroom and found Lewis there, conferring with the city prosecutor.

When Lewis joined Gerard on the bench behind the prosecutor, he didn't look happy, either.

"Why is this happening so quickly?" Gerard asked in a low voice.

"The faster this transpires, the less notice it will get. That must be why the catchers have agreed to a bench trial instead of a jury. Tempers on both sides run high."

Leaning nearer to Gerard, he muttered, "The prosecutor is aware of the unpopularity of bringing this case to court. He doesn't want to be seen as either pro–slave catcher or pro-abolitionist. If he and the judge could suppress this case, they would. But Blessing Brightman has too many powerful allies in the city and state, and everyone knows you come from Boston money and society."

Gerard digested this and felt like he was chewing glass. What did his family's money and influence have to do with this? He also devoutly wished he didn't have to be here. If he were going to miss work today, it should be to remain with Stoddard. But since Gerard was the one who'd insisted the men be charged, he had an obligation to testify.

"Don't expect much," Lewis finished.

Would these two go free? Was that possible? Gerard remembered how the slave catchers had jeered at Blessing and her family and broken the law without compunction. And the runaway—so young, miserable, and afraid. His jaw tightened.

The bailiff announced the stout, black-robed judge as he entered, and the proceedings began.

Gerard was called to the stand and sworn in.

"You were the one who brought these two men in?" the well-dressed prosecutor asked in an accusatory tone.

Gerard assented and then gave a succinct account of the men's attempt to carry out an unlawful search and seizure.

The judge addressed him in a scathing tone. "And you thought you were qualified to intervene?"

"I think it's the duty of every citizen to see that our con-stitutional protections are not violated, don't you?" Gerard kept his voice even, respectful.

"I'm asking the questions," the judge snapped.

Gerard stared at the man, letting his expression speak for him.

"Was there a runaway slave present?" the judge asked.

Gerard couldn't bring himself to lie on the stand. "Yes, there was a very young girl—"

"Why didn't you take custody of the runaway?" the judge demanded. "It was your duty as a citizen to escort her to a magistrate."

"I know that. But after subduing these two men, I was winded and couldn't take action. She got away before I could move." Also the truth, mostly. Of course, he hadn't tried very hard—or at all.

The judge glared at him.

The prosecutor frowned and looked unconvinced.

The defense attorney let loose a sound of derision.

Gerard wanted to punch a few more faces. But he kept his cool mask in place, unwilling to let them put him on trial. He waited in silence as if unconcerned. He watched the faces around him and guessed they were all trying to come up with a way to turn the charges onto him, make him the wrongdoer. But after a few strained minutes he was allowed to step down.

The defense attorney did not put his clients on the stand but used a lot of legal jargon and gave the impression that the two catchers had gotten carried away in the performance of a lawful errand.

The judge looked to the prosecutor, who did not object. Without further ado, the judge fined the two catchers ten dollars each and ended the trial with a bang of his gavel.

Lewis led Gerard through the courtroom. Out of the corner of his eye, Gerard glimpsed an unsettling figure in the back of the courtroom—a man with his hat pulled low so his face didn't show. Recognition shivered through him. Smith? Why would he show up here?

But Gerard didn't miss a step as he followed Lewis into the foyer and down the stairs.

Lewis paused at the bottom and grinned wryly. "Well, those two will probably be a bit more careful around Quakers with friends who know how to box."

Gerard nodded. "Do I owe you—?"

Lewis raised a hand. "I'm old friends with the Cathwells. No charge." The lawyer shook his hand and hurried away.

Gerard scanned the steps and saw no sign of Smith. If it had been Smith, no doubt the man had wanted him to notice and to let Blessing know he had something to do with this situation. Gerard could scarcely step outside his home without encountering the long reach of Smith's arm. The man's involvement in Gerard's affairs was nearing something he'd read about in a Boston newspaper, he realized.

It had been the account of a husband who had become convinced his wife was cheating on him. The paper had called the man's obsession an *idée fixe*. The man had ended up killing his wife and the next-door neighbor he suspected to be her lover. At the court case, many witnesses had testified to the innocence of the wife and her supposed lover, and the husband had descended into madness during the ordeal. He'd ended up in an asylum for the insane and later had been hanged.

Had the loss of Smith's mistress or something personal about Gerard or his family triggered Smith's fanatical behavior? Not for the first time, Gerard regretted ever dabbling on the docks or meeting with Smith. His desire to invest in a racetrack merely to spite his father now seemed juvenile and unappealing. He'd thought he could deal with men like Smith and remain free of consequence. He had learned his lesson the hard way.

But now he headed to work, hoping his boss would not be vexed at him for coming in late. Concern for Stoddard tightened around his lungs. Had Tippy survived the night?

❧

Gerard's day had not gone as he wished—any of it. After court, he'd gone to his place of business but left soon afterward in an unbelieving huff—dismissed from employment. He'd then come directly to Stoddard's house.

Tippy's life hung by a thread as fragile as a strand of a spider's web. The doctor, Blessing, and Aunt Fran hovered near her bed. Stoddard paced the hall and paused occasionally to stare into the room. Gerard could think of nothing sensible to say, so he merely paced with Stoddard till, both exhausted, they were forced to sit down. Then Stoddard's restlessness would rear up and they'd rise again and resume pacing. The only good thing he achieved on his cousin's behalf was bullying Stoddard into eating and drinking periodically.

And now, as evening fell and Gerard saw his aunt's exhaustion, he persuaded her to go home to bed. In the near dark, he walked her and her maid across the street and promised to come and get her if she was needed. Aunt Fran hugged him, looking desperately sad and weary. He left the maid, Shiloh, helping his aunt up the stairs to bed.

When he reentered Stoddard's house, Blessing met him in the front hall. Her hair uncovered and slipping from its pins, she looked strained but steady. Smudges from many sleepless hours darkened the skin under her eyes. Worry lines etched her forehead, and he wanted to smooth them away.

"Come to the kitchen, Ramsay," she murmured. "I'll fix us something to keep us going through the night. The doctor is resting in the spare room and Stoddard is sitting with Tippy." She closed her eyes as if gathering strength. "I persuaded the doctor that the man must be allowed some time alone with his bride."

Before he loses her. The additional phrase came unbidden to Gerard's mind, chilling him.

Blessing took him through the still house to the kitchen. The housemaid sat at the table, asleep with her head cradled in her arms. Blessing pressed a warning finger to her lips and then efficiently and quietly made a pot of tea and filled a tray with fragrant pumpkin muffins and butter.

She led him to the next room, a small breakfast nook. He lit the candles in sconces on the walls, and they sat down at the small table in the low, flickering light.

"I would have awakened Honoree, but I was afraid she might not fall back to sleep," Blessing murmured as if afraid of disturbing the solemn house. "She's been up around the clock since Tippy fell ill."

Gerard stared into his cup of creamy tea. All the words

he'd bottled up over the past two days bobbed to the surface, and the most immediate poured out. "The judge fined the slave catchers ten dollars apiece and chastised me for not bringing in the runaway."

She paused to sip her steaming tea. "What did thee expect in a city where only months ago the mayor encouraged race riots in order to drive free Negroes out?" Her reasonable tone grated on his raw nerves.

"Why didn't you tell me you and your family were involved with the Underground Railroad?" he accused, setting down his cup with a snap.

The candlelight caught the shine of her chestnut hair. Blessing stared at him, then calmly sipped her tea again. "Have a muffin."

Her response, so totally divorced from all that had happened to him today, prodded his temper. "Is that all you have to say?"

"I think it would be best if thee forgot the events of Saturday," she said primly, cutting a muffin in two and releasing the scents of cinnamon and nutmeg. "Thee ventured into my life—without being invited—and thee must accept the consequences."

Consequences. Her cool response burned inside him. "If I'm remembering correctly, you insinuated yourself into my affairs first." He knew he was being irrational, but the frustrations of the past two days goaded him.

"Would thee have preferred I let Smith take over thy life? Own thee?" She pressed her index finger over the muffin crumbs in front of her, gathering them and slipping the finger into her mouth. Then she picked up her cup with a sigh.

His ire leaped up another notch, probably because her point was more than valid. But a gentleman was supposed to come to the aid of any lady, not vice versa. And what rankled most was that he had invited Smith into his life, and in effect also back into Blessing's. He licked his dry lips. "I think he was there today. In court."

She halted her cup in midair. "Smith was there? Does thee think he really paid those catchers to come and harass my parents?"

"I don't know. But I think the man is becoming unhinged. Have you ever heard of an *idée fixe*?"

"No."

"It's an aberration of the mind—a person becomes obsessed with something or someone."

She gazed at him and slowly lowered her cup to the saucer. "An interesting and unnerving idea. Is he 'fixed' on thee or me?"

"I don't know. Maybe both."

She broke off a bit of muffin and buttered it thickly. "I told thee Smith wants to control people, and for some reason we don't know, thee might have become a trap to him."

"A trap?"

Chewing, she nodded but did not elaborate.

"I don't like turning around only to find him behind me."

"View it this way. He cannot do harm to others if he is focused on thee. And me." She pushed a muffin toward him and nibbled another bit of hers.

"Very comforting," he replied with thick sarcasm. "I lost my job today."

"What?" She put down her muffin.

"I was let go. I was late to work, and when I told my employer it was because I'd been to court to testify against two slave catchers, he told me he didn't want any man in his employ aiding runaways and breaking the law."

Unexpected tears poured from Blessing's eyes, and she bent her head, sobbing silently.

Instantly he regretted his words. "Don't cry."

She paid no attention to him, pushed away her tableware, folded her arms on the table, and hid her face in them, shaking with her tears.

Gerard did the only thing he could think to do. He rose and drew her up into his arms. For once she yielded and rested against him. She was so soft and scented with wisteria, as always, and her hair was silken under his chin.

Moments passed. Her sobs ebbed into weeping. He kissed her hair and began to murmur soothing sounds—not words, just the sounds someone long ago must have murmured to him. She looked up. Her tear-streaked face moved him. He kissed her.

A gasp caught in her throat and she stepped back, her hair now unloosed completely from its pins and sliding down to her shoulder.

He didn't want her to say anything about his kissing her. *I didn't mean to do that.*

"Tippy could die," she whispered, gazing at him, tears still trembling on her eyelashes.

Gerard nodded. He'd hoped she wouldn't refer to his lapse, yet now that she didn't mention it, he felt insulted.

"I'm sorry thee lost thy job, but thee will find another. Tippy could die," she whispered, wiping her tears with her fingertips.

He understood her meaning. Jobs were not life and death, at least not to him.

Then Blessing did something he did not expect. She returned to him and rested her head on his chest. "Ramsay, don't talk; just hold me. My heart is breaking."

He opened his mouth and then shut it. No woman, not even his mother, had ever turned to him for this degree of comfort. A wave of tenderness for this indomitable woman flooded him. He pressed her gently to him, enclosed her with his arms, and rested his cheek against her soft hair. Her moment of weakness gave him a strength he'd never known.

❧

MARCH 1, 1849

Tippy did not die. But she barely survived. Three nights after he'd held Blessing in his arms, Gerard finally had gone home to bed. The Quakeress hadn't given way to emotion again. She'd girded herself and battled alongside the doctor to save her friend's life.

In the full light of a new morning, Gerard felt somehow set adrift. Now that he'd lost his job, his normal routine was gone. He must make plans for what to do next. After a welcome bath and shave, Gerard shuffled down the stairs and went into the kitchen to beg food from Mary.

Mrs. Mather sat at the kitchen table. "I hear Stoddard's wife has survived."

"Yes, but she's very weak." He sank down in the chair adjacent to his landlady.

"I don't wonder. Mary, fix Gerard some scrambled eggs and toast. He looks depleted."

The cook began cracking eggs.

Mrs. Mather drew a letter from her pocket. "This came for thee this morning."

He accepted it, reading the return address. With a butter knife, he unsealed the wax emblem. His mother's handwriting was familiar but showed signs of her feeble state. She wrote, *I know you will want to come and be with me at the end, but please don't. I am unwilling to put you through that.* His gut tightened as he read what was probably her last letter to him. Tears wet his eyes.

"Bad news?" Mary asked, setting a plate in front of him.

"My mother is in failing health." Gerard's voice was husky. He drew in breath and banished the moisture from his eyes.

Mrs. Mather touched his hand. "I'm so sorry."

Mary poured him coffee and set that beside his plate. "I be sorry too. A mother is special." She shook her head and turned to Mrs. Mather. "I'll be leaving now, ma'am. I've got me shoppin' to do." With that, she left the room.

Gerard stared at his breakfast, now without appetite. The events of the past week had left him perpetually unsettled. But he picked up his fork. One had to keep breathing, keep eating, keep living.

"Oh, I forgot." Mrs. Mather rose and hurried from the room. She returned with another letter. "Yesterday, this also came."

Again Gerard recognized the writing. His father's. He opened it and read the terse note, demanding that Gerard do his duty as a son and return home. Gerard nearly crumpled it, but with his landlady watching him, he didn't. His father had used his mother's decline as a stick to prod Gerard—as if the man cared anything about her at all.

But the thought of his mother near death washed through him. Anger bowed to purpose. "Mrs. Mather, I will be going east for a while, but I'd like to keep my room here if I may."

"I have a special rate for that since no meals are involved."

"Excellent. I will leave on the morrow." First he must eat, and then he must visit his cousin once more. And Blessing—should he visit her? Their momentary encounter kept coming to mind. He respected her, admired her, but she was not a woman he would ever be comfortable with. How far would she go to further the causes of abolition or women's rights? Her determination seemed to know no bounds, an unsettling realization.

❖

Gerard called later that day at Stoddard's house to take leave of his cousin.

His eyes sunken and clothing disheveled, Stoddard clamped a hand on Gerard's shoulder. His cousin managed a weak imitation smile of greeting. "Tippy was able to keep broth down twice."

That this simple act should make his cousin rejoice caught Gerard in his throat. He nodded in reply.

"But every time I enter her room, she weeps." Stoddard's voice was hollow. And Gerard felt the pull of family. People were looking after Tippy. Who was looking after Stoddard? He knew that fell to him. "What have you eaten today?"

Stoddard stared at him, his brow wrinkled. "I think I had some coffee this morning. At the mention of cholera, our cook left us. Honoree has been trying to do meals as well as help with Tippy."

Gerard gripped his cousin's elbow and steered him toward the kitchen. The room was empty, but a pot of coffee sat warming on the woodstove. Gerard piloted Stoddard to a chair at the table. "Stay here. I'll find your maid."

"Don't bother her." Stoddard caught his arm. "She's sitting with Tippy."

Gerard looked around the kitchen helplessly. He'd never cooked anything in his life.

As if summoned by Gerard's desperation, Blessing entered through the back door carrying an oak basket laden with packages.

Gerard turned to her, and the sensations from their kiss washed over him in one overwhelming wave. He stood rooted to the floor.

Blessing glanced at him, then at Stoddard. "Does thee need help, Ramsay?"

Gerard had trouble finding his voice. "Stoddard hasn't eaten breakfast."

"To help Honoree, I just did the day's shopping," she said, setting down her basket.

He gazed at her, silently asking for help.

"I'll have breakfast done in a moment." Blessing bustled about, putting away the groceries. She waved him to the coffee-pot. "I'm sure thee can pour three cups of coffee. I have fresh cream."

He managed to find the cups and distribute the coffee. Soon Blessing had made Stoddard toast and eggs. The three sat at the kitchen table.

"I'm not really hungry," his cousin said.

"Stoddard, thy wife is depending on thee," Blessing said, touching the man's hand. "Please eat."

Stoddard reluctantly began to fork up his eggs.

Blessing gazed at Gerard and pointedly nodded toward his cousin.

Gerard for once read a woman's unspoken message. His cousin needed someone to look after him—and Gerard had already realized he was that someone. He sent her a look in reply that said, *I know.* "After breakfast, Stoddard, I think you need to take a bath and shave," Gerard said. "I took my own advice this morning and I felt better immediately."

Stoddard peered at him, rubbing his stubbly chin. "I appreciate your concern, but I don't think I am ever going to feel better."

"In this life there will be trials," Blessing murmured. "If we love, we suffer not only our own trials but those of our beloved."

"I would gladly have assumed Tippy's suffering," Stoddard said.

Blessing pressed a hand over his wrist. "I know. But right now thee must take care of thyself so thee can support her as she recovers. This will be a long recuperation. Anything could set her back."

Gerard didn't like the sound of that. Tippy might still die?

"What should I do?" Stoddard asked, his eyes moist.

"Eat thy breakfast and then take thy cousin's advice. I have already arranged for another cook and a maid. Honoree is a good nurse and should stay at Tippy's side. Thee will take her place when she must sleep and eat. I know I am intruding into thy business—"

"The help of a friend is no intrusion," Stoddard interrupted.

"I expect more help will arrive any moment," she said. "Tippy's mother will be coming over soon, and I'll stay as long as I'm needed."

"I'm here too," Gerard said, "as long as necessary." The words were the right ones, but he'd wanted to leave Cincinnati and go to his mother. She might pass away at any time, he knew, and he would have to leave. But until then, his path was clear. For the first time in his life he was considering others more than himself. *Seek ye first the kingdom of . . .*

A knock sounded at the back door, and at Blessing's call, two women of color entered, apparently a mother and daughter. Blessing greeted them and introduced them to Stoddard as his new cook and maid. The two donned aprons and began taking stock of the kitchen.

Stoddard finished eating, and Blessing instructed the new maid to begin heating water for his bath. Soon, along with the maid, Stoddard and Ramsay carried buckets of steaming water up to the spare bedroom, where Stoddard was staying until Tippy recovered.

Gerard returned to the kitchen for more water.

"I'm glad thee is here for Stoddard," Blessing murmured, standing very close.

He wanted her closer but at the same time didn't. "I was planning to head east tomorrow. My mother's in decline, but I'll stay as long as I can."

Blessing touched his arm. "I'm sorry to hear about thy mother. But I believe thee made the right decision, for Stoddard's sake."

285

Hiding his reaction to her gentle touch, Gerard didn't know how to respond, so he merely pressed his hand over hers. Their gazes locked, and awareness rolled through him. *Through her?* He pulled away abruptly. The pot on the stove top was bubbling. "I need to get this water upstairs."

Blessing said nothing but helped him refill the buckets. He headed up the stairs, trying not to spill either of the buckets. As he watched the quivering water, he thought back to the man he'd been the day he arrived in Cincinnati. He barely recognized that man and his motives. So much had happened. But in spite of it all, he couldn't shake his persistent antipathy toward his father.

He still needed to find out the truth about the house in Manhattan. But that must wait. If his mother changed her mind and summoned him to her deathbed, he would go, even if it meant leaving Stoddard. Otherwise, he was beginning to fear that he would not see her until her funeral.

Chapter 14

MARCH 12, 1849

A little more than two weeks had passed since Tippy had fallen ill. Now Blessing lurked just inside Stoddard and Tippy's parlor doorway. She was listening to the murmurs of Ramsay taking his leave of Stoddard at the bottom of the staircase.

Knowing Ramsay must pass this doorway as he left, she waited, hidden. She knew she should not be lingering here so she could say farewell to Ramsay. She tried to go deeper into the shadowy room, but she could not make herself obey this good sense.

Then he appeared before her, reaching for the front door-knob.

"Ramsay."

He turned to her and they both froze. He broke free first.

"I didn't know you were here. I was going to stop at your home and leave word that I had gone."

Memory of the night he'd held her in his arms kept her mute, wrapping around her heart. She nodded. The premonition that he was leaving and would not return welled up within her, a fountain of pain.

"I wouldn't be leaving if my mother weren't so close to the end of her life," he said. "And now Stoddard can manage without me."

She nodded again, feeling like an idiot.

"I know you'll watch over my cousin and his wife."

She cleared her throat. "Of course," she managed to say. "I'm sorry thee must face the loss of thy mother."

"We seem to be mired in the dark valley this year."

An understatement. She offered him her hand. "Godspeed."

Gerard received it and held on to it, searching her face. "Keep safe, Widow Brightman." He kissed her hand and then left swiftly.

In his wake, she remained in the parlor doorway, holding the hand he'd kissed to her cheek. A foolish gesture. In this moment, she confessed that the man from Boston mattered to her, and as much more than a friend. She'd let her heart be ensnared.

Closing her eyes, she prayed for strength. She'd already gone through the grief of losing her illusions about a husband and then losing the man himself in an awful event. Now she must endure similar circumstances again. She would sever this attachment before he returned—if he returned. *I will guard my heart more carefully in the future.* But that didn't help her aching heart now.

❖

MARCH 19, 1849

After the journey from Cincinnati, Gerard had spent the night in a modest New York City inn. He felt a bit guilty at not going immediately to his mother, but a telegram had reassured him that she was holding on. Now he stepped off an omnibus into the same neighborhood he'd visited in December. The early flowers—red tulips amid jonquils— were in bloom in the small yards, and the grass was greening up as if to spite his weltering confusion.

Different ploys bounced around in his head. How did one approach a complete stranger and ask about their relationship with someone? He kept reliving the moment he'd glimpsed his father walking into the house as if he lived there. How could that have happened?

Was the woman living here his father's mistress? But this looked like a quiet, residential neighborhood, not the locale for a lovebirds' nest. And the woman he'd seen in the garden looked like a respectable wife, not a mistress. Gerard's speculations chased each other around in a circle.

As if of their own volition, his feet carried him straight to the door he'd seen his father enter. He knocked without pausing for thought. Suddenly he was chanting silently, *Don't be home, please. Don't be—*

The door opened, and a pretty young girl of around seventeen stood before him. She had his father's large, dark, heavy-lidded eyes. Shock rippled through him.

"Yes?" the girl asked politely.

Gerard strained to find his tongue. "Good day." Words he'd considered but had initially rejected flowed from his rebellious mouth. "My name is Ramsay, and I'm looking for a distant relative, Saul Ramsay."

"Oh! Mother!" The girl turned. "Someone is here looking for Father."

For a moment Gerard's knees weakened. He grasped for his composure and caught the tag ends of it.

The same plump, middle-aged woman he'd seen last December bustled to the door.

"He says he's a Ramsay too," the girl reported.

"Well, come in, then!" the cheerful woman invited. "Are you related to my husband, Saul?"

"Yes," Gerard said. "Yes, I am."

❖

Standing in her old bedroom at her parents' house, Blessing was struck by the contrasts in life. She'd just spent weeks nursing Tippy, who was still too weak to get out of bed and who continued to mourn the miscarriage of her first child. A terrible loss. And now Blessing had traveled to her family's home to attend yet another wedding, the marriage of Caleb and Rebecca, though she was still uncertain about this union. Was it a happy event?

She and Rebecca found themselves alone in the girls' bedroom, Rebecca sitting on one of the three trundle beds and Blessing standing near the door. Everyone else was busy with preparations for the wedding later today and for the meal to celebrate it. Blessing listened to the mingling voices of her family and Joanna's loved ones.

Rebecca had been too shy to go to the meetinghouse for the usual Quaker wedding, so aged Brother Ezekiel, Joanna's grandfather, had ridden with Blessing to her parents' house. The wedding would be held with just family and immediate neighbors in attendance. Rebecca wore a new dress in a flattering shade of blue. Blessing's youngest sisters, twins Patience and Faith, had plaited wild violets into a circlet for Rebecca's hair—a lovely, simple adornment.

"You don't think I should be marrying your cousin." Rebecca's voice was thin and apologetic.

"That's not true." Blessing sought the right words. "I just want to be certain that thee is marrying him for more than protection."

Rebecca gazed out the small window at the green spring grass. "Caleb *will* protect me. That's true. And your family is so good to me. I had forgotten good people." She looked to Blessing. "I don't care that he can't hear. I think it has given him a tender heart."

"But does thee love him?"

"How does a girl know if she's in love with a man?"

The question was an arrow straight into Blessing's heart. She thought she'd been in love with Richard, but it had truly been an infatuation with a man who turned out not to exist. The dashing Richard had changed into a man who, when in his cups . . . She turned away from the memories. And ran straight into her confusion over Gerard Ramsay. Fortunately Rebecca was still speaking.

"When I'm with Caleb," Rebecca said haltingly, "I feel special. He is so gentle and kind. I trust him and want to be with him. That's all I know."

The girl's simple, honest words touched Blessing, convinced her that this marriage could be for the good. She walked to the girl and took her small hand. "That is what I wanted to understand." She realized her own sad marriage and her fear of falling in love unwisely a second time had tainted her perception of Rebecca and Caleb's relationship.

And she didn't trust herself, particularly when she was affected by her feelings for Gerard. "I'm happy for thee, and I know thee will be a good wife to my cousin."

"I've promised him I will begin to attend meeting with the family after we are wed." Rebecca looked into Blessing's eyes. "I'll feel clean then. Caleb's love will wash away my shame."

The girl's words pierced Blessing's heart deeper. She knew how shame and guilt could cling. But she claimed Rebecca's shoulders and spoke the truth the girl needed to hear, the truth Blessing herself needed to hear. "Only Christ can wash away thy sins."

"I know that. But the shame is just what's left over."

Again Rebecca's words went directly into the dark wound in Blessing's heart. She, too, suffered from what was left over. It had nothing to do with disbelieving God's forgiveness. She knew that somewhere deep in her heart, she had wished her husband dead so she could be free. And hadn't Christ declared that thinking a sin incurred the same guilt as doing it? She couldn't forgive herself for that. And Richard's decision to bequeath all his wealth to her had deepened her load of guilt.

Rebecca studied her. "I thought maybe the man who helped me that night you rescued me would come to the wedding. The one who stopped the slave catchers. That Mr. Ramsay."

Blessing pulled Rebecca close, not wanting the girl to see the pain in her own eyes. "His mother is dying. He had to go home to Boston to be with her."

"Oh, I'm so sorry."

I am too. I am too.

She hoped Gerard Ramsay would come back soon but knew it might be best if he was away awhile longer. She could not trust her heart again.

❖

As the woman led Gerard into the modest Manhattan house, he tried to appear calm and normal while his emotions rioted inside. He was shown to a chair in the simply furnished, homey parlor.

"Now, how is it you know my husband?" the woman asked.

"I am a distant relation, and while I'm visiting in the east, I thought I'd try to find some family. I had this address. I am from Cincinnati." He was too frazzled to make up any complicated lies.

"Oh, you've missed him. He's away on business again."

Gerard could only thank God he had missed his father. He couldn't endure a confrontation in all his confusion.

"Forgive me." The older woman offered him her hand. "I don't know where my head is some days. I forgot to introduce myself. I'm Bella Ramsay, Saul's wife, and this is our daughter, Lucille. Our son, Jeremy, is at college in Philadelphia. His father insisted he go there."

Gerard's head swam at this further revelation. Of course Saul would send his other son to a school far from Harvard, both Saul's and Gerard's alma mater. *I have a half brother. A half sister.* "I'm Gerard Ramsay." He shook the hands the ladies proffered, Bella's, then Lucille's. "My family moved to Cincinnati when I was younger." *Please, no questions.*

"I'm so sorry Saul's not at home. He's a salesman for a Boston firm and travels a great deal."

I'll bet he does.

Gerard clung to his self-control as Bella and Lucille insisted he partake of refreshments and listen to fond stories of Saul and his second family. He managed to eat the refreshments without gagging and to answer their innocent inquiries with vagueness and finesse.

He finally succeeded in escaping his newfound relatives, who urged him to come back anytime. He wondered what his father would say when they mentioned that Gerard Ramsay, a relative from Cincinnati, had visited here.

Outside, he hailed an oncoming omnibus. The most difficult thing to accept was the way Bella and Lucille had spoken of Saul Ramsay. Gerard was left with the unpleasant realization that his father had been a real father to this family, who obviously held him in respect and affection. How could he reconcile that with the cold way Saul Ramsay treated his bona fide wife and son? None of it made sense. *What am I going to do about this?*

❖

MARCH 22, 1849

Gerard had returned to Boston, but instead of going home, he'd taken a room in a modest inn. After the Manhattan visit, he'd expected to become angry. Instead he remained bewildered and disoriented, as if he'd been tossed in a blanket and landed on the ground hard. He found he couldn't make himself go to his parents' house—his father's house—quite yet.

Discovering Saul Ramsay's duplicity in Manhattan had fractured Gerard's peace of mind. He wanted to visit his mother but was afraid he would not be able to hold back his emotions. And in any event, she'd told him she didn't want him to see her in her extremity.

He had spent the past couple of days in the inn, barely leaving it. Thoughts of Blessing plagued him. He wanted to spill this puzzle into her nonjudgmental ear. But she was hundreds of miles away, and writing a letter wasn't the same as being in her understanding presence. Gerard could count on her to sympathize and console, yet he should not be seeking her solace. He reminded himself of his brush with her illegal activities and how they'd shaken him. Thinking of Blessing only stirred up his emotional turmoil further.

Finally he realized he had to talk to someone, and the only one who might understand would be the one who'd discovered Saul Ramsay's secret life in the first place. Gerard went to Kennan's family's home and asked for his whereabouts. He was given an address in Providence, so he boarded a coach to Rhode Island.

Late in the afternoon, he stood outside a seedy inn. He only hoped Kennan would be sober. He asked for the man and was led up to his room. It was a small chamber, barely large enough for a bed, a side table, and a chair.

"Gerard," Kennan mumbled as he opened the door. He dropped down onto the side of the rumpled bed, running his hands over his face. "What brings you here? I thought you were going to stay in Ohio."

Gerard sat in the only chair. "My mother is nearing her end. She may pass any day." He paused to stroke his taut forehead and the back of his neck. "And I had to find out the truth about that address in Manhattan. Did you know my father has a second family there?"

Kennan yawned and stretched. "That's what it looked like to me. Stuffy, upright Saul Ramsay—a bigamist." Kennan barked with laughter.

The sound jabbed Gerard. "I don't find it very amusing."

"So what is the plan?" Kennan rubbed his hands together. "Going to shove old Dad's face in it? Make him pay?"

Gerard stared at Kennan. "What?"

"Don't you see? This is excellent! You have power over your father now. He'll do anything to keep you from revealing his double life."

Disgust rolled up Gerard's throat. "I have never craved power over my father. I've only wanted freedom from him."

"Well, now you can have both. Or if you want to ruin him, here's your chance."

Kennan's words made Gerard pull back as if fending off a blow. "Kennan, my mother is near death. I will do nothing while she lives."

"Oh, I understand that. But after she's gone, let me know, and I'll be happy to help you take down your father."

It had been a mistake to come here. Gerard's stomach bubbled with turmoil. Kennan wasn't Stoddard; he hadn't grown up. Gerard's old friend had no idea how what he'd discovered in Manhattan could impact so many lives. How could he wound innocent Bella and his half siblings? Kennan had reduced it all to cheap revenge and blackmail. Gerard was beginning to see it was so much more.

❖

Blessing stood in the backyard of the orphanage, staring at the charred remnants of her carriage house. While she was away for Caleb and Rebecca's wedding and a couple days' visit with her family, it had caught fire.

"The neighbor over there," Adela explained, pointing to the east, "was up late with a toothache. He saw the fire and sounded the alarm. People came flying out of their houses in robes and slippers with buckets in hand and lined up here in the backyard by the pump. Then the volunteer firemen arrived with their pumper truck. They worked like mad pumping water onto the fire, but they couldn't save it."

Blessing heard footsteps, and Scotty appeared beside her and wrapped his arms around her knees. She reached down and patted the boy's head.

"We had a fire," the boy said sadly. "It was scary. Miss Adela made us line up in the front yard in our coats."

"God protected thee."

"Where's Mr. Ramsay? *He* shoulda been here to pertect us."

For a moment Blessing could barely breathe. A tourniquet tightened around her lungs. *Gerard.* If he were here, she would be tempted to bury herself in his arms and seek comfort as she contemplated how to keep the children safe. She struggled to maintain control.

"Mr. Ramsay's mother is very ill, Scotty." Blessing stroked the boy's soft, fine hair. "He had to go to be with her."

"I'm sorry his mama is sick."

Adela held out her hand. "Come on, Scotty. It's time I read you children a story."

Scotty released his hold on Blessing and accepted Adela's hand. But he continued glancing over his shoulder at her until they disappeared into the house.

The breeze carried the acrid smell of charred wood to her. The loss of the carriage house had not shaken her, but she feared the fire was not the result of any accident or natural cause. Smith again? Or was she letting fear overtake her? Fires happened every day for many different reasons. She shoved Smith out of her mind.

The vision of Gerard fighting the slave catchers came to her. She clamped her unruly mind against further thoughts of Gerard. And focused on planning her next step.

She had meant to begin looking for a new orphanage. Maybe she really needed to talk to a builder and buy some property farther out of the city. She'd originally chosen the present location because it was near Little Africa, which was a place of allies though often the target of violence, and near the docks, where she found many of her orphans. She sighed, considering this decision.

Gerard again tried to slip into her mind. She turned and walked briskly into the orphanage. No time to see Smith behind every bad event. No time for foolish longings. Time to make plans and carry them out. *Greater is he that is in me, than he that is in the world.*

❧

MARCH 26, 1849

Gerard stood in the gloom of his family's parlor, each window shrouded with funeral crepe. He didn't know if he could go through the restrained and affected protocol of his mother's visitation without exploding or fleeing. If anybody here truly mourned his mother as he did, he didn't know who it was. This artificial society mourning mocked his mother.

But for her sake, he must not make a scene. He wouldn't turn her obsequies into a carnival of emotions, wouldn't give everyone something shocking to gossip about. All the doors on the first floor stood open to accommodate the full complement of Boston's elite. They'd turned out to see and be seen.

Surrounded by cloyingly fragrant lilies, his mother lay in her ornate coffin upon a special pedestal made for this purpose. Every time he glanced at his mother's coffin, he was rent with grief. And every glance at his father sparked an outrage he was having trouble hiding.

Thus far Gerard had not been able to bring himself to approach his mother's casket, though everyone else, all dressed in sober black, paraded past the coffin, wiping their eyes and murmuring "appropriate" comments. The proprieties of death were being observed to the letter. And it sickened him. These people belonged to his father's life, not his. Or at least his father's *Boston* life.

"We are so sorry for your loss, Saul," yet another guest murmured to Gerard's father, who stood nearby. Each word of condolence to his hypocrite of a father plunged another needle into Gerard's mourning soul. He clamped down his fury. *If only Blessing were here.*

He banished the thought once again. A mourner approached him. He vaguely recognized this woman, who began shaking his hand. "I knew Regina from the time we were girls together. She had such a sweet heart . . . and such potential." The woman sent a sharp glance at his father.

He gripped the woman's hand. She was the first person who showed she understood how his mother had suffered after marrying his father. *And she doesn't know the worst.* "Thank you. My mother was special."

"I hear you've settled in Cincinnati," the woman continued.

"Yes. My cousin is there."

She squeezed his hand. "A good choice. A promising city, I've heard." Then she moved down the line and somehow, in the crush, managed to avoid speaking with his father.

Out of the corner of his eye, Gerard glimpsed Kennan and his family entering. Kennan must have used the death of a friend's mother to force his family to let him come home. Gerard's neck muscles tightened painfully. He didn't want a dispute at his mother's funeral. He owed Mother her dignity. He moved to intercept Kennan but was blocked by several new arrivals all eager to tender their sympathy.

Kennan, don't.

But his profligate friend ignored him and went straight to his father. "Mr. Ramsay, I know how much you'll miss your dear wife," Kennan said with rich irony in his voice, which was also unusually loud and somewhat slurred. Was Kennan never completely sober?

Gerard held his breath. *Kennan, that's enough here and now.*

Father thanked him with a face stiffened with disapproval.

Kennan chuckled but covered it with a cough and moved away. He avoided the coffin, found a chair near a window, and sat slumped against the straight back.

Touched by relief, Gerard remained where he was throughout the visitation, repeatedly checking the tall clock and

300

counting down to the time when the coffin would be taken to the cemetery for the graveside service, ending this travesty.

At last the grieving crowd adjourned to their vehicles. The satin-black hearse, pulled by black horses sporting dyed plumes and followed by a long line of carriages, arrived at the cemetery. Standing graveside, Gerard felt tears wash down his face, but he couldn't stop them and didn't bother to wipe them away. A son could weep at his mother's grave.

The minister spoke as her coffin was lowered into the ground. "'Thou wilt shew me the path of life: in thy presence is fulness of joy; at thy right hand there are pleasures for evermore.'"

While earth was cast upon the coffin, the minister continued: "In sure and certain hope of the resurrection to eternal life through our Lord Jesus Christ, we commend to almighty God our sister Regina Ann Ramsay; and we commit her body to the ground; earth to earth, ashes to ashes, dust to dust."

The words spoken over her coffin provided Gerard some comfort. He realized that, though his heart was an open wound, his mother—the one person who had loved him most—was with God, no longer suffering. What stabbed him was that his father had betrayed her. Though Blessing was miles away, he felt her comforting presence. She would have reassured him of God's love for his dear mother, a true Christian. But he shouldn't be thinking of Blessing at this moment.

❖

The horrendous day finally ended. He and his father entered their home. A solemn footman helped them shed their top hats, canes, and gloves in the foyer. This act of discarding the outward signs of mourning liberated him in some way, released him. He followed his father into his second-floor study, finally ready to vent his rage.

His father sat behind his desk with a sigh.

The sound goaded Gerard into speech. "Well, you're free now," he snapped.

Saul looked up, frowning. "Do we need to have a display of emotions tonight? I'm quite fatigued."

"Really?" Gerard clenched his fists. "Burying your wife has left you 'fatigued.' What a pity." Every syllable dripped sarcasm.

Saul rose. "I'm going to my room. I'm not in the mood for an outburst."

Gerard blocked his exit. "Are you in the mood for bigamy?"

His father froze by his chair.

Gerard stared into his father's wide eyes. "I know about the house in Manhattan."

Saul stumbled back and slumped into his chair. "What? What house in Manhattan?"

Gerard let loose a sound of disgust. His father was going to try ignorance—really? He moved onto the balls of his feet, ready to fight and wanting to pound the man. "I met Bella and Lucille."

His father's mouth opened, but no words came forth.

Gerard slammed his fist onto the desk. *"Well?"*

Tears welled up in his father's eyes and poured down his cheeks. The ever-dignified Saul Ramsay buried his face in his hands and sobbed.

Bemused, Gerard listened to the sound, something like

the whimpering of a puppy separated from its mother. He'd never imagined his father like this, sobbing and defenseless.

His father's vulnerability pulled the plug on his rage, and it drained out of him. Exhausted by his own rampant emotions, he sank into the chair on the opposite side of the desk. "Why?"

A long silence ensued.

"Why?" Gerard prompted again, wanting to hear, not wanting to hear.

"I just desired a little happiness," his father muttered, not looking at him.

Gerard snorted. "So you committed adultery, misled two women, and fathered an illegitimate son and daughter," he sneered, his anger resurfacing. "So you could have a little happiness."

"Don't."

"Don't what? Speak the truth?"

"You've always hated me," his father said.

Gerard stared at him. "Did you ever give me a reason to love you?"

"I'm your father."

"You're right. No son is born hating his father. You know that. So I have to love you, and that means you can do whatever you want—is that it?"

"My family in Manhattan is the only thing I've ever done just for myself," Father snapped, looking resentful. "Ever since I was born, it's always been all about doing my duty to the family, to the business, to society, to the church. I wanted a life of my own. And so I created one."

"Mother didn't have that option. You held her fast. Why did you marry her if you didn't want her?"

The man glared at him. "My father insisted our family needed the infusion of capital that marrying Regina would bring."

"Did you even like my mother?"

He shrugged. "I always gave her everything she wanted—"

"Except for love and devotion." Gerard didn't know how much further he could go with this conversation. Each word scored his throat. "Then you tried to do the same thing with me. Tried to marry me to a banker's daughter."

"I gave you plenty of time to fall in love with someone." His father sounded aggrieved. "Your life was going nowhere. It was time you settled down."

Blessing's face entered his consciousness, bringing with it feelings he didn't want to acknowledge. "And if I said I'd fallen in love with a radical suffragist Quakeress, you would have welcomed her to the family?"

His father sat up, looking alarmed. "What?" The words must have shaken him. Saul Ramsay had evidently learned nothing from this confrontation.

Gerard rose. "Don't worry. I doubt she'd have me anyway."

"Wait. What are you going to do? I can't . . . The truth would kill Bella—and the children." He flung up a hand. "They are blameless in this."

Gerard halted, his father's words settling in him like concrete. He knew that Bella and her children didn't deserve scandal and shame. He couldn't hurt his father without making them suffer. And there was already too much suffering in this world and in this family.

"When I visited them in Manhattan, I identified myself as Gerard Ramsay, a distant relative from Cincinnati. I shall contact them no more." He paused to draw in fresh breath, suddenly exhausted. "Stoddard's wife has miscarried and is still recovering. He needs me." The way opened before Gerard. He wasn't trapped here in this mire. "I'm going back to Cincinnati to live my life." Gerard had no more words. He lifted a hand and walked out.

As he picked up his gear in the foyer, he thought of Kennan. He must stop him from airing this scandal in public—of that he was sure. Gerard couldn't see much of his way forward, but he knew Kennan was capable of anything. He'd proven that the night he'd drugged Gerard at Smith's bidding.

Gerard took a cab straight to Kennan's family home and found his onetime friend still there. In the family garden, Kennan greeted him with a broad grin. "So what's the plan?"

"I'm going back to Cincinnati. And I don't want to expose my father." He tried to come up with an excuse. "It's too soon after Mother's parting. It would shame her memory."

Kennan's grin faltered, his mouth drooping open. "What? You have him in your grasp at last. You can get anything from him. *Anything.*"

"There is nothing I need from him. He doesn't have anything I want."

"You don't want the family fortune?"

Gerard shrugged. "I have a life in Cincinnati, and I'll find another occupation there. I'm not coming back east. I'm warning you not to make my father's bigamy public nor to use it against him. Even though my mother's dead, I don't want people to know how Father disrespected her." Though what leverage he had to stop Kennan, he didn't know.

Kennan's jaws moved as if he were chewing wood. "I don't get it."

Gerard gripped Kennan's shoulders. "I am my own man. Not a puppet attached to my father and his wreck of a life. Kennan, you need to break free too."

"I am free." Kennan jerked out of Gerard's grasp. "I do what I want, when and where I want."

"Living in the bottle is what you want?"

"Don't preach to me," Kennan growled, stepping backward.

"We've been friends since we were boys. Do you think I want to see you go down to delirium tremens or early death?"

Kennan took another step backward. "You're not the Gerard Ramsay I knew."

"Thank heaven," Gerard said, recognizing the truth. "Good-bye, Kennan. I wish you well."

"Go to hades."

"No, Cincinnati is far enough for me."

Kennan jeered wordlessly.

Gerard walked out of the garden and hailed a cab. He could be home in a week if he left in the morning. A longing to be near Blessing once more worked in him like a magnet. He resisted its pull. That was the only danger in returning to Ohio.

Commendable in many ways, Blessing was a woman devoted to causes, a woman who wouldn't welcome marriage and its obligations—especially after a marriage that seemed to have caused her suffering. And she didn't blink at breaking the law. In contrast, all he wanted now was peace. And Blessing Brightman was not a peaceable woman. Yet he was unsure what to do about this misguided attraction to her.

Chapter 15

The spring breeze played with Blessing's gray bonnet ribbons. The middle-aged land agent, another Quaker, walked beside her through the open field decked with tender green leaves, grass, and wildflowers—tiny lavender and yellow violets, white trilliums, and bluebells. The world around rejoiced. Inside, she mourned. Gerard had been away for days now, but it felt like much longer. *I can't think of that.*

"This property is well drained by the creek at the back," the land agent said, pointing toward the line of budding trees and shrubbery lining the small creek. "It's on the Lebanon Road, but there's enough land to set the orphanage and its grounds far back."

Blessing struggled to keep her mind on task, on the new

orphanage. "It looks like a good place—plenty of room for the children."

"And there are no near neighbors." He left unsaid that people usually didn't want an orphanage in their vicinity.

"Good."

"Thee is planning on closing the other orphanage in town?" he asked as they walked through the wild grass toward his open gig for the short ride back to town.

"I will keep that house as a kind of receiving center for orphans," she said, letting him hand her up into the gig with care. "And it's convenient for other activities too."

He exchanged a glance with her. He was also involved in the Underground Railroad.

"I am done looking," she said. "I think this acreage will suit my purpose. Close to town but not right in town, and it's large enough for now and the future."

"A good decision." He climbed onto his seat in the gig. "I will make certain we get it at a reasonable price."

She thanked him and he slapped the reins, turning them back to town. She closed her eyes and tried to direct her thoughts away from Ramsay. He might not come back to Ohio. And even if he did, she would have no more to do with him on a personal level. He had become too important, too tempting. And she, too weak.

❧

APRIL 2, 1849

Gerard rode beside the drayman from the riverfront to the bluff on this bright April morning. This was the third time he'd arrived in Cincinnati but the first time he felt as if he'd truly come home. A satisfying reaction. Yet he suffered from wanting what he couldn't, shouldn't have. Everywhere he turned at the docks, he saw the phantom of Blessing.

He forced her from his mind and began planning. He needed to find a new position. He'd inherited his mother's portion, the money settled on her in the marriage agreement between the two wealthy families, so he didn't need funds, but he needed to occupy himself and to begin forging connections here, where he'd make his life. Nonetheless, what he'd left behind—his father's duplicity and his uncertainty over Kennan's discretion—continued to plague him. How could he trust a man so often in a drunken state? He had no choice but to do so, however. Kennan would have little reason to blackmail Saul Ramsay—unlike Gerard, he was once again living comfortably off his family's estimable resources. Gerard also doubted Kennan had the ambition for such a scheme.

Gerard himself wanted a fresh start, not one tainted by extorting funds from his father. And he didn't hate Bella, Lucille, or Jeremy; he wished them no harm. He'd suffered from his parents' unhappy union. Why should more people suffer in the wake of Saul Ramsay's selfish decisions?

The drayman drove Gerard and his valises toward Mrs. Mather's, rumbling over the uneven road. Imagining the widow Brightman on every corner was a torment. The thought of seeing her lifted him even as other memories of these streets pressed him down—catching Theodosia as she jumped from a window, testifying against the slave catchers in a biased courtroom. After these past few tumultuous months, he craved peace.

And if he let it, time would gradually erase Blessing from his mind. He just needed to get busy, find employment, and begin cultivating a new life here. He would visit Stoddard today and ask him for possible leads on a new position. Surely Stoddard, with his connection to the Foster family, would be able to point him in the right direction.

❧

Later that day the maid Honoree let Gerard in at Stoddard and Tippy's front door. He'd been eager to see his cousin and ascertain the state of Tippy's health. But as he stepped inside the door, remembrance of the time he'd spent here with Blessing rushed through him. The hope that she'd be in the house tried to rise, but he cut it off. If she was here, he would leave as soon as possible.

"Hello, Mr. Ramsay." Honoree relieved him of his hat and gloves, and he deposited his cane in the umbrella stand by the door.

"How is Mrs. Henry?"

Honoree looked serious. "She is some better, sir. Will you wait in the rear parlor? I'll go get Mr. Henry."

He entered the small parlor and stood, gazing out the window. Footsteps on the hardwood floor alerted him. He turned as his cousin entered.

"Gerard." Stoddard greeted him with outstretched hand.

"Cousin." Gerard clasped hands with the man, grateful for at least one friend and relative still true. "How's your bride?"

Looking haggard and disheveled in his shirtsleeves, Stoddard waved him to a chair. He let out a labored sigh as he sat across from Gerard. "It's difficult."

"But she's better, isn't she?"

Stoddard tried to look hopeful and failed, his features tensing. "Some, but her convalescence is slow. If it had just been a miscarriage, she'd be up by now. The doctor said the cholera has made her . . . weaker."

Gerard read the worry etched deeply into Stoddard's face. "But she will recover?"

His cousin bent forward, clasping and unclasping his fingers. "I hope so, eventually, unless some other contagion lays her low again." Stoddard scrubbed his face with his hands. "She's in low spirits too."

"I imagine she would be," Gerard said with true sympathy. A young woman would take the loss of her first child hard, especially a caring person like Tippy.

"I feel helpless," Stoddard admitted, looking into Gerard's eyes. Then he roused himself. "I'm sorry. I'm focusing on my own troubles. You just lost your mother. And I regret I wasn't able to attend my aunt's funeral."

The mention of this slid in like a blade. Gerard hoped his grief didn't show. "She's no longer in pain." *In so many ways.*

Stoddard nodded.

Aunt Fran appeared at the door. "Gerard." She held out both hands.

He rose, claimed them, and drew her into the room.

"I was so sorry I couldn't go to Regina's funeral," Aunt Fran said.

"You had more pressing obligations." Gerard gently squeezed her hands to emphasize his point.

Then Blessing stepped through the doorway. She wore one of her simple gray dresses and a white widow's cap. Her plain attire only highlighted her warm brown hair and blue eyes. Her presence filled the room before she was even inside it.

The sight of her shot through Gerard, bringing him fully alive. Fully wary. He forced himself not to move toward her, though his whole body felt the pull. "Widow Brightman," he murmured with a formal bow of his head.

She paused in the doorway, nodded to him, and then entered, looking away from him. "I require thy help, Stoddard. I think Tippy needs some fresh air and sunshine—*must have* some to begin to heal. She has argued with me but I'm ignoring her."

Aunt Fran, also in sober gray, nodded in vigorous agreement, making the ribbons of her own white widow's cap bounce.

Stoddard looked from one to the other.

"I've asked Honoree to dress her in a housecoat and slippers," Blessing said. "And I want thee to carry her into the garden, Stoddard."

Stoddard hesitated, looking uncertain.

"Son, do what Mrs. Brightman says," Aunt Fran urged. "Tippy does need sunshine and fresh air—not only for her body but for her mind. If she lies in that bed much longer, she will never be the same."

"Now," Blessing instructed. "Please, Stoddard."

Gerard felt the strength of Blessing's will and insight. She could be trusted to do only good for Tippy.

Stoddard walked between the two women and up the stairs, and Gerard trailed after him in support.

Tippy's wan appearance dismayed Gerard. She'd lost too much weight and her skin looked pasty white.

Tippy wept and begged, but Stoddard lifted her from bed and carried her down the stairs, ignoring her protests.

Blessing and Aunt Fran had already gone out into the garden and prepared a high-backed wicker chair with cushions and a light blanket. Stoddard set his wife carefully onto the chair in the sun and pushed the matching footstool under her slippered feet.

Gerard hung back while Aunt Fran and Blessing arranged the blanket over her and spoke soothingly to her.

Tippy closed her eyes, moist with tears. She rested her head against the chair and trembled.

"Tippy," Blessing said, "the grief will remain, but spring is here and it's time to begin again the task of living. Thee has a husband who needs thee. And family and friends who want thee well."

Tippy nodded, pressing her teeth down on her quivering lower lip.

Aunt Fran sank into the chair beside her daughter-in-law. She patted Tippy's hand, murmuring comforting words.

Finally Tippy opened her eyes and held out her other hand toward Stoddard.

He gripped it and drew it up for a kiss. "We'll do," he said simply.

"Yes." Tippy gazed at him.

Aunt Fran rose. "I think it's time I went home for a bit." She led Blessing and Gerard back into the house.

"Thank you so much, Mrs. Brightman," Aunt Fran said inside. "I've tried to get her out of that bed for almost two weeks."

Blessing pressed her cheek against Aunt Fran's. "I must go to the orphanage."

"I'll walk you partway," Gerard said, startling himself. He'd had no intention of being alone with her.

Blessing stared at him.

"Walk me home first, Gerard," Aunt Fran said. "I'm going to sit in my garden and enjoy the sunshine too."

In the foyer the three of them donned their hats and gloves, and Gerard accompanied his aunt to her gate.

"Don't let this woman slip through your fingers," Aunt Fran whispered to him there. "Your mother would have loved her."

He tried to ignore the irritation this comment provoked, which was directed more at himself than at his aunt.

He caught up with Blessing, who had already begun walking. "I'm glad Tippy has you for a friend." Even as he spoke the words, he wanted to kick himself. So much for avoiding the woman.

"I'm glad Stoddard has thee as a friend as well as a cousin. I'm very sorry for thy loss."

So the two of them, who had faced down Smith together, were reduced to this, polite parlor conversation. "Thank you."

They walked in silence past the now-familiar houses on Stoddard's street.

She cleared her throat. "What is bothering thee? Thee looks as if thee is carrying the world on thy back."

Picturing his father's second house in Manhattan, he shut his eyes and then opened them. "Something I must deal with myself." He found he couldn't confide it to her after all.

Blessing repeated the words silently. *"Something I must*

deal with myself." Attraction to this man was definitely the something *she* must deal with herself.

The two of them walked together as far as the street that led to Gerard's boardinghouse.

"I'll leave you now," he said.

"Yes, good-bye." She offered him her hand.

He shook it and turned away.

She watched him start back down the street. *Good-bye, Gerard Ramsay. I'll try to make certain we don't run into each other again.*

❧

APRIL 30, 1849

On a balmy evening Gerard found himself in the familiar auditorium at Lane Seminary to hear Frederick Douglass. The crowded hall buzzed with voices. Gerard had argued with himself for days but had not been able to keep himself from attending tonight's lecture.

He did indeed want to hear the notable abolitionist, this courageous man who had run away from slavery and later earned enough to buy his freedom.

Yet Gerard knew that in reality he'd come here to glimpse Blessing. Almost a month had passed since they'd seen each other at Stoddard's. Gerard had kept himself busy and only called on his cousin when he knew the house would be without other visitors.

Tonight he could at least see her, but in the protection of a crowd. He would make sure not to chance a private word.

Except that the widow Brightman did not come.

Settling back to listen anyway, Gerard found Douglass, a

tall, imposing man, to be a spirited and interesting speaker. When the man said that a discussion of the rights of animals would be regarded with far more complacency than would be a discussion of the rights of women, Gerard gasped. And he wasn't the only one in the audience.

Douglass went on to connect women's rights to abolition and stated the position of the *North Star*, his periodical: "We hold woman to be justly entitled to all we claim for man."

Gerard listened with his whole mind to a man he formerly wouldn't have paid a moment's attention to. However, the evening fell flat because Blessing Brightman had not come. With whom could he discuss this man's ideas?

In the general commotion at the end of the lecture, Deborah Coxswain, the white-haired woman who'd attended *Hamlet* with him in Blessing's stead, approached him. "Where is Blessing? She told me that nothing would make her miss tonight's lecture."

"I expected to see her too." He'd come to spend an evening near Blessing, and evidently this woman knew that. *Whom am I trying to fool?*

"I hope she isn't ill," Deborah said, sounding worried.

Alarm rippled through Gerard. Why hadn't she come?

"I'll go and check on her," he assured her without hesitation. Nothing could keep him from investigating what had prevented Blessing from coming to hear Frederick Douglass. How many times had she brought up his name to Gerard?

He first walked to her house.

"No, she isn't here," Salina told him. "She must have stayed late at the orphanage. If you find her there, tell her I sent her supper home with our maids. So she best not expect to find it here."

Gerard shook his head, certain only Blessing would employ such a tart housekeeper.

He headed for the orphanage, a deep foreboding growing within. But perhaps Blessing had simply gotten caught up with one of her causes tonight. Another escaped slave? Another fallen woman? Soon the orphanage lay just ahead. At nearly ten at night, there were no lights on upstairs. The children and their nurses must be abed. He edged around to the rear.

Yes, low lamplight glowed from the kitchen windows and one of them was cracked open, but all the curtains had been pulled shut. He hesitated. Did this have something to do with the Underground Railroad? Did he really want to become involved in illegal activity a second time?

He stared at the curtained windows, listened to the quiet street noises. Finally he decided. He could not go home without seeing Blessing and making certain she didn't need help—even if it was help in breaking the law.

In the dark he pushed the gate open silently and stepped into the back garden, his senses alert. Movement rustled near him—a shadowed form. He shifted his cane, ready for any attack.

Then he realized the figure was a woman. He doffed his hat automatically.

"Oh, you're a gentleman; oh, help," the woman whispered, sounding panicked. "I don't know what to do. He's in there with her."

"Who?"

"Smith."

Chapter 16

SMITH. The name sucked away all sound, and Gerard couldn't breathe. Fear for Blessing's safety dragged him back, and he fought for air. His hearing and breathing, his will returned. "Are you certain?" he whispered.

"Yes. I was just leavin' after visitin' my nephew and then talkin' with Mrs. Brightman. My Danny's an orphan here. I glanced over my shoulder, I saw Smith go in, so I snuck back. I mean, the man never does anybody good. I peeked in the window. He's in there with that kind lady. I don't know what to do." The woman's voice was tinged with infectious panic.

"I'll do what I can," Gerard said, resisting the fear emanating from the woman's voice. "Go for the night watch."

She slipped out the gate.

Gerard took a deep breath and readied his pistol to come out at a moment's notice. Nonetheless, he didn't want to plunge in blindly, wildly. Such action might endanger Blessing further. He edged nearer to the open window, where he could hear voices but see nothing more than the shadows of the two people inside. One was standing, one sitting. Why had Smith come here? More intimidation? Or something worse?

Closer now, Gerard heard Smith taunting Blessing. "You hold a grudge against me for your late husband."

What about her husband?

"I don't hold grudges," Blessing replied. "Thee does."

Smith snorted. "Mrs. Sanctimonious, admit it here. You hate me. And it all started with Richard Brightman."

"I hate no one. But I do hate what thee does and what thee did to my husband."

What did Smith do to her husband?

"Your *late* husband was a grown man. I didn't make him do what he did."

"Thee knew—and I learned, to my sorrow—that sin is addictive. Richard could not stop the drink nor the liaisons with the women thee introduced him to. Nor the gambling and opium he began to crave." The widow's voice was harsh.

"Well, at least I didn't kill him," Smith mocked.

What? Gerard was more certain than ever that Smith had lost his mental faculties. But he couldn't help recalling what the men at his long-ago racetrack dinner had insinuated about Richard Brightman's death. He tried to shake it off but listened more closely.

"Thee thinks I'm guilty of murder?" Blessing's voice trembled at first but then grew stronger. "My husband came home from one of thy 'establishments' inebriated and fell and broke his neck."

"That's what you told the police, but I've always suspected—"

"Thee wants to paint everyone with the same tar as thyself," Blessing cut in. "Why do I vex thee so much?"

"Where is Jewel?" he demanded.

So that was what had brought Smith here in this savage state of mind. Gerard wavered between staying where he was and moving to confront Smith immediately. But what if the man had a weapon? He could use it on Blessing long before Gerard could confront him.

"Thee keeps asking me that. And I say again, I do not know where Jewel is. If thee wanted to keep her, thee should have taken better care of her."

The sound of a fist hitting wood. Gerard jerked back.

"I took care of her," Smith declared. "I gave her everything."

"Then why did she leave?" Blessing's voice remained cool.

The fist hit wood again. "I want to make it right."

"I doubt thee could. I heard the rumors. It is said thee smothered thy own newborn son—thy and Jewel's son."

Gerard felt ill. *Dear God, no.*

"If that were true—" Smith's voice had descended to a tiger's growl—"I did the child a favor. Can you see me as any child's father?"

"Thee could have brought the baby to me. I would have cared for him."

"Yes, such a good work of charity," Smith said, his voice dripping with acid. "I'd rather have my son dead than raised as someone's bastard in an orphanage."

"Did Jewel agree?"

The fist slammed down a third time.

Gerard measured the distance between his position and the back stoop, gauging how quickly he could get inside. Yet he once again cautioned himself against acting rashly. When would the watch arrive?

"I gave her everything she wanted," Smith repeated as if flailing for words.

"She wanted her child."

Smith rumbled with anger, menacing. "You believe in heaven. Any child of mine is better off there."

"Is that what thee thinks of thy life? Has thee considered where thee might go?"

Gerard waited to hear the fist hit the table again. But only silence followed, ominous silence.

"I . . . hate . . . you."

"I know." Blessing's tone had saddened.

"Why aren't you afraid of me? You should be begging for mercy."

Gerard lifted onto the balls of his feet, ready to move.

"Why is thee here?" she asked.

Smith slurred an imitation of a laugh. "I'm going to kill you so Ramsay feels how I do. I'm going to rob him of the woman he loves."

Gerard's scalp tightened. Sheer terror rippled up his spine.

"Thee thinks Gerard Ramsay loves me? He doesn't."

Smith barked another travesty of laughter. "You said it yourself. Sin is addictive. The man lusts for you."

"But thee thinks thee loved Jewel?"

"I love her," Smith insisted.

"Love can survive almost anything yet can be so fragile

too. Did Jewel love thee? Or did she just submit to thee because she had no choice?"

Smith bellowed with rage.

Tingling with fear for Blessing, Gerard edged toward the door. He could no longer wait for the watchman who might never come.

"Why was Gerard Ramsay so significant a target to thee?" Blessing asked. "Why is it so important to hurt him?"

Gerard froze. He'd wondered this too.

"Because he was born with everything!" Smith declared. "Wealth, position, a family! Everything I should have been entitled to."

What? Why should Smith have been entitled to my life?

Smith raved on. "And he was willing to throw it all away— for what? To embarrass his father? He's a fool. He deserves judgment."

"Why does that concern thee? He isn't the first to treat his birthright with scorn. My husband was a sad example. Is that why he became one of thy targets too?"

Peering through the edge of the curtain at the last window before the porch, Gerard finally glimpsed Smith. He was holding a pistol trained on Blessing, who sat at the table with a sleeping baby in her arms. Smith's hair was wild and his eyes were unnaturally bright.

Stark terror electrified Gerard.

"Ramsay—" Smith said the name with loathing—"galls me because I deserved what he readily despised. Smith isn't my real name—not the name I should have borne. My father was a Boston Brahman too, just like Ramsay's father. They were neighbors. But my mother was merely an Irish maid in his house."

"So that is the seed of thy jealousy." Blessing's tone was sympathetic, which somehow didn't surprise Gerard. "I'm sorry thy mother was mistreated."

"He supported us, visited us, but walked by me on the streets of Boston as if I were a stranger not worthy of even a nod. Do you know how that made me feel?" Smith's voice vibrated with fury. "When I was a child, my mother took me to see his big house on Beacon Hill. And across the street I saw the Ramsay house and a boy playing there. I went back many times before I left Boston. I observed Gerard Ramsay many a day, a privileged, legitimate son. Not like me, the bastard. It wasn't fair!" His last words sounded deranged.

It was time. With as much stealth as he could, Gerard ran up the steps and onto the back porch. He entered the kitchen, his pistol drawn. "Smith," he challenged, "put the gun away." Gerard raised his Colt to protect Blessing.

Just then the night watch called out, "Police!"

Smith swung his pistol toward his head and pulled the trigger.

Gerard charged forward. *No!*

The gunshot exploded, deafening.

Blessing screamed. She leaped from her chair, the baby clasped to her, wailing.

Smith's body hit the floor hard.

The night watch charged into the room, gun drawn. "What's happened? Who's shooting?"

Gerard tried to go to Blessing. But the night watch stood between them—only the first of many of the watch to come thundering into the kitchen.

The woman who'd alerted him about Smith entered and

went to Blessing's side. "Are you all right, ma'am? He didn't hurt you?"

The orphanage staff piled into the room, wearing hastily donned robes. And then came neighbors, pounding on the front door and running in the back door. More police crowded in as well.

Gerard looked across the jammed kitchen and tried to catch Blessing's eye. She was trembling, her face downcast. The sight caught him, and all he wanted to do was draw her into his arms. But the police investigating Smith's suicide intervened, keeping them apart.

Someone placed a sheet over Smith's body. Blessing was led away by the orphanage staff. At last allowed to sit at the kitchen table, Gerard provided an account of what had taken place to the first night watch, then to a second one of higher rank, and finally to a deputy sheriff.

When the sheriff himself, who'd just arrived, demanded yet another recital, Gerard balked. "That's enough. I have already given my statement to three other officers. They took notes. You can read their reports." He rose.

The sheriff laid a hand on Gerard's arm.

Gerard pulled from the man's grasp. "Smith killed himself," he snapped. "If you need to hold someone responsible, arrest him. Now why don't you all leave and take this body with you? This is an orphanage with women and small children in residence. They need quiet."

The sheriff grimaced. "Don't leave town."

Gerard glared at the man. "Don't be foolish." He left the kitchen and the diminishing crowd that remained.

In the parlor Gerard was met by a young woman of color.

"Where's Mrs. Brightman?" he asked.

"I sent her home in her carriage," the girl said. "She was pretty overwhelmed by all this."

He nodded. "I'll go there, then."

"You can, but she may need her sleep."

Gerard didn't reply but walked to the front door and let himself out. No power on heaven or earth could keep him from going to Blessing. Nearby in the moonlight a police wagon had arrived and two men were carrying a sheet-covered stretcher to it. Gerard sorted through all he'd overheard, but one question clamored for an answer. Why had Smith shot himself?

❖

Blessing sat in her rear parlor, wrapped in a large knit shawl. Salina, in her red print robe and leather slippers, had built up the fire and bullied Blessing into sipping a medicinal glass of sherry. Smith's anguished expression glimmered before Blessing's eyes like the firelight.

Salina stood over her until she had slowly downed the restorative, and then the housekeeper accepted the empty glass. "Now you sit and rock. That will help too."

The brass knocker on the front door sounded, insistent.

"I bet I know who that be," Salina said as she turned to answer the door. "'Bout time."

Blessing heard Salina open the door and say from the foyer, "Well, Mr. Ramsay, what took you so long?"

Rapid footsteps hurried down the hall. Ramsay appeared at the doorway, the fire illumining his face. "I came as soon as I could get away from answering police questions. How are you?"

Blessing burst into pent-up tears, shocking herself.

He lifted her from the rocker and pulled her to him.

From the hall, Salina gave a murmur of approval and shut the door quietly but firmly.

Blessing buried her face in Ramsay's chest, clutching his coat. His bracing arms encircled her. To be honest, she wanted to be in Ramsay's arms, but she knew she couldn't begin to depend on him. Smith's words tonight about her late husband had brought up all the unhappy memories of the past: the pain of loving Richard, of watching him slowly, inexorably destroy her love for him. And then losing him so tragically.

"I'm so sorry you had to see that, suffer that," Ramsay soothed near her ear.

"I'm so sorry that man was tortured enough to kill himself." She pulled back, forcing herself to break away. "Why did he do it? I would never have guessed he'd take his own life."

Ramsay claimed her hand. "We can never know, but perhaps in that instant he realized that this time he'd go to trial, face public humiliation. He was threatening to murder a prominent lady. Or . . ."

"Or?"

"Or maybe he couldn't face living his own life anymore." He recalled what he'd overheard Smith say about his illegitimate birth and his longtime envy of Gerard. The thought occurred to him that one never knew who might be watching and judging one's life. He considered his visit to the Manhattan house. Bella and her mother had no inkling of what he'd felt sitting in their parlor, listening to them talk about their beloved husband and father—the father who both claimed and rejected him.

Needing her closer, he tugged Blessing toward him and stroked away the stray hair from her face, disturbing her widow's cap. It fell to the floor, and her rich, dark hair glimmered where it caught the light. He gazed at her, forgetting that he wasn't to want her. *I do want her, want to be with her.*

These feelings prompted thoughts of Smith, of his cruelty to Jewel. Gerard understood a little of what Smith had felt at being deprived of the woman he needed. Obviously losing her had cut the last thread to the man's sanity and driven him to violent threats and a violent end.

"If what you heard about what Smith did to the child is true . . ." Gerard shied away from the loathsome idea. "In any event, he'd lost the woman he loved and he knew it was his fault, his grievous sin," he said. He couldn't ignore his own yearning tonight. He wanted to kiss this woman, and he was going to.

❧

Blessing saw Ramsay's mouth lowering to claim hers. She felt herself leaning forward, anticipating his lips, soft and insistent—

She tugged free with a silent gasp.

He gazed at her with such longing she had to stiffen her resolve, turning toward the fire. The two of them had no future together. "I always tried not to provoke Smith," she said, unable to stay silent, "but he was so wicked and caused suffering for so many." *For Richard and me.* She sank back into the rocker and pulled the shawl around her, still palpably chilled by tonight's events.

Again her mind conjured up her sad marriage. All the

times Richard had vowed to be free of alcohol and gambling and other women. And all the times he'd failed. All the times Smith had lured him back to the docks, introducing him to sinful pleasures that could excite him in new ways. She shuddered, admitting to herself she had retained a grudge against Smith. Maybe he'd been right to accuse her of hating him.

Ramsay sat in the rocker opposite her, his gaze beseeching her to let him come closer. "I overheard most of what Smith said in the minutes before . . ."

Was he asking for an explanation about Richard? She could not, would not speak to this man about the husband who had abused her and followed a path to destruction—and bequeathed to her all his wealth out of guilt and shame.

She turned the conversation toward Ramsay. "Now we know why Smith hated thee in particular."

"I was listening outside, hoping the night watch would come. I heard everything. He indeed wanted to destroy me. And you're the one who stopped him. Where would I be if you had not deterred his plans?"

Blessing wouldn't respond to that. It would only bring them closer. "Sometimes the evil in this world weighs me down," she said, redirecting the conversation and trying to keep her feelings hidden, difficult though it was. Witnessing Smith's suicide had stripped away her outer shell. She must be wary.

"What can I do to help you? You shouldn't have been subjected to this dreadful incident."

His words were exactly what a gentleman was expected to say to a lady who'd witnessed something unpleasant. Of course, Smith's suicide was far from merely unpleasant. But Ramsay's falling back onto propriety somehow steadied her.

She gazed at him, pulling up her reserves. *I am not a sheltered lady.*

She looked him in the eye. "Thee forgets that I am the woman who walks the docks at night, trying to find those who can still be rescued." She lifted her chin. "I've seen violent death before. Sadly."

"I wish that weren't true. But I know I can't change you."

His final words endangered her resistance to him most of all. Of all the men she'd known, this one understood her the best, better than Richard ever had.

Again she averted the discussion from herself. "So Smith's *idée fixe* didn't start when thee arrived in Cincinnati. He'd envied thee long before that."

Gerard snorted. "Appearances can be so deceiving. Smith never met my father. I may be his legitimate heir, but my father has never loved me."

The stark words saddened her. "I'm sorry to hear that. I've always been fortunate in my parents."

He nodded in the low light.

She needed him to go before she had another weak moment. "Ramsay, I really don't want to talk more."

"Would you like me just to sit with you? We don't need to talk."

She tried to say she didn't require his presence, but she couldn't bring herself to tell an outright lie. "Yes, thee may stay and sit."

He assented.

She found she couldn't send him away. His nearness was calming her, stabilizing her. "Please stay till I can go up to bed."

"Very well."

The firelight flickered on the rose-papered walls. The silence of deep night settled over them. Though Blessing relaxed in Ramsay's comforting presence, she prayed she would have the strength to resist her feelings for him.

No one must know the truth about the guilt she carried and would never be free of, least of all this man who was becoming so much more than she could have thought possible at their first meeting.

❧

MAY 1, 1849

Reports of Smith's suicide hit the streets in the newspaper *Extras* the next morning. Any doubt that Mr. Smith had held notorious sway over many men could no longer be denied, and death by his own hand made for a sensational story. Newspaper reporters, notebooks in hand, gathered around Mrs. Mather's front door, asking for Gerard.

After a hastily eaten breakfast, Gerard faced them on the front porch and gave a succinct and guarded statement about Smith and his death. They clamored with questions. He answered a few and then asked them to leave. There was nothing more to say.

The raucous and insistent newspapermen refused to leave, perhaps scenting much more gore or drama for their columns. Finally the watchmen, prompted by complaints from the neighbors, had to disperse them. Gerard, inside the front door, faced Mrs. Mather. "I'm sorry. I seem to always be your most troublesome boarder."

She ignored his apology. "Thee had best go quickly to Blessing's home. I'm sure they are harassing her too."

"Why didn't I think of that?"

"No doubt because thee mistakenly thought that those men wouldn't bother a lady," Mrs. Mather replied with a touch of sarcasm. "Mary and I will stay in today and lock the doors and pull down the shades. That should keep unwanted reporters away."

He grinned. "You're a Trojan, Mrs. Mather."

She blushed. "Go and protect Blessing from those vultures."

Gerard donned his coat, hat, and gloves and, gripping his cane, headed to Blessing's house. From a discreet distance, he found it shut up tight with the curtains drawn. Without calling attention to himself, he made his way to the orphanage instead.

There he found a guard standing at each gate and door—large men of color and a few white men dressed in Quaker attire. One of the former recognized Gerard, and he was allowed inside.

Blessing sat in the parlor with several noisy and lively children playing around her. She looked much more relaxed than he had expected.

Scotty immediately accosted Gerard. "Mister, something bad happened last night."

Gerard stooped down and looked Scotty in the eye. "I know, but you're safe today. No one is going to do anything bad again."

Scotty leaned against him, and Gerard patted his shoulder awkwardly. "Now why don't you go play jacks?"

The child pressed closer to him.

Gerard gave in. He swept the boy up into his arms, picked

his way through the children playing on the parlor rug, and set Scotty on his lap as he sat across from Blessing.

He almost asked if she was doing well, but that sounded insipid. "I'm glad to see you this morning," he substituted.

She smiled but didn't reply.

And that was how the remainder of his visit proceeded. Blessing had erected a wall around herself and wouldn't let him in. Finally he set Scotty down and bid her a polite good day.

As he left, Gerard couldn't figure out if he'd done something to offend her or if she was still suffering some form of shock. He recalled holding her last night and realized that he longed to embrace Blessing again to comfort her—and perhaps comfort himself.

❧

After leaving the orphanage, Gerard didn't know where he was going until he reached Stoddard's house. He knocked on the door, choosing not to analyze his motives. Stoddard was probably at work already in any case.

Honoree answered. "Oh, sir, I am that glad to greet you. Miss Tippy is worried about you and Miss Blessing. Mr. Henry left for work before we saw that story in *Extras* about what happened last night. Is Miss Blessing all right?"

"I just visited her at the orphanage. She is doing well." He realized he'd come seeking comfort but now would be providing news and solace to Tippy and her household.

Honoree did not look convinced. "Did you want to see Miss Tippy?" Her simple request concealed the real message, a plea for him to console Tippy with information.

Then Tippy's voice floated down the hallway. "Gerard, please come and visit me."

Gerard could not say no to Stoddard's beloved, who was still recovering. He let Honoree relieve him of his accoutrements, and she led him to the garden off the rear parlor.

Tippy sat in the same white wicker chair as usual, but she appeared much better than she had the day Stoddard had carried her here against her wishes.

Gerard was moved to kiss her proffered hand in welcome. "I am glad to see you looking so much healthier."

Tippy smiled. "Do sit. Honoree, bring him some refreshment, please."

Gerard sat in the chair adjacent to Tippy's, glancing at the fresh greenery and flowers everywhere. "Your garden is beginning to thrive."

"I have started digging in the dirt," she said with a laugh. "It's good for the plants and for me. Now, what is this I read about that man Smith?"

Gerard did not want to tell her, but she'd find out soon enough anyway. He gave her a brief report of events without embellishment.

Tippy stared at the house next door over his shoulder. "You care for Blessing, don't you?"

He hadn't expected this question and didn't reply.

"She cares for you, too," Tippy continued.

He still kept silent.

"Since she lost Richard, I've not seen her drawn to any man as she's been drawn to you. Blessing is one of the most special people I've ever known." Tippy looked into his eyes. "If you let her slip away from you, you will regret it."

The truth of her words settled over him and then sank in like a gentle rain on soft earth. "I don't want to let her go," he admitted. "But she has been pushing me away."

Tippy glanced downward. A woodpecker nearby was pounding his beak into a tree. "She never speaks of her husband. But it was not a happy marriage." Tippy looked to him again. "After her period of mourning ended, many men fixed their interest on her, but she never gave anyone a second look. Till you came."

"You hold a grudge against me for your late husband." The words Smith had taunted Blessing with came back.

"What kind of man was her husband?"

"He inherited two breweries and much valuable land from his father when he was only twenty-two. He was *very* handsome and charming."

"But what kind of man was he?" Gerard repeated.

Tippy almost lowered her gaze again but lifted her chin instead. "I never liked Richard Brightman. I think he was drawn to Blessing because she was his complete opposite. He was weak and she was strong. Perhaps he thought she could save him from himself."

Tippy's blunt assessment set Gerard back on his heels. A woman like Blessing married to a man who was weak? A wealthy young man perhaps more foolish than Gerard had been before he'd met Blessing. He recalled that Smith had completely ensnared the man. "No wonder," he murmured.

"What?"

"Nothing." But in his mind he completed the thought. *No wonder Blessing fought to keep me from Smith.* He fell silent.

Tippy closed her eyes as if fatigued by the conversation.

Gerard listened to wheels and footsteps passing on the street and the chirp of baby frogs in the garden pond. A blue jay chided them from a nearby tree. Gerard found himself equally agitated and exhausted by the events of the previous night. And the truth about his father's duplicity intruded, reminding him of the sad loss of his mother. So much pain, one thing on top of the next.

Before cool gloom could drag him down, he pulled himself together. "What should I do?"

Tippy opened her eyes and blinked. "Do you love her?"

Her words galvanized him. He didn't need to answer the question. "Thank you." He rose and impetuously kissed her forehead. "Get better. Stoddard needs you."

"No more than I need him."

Gerard lifted his hand in wordless farewell and started out, still trying to come to a plan, a course of action. At least he knew what he had to do about Blessing. Words must be said.

❖

After a day spent in the company of her orphans, Blessing felt more like herself. She waved good-bye to Adela and walked through the back garden to her carriage. She would never have to worry about Smith again, and her work at the docks could commence once more. She should have felt relieved, but she didn't. Though she continually shuttered her mind against Gerard Ramsay, he still managed to remain with her always.

Judson opened the carriage door for her and helped her inside. Blessing sat back and found herself facing Ramsay. She gasped.

"I didn't mean to startle you," he said. "But I wanted to make sure you got home safely. Reporters are still lurking."

"My driver would have taken care of that." Her words came out sharply.

"He needs to be busy with the team. Don't worry. I know you're tired. I'm just seeing you home."

What could she say to that? She could hardly order him from the carriage.

They rode in silence. Unfortunately he was correct. When the carriage pulled up to her gate, reporters loitered there.

"Allow me," Ramsay said as he opened the door and stepped outside. Brandishing his cane, he shooed away the reporters, guided her through the gate, and shut it behind them.

She tried to come up with a polite way to send him home. But she could not think of anything that wasn't rude or unappreciative.

Salina met them at the door. "I'm glad to see you brought her home safe, Mr. Ramsay. I'll bring tea to the rear parlor for you two."

Never had Blessing wanted to shake Salina before, but she did now. She sent her housekeeper a severe glance. Then she walked into the foyer and left her bonnet and gloves there. Ramsay did the same with his own trappings and followed her into the rear parlor. She sat down and allowed Salina to bring in the tray with the teapot, sandwiches, and small cakes. She would let the man take tea with her, then bid him good evening.

Blessing poured a cup for each of them and passed his over.

He accepted the cup but just held it in his hand, gazing at her. "Blessing, I love you."

His words, spoken so calmly and plainly, took her unaware. She opened her lips but shut them before she could say anything that might lead him on.

In the silence she heard a frantic dog barking outside the open window. The sound echoed her own turmoil at his declaration.

"I have tried to deny this for weeks," he continued in a voice as relaxed as if he were discussing the weather. "I have never sought to fall in love or to marry. You're not at all the kind of woman who will make for an easy life. Your ideas are radical. You break the law. You live dangerously." He lifted one hand in surrender. "But I've fallen in love with you."

Still she kept her lips pressed together and stared out the window over his shoulder. A red squirrel alighted on a nearby branch, making it quiver. Moments passed.

"Blessing, I have just declared my love for you. You must have some reaction."

"I cannot marry thee."

"Why?"

"Thee is not a Quaker. I would be put out of the meeting again. I cannot face that."

"I—"

"If I marry again, I would lose all my legal rights," she said, forestalling his reply. "I cannot do that again either."

"I—"

"If I married, my husband and perhaps children would become my focus, not the work I want to accomplish. I would lose everything—my independence, myself."

He gazed at her. "I hadn't thought of any of those matters."

He took a sip of his hot tea as if considering her words. "I'm not going to give up."

"I will not change my mind," she said and paused to sip her tea as well. Her explanations bolstered her resolve. Everything she'd said was true. "If I were to marry, I would have everything to lose. I will not lose again."

"Can you say that you have no feelings for me?"

She looked away, unwilling to answer him. *What does it matter if I have feelings for thee?*

Again silence fell. She chafed in it and wished he would leave.

But he merely drank his tea and began nibbling at the refreshments. "Tell me about your afternoon. How are the children?"

His persistence exasperated her. "Does thee care? Really care?"

"Yes, I do care about the children. Please, inform me."

He had given up the previous train of conversation, and she was relieved. Yet she wished she weren't caught between wanting him to stay and wanting him to leave her life altogether. *Ramsay, how am I going to convince thee I cannot afford to love thee?*

Chapter 17

"I'm glad you came, Gerard." His aunt greeted him at her front door.

"Your note just said, 'Please come soon.' What is it, Aunt Fran?"

"I need to do some shopping and wanted an escort."

Gerard stared at her. His aunt had summoned him to take her shopping?

"Shiloh!" Aunt Fran called over her shoulder. "I'm going out with my nephew on that errand we discussed."

"Yes, ma'am!" Shiloh's voice came from outside, through the open rear window. "I'm weeding the garden."

"Good girl!" Aunt Fran tied on her bonnet, pulled on her gloves, and handed Gerard an oak basket.

He put the handle over one arm and offered her the other.

Soon they were walking side by side toward the business district.

"I needed a walk, needed to do something other than visit Tippy and sit in my garden, stitching." Her lower lip twisted down. "I had expected to be sewing many little gowns about now." The last words were spoken stiffly, painfully.

Gerard did not want to talk about the lost grandbaby. "So what do you need at the stores?"

"Nothing. I need absolutely nothing, but Tippy heard of a new widow who has been left with five youngsters, and I want to take her a basket of food and see what else she might need. We're not the only ones in the city who have lost loved ones this year."

"Good grief, you've been influenced by—"

"By my lovely and caring daughter-in-law . . . and Blessing Brightman. Certainly. I just wish I'd left Boston immediately after my second husband died. I am free of the past at last."

Gerard didn't know how to respond to this.

"I have more in common with Blessing than you know. Your mother was the dutiful daughter and married the man her parents chose for her. I, on the other hand, fell in love with a fine but penniless man, a poet. We eloped."

Gerard stopped midstep. "Eloped?"

"Yes. Shocking, isn't it? It was all hushed up, of course. A Ramsay eloping? And my parents and older brother—your father—were so relieved that Stoddard wasn't born until we'd been married over a year. They never managed to drag my first husband into the family business, but he got a respectable teaching job and was able to support me and our son. I always felt a bit guilty over your mother, though. If I'd married a wealthy man, maybe your father wouldn't have been forced to marry Regina merely for what she brought with her."

Gerard's head swam. "Why are you telling me this?"

"Because you have been at loggerheads with your father since you were a child. Which I quite understand. Saul and I have also never seen eye to eye, but in his own way he has done his duty to me. To remove my young son from my second husband's house where he was not welcome, Saul sent Stoddard off to school and enrolled you at the same time so he wouldn't be alone."

"That's why he sent me away to school!" Shock quivered through him.

"Yes. I never asked him to, Gerard. But frankly it was the right decision at the time, and not only for Stoddard's sake. We almost lost your mother that year—she could hardly rise from her bed. She couldn't have been a mother to you for several years after that severe bout of her ailment."

The thought that his father had not sent him to school out of selfishness or spite—but rather for nobler reasons—astounded Gerard. He still couldn't move.

"Let me explain how it was." His aunt tugged at his arm and they began walking again.

He obeyed but could barely feel his boots touching the ground.

"My dear love, Stoddard's father, had died of cholera, and when I could no longer stand living with my parents, I allowed them to finesse me into marrying a much older and reasonably wealthy man I didn't love. Eventually, I discovered that my second husband married me only to gain an heir. But

I never gave him a child, and in the end, ironically he made a will leaving all his wealth to Stoddard, the stepchild he'd avoided for over a decade."

Gerard chewed on this new perspective of the past.

As they arrived at the grocer's, Aunt Fran's confidences ended. She walked to the counter, and presently the basket on Gerard's arm was filled with staples such as eggs, cornmeal, salt, pepper, sugar, and flour.

Gerard wanted to ask many questions but couldn't find his tongue. For the first time he began to view his father as a person like him who'd made choices—some good, some bad—and then lived with them.

Outside again, Aunt Fran pulled out a slip of paper and read the address. Moments later they were entering the neighborhood of Little Africa.

"I presume the new widow is a woman of color," Gerard commented, noticing the aftermath of the riot still plainly visible in the rubble littering the streets and the handful of burned-out dwellings.

"Yes, though I'm sure if I looked, I could find a needy widow in most any part of this city. Maybe that will be my work." Aunt Fran glanced around and approached an older man sitting on a bench at the front of his modest home. She inquired about the widow's address, and he rose, directing them to the right house, a one-room cabin that looked like it had been built by an original Ohio pioneer fifty years ago.

A young woman opened the door and stared at Gerard and Aunt Fran.

"Blessing Brightman gave me your name and said you needed help," Aunt Fran said by way of introduction.

"Miz Brightman sent you?" the woman replied.

"Yes. I brought some items that any housewife can use, but what else do you need?"

Gerard entered the cabin and joined the widow and Aunt Fran, seated on kitchen chairs.

Just like Scotty at the orphanage, the woman's children gathered around Gerard's knees, staring up at him. One of the little girls climbed onto his lap. When her mother protested, Gerard smiled and raised a hand. He began talking to the children about whatever they brought up.

"What I really need is work," the widow said finally. "I can sew real good and I bake a good cake."

"I will spread the word," Aunt Fran said.

"Thank you, ma'am. That's kind of you."

A few more minutes of conversation, and Gerard and Aunt Fran bid her good day.

When they were a couple of blocks along, Gerard finally found the words he wanted to say. "Why didn't you tell me all that about your past earlier?"

She paused and eyed him with a mix of amusement and exasperation. "You don't know?"

He shook his head no.

"My dear nephew, I'm sure that you want to marry Blessing Brightman. And it is by far the most intelligent thought you've ever had. Now, my advice: you need to figure out what is stopping you. Is it your past? Is it something else? Whatever it is, fix it."

No, *he* wasn't the one stopping matters, but he didn't say that. "Fix it?" Fix Blessing Brightman?

"Yes, exactly." She began walking briskly toward home.

He grumbled silently but hurried to keep up with her, the now-empty oak basket banging against his side. The discomfort mimicked his frustration over Blessing's refusal to entertain his proposal.

Then, as he kept pace with his aunt, who appeared to be in a great hurry to get back to her home, he thought about her advice—*"Fix it."*

How was that possible in such a situation? Could he fix all the obstacles between himself and Blessing on his own?

❧

MAY 16, 1849

Bouncing the eight-month-old, squirming-to-get-down Daniel Lucas in her arms, Blessing watched as the judge signed the papers making the baby her legal son, her legal heir.

In the judge's chamber, Tippy and Stoddard stood to one side of her. Tippy was pale and thin but smiling at this occasion, her first time in public since her convalescence. Ducky Hughes, wearing an obviously new dress, stood on Blessing's other side.

And behind her gathered Blessing's beaming family, who'd all come to celebrate the new member of their family. Rebecca clung to Caleb's arm; this was her first family gathering away from Sharpesburg. She'd been worried about coming so close to the docks but had decided to be brave. She had a husband with a large family for protection now.

Yet, for Blessing, a persistent weight overlaid today's joy. She crafted a smile and brought it to her face. Gerard Ramsay would not be here with her for this happy moment. She disliked this reality but could not deny it.

The judge finished the paperwork and said, "I hope this child realizes what you've done for him today. And never causes you to regret it."

The implied judgment that a bastard orphan would probably only cause her grief nettled Blessing like a sharp stone in her shoe. She mentally shook it out. The conflicting emotions of today clogged her throat.

"He's one lucky child indeed." It was Ramsay's voice, coming from behind.

Trembling within, she whirled around to see him just inside the room, leaning against the doorjamb nonchalantly as if he'd been invited.

Tippy leaned close. "I told Gerard about today," she whispered into Blessing's ear. "It's time you faced him. Don't be foolish. Gerard Ramsay isn't Richard Brightman."

Her friend's words startled her, made her mute. But fortunately the agenda for the day had already been set. She moved forward with it, ignoring—or trying to ignore—Ramsay's presence.

Soon everyone sat around Blessing's dining room table for a festive meal. Blessing had been annoyed to see that even before they'd arrived, Salina had set a place for Ramsay at the table. Everyone seemed to be one step ahead of her.

❖

For his part, Gerard let Blessing hide behind her family and the occasion, biding his time. If nothing else, the way she refused to look at him said tomes and revealed her awareness of his presence. *Oh, Blessing, you're acting like a silly schoolgirl.* He found it charming.

The legal document he'd commissioned Alan Lewis to draw up warmed his pocket. He couldn't wait to witness Blessing's reaction to it.

Finally the meal—capped by a sumptuous wild-strawberry cake topped with fresh whipped cream—had been fully appreciated, the well wishes had been spoken, and everyone left, all casting parting glances at Blessing and him.

While Blessing walked her parents to their wagon, Gerard purposefully moved to the rear parlor, settled in, and waited for Blessing to capitulate and come deal with him. Alone.

She finally entered the room. "Ramsay," she reprimanded him politely, "I'm very much fatigued, so I must ask thee—"

With aplomb, he lifted the prepared document from his inner pocket and handed it to her. "I need you to sign this." He read the surprise and reluctance to accept it in her expression, so he shook the paper, insisting she take it.

Blessing finally claimed it as if picking up a snake by the tail. After glaring at him for a moment, she sat in the chair opposite him. She nervously smoothed the document on her lap.

"You'll have to read it. It can't speak aloud," he teased.

Frowning, she bent over the legal document.

Gerard watched intently for her reaction.

As she read, her lips parted in disbelief. At the end she looked across at him and then down again. "I don't understand."

Her tentative response energized him. "What's not to understand? I am in love with you, Blessing. I want to marry you."

She tried to interrupt.

He refused to let her. "You said if you married, you would

give up your independence, lose all your legal rights—and you were correct. The way the laws now stand, your point is valid. I don't like it, but we must work with what we have." He pinned her with his gaze. "So I've promised in this agreement that I will never treat you as if you're of less value than I am merely because you were born female."

She began to speak.

He held up a hand, forestalling her. "I will never expect you to become my shadow, to become powerless. As the document states, I will not claim any right to control or possess the property you bring into the marriage, and I grant you complete partnership in whatever property I have or will gain."

Blessing felt her eyebrows rise with each statement he made. Still, she could not miss the fact that his words were confident but his tone revealed not only how important this agreement was, but also how important she was to him. "Ramsay, I—"

"Your family's lawyer, Alan Lewis, assures me that this document would stand up in any court. You will lose nothing by marrying me. And I hope you might gain something. I'm not much, but I love you." He cleared his throat, then waited for her response.

Pressing her lips shut, Blessing gazed at him. Why had he done this, stripped away her defenses? And then her stomach began to churn. With this unexpected act, he'd taken away one of the main protests she could voice in opposition to marrying him.

The more private reason she could never trust herself to marry flared within. She felt as if the power of it were dragging her down. Her pulse throbbed in her temples.

"You look ill, Blessing."

She grasped for another objection. "If I marry thee, I will be put out of the meeting again."

He stared at her, considering this.

And Blessing was relieved. Gerard Ramsay would never become a Quaker. She was safe.

"Blessing, I have always vaguely believed in God but have not often felt close to him. I think that had to do more with my father than the heavenly Father." He glanced down. "Perhaps the man I've become since meeting you would fit better in your meeting than the man I was before. Hearing Frederick Douglass, James Bradley, and especially Sojourner Truth . . ." He shook himself. "I can't shut away what their words revealed. I can't forget the look on that young female slave's face that day at your parents' home. Or the mocking and cruelty of those slave catchers. I'm not the same man I was when I stepped off the steamboat here last September. I confess now that God is real and demands that we be real too. And you must see I'm finally aware of more than just myself, my petty problems. I will give your meeting a try, Blessing. And not only for your sake . . . for my own."

Nonplussed, Blessing stared, cornered. "I'm sorry. I cannot marry again."

"Why? What do you have to lose now?" He edged forward on his seat.

Her mouth stuttered, opening and closing several times. "I-I . . ."

Ramsay studied her. "Smith knew your husband."

The mention of that man jolted her. She gasped.

"Is that why you won't wed a second time? Because

Brightman ignored your advice and became a puppet of Smith?" He pressed her with his words, but he did it with compassion, in a way she couldn't rebuff. Tears wet her eyes and her resistance began to melt. Not only had Ramsay changed over the past months; she now knew she had as well. She'd fallen in love against her will. Her resistance collapsed.

"Ramsay, I married unwisely. I was so young, barely eighteen. I was swayed by the promise of life in the big city, dazzled by Richard's good looks, charm, and wealth. He pursued me single-mindedly, relentlessly. Richard Brightman opened an entirely new world to me. . . . I only knew him a few months before we married—against my parents' counsel."

"What happened?" he asked, so gently.

She pressed a handkerchief to her moist eyes and pursed her trembling lips. She did not want to explain, but this was Ramsay.

He'd helped her rescue Rebecca, who was now a member of her family.

He'd saved Theodosia and her children in the riots.

He'd played ball with the orphans.

He'd liberated the young runaway from the slave catchers.

He'd comforted Stoddard when they'd nearly lost Tippy.

And now he'd proposed marriage and offered to protect her rights in writing.

He deserved the truth.

She gathered her courage and will. "Richard always meant well, but he could not handle his liquor. And when he drank, he became mean and belligerent, a completely different person from the cheerful, easygoing man I thought I'd married. He became . . . abusive with me . . . physically."

Gerard blanched but said nothing, not wanting to stop her flow.

"He promised each time this happened that it was the last time." She sighed in little hitches. "But Smith made certain—" her tone hardened—"that various temptations always brought Richard back to the docks."

Gerard took her hand for a moment. "Thank you for revealing that to me." *Thank you for fighting Smith on my behalf as I took dangerous chance after dangerous chance in becoming involved with him.*

She nodded and looked down. All the truth must come out now. She needed to give Gerard all the facts before they made an irrevocable decision. "Did thee hear Smith accuse me of killing my husband?"

"The man was deranged."

Blessing drew in a deep breath, preparing to expose what she'd never revealed to anyone else. But after going to such lengths to propose marriage, Ramsay deserved her honesty.

"The night my husband died, he came home drunk yet again. He'd promised me he would come straight home from the brewery that evening and not go down to the docks. But as I waited, I finally decided I would leave him. I would humble myself and go home to Sharpesburg and live with my parents. It was in the early hours of the morning, and I met him on the second-floor landing."

Gerard couldn't speak for the suffering he read on her face, heard in her voice.

"I told him I was leaving him, and we fought. He was cursing me and . . . striking me. I had never hit back before, but this time I did. I shouldn't have. It surprised him and put him off-balance. He staggered and fell down the stairs. He broke his neck at the bottom." She inhaled a sharp breath. "He died instantly."

Gerard put his hands over his eyes as if he could shut out the image she'd portrayed. "Oh, Blessing."

"I never meant to hurt him. I just reached the end of my rope and struck back. I know I didn't intend for him to die. If he'd kept his promise to me and come home early that evening as he should have, he wouldn't have died. And if he'd come home sober, he wouldn't have been unsteady on his feet."

She wiped away her tears but they continued to fall. "Nor would he have been argumentative. I married a man I shouldn't have. And then he died while we fought. All these things I know. And most important, I know God has forgiven me. Yet I can't get over . . . the guilt." Her voice broke. "What's left over," she echoed Rebecca's words.

Gerard sat silently, going over her revelation, considering what to say. The sound of Blessing's subdued weeping twisted his nerves. "I understand your guilt," he began. "A woman like you with a very tender conscience would of course feel guilt. However, I doubt any honest grand jury would even indict you, when the incident was clearly accidental and the result of defense against bodily harm. But what does this matter to me? To us?"

She lifted a bewildered gaze to him. "What?"

Certainty surged through him. "I won't dismiss your feelings. But why should we pay the price for your first husband's incredible stupidity? He was married to a woman like you and he preferred Smith and his enticements? *Please.* I was foolish at first but I was able to learn. I want you for my wife, my helpmeet, my joy for life. Are you going to let Smith win this final battle—from his grave?"

Blessing blinked away the moisture in her eyes.

"I am committed to the orphanage, as you know," he continued. "And I'll work with you for women's suffrage and abolition. I will not violate your rights and am willing to attend the Quaker meeting with you, to seek Christ and ask God to make himself known to me. I'm offering you my heart and my commitment for life. Will you turn away? Are you going to be as foolish as your husband?" He leaned forward and tapped the paper in her lap. "Sign this agreement and we'll begin planning our wedding."

She clasped her handkerchief like a lifeline.

A moment passed as he let her digest what he'd just said. Then he continued, "Why should what happened in your past make us miserable?"

Her expression changed as if a light had been kindled within her, rays of sun bursting through storm clouds. "I hadn't thought about it that way." She eased forward. "Smith took his own life and destroyed so many others', but not ours."

Gerard couldn't hold back his joy. It filled him, warm and buoyant. "Good, because I'm not going to take no for an answer. And people might talk if they see me carrying you kicking and fighting to our wedding."

Blessing laughed, and it felt good, a release of tension. Joy lifted her to her feet. The paper fell to the carpet, and she knew she wouldn't have to sign it. Gerard meant every promise. She opened her arms. "Gerard, kiss me."

Gerard sprang to his feet and pulled her close. "I am happy

to obey you, ma'am." He folded her into his arms with all the tenderness he felt for her. He kissed her once lightly and then drew her tighter to him and kissed her again, promising everything with his lips.

Blessing at last gave in to the urge to draw near. She let herself lean against this man who offered her so much more than love. He pledged her respect and equality. Surely that was a true sign of a changed heart—two changed hearts, hers as well as his.

❖

Later that evening at the desk in his room at Mrs. Mather's boardinghouse, Gerard penned a letter.

Dear Father,

I am writing to tell you that I am going to marry Blessing Brightman. I'm sure you recall her from Stoddard's wedding. I will be working with her in her many causes and helping manage her considerable business holdings.

I will invite you to the wedding, to take place in July, but will not be insulted if you don't come.

I have some advice for you. I suggest you sell the family business—I'm never going to take it over; I will never return to Boston. Then you should go to Manhattan. Live your life with your other family. I liked Bella and Lucille. Tell them you've retired from your enterprise, and spend time with them and enjoy their company. Why waste more time away from

*them? You might even find them understanding
if you confessed the truth. I do not know. That's up
to you.*

*I remind you that, when I visited, I told them
my name and that I was a distant relative visiting
from Cincinnati. That is the truth. We've always
been distant relatives. I have resented you for most
of my life, but I am free of that now. And I want you
to be too.*

*Confess your sin to God and he will forgive you.
Don't let the past ruin your life. I'm not.*

*Yours sincerely,
Gerard*

He read it over, sanded and sealed it.

Kennan came to mind. Would he keep the secret? Gerard could only hope. However, it was his father's worry, his father's guilty sin. He had done what he could to dissuade Kennan from speaking out.

Gerard was free. No longer a slave to his hatred of his father or to the past. He imagined his mother, and she was smiling and clapping. *Mother, you would have loved Blessing. I do.*

Epilogue

Blessing stood before the freestanding full-length mirror in Tippy's bedroom. Blessing had ordered a new dress for her wedding—she'd chosen a deep royal blue and allowed herself to have it made in the latest style.

Tippy, who'd insisted on hosting the wedding, came into the room and stood beside her. Tippy also wore a new dress in a shade of lavender lovely with her blonde hair and light complexion. "We're pretty, aren't we?"

Chuckling, Blessing pressed her cheek to Tippy's. Tippy was still very thin from her ordeal, but her color had come back and she was getting stronger in spite of the heat of July.

"On this same day last summer in Seneca Falls, we would never have believed this could happen, would we? That you'd be marrying Gerard Ramsay today?"

That was exactly why Blessing had chosen this day for her

wedding. "And who would have thought we would become cousins by marriage?" Blessing slipped her arm around Tippy's tiny waist. "Our children will play together."

A shadow crossed over Tippy's face.

"I'm sor—"

"No," Tippy cut her off, "I'm fine. Yes, our children will play together. Now let's not keep the men waiting. The heat of the day is already building." Tippy led her down the stairs and handed her a bouquet of daisies and pink roses.

Blessing's father, in his best summer suit, was waiting at the bottom of the stairs. He offered her his arm and kissed her cheek. "You look beautiful," he signed.

She blinked away tears as she signed, "I'm so glad thee, Mother, and the family are here for this wedding."

"We are too," he replied, and escorted her into the parlor. Only Tippy, Stoddard, Aunt Fran, and Blessing's and Joanna's families were in attendance at the private ceremony. Gerard had been attending the meeting for the past two months, and he had already begun speaking to the elders about joining. Since Gerard had stated his sincere intention and proven faithful thus far, the elders had agreed that this private ceremony could take place.

By the cold fireplace, next to the Presbyterian pastor from Tippy's church, Gerard gazed at her as she took her place before him. She read the love in his eyes and drew in a deep breath so she wouldn't cry. Her heart rejoiced, and she wished for once that she had a voice to sing.

Then Aunt Royale broke the solemn silence and, as if reading Blessing's thoughts, began to sing, "'In that great gettin' up mornin', fare thee well. Fare thee well.'"

And suddenly everyone was smiling. Blessing knew finally, fully, that she was forgiven and could look forward to a future filled with love and Gerard Ramsay. She sang in her heart, sang away the regret of the past: "'Fare thee well. Fare thee well.'"

HISTORICAL NOTE

As I researched this book, I found myself appalled by many nineteenth-century facts of life and events, primarily race riots and lack of women's rights. First of all, would a mayor really incite a riot?

Yes. In very real events, after an abolitionist press had been destroyed in downtown Cincinnati, Harriet Beecher Stowe, a resident of the city at the time, wrote, "The mayor was a silent spectator of these proceedings, and was heard to say, 'Well, lads, you have done well, so far; go home now before you disgrace yourselves'; but the 'lads' spent the rest of the night and a greater part of the next day (Sunday) in pulling down the houses of inoffensive and respectable blacks."

And in a quote from an 1888 biography of Stowe, she recalls: "During the riots in 1836, when . . . free negroes were hunted like wild beasts through the streets of Cincinnati . . ."

This was just one riot. Race riots took place in Cincinnati in 1829, 1836, and 1841. As a novelist, it's my job to dramatically portray events, not merely report them. So I transported what happened in 1836 to the year 1848.

If the attitude in the city toward black residents had changed in the twelve years between 1836 and 1848, I would not have felt free to move the event. However, the prejudice against free blacks had remained unchanged and, in fact, might be said to have increased. Cincinnati wanted trade with the South. The South resented the city's being a pipeline in the Underground Railroad, and these kinds of tensions were among the factors that eventually led to the Civil War.

Also, I again point out (as I did in *Honor*, the first book in this series) the injustice of widows not automatically inheriting property. Blessing only inherited her husband's property because he unexpectedly made out a will in her favor.

Otherwise his wealth would have gone to his nearest male relative, which could be a woman's eldest son. If the son was still a child, a trustee would have been appointed to oversee the estate until the child came of age. These laws, which now seem medieval, only began to change in the US in the mid-1840s. Michigan and New York State were two of the early adopters, giving widows the right to inherit and control property.

When I quoted Frederick Douglass saying that a discussion of the rights of animals would be met with more complacence than a discussion of the rights of women, I did not make that up. I know that, as a twenty-first-century woman, this is hard to believe. But sadly it's true. The words attributed to James Bradley and Sojourner Truth are also historically authentic. You can readily find the full text of their respective speeches by searching for them online.

Wives in the nineteenth century were legally invisible. A

wife could not own property, keep her own wages, or complain if her husband beat her. Seen as less competent than men, women could even get away with certain crimes if their husbands were present—similar to our modern laws about juvenile crime.

If you've never read the articles of the Declaration of Sentiments, which discusses all these inequities and was passed at the Seneca Falls Convention, where the story of Blessing and Gerard begins, you should. Here's one address where you can find it: http://en.wikipedia.org/wiki/ Declaration_of_Sentiments. It's also available, I'm sure, at your local library.

I was especially struck by the sentiment that discusses a double standard:

> [Man] has created a false public sentiment by
> giving to the world a different code of morals
> for men and women, by which moral delin-
> quencies which exclude women from society,
> are not only tolerated, but deemed of little
> account in man.

To put it less formally, while a young man was expected to sow his wild oats, any similar indiscretion could banish a young woman for life from respectable society, "ruin" her. This is one of the injustices that Blessing chooses to work against.

She knows that the majority of women who work in the brothels and walk the streets at the riverfront did not go there from choice but often after being abused or abandoned by men—or because of a lack of opportunity for education or meaningful work that paid enough to live on, another point included in the Declaration of Sentiments.

And in light of her unhappy marriage, Blessing resents the fact that an abused woman has no legal recourse. At that time, if a woman sued for divorce, she could literally be put out on the street with no way to support herself and could lose all rights to her children. Chilling, isn't it?

I'm old enough to remember my own mother telling me that her mother was already a married woman with children when she gained the right to vote. Her point was that I should never miss voting in any election or I would be showing disrespect to those who had spent their lives working to raise the status of women.

Blessing, as many other women did, decided not to accept the status quo but to work to change the laws that not only bound slaves but also women of any color. I'm sure Christ, who loves us all, approved of work like hers.

In our modern world, it's hard at times for me to believe that women on many continents are still abused and live subordinate lives without education or rights. I hope that when you consider organizations to support financially, you will choose some missions that are committed to bettering the status of women. God doesn't love and respect one skin color over another any more than he loves men more than women.

To quote Galatians 3:28—"There is neither Jew nor Greek, there is neither bond nor free, there is neither male nor female: for ye are all one in Christ Jesus."

BE ON THE
LOOKOUT FOR

Faith

BOOK THREE IN THE

QUAKER

BRIDES

SERIES

AVAILABLE SPRING 2016

TYNDALE
FICTION

www.tyndalefiction.com

Chapter 1

Each time her grandfather struggled for another breath, Honor Penworthy's own lungs constricted. She stood beside the second-story window, trying to breathe normally, trying to catch a breeze in the heat. Behind her, the gaunt man lay on his canopied bed, his heart failing him. How long must he suffer before God would let him pass on?

Outside the window stretched their acres, including the tobacco fields, where dark heads covered with kerchiefs or straw hats bent to harvest the green-speared leaves. High Oaks—to her, the most beautiful plantation in Maryland. She felt a twinge of pain, of impending loss.

"The edict was impractical. And your . . . father was a

dreamer. But at least he had the sense to realize his irratio-nal decision must be kept secret. Doesn't that tell you not to carry it out?" Each word in this last phrase slapped her, and each cost him.

Unable to ignore this challenge, she turned. In her grandfather's youth, the Society of Friends had dictated that all Friends should free their slaves. "My father re-mained Quaker." She said the bare words in a neutral voice, trying not to stir the still-smoldering coals.

"I remained a Christian," he fired back. "My forebears chose to leave the Anglican church to become Quaker. I chose to change back."

He'd made that choice because the Episcopal church didn't press its members to emancipate their slaves. All of the other Quakers in the county had left except for a few older, infirm widows—women who'd lost control of their land to sons. As a single woman, however, Honor could inherit and dispose of property legally.

Honor returned to his bedside. At the sight of her grandfather's ravaged face, pity and love surged through her.

As she approached, her grandfather's mouth pulled down and his nose wrinkled as if he were tasting bitter fruit.

Torn between love for her father and for her grand-father, she didn't want to fight with him, not now. "My father loved thee," she said to placate him.

"That is beside the . . . point. He should *never* have asked that promise of you. It was cowardly." He panted from the exertion.

Honor gazed at him levelly. The memory of her father's untimely and unnecessary death still had the power to sweep away her calm, but one couldn't change history. Her grandfather's comment could lead them into harsh recriminations. And it proved that he knew he'd done wrong and had chosen the wide way, not the narrow gate. She chose her words deftly. "I believe that my father was right."

Grandfather's mouth tightened, twisted, not only because of her recalcitrance but also from a sudden pain. He gasped wildly for breath.

If only it weren't so hot. She slipped another white-cased down pillow under his chest and head, trying to ease his breathing. She blinked away tears, a woman's weapon she disdained.

"How will you . . . work the land without . . . our people?" he demanded in between gasps.

"Thee knows I cannot. And that once they are gone, there will be no way I can hold the land." She said the words calmly, but inside, fear frothed up. Freeing their slaves would irrevocably alter her life.

He slapped the coverlet with his gnarled fist. "This estate has been Penworthy land for four generations. Will you toss aside the land your great-great-grandfather cleared by hand and fought the Cherokee for?"

Honor felt the pull of her heritage, a cinching around her heart. "I know. It weighs on me," she admitted.

"Then why do it?"

He forced her to repeat her reasons. "I gave my father my promise, and I agree with him."

Her grandfather made a sound of disgust, a grating of rusted hinges. Then he glared at her from under bushy, willful brows. "Things have changed since your father left us. Did you even notice that our bank failed this year?"

The lump over Honor's heart increased in weight, making it hard to breathe. "I am neither blind nor deaf. I am aware of the nationwide bank panic."

"Are you aware that we've lost our cash assets? We only have the land and the people to work the land. And debts."

"Debts?" That she hadn't known.

"Yes, debt is a part of owning a plantation. And I'm afraid last year's poor crop put us in a bad situation even before the bank panic."

Honor looked into her grandfather's cloudy, almost-blind eyes. "How bad?"

"If you free our people and sell the land, you will have nothing worthwhile left."

A blow. She bent her head against one post of the canopied bed. The lump in her chest grew heavier still. "I didn't think emancipation would come without cost."

"I don't believe you have any idea of how much it will cost you." Disdain vibrated in each word. "Who will you be if you free our people and sell the plantation? If you aren't the lady of High Oaks?"

She looked up at the gauzy canopy. "I'll be Honor Penworthy, child of God."

"You will be landless, husbandless, and alone," he railed. A pause while he gathered strength, wheezing and coughing.

Honor helped him sip honey water.

"I don't want you in that vulnerable position," he said in a much-gentler tone, his love for her coming through. "I won't be here to protect you. You think that Martin boy will marry you, but he won't. Not if you give up High Oaks."

Alec Martin had courted her, but no, she no longer thought they would marry. A sliver of a different sort of pain pierced her.

The floor outside the door creaked, distracting them. Honor turned at the sound of footsteps she recognized. "Darah?" she called.

"I want to see her," Grandfather said, looking away.

Honor moved quickly and opened the door.

Darah paused at the head of the stairs. She was almost four years younger than Honor's twenty-four, very slight and pretty, with soft-brown eyes and matching brown hair.

"Cousin, come here. Our grandfather wishes thee."

Darah reluctantly glanced into Honor's eyes—at first like a frightened doe and then with something else Honor had never seen in her cousin before. Defiance?

Darah slipped past her into the room. "Grandfather?"

He studied his hands, now clutching the light blanket. "Honor, leave us. I wish to speak to Darah alone."

Why? Worry stirred. She ignored it. "And I must see to a few of our people who are ailing." Honor bowed her head and stepped outside, shutting the door. She went down the stairs to gather her medicine chest, remembering that later she must meet with the overseer. The plantation work could not be put aside because her grandfather's heart was failing. She tried to take a deep breath, but the weight over her heart would not budge.

Honor hated to see her grandfather suffer, and she hated to disappoint him. But her course had been set since she was a child. She shuttered her mind against the opposition she knew she would stir up.

DISCUSSION QUESTIONS

1. What were Blessing's reasons for marrying Richard Brightman?

2. Do you believe Sojourner Truth had a vision of Christ? Why or why not?

3. Why does Gerard think he needs to save Stoddard from Tippy? What does he believe he is saving his cousin from?

4. Why do you think only a thin minority of Christians in the mid-nineteenth century championed abolition and women's rights?

5. In this novel, Blessing works to lift abused women up and give them back their self-respect. But children of both sexes were hurt by society's expectations. Which male character is mistreated by his father? What is the result?

6. Aunt Fran surprises Gerard when she explains his father's motivation for sending him to boarding school. Have you ever discovered facts about your childhood or family that explained decisions and behavior you'd misunderstood?

7. Have you experienced discrimination for your gender, race, or some other aspect of your identity? What happened? What advice would you give others who face this sort of discrimination?

8. Though the laws have changed since Blessing's day, there is still tension between women and men—in the workplace, for example. Why does this controversy continue?

9. In the 1840s, men's sexual indiscretions were often treated more lightly than women's. Does this double standard hold true anymore? What does today's society expect from young men and women? How have things changed for each gender, and how have they stayed the same?

10. If you lived in 1848, would you have attended the Seneca Falls women's rights convention, like Blessing and Tippy? Or would you have condemned it, like Gerard? Why? What do you imagine would have been the most interesting aspect of the convention?

ABOUT THE AUTHOR

LYN COTE, known for her "Strong Women, Brave Stories," is the award-winning, critically acclaimed author of more than thirty-five novels. Her books have been RITA Award finalists and Holt Medallion and Carol Award winners. Lyn received her bachelor's degree in education and her master's degree in American history from Western Illinois University. She and her husband have two grown children and live on a small but beautiful lake in northern Wisconsin. Visit her online at www.LynCote.com.